Overworld
The Dragon Mage Saga
Book 1

OVERWORLD
The Dragon Mage Saga
Book 1

Rohan M. Vider

COPYRIGHT

Overworld (The Dragon Mage Saga, Book 1)
Copyright © 2020 Rohan M. Vider.

All rights reserved. This book or any portion thereof may not be reproduced or used in any manner without the express written permission of the publisher, except for the use of brief quotations in a book review. If you would like permission to use material from the book (other than for review purposes), please contact rohan.vider@gmail.com.

Second Edition
Revision 2.0

This is a work of fiction. Names, characters, places, and incidents either are the products of the author's imagination or are used fictitiously. Any resemblance to actual persons, living or dead, businesses, companies, events, or locales is entirely coincidental.

Acknowledgments

Thanks to my wife and two children. This book, as usual, is dedicated to you.

Also, thanks to my cover designer, Maria Spada, and my editors, Karin Cox and Josiah Davis for their sterling work and professionalism.

Finally, thanks to all my readers, who have made these stories possible.

BOOKS BY ROHAN M. VIDER

The Dragon Mage Saga
Overworld, Book 1
Dungeons, Book 2

The Gods' Game
Crota, the Gods' Game Volume I
The Labyrinth, the Gods' Game Volume II
Sovereign Rising, the Gods' Game Volume III
Sovereign, the Gods' Game, Volume IV
Sovereign's Choice, the Gods' Game Volume V

Tales from the Gods' Game
Dungeon Dive (Tales from the Gods' Game, Book 1)

OVERWORLD

THE DRAGON MAGE SAGA, BOOK 1

A magic apocalypse.
A new world.
Elves, orcs, dragons.
And at the center of it all: THE DRAGON MAGE!

Earth is doomed and mankind has been exiled to Overworld, a strange world ruled by the Trials. Jamie Sinclair is a young man with unique gifts, and it falls to him to find a way for humanity to survive Earth's destruction and build a new home in Overworld.

Can Jamie save mankind?

The Trials is no game. Join Jamie as he struggles through its brutal challenges while wrestling with his new magics and Overworld's game-like dynamics.

Read the award-winning epic fantasy of one man's journey to save humanity today.

PRAISE FOR BOOK 1 OF THE DRAGON MAGE SAGA:

"*A fantasy RPG come to life, Overworld is a particularly fun and readable adventure...*" —**manybooks.net**

"*It is beyond entertaining. I felt like I was part of the story.*" —**readersfavorite.com**

"*I LOVED THIS BOOK, plain and simple.*" —**Under The Radar SFF Books, fantasy blogger.**

"*A fast-paced action-adventure that lovers of books like Ready Player One will be thrilled with.*" —**reedsy.com**

"*Once I got started I couldn't put the book down.*" —**booksirens.com**

Author's Note

Dear Reader,

Thank you for reading the **Dragon Mage Saga**.

A cautionary word to those of you unfamiliar with the genre; this is a story based in a game-like world. It contains elements common to CRPG and MMO computer games, but knowledge of such games is not necessary to enjoy the story.

I encourage you to drop me a message on anything related to the Dragon Mage Saga or otherwise. Please also let others know what you think about the book by leaving a review on www.amazon.com and www.goodreads.com.

Most importantly, I hope you enjoy the book!

Best Regards,

Rohan M. Vider
Support me on PATREON

Contents

Overworld iii
Copyright iv
Acknowledgments v
Books by Rohan M. Vider vi
Overworld vii
Author's Note ix
Contents x
Chapter One 1
Chapter Two 9
Chapter Three 15
Chapter Four 24
Chapter Five 30
Chapter Six 35
Chapter Seven 43
Chapter Eight 54
Chapter Nine 62
Chapter Ten 70
Chapter Eleven 75
Chapter Twelve 84
Chapter Thirteen 94
Chapter Fourteen 103
Chapter Fifteen 113
Chapter Sixteen 121
Chapter Seventeen 128
Chapter Eighteen 135
Chapter Nineteen 144
Chapter Twenty 154
Chapter Twenty-One 165
Chapter Twenty-Two 177
Chapter Twenty-Three 192
Chapter Twenty-Four 202
Chapter Twenty-Five 211

Chapter Twenty-Six	223
Chapter Twenty-Seven	239
Chapter Twenty-Eight	252
Chapter Twenty-Nine	259
Chapter Thirty	271
Chapter Thirty-One	279
Chapter Thirty-Two	287
Chapter Thirty-Three	301
Chapter Thirty-Four	312
Chapter Thirty-Five	317
Chapter Thirty-Six	326
Chapter Thirty-Seven	339
Chapter Thirty-Eight	346
Chapter Thirty-Nine	355
Chapter Forty	365
Chapter Forty-One	370
Chapter Forty-Two	375
Jamie's Player Profile	380
Afterword	xii
General Definitions	xiii
Trial System Definitions	xv
List of Locations	xvii
List of Notable Characters	xviii

CHAPTER ONE

30 APRIL

> *"Life is not fair. And neither are the Trials."*
> —Anonymous player.

"Jamie, come quickly. You have to see this!"

Mom's cry of alarm was muffled by the oversized headphones I wore, but even so, her distress filtered through my clanmates' panicked voices over the team chat.

Our battle against the world boss was not going well. *Now it'll go even worse,* I thought, as I rose out of my chair.

"Guys." I broke through the team's frantic chatter. "Mom's in trouble. I gotta go." I ripped off my headset, ignoring a last-minute jibe from my friend Eric about being a twenty-four-year-old "Momma's boy." There was no helping it; she needed me.

"What is it, Ma?" I hobbled into the lounge as fast as my gimp leg would allow.

"The news!" My mother was curled into a ball on the couch, looking even smaller and more anxious than usual in the cramped room.

The... news? I stifled a groan. Had I just abandoned my clan's epic fight for the latest media craze? *The guys won't let me live this one down.* "It's just the news, Ma. Bad stuff happens all the—"

"Shush, Jamie. Listen!" Mom clutched blindly at my arm, her eyes fixed on the television screen.

She hasn't heard a word I said.

"Look!" She pointed a trembling finger at our battered TV.

I sighed. I wasn't going to get back into the fight until I calmed her down. Besides, it was probably too late. A man down, the clan must have been wiped out by now. I followed her gaze—and blinked.

"... it's the breaking news of the hour," the news presenter reported. "Ninety-foot-tall structures of unknown origin have appeared all over the world. Experts believe..."

Overworld, Book 1 of the Dragon Mage Saga

The presenter's words faded away as my attention was drawn to the images displayed: a close-up of one of the objects in New York's Central Park. Expanding from the ground up, as if it had stood there for eternity, was a most absurd and unnatural structure.

The artifact—*what else to call it?*—was of silver metal with a faint tinge of red. The perspective of the background made it clear the object was immense, yet its design was disturbingly simple: four metal pieces arranged in a rectangular shape. It could have been mistaken for a window frame or doorway, if not for its size and composition.

What is that metal? Some sort of steel?

I scratched my head, confused. Was this a prank? Why would anyone create the object, much less place it in the middle of a city? I patted Mom's hand, and then slipped out of her white-knuckled grip and limped closer to the television, leaning forward for a better look.

My initial assumption had been wrong.

The artifact was not as simple as it appeared. The inside wasn't empty; instead, it was filled with a near-translucent, shimmering curtain of red. The crimson-touched metal borders were not plain either. Inscribed on their surface, barely visible in the less-than-ideal resolution of the broadcast, were flowing patterns that resembled writing of some unearthly origin.

Frowning, I leaned back.

"What is it?" Mom's voice was strained.

"I don't know, Ma," I murmured. *Fake news*, I decided. I pulled out my cell phone and searched the web for corroboration, listening to the broadcast with half an ear.

"... what do you make of it, Timothy?"

"I don't know, Janice. This has to be a hoax, but with more than fifty confirmed sightings across the globe, it is a pretty elaborate one, not to mention expensive."

"A hoax, Timothy? I mean, the sheer scale of the resources required to pull off something like this... it defies belief. And what would be the point?"

"What else could it be, Janice?"

"You don't think there is anything to what our commentators are saying? For the folks at home who may have missed our earlier interviews, some experts believe the objects are of extraterrestrial origin."

"Aliens! Be serious, Janice." Timothy gave an amused chuckle and waved his arms vaguely above his head. "Even if there *were* aliens out there, surely they would have smarter ways of initiating contact than putting in what look like, for all intents and purposes, big metal windows?" He shook his head in disbelief. "The very notion is absurd."

I tuned out Janice's reply.

There was no point paying attention to the newsfeed. Clearly, the presenters were as clueless as I was. But as far-fetched as it sounded, the existence of the structures was indisputable.

Multiple web sources confirmed sightings of at least fifty-three artifacts. And while Internet pundits, bloggers, and forum-goers were uncertain about the structures' origins, no one was questioning the authenticity of the sightings. That the structures existed was accepted fact—even on the Internet.

Multiple theories about the objects were already circulating. Some believed the artifacts to be the work of aliens; others thought they were clever illusions created by the government. Some suggested the inscriptions were ancient Egyptian hieroglyphics; others thought they signaled the return of Atlantis. And those were the saner hypotheses.

"Jamie, what is this all about?" Mom's voice trembled. "How can any of this be happening?"

I looked up from my cell phone to her stricken face. "I don't know, Ma," I repeated.

I limped back to her and took her careworn hands, calloused and wrinkled from decades of back-breaking work, into my own.

"Whatever these strange artifacts are, no one understands their purpose... yet." I squeezed her hands reassuringly. "The government will figure it out soon."

"What do we do?" she asked, trembling.

I kept my face impassive, careful not to betray my concern for her and for the situation of the world outside. Mom's mental state was precarious most days, and today's shocking news had made it worse than usual.

Life had taken a toll on her. Despite having almost no education to speak of, no family, a deadbeat husband, and one hungry kid to feed, clothe, and educate, she had succeeded in providing me with the opportunities she had missed.

She worked two jobs—sometimes three—to fund my education. Now, at the age of twenty-four and a working professional, it was my turn to take care of her, although I couldn't help but worry I was failing.

Day by day, despite all the doctors and medication, Mom's condition deteriorated. A form of dementia, the doctors called it. Give the meds time to work, they said. She will recover, they said.

But it had been nearly a year since Mom had stopped working—nearly a year of endless medication—and her condition only seemed to worsen. I squeezed her hands again. I could not afford to lose her.

"Come sit, Mom. Let's watch the news together. I'm sure this will all turn out to be a big mistake. A hoax," I said, quoting the presenter.

But I did not believe it myself.

*** * * ****

Three days went by, and no one was closer to solving the mystery of the artifacts. Every day, more of the objects appeared. By the end of the third day, every town and city in the world had one.

The artifacts, though, were not identical.

While they all shared the same basic characteristics—rectangular design, identical dimensions, and borders inscribed with alien runes—observers had noted there were nearly as many shimmering green structures as there were those with a curtain of red. Artifacts of other colors were also witnessed. A small but significant percentage of the objects had translucent fields of orange, blue, and black.

Even our town, small as it was, received one. Staring out my bedroom window gave me a clear view of the mammoth structure that had appeared yesterday in the parking lot of the town's only shopping mall, some two hundred meters away.

Like officials all over the world, our mayor had no idea what to make of the artifact, or what to do about it. Eventually, he settled on cordoning off the area and ignoring its glaring presence.

But that had not stopped the curious and bold from exploring. Even now, many of the town's residents wandered around the structure, touching its textured surface, which scientists had confirmed was of unearthly origin.

The more adventurous souls had even stepped through its shimmering curtain. Despite reports from across the globe that the translucent field had no noticeable effect on human or animal anatomy, I considered it a foolish risk.

Although I itched to take a closer look at the strange artifact, Mom's worsening anxiety meant I could scarcely leave her sight.

Thankfully, my boss was an understanding soul. I had been forced to call in sick and had spent every day in front of the television with Mom, soothing her worry.

It was no surprise then that I was slumped on the couch, gazing listlessly at the TV, when the commentators' endless—and fruitless—speculation was interrupted by a momentous event.

"I'm sorry, Doctor Theisen." The anchor, Janice, cut off a commentator. "We have to interrupt with a live broadcast from New York City, where a most extraordinary event is taking place." The newsfeed jumped to a reporter, who was shifting from foot to foot. "Rebecca," continued Janice, "can you tell us what is going on there?"

Rebecca bobbed her head. "Yes, Janice. If the appearance of the structures was not astonishing enough, events have turned even more bizarre. Across the world, faces have been spotted in the artifacts—even in the one in New York!"

"I'm sorry, Rebecca. Did I hear you right?" asked the anchor. "Did you say *faces?*"

"I did, Janice," Rebecca babbled. "To be clear, a two-dimensional image of a face, not an actual one. Our experts now believe the artifacts are some sort of visual projection device. But the most amazing aspect is that the face bears no human resemblance. By all appearances, it is of alien origin!"

"I'm not sure I understood you—"

"Sorry to interrupt, Janice. We have just been told that the alien has begun speaking through the London artifact, and in English too! Yes, you heard right, the alien has started communicating in a language we can—"

The reporter broke off and held up a hand, listening intently to her earpiece. "Apologies to you and our listeners, Janice. We have more information coming through. My producer tells me the alien is now also speaking from the structures in Washington and Berlin. We anticipate it will do so from the New York artifact soon as well. Stand by while we take you to a live feed!"

What the—? I jerked upright on the couch.

"This can't be true, can it?" Mom's nails dug into my arm. "It has to be a sick joke."

I patted her arm absently, keeping my eyes on the screen. Mom was right: it sounded too preposterous to believe. Surely, the reporter was mistaken. Nonetheless, it was riveting to watch.

A second later, the newsfeed jumped to an aerial shot of the New York artifact. I leaned forward. Within the hazy red curtain of the structure, I beheld a face—an *inhuman* yet distinctly humanoid face.

My jaw dropped open in astonishment. The alien's features were *instantly* recognizable to me, courtesy of a lifetime spent reading science fiction novels and playing RPGs. With flaring nostrils, two tusks protruding up from its lower jaw, and deep-set sunken eyes, the face was the spitting image of an... orc.

An orc? The aliens who had caused strange artifacts to appear all over Earth were orcs? I shook my head in disbelief.

Mum's face had gone pale. She stared at the TV, transfixed by the image on display. "What *is* that thing?" When I didn't respond, she turned my way and noticed my own reaction. "What is it, Jamie? Do you recognize the creature?" she asked, correctly interpreting my expression.

Before I could answer, the orc spoke in a low rumble that hinted at leashed power. "People of Earth, I am Warlord Duskar Silverbane, chieftain of the Fangtooth tribe and supreme ruler of the Orcish Federation." He paused dramatically. "And now Earth. By the laws of Overworld and the Trials that govern it, I claim your planet and you, the humans that infest it, as mine."

Duskar's unpleasant smile carried the promise of suffering to come. "You doubt my words. I can smell your rebellious thoughts from here. But you will learn. Serve or die—that is the only choice before you. Yours is not the first world I have laid claim to, nor will it be the last."

His chuckle reverberated ominously from the artifact. "By the dictates of the Trials, there are a few facts I am obliged to convey. Listen closely. I will not repeat myself.

"Your world is being subsumed into Overworld. In two weeks, the process will be complete. Thereafter, your planet shall cease to exist. It will be gone from the universe. Its energy, matter"—Duskar bared his filed teeth in another ugly smile—"and all its plentiful creatures will be absorbed into Overworld as grist to fuel the Trials.

"If you do not wish to be consumed along with your world, you will enter the gates before then." Duskar's clawed hand gestured lazily at the borders of the artifact rimming his image. "The gates will open tomorrow and remain open for exactly two weeks. My men will await your arrival and take your oaths. Only those who pledge loyalty to me will be allowed into Overworld. Those who resist will be put to the sword. And if you think deceit will save you, think again. The Trials take pledges *very* seriously." He sneered. "You will not enjoy the consequences of severing your oath, believe me. Goodnight, humans."

Duskar's face vanished, and the newsfeed cut back to the speechless anchor, whose mouth worked soundlessly until she finally said, "Well, there you have it—"

I switched off the television and swung to face Mom.

"What do we do, Jamie?"

"I don't know, Ma." I stared out the window at the distant gate. "I just don't know."

CHAPTER TWO

03 May

> *"We shall rule Overworld. If not today, then tomorrow. This, I promise you."*
> —Duskar Silverbane.

As it turned out, Duskar was not the only alien the world got to see that night. Following on the heels of his speech, another, more palatable one was given from the gates of shimmering green.

"People of Earth, most of you have no doubt heard the words of the tyrant, Duskar," said the woman on the screen.

Mom and I were glued to the television again. Like Duskar before her, the woman's skin was tinged green, but her other features couldn't have been more different. Her ears peaked to a point, her face was thin and sharp, and her wide, round green eyes sparkled with fury.

Unsurprisingly, given her looks, she identified herself as an elven queen—Ionia Amyla, "leader of the free elven people of Overworld," to be exact.

"While Duskar spoke true," Ionia said through thin lips, "the wretch has not given you all the truth. Your world is being forcibly consumed at the *behest* of Duskar. The tyrant has initiated the process without your consent—a most heinous crime, but regrettably one that cannot be reversed."

The elven queen bowed her head so her flowing green locks shielded her gaze, but not before revealing eyes heavy with sorrow.

I frowned. The gesture seemed deliberate, and a tad too artful to be natural. *Just how practiced was Ionia's speech?*

The elven queen lifted her head again and continued, "It is the practice of the Elven Protectorate to only voluntarily subsume new worlds. However, now that Duskar has begun the process, it cannot be stopped. The best I can offer you is the opportunity to join our cause and escape a lifetime of slavery under the orcs.

Overworld, Book 1 of the Dragon Mage Saga

"Many of you must be wondering about Overworld. I will tell you what I can." Ionia paused, clearly gathering her thoughts. "Overworld is an ever-shifting land created by the long-vanished Elders in a dimension removed from your own. Just as you are being assimilated now, many millennia ago the orcish and elven people were also brought to this world.

"Even after centuries, we can only guess at the Trials' ultimate purpose, but one thing is certain: the Trials have fashioned Overworld into a test, one with the objective of evolving its inhabitants into stronger images of themselves. *Why* however, remains a mystery.

"Know that if you enter the Trials, you journey into a world of conflict, a world in which you will be constantly challenged. Overworld is a harsh land. Survival will be difficult, if not impossible on your own. Know, too, that if you choose to accept our aid, my people and I will assist you every step of the way." Ionia's lips widened into a benevolent smile, entreating us with both her beauty and her words.

She is trying too hard, I thought, my suspicions hardening. Something seemed off about Ionia's mannerisms, as if her speech was staged to appeal to a trapped, confused population. Was Ionia truly altruistic, or did the elves have less noble motives for coming to our aid?

I knew what my money was on.

"As new entrants into Overworld, your species will not be entirely without protection," the elven queen continued. "The Trials have granted humanity its own territory. This land, the newly created Human Dominion, will be seeded with wildlife and monsters from all over Overworld and its multitude of subsumed worlds. The Human Dominion will be shielded for exactly one Overworld year, during which time, it will be protected from invasion."

Ionia raised a cautionary finger. "But do not think this means you are safe. The monsters and beasts in humanity's territory are dangerous. You will find your fledging outposts and camps overrun time and again. And that is not all. Duskar, as the initiator of your world's assimilation, is mankind's Patron."

The elven queen all but spat out the last word. She took a calming breath before continuing. "The Trials permit Duskar alone to send troops into the wilds of your Dominion, both to protect and police humanity. Do not despair though. The elves have won the honor of serving as one of humanity's Sponsors. While this does not grant us the same rights as Duskar, the Trials allow us to create cities within your Dominion to shelter humanity from both its Patron and the dangers of Overworld."

Ionia directed her green-eyed gaze into the camera, staring right into my—and every other watching human's—eyes. "I implore you to enter Overworld through one of the elven gates. If you do, you will find yourself within one of our sponsored cities. I promise no pledges of loyalty will be demanded from you. My people will do everything to help you. We will provide you with shelter in return for a fair exchange of goods and resources. Goodbye, and fare thee well, humans."

* * *

The elven queen's speech caused as much consternation as Duskar's had. Every major media and news outlet spent countless hours replaying her words and dissecting the meaning beneath.

But more than the words themselves, experts mulled over the minor miracle that *everyone* who heard the orcish and elven leaders understood them—even those who spoke no English.

Initial reports had been wrong. The Overworlders' speech was not English, nor was it Russian, Chinese, or any language known to humans; yet, amazingly, everyone who heard the Overworlders understood every word. It had human scientists flummoxed and the craziest claiming it was magic.

The Internet, too, was rife with speculation. A new and "fresh" article, blogpost, and forum post appeared every minute, each fixated with the orcish and elven leaders' speech and mannerisms.

The web revealed there was apparently a third speech, too. It went largely unnoticed by the media, but was already causing a stir among select individuals.

My cell rang insistently, and I glanced down at the screen. *Eric.* He had called three times already. Engrossed in the broadcast of the elven queen's speech, I had somehow missed his calls.

"Hi," I answered. "You watching this? First orcs, now elves... what is the world coming to?"

"You haven't seen anything yet, man." Eric chuckled, but worry sliced through his tone.

About to launch into my own analysis of Ionia's speech, I paused. "What do you mean?"

"You heard the gnomes yet?"

"Gnomes? You're pulling my leg!" But I already knew he wasn't. If there were elves and orcs, why not gnomes?

"Nah, man. I'm not. The gnomish leader gave a speech too. I take it you haven't heard it yet?"

"No," I replied. "For some reason, there is no footage of it on the news. I've been trying to find a recording on the web."

"Well, you gotta watch it."

"Which gates belong to the gnomes?" I asked. We had learned that the color of the artifacts indicated the controlling species. Duskar's speech was broadcast from the red gates, and Ionia's from every green structure.

"The blue ones," Eric replied.

"Ah," I breathed. The blue artifacts were the least numerous, which explained why footage of the gnomish leader's speech was scarce. It was likely that no reporters had been in a position to film the speech, which left me wondering about the orange and black gates. No speeches had been broadcast from them yet. *Which species control those gates?* We would find out soon enough, I suspected.

"So, what did the gnomes say?" I asked Eric. "Something different?"

"You could say that," he chuckled nervously again before breaking into a bout of laughter that left me scowling. I pulled my cell away from my ear and stared at it.

Eric was my best friend, but sometimes I wanted to strangle him. "Come on, don't leave me hanging. What did you hear?"

His laughter sputtered out. "The gnomes," he finally gasped, "claim to be the first Overworld species to have discovered Earth. They *claim* that they have been preparing humanity for voluntary assimilation for the past few centuries. They *claim* to have injected their own stories into human history—can you believe it? The gnomish leader was quite upset with the orcs and went to great lengths to accuse them of stealing the gnomes' Patron rights before Earth's assimilation could be completed."

"All right," I said, perplexed. "That's mildly interesting, I admit, but not worthy of much attention considering everything else that has happened."

"Oh, I haven't gotten to the best part yet. Do you want to guess how else the gnomes have been readying humanity for Overworld? In the last few years, at least?"

"No, Eric, I don't want to guess," I growled. "Just spit it out."

"You're no fun, man," he lamented.

"Eric—"

Knowing me too well, he headed off my impending explosion before it began. "All right, all right, I'll tell you. The gnomes haven't just altered our myths and legends, they have also influenced our gaming culture—or so they claim."

"What?"

Eric chuckled, sensing my confusion. "You heard right, buddy. According to the gnomes, they've guided video game development on Earth to provide humanity with a basic understanding of the Trials' principles before we entered Overworld. And that still isn't the best part."

"Oh?" I struggled to be patient, knowing that Eric's annoying flair for the dramatic meant he was purposely dragging out the mystery. I hurried to my laptop and began typing in search words.

"You betcha!" he exclaimed. "They've uploaded what they're calling the Trials Infopedia onto the web. It's really something, this Overworld. Kind of makes me want to go in already. I swear you're gonna fall off your chair when you see—"

I ended the call as the search results appeared. *Maybe that'll teach him*, I thought with a chuckle of my own. I didn't hold out much hope, though. The oddest things amused him. He was probably laughing at my reaction right now. Banishing Eric from my thoughts, I turned my attention to the webpage containing the gnomes' data on the Trials.

As I scrolled through the information, one thought kept occurring to me. "It's a game," I whispered breathlessly. "Overworld is a goddamn game."

Chapter Three

03 May

"There is something troubling about the humans. We must keep a close watch on them."
—Ionia Amyla.

I stayed up late that night.

After Eric's call, Mom and I had watched a recording of the gnomish leader's speech. Mom had long since fallen asleep on the couch, but I remained at my computer, poring over the Trials Infopedia.

I still had no idea what to make of Overworld, Duskar, Ionia, or the gnomes' information. It all still felt like a hoax to me—I mean, who could believe the world was going to end in two weeks? The gnomes' "data" only deepened my belief that it was an elaborate lie.

But, fake or not, the information in the Trials Infopedia was as fascinating as it was dense. The wiki's webpages could have filled a dozen encyclopedias twice over. It would take months to sift through the mountain of information. I started by skimming through the thoughtfully provided synopses.

According to the wiki, Overworld was a land controlled by a Game: the so-called Trials. At least, that's how I interpreted what I read.

Overworld was supposedly filled with dungeons, monsters, resources, and regions called Dominions. Each Dominion was the territory of a single species and expanded or contracted as that race's players gained or lost ground, or as factions within the territory revolted or joined other Dominions.

The Trials appeared to have no purpose other than advancing the players on both an individual and species level. But for all that the Trials was seemingly a game, it contained no game constructs or artificial intelligence. Every player was a thinking being, and every monster and beast a living, breathing creature, even in the dungeons.

The most intriguing aspect of Overworld, though, was its leveling system. It was completely open-ended, with no classes, item restrictions, level caps, or limits to the number of traits a player could obtain. And in that way, it differed strikingly from roleplaying games here on Earth.

The game mechanics—or 'Trials' as the Overworlders called them—made no attempt at balance. They focused purely on measuring a player's achievements and rewarding them with knowledge and physical enhancements.

And that was the extent of the Trials' interference.

There were no system-generated quests or items. Everything was controlled by players as they struggled for survival, whether as individuals, nations, or factions. It was a player-driven world in an environment as intriguing and unbalanced as it was brutal.

I realized then that there was nothing fair about Overworld. Humanity's entrance into the Trials reeked of injustice, and assuming this wasn't some bizarre fabrication, I knew that neither Mom nor I could expect any mercy. And neither could humanity itself.

Perhaps Overworld is not a game after all, I mused. Maybe, Ionia had spoken true and the Trials reflected what Overworld actually was: a training ground. *But to what end?*

"What will it take to survive in such a world?" I murmured, glancing again at the screen I had been staring at for the last hour.

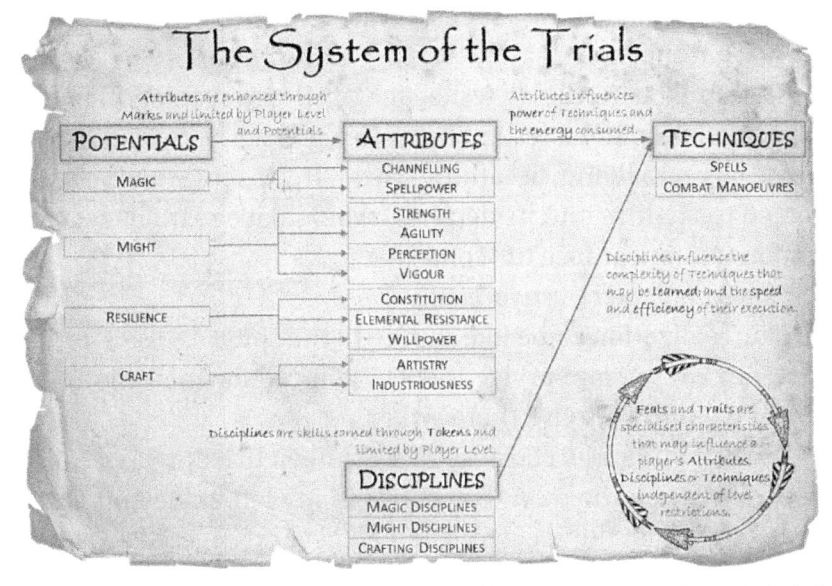

The System of the Trials

Attributes are enhanced through Marks and limited by Player Level and Potentials

POTENTIALS
- MAGIC
- MIGHT
- RESILIENCE
- CRAFT

ATTRIBUTES
- CHANNELLING
- SPELLPOWER
- STRENGTH
- AGILITY
- PERCEPTION
- VIGOUR
- CONSTITUTION
- ELEMENTAL RESISTANCE
- WILLPOWER
- ARTISTRY
- INDUSTRIOUSNESS

Attributes influence power of Techniques and the energy consumed

TECHNIQUES
- SPELLS
- COMBAT MANOEUVRES

Disciplines influence the complexity of Techniques that may be learned, and the speed and efficiency of their execution.

Disciplines are skills earned through Tokens and limited by Player Level.

DISCIPLINES
- MAGIC DISCIPLINES
- MIGHT DISCIPLINES
- CRAFTING DISCIPLINES

Feats and Traits are specialised characteristics that may influence a player's Attributes, Disciplines or Techniques independent of level restrictions.

Depicted in a single succinct diagram was the Trials' measurement system, with its four key aspects: Potentials, Attributes, Disciplines, and Techniques.

Disciplines were skills—knowledge that could be directly acquired from the system. There were hundreds of Disciplines, and no restrictions on which ones a player could learn, although there were three limiting factors.

One, a player was granted only five Tokens for every level he advanced. These could be used to advance a player's Discipline in whatever manner desired, but the limit of five Tokens was a hard restriction that could only be lifted by rare Traits.

Two, the effectiveness of a player's Techniques—or abilities— was determined by both his Disciplines *and* the related Attributes.

Attributes enhanced a player's physical and mental characteristics through the use of Marks, and a player only received two of them every level.

Three, most importantly, Attributes were *not* freewheeling characteristics; instead, they were limited by a player's core nature: his Potentials.

All Potentials were locked from birth, determined by the die of fate. There was no way to change them. If you had no Potential for

Magic, you couldn't cast spells. It was that simple. Your Potentials were what they were.

It seemed a needlessly cruel and arbitrary system, making me sure that, despite its resemblance to a game, Overworld was *not* a game. It was a living, breathing world. If, by some madness, I was forced to venture into its depths, I would have to hold fast to that understanding or face the consequences.

But I can't enter Overworld.

The realization came like a knife to the spine.

Mom would not survive there. I glanced down at my hobbled foot. I wouldn't survive there either.

My crippling was courtesy of a drunken driver who'd failed to keep his car on the road. The bones in my left ankle and foot had been crushed in the accident and had never recovered properly.

Despite running herself ragged, Mom had not been able to afford anything more than the most rudimentary of surgeries to mend the damage. Now years later, the bones had fused together, leaving me hobbled for life.

In many ways, the accident had been harder on Mom than me. I knew she had never forgiven herself for not being able to provide me with the care I needed. And if I had to guess where her slow decline of mental health had begun, it would have to be there.

I swallowed back the memories. My handicap did not bother me anymore. I had lived with it for so long that I could barely remember a time when I could run or jump freely. But how would I ever survive on Overworld?

I shook off the grim thought. Duskar's ultimatum had to be nonsense, didn't it? The notion that the world would end in two weeks felt preposterous. *It has to be a hoax.*

As thrilling as Eric clearly found the prospect of Overworld, entering it simply wasn't for me. Stifling yet another yawn, I got up and headed to bed.

✳ ✳ ✳

I awoke with a pounding headache and turned my bloodshot gaze to the clock. It was 7 am. I had only managed four hours of sleep.

With a groan, I flopped back onto my bed, determined to close my eyes and let sleep claim me, but it was no use.

A honking car horn, birdcalls, streaming sunlight, and Mom clattering in the kitchen all defeated my attempts.

Accepting the inevitable, I sat up and limped to the bathroom. Leaning over the sink, I stared at my haggard appearance. Hazel eyes peered back at me from a face with too many age lines for someone who had just turned twenty-four. Too many responsibilities, too many bills to pay, and not enough hours in the day.

At least until a few days ago.

Now I had more time on my hands than I cared for. "What do we do today, Jamie?" I asked my reflection, but it was no more enlightened than I was. I rubbed at my chin, its dark-brown stubble was getting ragged. I needed a shave. *Tomorrow*, I decided. *Or the next day.* It wasn't like I was going anywhere.

After finishing my morning ritual, I tottered back to my room. My gaze drifted from my computer to the columns of books stacked from floor to ceiling.

No gaming today.

None of the hundreds of games installed on my machine sparked my interest, not after reading the Trials Infopedia. Tilting my head, I studied the pile of novels. Perhaps I would read today. It had been a while since I'd lost myself in a good book.

"Jamie!" Mom called from the lounge. "Are you finally awake? Come see what's on the news!"

I groaned quietly. *What now?* I was damnably tired of hearing about the artifacts, but I didn't let my ill-humor color my voice as I called, "Coming, Ma. Be there in a minute."

Grabbing a well-worn copy of my favorite novel, I made my way into the living room and sat beside Mom on the couch. Her color was better—her face was less pale and her eyes sparkled with interest.

Contrary to my expectations, yesterday's news had raised her spirits. *Perhaps I can even return to work tomorrow*, I thought with cautious optimism.

"It's the New York gate. Something is coming through!"

"What?" I swung my gaze back to the television. It was true. Reporters on the scene were gesticulating wildly as they filmed a small column of orcs passing through the gate. They carried a cloth banner bearing the insignia of a single fang. Duskar's men, I guessed.

Federal agents and military personnel rushed to surround them, guns drawn on the self-declared enemies of humanity.

For my part, I was simply amazed that the artifact actually *was* a gate. If the orcs were here—on Earth—they had to have come from somewhere, and that somewhere had to be Overworld.

So... it really exists.

If the aliens weren't lying about Overworld's existence, the gnomes' description of the Trials system was probably correct too. I pushed down the trepidation and excitement worming through me.

It is not for me, I reminded myself. *Or Mom.*

Wrenching my thoughts away, I studied the orcs and the dozens of government personnel around them.

The Overworlders were green-skinned giants, half-again as tall as the average human and with hands as large as most men's heads. Each orc was armored in a mountain of steel and carried an arsenal of weapons: swords, axes, and war hammers.

Their attire did not surprise me. The Infopedia had suggested Overworld was a technologically backward world, albeit one with magic. The wiki's claim of magic hadn't shocked me either. How else to explain the gates' appearance?

The orcs' stature also made it easy to understand why they were one of Overworld's dominant species. *They must make fearsome warriors on Overworld... but they'll stand no chance on Earth.* The armor each behemoth wore wouldn't protect them against the fury of modern weaponry.

I leaned forward in anticipation. The orcs were about to be taught a lesson they wouldn't soon forget.

An army colonel hollered at the orcs to drop their weapons. The green-skinned giants ignored him, forming twin lines and marching forward.

I noticed they were making directly for the largest concentration of defenders. The colonel shouted more orders, and his soldiers pulled back.

The orcs kept advancing. "Halt!" the human officer yelled again, but once more the Overworlders ignored him. Disregarding the weapons pointed their way, they ploughed through the defenders' barricades.

The colonel had had enough. Abandoning further attempts at reason, he ordered his men to fire.

Chaos ensued. The broadcast devolved into a blur of half-caught movement, smoke-filled fury, screaming civilians, and unintelligible commentary.

I clenched my hands, waiting for order to be restored. Finally, the camera's field of view cleared.

Mom's eyes widened in disbelief.

Shielded beneath a transparent ruby dome, the orcs were unharmed. The force field—because that was what it surely had to be—originated from the raised wooden staff of the lead orc.

That orc, while steel-clad like his fellows, bore only one weapon: a wooden staff. His armor, too, was different. Where his fellows' breastplates were plain, his was adorned with runes similar to those inscribed on the gate.

A mage?

The warriors behind the mage stared in angry confusion at the soldiers, who, observing how little effect their rifles had, backed away.

Evidently, the Overworlders had never seen human weapons before, but it was equally clear they were unimpressed. The largest orc raised his massive two-handed axe and bellowed furiously, causing the remaining civilians to flee.

The warrior stepped forward to charge the soldiers, but the mage placed a hand on the axeman's arm, and he fell back into position.

The colonel, however, was not done. Spitting orders into his radio, he called in the waiting armored tanks. Their turrets lifted and rotated into position, but before the final order to fire could be given, the orcs vanished.

The colonel and the reporters scratched their heads in confusion.

I did likewise. *Where'd they go?*

* * *

It did not take long for the world to find out.

Contrary to the media's military commentators, who had vocally asserted that the orcs had fled—scared off by humanity's might—the orcs had not retreated. Instead, we learned they had teleported themselves to an apartment a few blocks from the gate, where, for some inexplicable reason, they abducted its sole occupant.

News crews rushed to the scene, but the orcs were gone long before the cameras arrived, leaving the unhappy reporters with nothing to film but the destruction the orcs left in their wake.

And there was a lot of it.

The green-skinned invaders made no attempt to disguise their presence. Bodies of innocent bystanders cleaved in half, smashed walls, and busted doors bore testament to the orcs' proclivity for violence.

I gripped Mom's hand, staring at the orcs' gruesome handiwork. It finally drove home the reality of the last few days.

Earth had been invaded by hostile aliens!

And we were helpless to stop them. I glanced at Mom. Her jaw was clamped shut and her eyes flitted restlessly across the TV. She was scared. Petrified, but doing her best not so show it.

How was I going to protect her? Only now did I realize that I might need to physically shield her from the violence the invaders brought. But how? Guns were of no use; the military had proved that.

I stared down at my arms. Once, I had prided myself on my athletic ability. But after the accident I had shied away from physical activities and turned my mind to academic pursuits.

And now, I thought bitterly, *I am in no condition to protect myself, much less Mom.*

What do I do?

CHAPTER FOUR

05 May: 12 days to Earth's destruction

> *"My colleagues believe the humans are dangerous. I disagree. Certainly, they are a violent and bloodthirsty species, but they also possess a capacity for greatness and ingenuity that I find remarkable. In time, the humans may prove to be our salvation."*
> —Arustolyx, gnomish archaeologist.

The next day, the second since Duskar's ultimatum, the other gates also opened, and humanity was treated to its first sight of elves, gnomes, fiends, and svartalfar. While humanity's encounters with the elves and gnomes were peaceful, first contact with the fiends and svartalfar—dark elves—was decidedly not.

Both encounters made the New York incident with the orcs appear tame by comparison. The fiends, who were diminutive, scaled, and hoofed humanoids with a long central horn sloping backward from their heads, emerged from the orange-tinged gates in a fury of flame and fire. They immediately set upon everyone near the Paris gate, civilian and military personnel alike.

In short order, the hapless French armed forces guarding the gate were slaughtered, and the city of Paris was set aflame before the fiends, like the orcs before them, disappeared.

The svartalfar were more... refined... in their butchery. With skin the deepest shade of blue, colorless eyes, and shocking white hair, wherever the dark elves emerged from their black gates, they wrought destruction on a staggering scale.

It took only *three* svartalfar mages, wielding magical whips of freezing light and calling down the fury of an ice storm in the middle of summer to turn the entire city of Tokyo into a frozen wasteland devoid of life.

I watched the televised mass murders in a state of stunned shock. What possessed the Overworlders to slaughter so indiscriminately? Was it not enough that our world was to be consumed by theirs? Why did they have to kill us so wantonly as well?

"How can any of this be real?" sobbed Mom in anguish.

"I don't know, Ma," I replied. It was a response I was drearily tired of, and it was past time that I rectified my ignorance. "We have to stop assuming that the happenings around the world won't affect us. We have to get ready," I finished grimly.

Mom's face scrunched up in confusion. "But ready for what, Jamie? How do we prepare for the end of the world?"

I took her hands in mine and stared into her eyes. "We have to behave as if everything that orc Duskar said was true. We have to assume we will be forced to enter this Overworld, and we have to plan for how we will survive there."

Mom's hands trembled as her anxiety peaked. "Jamie, I can't. I don't—"

"I know, Ma," I said gently, "but we have to try. The world has changed, and the end may be near. We can't go on as usual. Will you help me? Please."

"All right, Jamie." She took in a tremulous breath. "Where do we start?"

"Research," I said without hesitation. "Do you remember the gnomes' broadcast?"

Mom tilted her head in thought. "The race of short, chubby people?"

"Yes, that's them. Eric found a wiki that they put on the Internet—or said they did. Our first task will be to learn everything we can from it."

Mom nodded.

"The more we learn about Overworld, the better prepared we'll be to face its dangers." I waved my hand over my body. "Even with our handicaps," I said wryly, "the information will benefit us. Knowledge is power."

"Oh, Jamie." Mom's eyes filled with tears, as they did every time I made mention of my disability.

I cursed myself for my momentary self-pity. I needed to keep Mom focused, and she wouldn't focus if she was dwelling on things that couldn't be changed. I rose to my feet and pulled her up with me.

"Come on, Ma." I led her to my computer. Sitting her down in my chair, I opened the Trials Infopedia. "This is the wiki page I told you about. Start reading, don't rush, and ask me about anything you don't understand."

"Where do I begin?" Mom stared at the bewildering array of menus and submenus.

"Just the overviews for now," I said, pointing out the relevant sections on the screen. "We'll tackle the rest later."

"All right." Determined, Mom pulled on her reading glasses. She glanced at me. "What are you going to do?"

"I'm going to figure out a way to get us to a gnomish gate."

After ensuring she was all set, I left Mom to her research and went into the kitchen. Pulling out my cell, I dialed Eric. He answered immediately.

"You've seen the news?" he began without preamble.

"Yep." I leaned back in my chair. "I think it's time we took this seriously."

"I couldn't agree more, my man. Emma is going crazy over here." Eric's girlfriend shared his tiny apartment.

"What? You mean she's not taking the coming apocalypse well?"

Only with Eric could I be this glib. We had been friends since forever; he understood me better than anyone and he knew as well as I did that sometimes only humor could ward off the horrors life threw at you.

"No, she is not," he replied with a laugh. "How is your Mom doing?"

"She's... managing."

"That's good." I heard his sigh of relief. In spite of his teasing, Eric had helped me through the worst of Mom's episodes. He knew how bad it could get. "So, what are you thinking?"

"We have to assume we'll have no choice but to abandon Earth. Our best bet will be to enter Overworld through a gnomish gate."

"My thoughts exactly," he agreed.

"I haven't been keeping track of the gate locations. We'll have to find the nearest one—"

"Way ahead of you there, bud. I've already checked. There's a gnomish gate in the city next to mine, less than five miles away." He paused, but then added reluctantly, "There aren't any near you, though."

"Damn!" Eric and I no longer lived in the same town. While I had stayed behind in our hometown, Eric had traveled to the city in search of a job. "How far away is the closest one to me?" I asked, chewing my lip.

Eric was slow to answer, which only heightened my concern. "The gnome gates are few and far between," he explained. "They're a much smaller Dominion than the orcs or elves. The last time I checked, there were only four hundred and twenty-seven confirmed sightings of gnomish gates worldwide."

"Quit stalling, Eric. Just tell me."

He blew out a breath. "The nearest gnomish gate to you is the one near me."

I swallowed. That was a few hundred miles away. Getting to the gate was not going to be simple, but I would manage it. Somehow. "We'll get there," I promised.

"I know you will," said Eric confidently. "I'll wait for you."

"Damn right you will!" I exclaimed. Then added more soberly, "But in all seriousness, only wait as long as you can. Go if you have to."

"I won't leave you, Jamie," he said with quiet conviction.

I choked down emotion. Eric's loyalty still caught me by surprise at times. "We have to contact the others," I said, changing the topic.

"The others" were the rest of our gaming clan and our closest friends. We had been playing together for years. Considering the nature of the Trials, I thought gamers would best understand the strange new world and its mechanics.

"You're right. The more we band together, the better our odds of survival. Leave it with me. I'll contact the gang. You figure out how to get to the gate."

"Right. I'll call you tomorrow after I've checked what's what. After that, we can confirm our timelines."

"Wait, Jamie, before you go ... Did you see the latest gnomish broadcast?"

"No. Why?"

"You gotta watch it. Their representative explained what the orcs, fiends, and svartalfars are up to. The destruction wreaked in Paris and Tokyo wasn't as senseless as it seemed. The two races were securing the gate for their retrieval parties."

"Retrieval parties? What are they retrieving?"

"Not what—who. The orcs, fiends, and svartalfar are hunting down those with an affinity for magic and forcibly abducting them. Even the gnomes and elves are aggressively recruiting, although more peacefully than their counterparts. The elvish and gnomish representatives have offered generous rewards for humans with Magic Potential to join their cause."

I scratched at my beard, confused. "But why bother with any of that?"

"How much of the Infopedia did you read?"

"Not much," I admitted. "So far, I've only managed to get through the overviews."

"Then you know a person's Potential is fixed, right?"

"Sure, but what does that have to do with anything?"

"Everything! You see, magic is scarce in Overworld—rarer than a fish on dry land. All the Dominions will risk war for the chance of getting their hands on more mages. The Overworlders are using this opportunity to increase their contingent of magic users by dragging humans with Magic Potential into their service."

"How are they finding them?"

"That, I don't know. The elves and gnomes weren't clear on that part."

"Hmm," I mused, chewing my bottom lip in thought. I understood the implications. If any of our friends had Potential for magic, it would improve our odds of survival in Overworld, but it would also paint a target on our backs.

Is there any way we can determine who has Magic Potential? Evidently, I would need to spend more time wading through the Trials Infopedia. If answers could be found anywhere, it was likely there.

Returning to the present, I said, "Thanks, Eric. I'll make sure I watch the broadcast. Take care, my friend."

"Bye, Jamie."

CHAPTER FIVE

05 May: 12 days to Earth's destruction

> "Sir. There have been 10,214 confirmed Overworld gate sightings worldwide. Of the gates identified, the orcs control approximately forty percent, the elves roughly thirty percent, and the gnomes less than five percent.
> "While the gnomes seem the least threatening of the alien species, judging by gate numbers, they also appear to be weaker than the elves. Our analysts are of the opinion they will make for poor allies.
> "It is my department's recommendation that an alliance be sought with the elves instead."
> —Classified intelligence report.

After firing up my laptop and setting a jug of coffee to boil, I set up shop in the kitchen and got to work. It did not take me long to find what I was seeking in the Infopedia.

The wiki was admirably well-indexed and sorted. However, the answer was disappointing. All players in Overworld had a Technique called *analyze*, which revealed another player's Potential to them. This, of course, was no help to me or any other human still on Earth. We would have to enter Overworld and undergo the Trials Initiation before we obtained the same Technique, but by then, we would presumably know our own Potentials already.

Closing down the wiki page, I turned my efforts to my next vital task: figuring out how to get to a gnomish gate safely; this proved more arduous than expected.

The world had descended into chaos.

After the attacks by the orcs, fiends, and svartalfar, Earth's nations had declared war. All over the world, militaries had launched strikes against the Overworld gates. They had thrown everything they could at the artifacts, from small artillery fire to air strikes—and even a nuke in the case of one Chinese gate. All to no avail. The gates were impervious to our weaponry.

The military failures did not go unnoticed by Earth's civilian population.

When people realized their governments had no effective means of protecting them, mass hysteria ensued. Airplanes were grounded, shopping malls were closed, highways were blocked off, shops were looted, and millions stampeded away from the orcish, fiend, and svartalfar gates to the benign-by-comparison elvish and gnomish ones.

Given the anarchy reigning in the world at large, traveling cross country was out of the question. Passage by air was impossible, and traffic on the highways had come to a grinding halt. For me and Mom, hiking a few hundred miles was not an option.

I was left with no choice but to search for an alternative gate.

Thankfully, digital communications had been left untouched by the chaos overturning the world, so I was able to pull up the location of all nearby Overworlder gates.

I groaned as I studied the information. Mom and I had no luck. Other than the orc gate in our town, no other gates existed within a day's walk.

The next nearest—an elven one, fortunately—was twenty miles away. At the rate Mom and I could walk it would take us at least two days, if not more. But there was no help for it. If we wanted to survive, we would make the journey.

Heaving a sigh, I limped to the window and peered out. Everything was relatively peaceful outside. Our rural town, isolated by distance, remained largely untouched by the anarchy afflicting the world. But I knew it wouldn't last. In days or hours, the rampant panic would come here too.

And before it did, I had to get ready.

I hadn't left the house in days, and it was finally time I did. I walked to my room and popped my head in. Mom was engrossed in the Trials Infopedia. "Ma, I'm going to the mall."

She turned to face me. "What? Why? We don't need anything."

I briefly contemplated lying, but the sooner she knew the truth the better. "The closest Overworld gate is twenty miles away. We're going to have to walk to get there. I have to go out and get the supplies we need."

Before there is nothing left to buy, I thought, but left the words unsaid. Some truths were better left unspoken.

"All right," she said, though she seemed uncertain. "If you think it's necessary."

"I do," I said. "Don't worry. I won't be long."

※ ※ ※

The town was subdued as I walked into it.

Remarkably, other than the local militia, no one appeared disturbed by the happenings in the rest of the world. The militia captain, an aging veteran who had seen more than his share of warfare, had set up a round-the-clock watch on the gate.

Captain Hicks didn't have the men to cordon the gate off completely—not that the mayor would have allowed it—but he made sure the area was kept under guard.

The good captain had even hauled a battered armored tank out of whatever junkheap it had been consigned to and returned it to some semblance of service. *Gods*, I thought as I limped passed the relic on the way to the mall, *where did Captain Hicks get that thing? And does it even work?*

Despite the militia's vigilance, everyone else believed what had happened elsewhere couldn't happen here. I shook my head at their blind faith, and went about my business.

Although the orc gate was within the mall parking lot and I itched to explore it, I stayed well away. Now wasn't the time to tempt fate. If an orc party unexpectedly exited the gate, I had no doubt they would execute everyone nearby.

I bought everything I could think of, and quite possibly more than Mom and I needed: camping gear, batteries, guns, and enough food for two weeks. We wouldn't set off for the gate immediately—there was plenty of research to do—but in the interim, I didn't want us to run out of supplies.

I hoped I wouldn't need to use the guns. The last thing Earth needed was more people killing each other, but human nature being what it was, I did not doubt there would be those who would prey on the weak and unprepared. I was determined that would not be me and Mom.

Later that night, I called Eric again. "Hi, mate. I got bad news."

"I know," he replied. "I've been following the news reports. The world's gone to shit. There's no way you gonna make your way cross-country to get here." He fell silent for a moment. "What are you going to do?"

"There is an elvish gate twenty miles away. Mom and I will make for it."

"That's great." I could tell from Eric's voice that he was beaming with happiness. "Better the elves than the fiends or orcs, or God forbid the svartalfar."

"Yes," I said, agreeing wholeheartedly.

"Did you get rations and supplies? The shops here are gutted. Emma and I barely found enough food to get us through the week."

"People here are still in denial. I've stocked up. The store will deliver everything tomorrow. What news from the rest of the crew?"

"Not good, man." Unhappiness crept back into his voice. "Half of them can't make it. They're either too far away from a gate, or they have their own families to take care of."

"Oh," I said, sharing his disappointment. "And the other half?"

"I couldn't reach most of them. The two I did reach, Doug and Michael, will join us with whatever friends and family they can rustle up."

"That's great." I was pleased Eric and Emma wouldn't be alone; not like Mom and me. After a moment's silence, I asked, "When do you plan on leaving for the gate?"

"Not for a few days at least. I want to learn as much as I can from the wiki before we set out. Too bad the gates won't let us transport anything but ourselves through, otherwise I would carry a stack of notes with me."

According to the wiki, new players couldn't take anything on their journey into the Trials. We would lose even the clothes on our backs when we entered Overworld. I couldn't help wondering how though, how the Overworlders were making the same trip with all their gear. It bore looking into.

"What about you?" asked Eric, interrupting my musing.

"Me? I've been thinking along the same lines as you. We'll give it about a week and learn everything we can from the wiki first. Who knows, maybe the world will return to order before then." Though I doubted it.

"I hope so too." Eric fell silent again. We both felt in a sense that this was goodbye. We might never see each other again. Our paths were diverging, and who knew how far apart we would find ourselves in Overworld, once we entered our respective gates. "We need to find a way to communicate with each other once we get there," I said at last.

"Definitely. I'll make that a priority in my search of the wiki."

"Me too," I said. "All right, then… good night, Eric. Take care of yourself."

"You too, man," he replied. "And, Jamie… If I never see you again, just know—"

"I know, Eric," I murmured, hearing his choked-off sob on the other end. "Thanks for everything. I will never forget everything you've done for me."

"Me neither, my friend. Stay safe."

CHAPTER SIX

06 MAY: 11 DAYS TO EARTH'S DESTRUCTION

> "Sir. All attempts to establish contact with the svartalfar have failed. They slaughter our envoys on sight. We have been forced to conclude that negotiations with the Overworlder races are impossible and recommend discontinuing this line of investigation."
> —Military report.

The next few days passed in a blur.

To my great relief, all the goods I ordered were delivered the next day in full, without any surprises. After making sure I understood how all the equipment worked, and packing backpacks for both Mom and me so we could leave at a moment's notice, I dove into the Trials Infopedia, only venturing up for air to eat or sleep.

I spent days learning about Overworld and its history. It seemed there were far more intelligent races on Overworld than the five who had created gates to Earth. The others were races whose Dominions were too far from wherever the Human Dominion had been founded, or who had played no part in assimilating Earth.

There was one bit of Overworld lore that caught my attention in particular. It was a reference to the Elders, the beings responsible for the creation of Overworld and the Trials themselves.

The gnomes called them dragons.

I gathered from the Trials Infopedia that the Overworld dragons bore a striking resemblance to the dragons of human folklore. Earth's earliest dragon tales, dated back thousands of years, but it seemed impossible that the gnomes had been tinkering with human myths for that long. Were the Overworld dragons and Earth's dragons one and the same? If so, how could that be?

Answers to the mystery would not be easy to find either. According to the wiki, the Elders had vanished millennia ago. It was still an intriguing bit of lore and it quickened my interest in Overworld and its history.

Mom, to my secret relief, was as captivated by Overworld as I was. Immersing herself in the Trials Infopedia with relish. Every day, she grew a trifle more confident, a touch steadier, and by midweek, she appeared to have left her anxieties behind her.

My study of the Trials Infopedia advanced steadily, if slowly. By the end of the first day, I knew there was no way I could memorize even half its information in the time available, forcing me to prioritize.

Regardless, as the week advanced, my confidence grew. Assuming Mom and I managed a decent start, we could survive Overworld. I was sure of it.

But even as we stayed cooped up at home, things in the world outside deteriorated. Abductions by the evil Overworlder civilizations—as I had come to think of the orcs, fiends, and svartalfar—continued unabated. Every day, there was a new story of another human taken prisoner, another home destroyed, or another military defeat.

News from our scientists painted an even bleaker picture. Researchers from around the world published a flurry of papers with data that, to the dismay of many, supported Duskar's predictions: the world was ending.

Earth's seismic and volcanic activity had spiked so severely that geologists predicted natural disasters on an unprecedented scale less than ten days from now. Scientists were unable to pinpoint the cause of the instability, but all agreed that an unknown force was manipulating the Earth's core.

Understandably, the news sent shockwaves across the world, and hastened humanity's exodus through the Overworlder gates. Some did not even bother distinguishing between the Overworlder races, entering whichever gate was nearest.

The news, while disturbing, was not catastrophic enough to affect my timeline. Mom and I could still enter Overworld with time to spare. We planned on setting off for the elvish gate in two days, which by my calculations left us four days to make the trip before Duskar's ordained end of the world occurred. Four whole days, I felt, gave us a comfortable margin of security.

But the day before we were due to leave, as Mom and I were finishing our preparations, disaster struck.

* * *

12 May: 11 days to Earth's destruction

I was in my room, staring fixedly at my screen and trying to ignore the glare peeking through my curtains, when Mom's shout broke through my thoughts. "Jamie!"

"Ma?" I called, deeply absorbed in an obtuse paragraph on the workings of dungeons in Overworld, and hesitant to leave my chair.

"It's the gate—it's opening!"

"Again?" I responded, thinking she was watching the news. "How many orcs came through this time?"

There was a moment of shocked silence as Mom processed my response. "No, Jamie, not on the telly! The one in town!" she yelled.

What?! I bolted upright and raced—well, shambled—straight to the lounge. The portal in our town had never opened from the Overworld side, and everyone in town had begun to think it never would. A few braver souls had entered its depths and vanished, evidence enough that the gate worked.

But no orcs had appeared—proof, the town gossips said proudly, that our town was too inconspicuous for even the Overworlders to bother with.

I stepped up to Mom's stiff form at the window and peered outside. Most of the townsfolk were still asleep, but the few who weren't were sprinting away from the gate. Captain Hicks's troops were in turmoil: dashing for cover, or unshouldering and readying their weapons. I swallowed nervously. All this activity seemed proof enough, but I searched on.

Then I saw them.

Beyond the frenetic militia, loomed the orcs' distinctive, green-skinned forms. My stomach clenched.

Why are they here?

But I knew the answer: to abduct someone. Whoever the unlucky individual was, there was little hope of resistance. In the countless abductions reported over the past few days, there was not a single mention of a failed attempt.

"Ma, keep watch. I'm grabbing the backpacks," I yelled over the sounds of erupting gunfire as the militia engaged the orcs. "We leave now!" I hurried to the closet where I had stored our backpacks.

The town was no longer safe. I wished Captain Hicks and his men the best of luck, but they were already doomed, and I wasn't about to let us share their fate. *We should have left earlier, when we had the chance. Damn it!*

"Jamie!" Mom's bone-chilling cry of fear, like nothing I had ever heard before, made me swing around.

"Wha—?" The words died in my throat, and my face drained of color. Lurking outside our house were two of the green-skinned monsters.

The orcs were here.

"Quick, Ma," I shouted. "Run—"

But it was too late.

The door and the surrounding wall shattered, and two nine-foot-tall giants barged in. The first, an armored brute with one chipped tusk, wielded a hammer nearly as tall as I was. He locked eyes on Mom as he advanced.

I limped back into the lounge, fumbling for the gun in my backpack. Forcing myself in front of her, I screamed, "Leave my—"

My useless words were cut short as a massive fist seized me and effortlessly lifted me into the air. My legs dangled as the orc raised me higher, for inspection. The behemoth shoved his face into mine.

He is going to eat me! my mind screamed.

But the orc only took one long sniff before grunting dismissively and tossing me out the window. The pane and wooden bars shattered—no obstacle to my violent momentum.

I rolled to a stop on the front lawn, surrounded by broken glass. Dazed, battered, and sporting a host of stinging cuts, I was otherwise whole.

My thoughts frayed, I pushed myself upright on trembling limbs and saw that I lay at the feet of three more orcs, all observing my struggles in contemptuous silence. The staff one of them bore identified him as a mage.

Mom shrieked.

No!

Orcs forgotten, I whipped around in time to see Mom's tiny form sail through the same window I had. My heart stalled at the sight, but at the twitching of her crumpled form, I began to breathe again. She was alive. Like me, she was covered in cuts and bruises, but she had survived.

Wood cracked again as the two armored giants punched another hole in our abused house on their way out. I threw myself protectively over Mom as the pair lumbered past. Ignoring us, they made for the line of waiting orcs.

My heart thudded in painful relief. But it was short-lived. Our straits were dire. *This isn't good, Jamie, not good at all. How are you going to save Mom?* I had no answer.

"These two were the only humans inside, Shaman," reported one of our captors, his voice barely more than a growl.

The shaman stroked his chin with one clawed hand—carefully manicured I noted, inanely—and studied Mom for a silent second before flicking his gaze back to me.

His eyes narrowed. Pinned by his stare, I huddled down, my mind worked frantically. A moment later, rocking back, the orc's eyes widened in shock. "Impossible!" he exclaimed.

The other four orcs tensed and set cautious hands on their weapons. "What is it, Shaman?" asked the brute to the shaman's left. He was larger than his fellow warriors and his armor more elaborately decorated.

"His Magic Potential, Pack Leader. It's like nothing I've ever seen before!"

"Hrnn," grunted the pack leader in disinterest, and relaxed from his alert posture.

"You don't understand," replied the shaman. "The warlord himself will reward us for this!"

Not even that sparked the pack leader's interest. "What about the other one?" He pointed his axe at Mom. "Do you need her?"

The shaman flicked his hand dismissively. "No. Kill her."

"What? No!" I screamed, shielding Mom with my body. "I'll do anything you want. Just don't hurt her!"

Ignoring me, the pack leader advanced steadily forward. "Please, please—" I begged.

Rough hands grabbed me from behind and flung me away. I tumbled to a stop, face-first in the grass.

"Careful with him, you fool! His hide is more valuable than yours!" the shaman shouted, berating the offending warrior.

"Jamie?" Mom's bewildered cry was little more than a whisper, barely audible.

"Ma! I'm coming!" I yelled, scrambling to my feet.

I was too late. An eternity too late.

The pack leader's axe slashed into Mom. And then out again. "No!" I shrieked, staggering forward. *It can't be. It isn't real. Mom can't be...* But the axe's wet *squelch* as it struck unresisting flesh refuted my denial.

I dropped to my knees in time with her body's soft *thud*, hearing over and over again the sound of axe on flesh.

"What have I done?" I moaned. Wrapping my arms around myself, I rocked mindlessly back and forth. *Oh, Mom, I'm sorry. I'm so sorry.* Why had we not left days ago? Why had I kept us here?

My head throbbed, and agony exploded behind my eyes. *This can't be real*, I thought. I fled the pain, fled myself, and watched—a spectator only—as the pack leader bent over my mother.

Numb with disbelief, I ignored him, my gaze fixed on Mom's feet and her floral-patterned dress. It had been her favorite.

A single rivulet of crimson trickled down Mom's body.

I wept, lacking the courage to follow the disturbing line of scarlet back to its source.

More streaks joined the first.

And despite my denial, reality intruded. The rivers of red transformed into a tide that seeped into Mom's once-pristine dress, marring it with ugly splotches.

It was blood. *Her blood.* I swallowed, unable to hold myself apart any longer. I looked up.

The pack leader was wiping his axe clean on Mom's clothes.

Horror lashed at me, and my vision turned red. In a haze of fury, I surged to my feet. Uncaring of the orcish warrior standing guard over me, I threw myself forward.

The orc reached for me, but I twisted away. Rage fueled me as I charged the pack leader, intent on wreaking vengeance for the one person whose life mattered more than mine.

Another orc stepped in my way. I dodged, but I failed to evade his grasp completely. His hands clutched at my shirt, but with a mighty heave, I wrenched free. Snarling, I resumed my charge, then staggered to halt as I caught sight of Mom's corpse—headless.

Why hadn't I noticed that before?

Twisting my head, I searched frantically for the rest of her. Two feet away, I spotted her severed head. I slumped to my knees, all life draining from me, transfixed by the frozen horror of her expression.

For as long as I live, I will never forget that last sight of my Mom: her eyes unnaturally wide and staring sightlessly; her nostrils flared wide in fear; and her mouth gaping open in a wordless scream of terror.

Oh, Ma.

Caving under the weight of my grief, I sagged listlessly and bent my head to the ground.

Mom was dead. She couldn't be. But she was.

A heavy foot thudded down on top of Mom's skull. The pack leader.

"Get up, you sniveling worm," he snarled. Winding his foot back, in an act as foul as it was sickening, the orc booted her away.

I lifted my bloodless eyes to stare at the orc. Had he not desecrated Mom enough? Why heap further perversion on her?

This monster cannot be suffered to live, whispered the voice of cold hatred in my head.

My rage reignited, and all reason fled. Bounding to my feet, more animal than human, I leaped onto the shocked warrior and clawed at his face.

Kill him. I will kill him, I vowed, seething with hatred.

Blows thudded into me, but I ignored them, feeling no pain. I raked my nails along the orc's face, carving deep furrows into his skin.

"Gently, you fools!" the shaman screamed. "Don't kill him!"

More blows landed, likewise unheeded. I had a singular purpose: to kill the green-skinned monster before me. Wrapping my legs firmly around the pack leader's neck, I tightened my grip and clawed my fingers deeper into his eyes.

The blows stopped. *Yes!* I exulted. *He is mine now.* I pushed harder, trying to gouge the orc's eyes out even as his tusks ate into me.

The shaman entered the fray, and something—not a blow—struck me from behind. My vision blurred. *No!* I wailed. *I can't die. Not yet. I must kill him.*

But my will alone was insufficient to hold the darkness at bay, and consciousness fled.

CHAPTER SEVEN

12 MAY: 5 DAYS TO EARTH'S DESTRUCTION

> *"Gentlemen, we must face reality: humanity has been subjugated. We cannot do anything to save Earth's millions, but we can still save ourselves. We must negotiate with the Overworlders."*
> —Unknown politician.

Awareness returned slowly.

With it came voices, reaching my ears as if muffled by great distance.

"We can't take him through the portal like this. His wounds are too severe. He will never survive."

"Who cares! Blasted human. How *dare* he attack me."

"Perhaps you shouldn't have enraged him, then," growled the first voice. "What were you thinking?"

The second grunted. *The pack leader*, I thought as memory returned. *He is still alive.* I despaired. Mom was dead, and not only had I failed to save her, but I had also failed to punish her killer. I choked back spiraling grief and bitterness.

Keeping my eyes closed, I followed the conversation of the two listlessly.

"What do we do now?" asked the pack leader.

"Send one of your men back to fetch healing ointments, or better yet, one of the healers."

"Healing ointments?" The pack leader sounded skeptical. "Is he really worth all *that*?"

"Listen to me, you fool! He is worth more than *all* our collective hides. If the warlord hears we let him slip through our fingers, we will suffer for it."

"As you wish," said the pack leader, his voice tight with anger. I almost smiled. Anything that made that killer unhappy made me happy.

Their voices faded as they walked away, and with nothing else to hold me to consciousness, I retreated into the comforting embrace of sleep.

Mom is dead, I thought forlornly, as darkness claimed me again.

* * *

When I next woke, it was to the smell of pungent herbs. I wrinkled my nose at the odor. Too late, I remembered that I was in enemy hands and could be under observation.

"Good, you're awake. Open your eyes," said the shaman.

I debated ignoring him. *The orcs have already done the worst they can to me*, I thought in painful realization. *What else is left for me in this life? Why not let it all go?*

"I know you are awake. Open your eyes. Now! Or I will order Yarl to kill more of your kind. He will take great pleasure in it."

"Yarl," I whispered, tasting the feel of the orc's name on my tongue. *So that is his name.* I swallowed back grief. The pack leader's name reminded me that I had failed, that Mom's killer was still alive.

Beyond that, I still had a purpose: to kill Yarl. To kill them all.

There is time yet. The orcs obviously believed me of some value, and while my first opportunity at revenge had been squandered, vengeance was still within my grasp.

I let my rage cool. Haste was my enemy. My first failure had taught me that. I would not avenge Mom with hot, impulsive action. Cold calculation—that was what I needed.

I must be like stone. Grieve later, I told myself. *Now, I must harden myself.* Drawing in my anguish and loathing, I locked it away in the dark recesses of my mind, letting it fester. With time, it would harden into a ball of fury that, when the opportunity presented itself, I would unleash.

Feeling my emotions drain away and equilibrium return, I opened my eyes and glared balefully at the shaman looming over me. "What do you want?" I spat.

The orc only smiled in the face of my anger. "You are feeling better, I see. Good. We have wasted enough time in this benighted world of yours. Sit up."

I sat, groaning with the effort. My back and arms felt as if they had been beaten to a pulp, and my face... I lifted my hands to probe the spot where the skin had been ripped open by Yarl's tusks.

The shaman slapped away my hands before I could make contact. "Don't do that! You will disturb the salve. The wounds still need to heal."

Why was I of such value to them? Then I remembered the conversation I'd overheard, and the jobs orc bands like this one were tasked with. *I must have Magic Potential.*

Good. I could use that.

A furious hissing sound pierced the air. I looked up in time to see a burning projectile crash into the shimmering barrier of red above us. The world outside disappeared as the dome's surface was momentarily consumed by a conflagration of sound and blinding white light.

I flinched. Yet neither the heat nor the flames from the explosion pierced the shaman's magical shield.

"Your countrymen," grunted the shaman, unperturbed by the incoming fire. "They have been throwing flaming rocks at us for the past hour. The fools don't learn. They will never get through my shield," he said with a hint of pride.

Artillery fire. Captain Hicks must have finally managed to get the decrepit and obsolete tank operational. *How long have I been out?*

I took in my surroundings. The orcs hadn't moved me. We were still outside my home. *Former home*, I thought bitterly. Whatever happened from here on out, I wouldn't be going back to it.

A second mortar shell cracked against the shaman's shield. This time, I ignored the impact and kept my eyes fixed on the orc.

As hard as he tried to hide his reaction, the shaman's start of surprise and swift upward glance betrayed his concern.

Ah, the orcs aren't invincible after all. God bless our bloodthirsty militia captain. Maybe he and his band of crazy old men could do what the country's military couldn't and kill some of the loathsome creatures.

My gaze dropped to a crate lying next to me. The wooden box didn't belong to me or Mom, and I'd never seen it on our lawn before. Where had it come from? I peered inside and gasped involuntarily.

The shaman noticed both the direction of my gaze and my reaction. "Some of your people's strange firebombs. Yarl collected a few. The fool wouldn't listen to me when I told him they wouldn't survive the transition through the gate. Do you know what they are?"

I shook my head, feigning ignorance as a glimmer of an idea took shape. To distract the shaman from the object of my interest, I asked, "What do you want?"

The longer I kept the shaman talking, the better. His shield couldn't last forever. Surely, sooner or later, it would sustain too much damage to remain in place?

But whether he was concerned by the falling mortar shells or not, the orc shaman appeared in no hurry. Taking his time, he scrabbled in his pouch before pulling out a medallion. "Hold this."

I eyed the object with suspicion. It was a gold disk inscribed with the Overworlders' strange runes on both sides. "What is it?" I demanded.

"Take it," repeated the shaman, ignoring my question. "If you do not,"—he gestured behind him—"I will get Yarl's soldiers to hold you down while I force you to comply. I do not need your consent."

My gaze slid beyond the shaman. Four orc warriors waited there, with Yarl at their fore. With his arms folded, the pack leader glared at me from under hooded eyes. But the effect was spoiled by the ribbons of blood decorating the warrior's green face.

I smiled, and even managed a chuckle on seeing his scarred visage. Yarl's scowl deepened, and he seemed poised to leap at me. Not wanting to give the orc the chance to vent his frustration on me, I grabbed the medallion from the shaman's hands.

The object was cool and fit neatly in my palm. I studied it more closely. Thousands of tiny runes were inscribed across its entire surface, but despite the decorative alien script, the medallion looked little different from an oversized coin. I frowned.

What is this thing? And why does he want me to hold it?

"Close your fist around it," demanded the shaman.

I glanced up at him. The orc's gaze was fixed on the medallion, but his face hardened as he noticed my hesitation. "Now!" he growled.

I didn't have much choice, I knew. My gaze flicked to the wooden crate. *Not yet.* With a small shrug, I complied with the shaman's order.

I froze as my fist closed around the medallion. Heat flared out from the object, into my body. "What the hell—"

I broke off as my vision blurred and a wave of nausea passed over me. I swayed, but before I could fall, the dizziness faded and my vision cleared.

I blinked. Then blinked again.

Words floated in the air.

... loading Trials Key successful. Basic interface installed. Analyzing host entity...

I gaped in amazement at the text superimposed on my sight. It was as if a window had unfurled in my mind, and words had spilled out.

Before I could make sense of the words, the Key in my hand grew hotter and further tendrils of energy snaked into my body.

Analysis complete: host complies with all requirements. Entity identified as Jameson Sinclair. Planet of origin: Earth. Species: *Homo sapiens*. Age: 24 years. Designation: Candidate, suitable for entry into the Trials.

Core ready for installation.

What is this? I wondered. *The Trials? Have I been made into a player?* Distracted by the Key's strange effect, I was slow to react when the shaman raised his hand. In response to the orc's gesture, the runes on the Key *lifted off* and seeped into my skin.

I blinked. The runes were inside me! I could *feel* them. In a slow march, they made their way through my palm, up my hand, and into my head.

I swayed again. My head felt fuzzy. More runes gathered in my mind, increasing my sense of disorientation, and I shuddered.

What's happening to me?

Runes poured into my head until it seemed as if my awareness was bursting with them. They formed patterns—patterns with forms I was on the edge of understanding.

I strained to focus. The runes began to make sense. Almost... I grasped their meaning. Then, the last rune entered my mind.

And my consciousness exploded.

Trials Key activated by shaman Kagan Firespawn. Commencing Trials core installation...

Core embedded...

Player basic data updated...

Species Traits unlocked...

Language: Overworld standard loaded...

Temple access granted...

Status updated...

Verifying configuration...

Core installation done: Induction completed.

I doubled over, gasping for breath. My heart thudded, and my pulse stuttered. I felt different.

Energized.

Depleted.

My awareness expanded. I was not alone in my mind anymore. Something else was in me.

I sensed a connection to something other, something that brushed the edges of my mind, a great nebulous... machine?

It is the Trials, I realized.

That was what I sensed—the Trials roots sinking into my mind. I shivered. When I read the wiki, the Trials had been an abstract concept. Now, feeling its interface reside in my mind and its tendrils coursing through my body, I realized how otherworldly it was.

What is it? A being? An entity? A machine?

I wasn't sure. Whatever the Trials was, it was so foreign I could scarcely comprehend it.

And now I'm connected to it forevermore.

More words appeared in my vision. Straightening, I raised a tentative hand to my temple as I read the message.

Introductory message: Jameson (Jamie) Sinclair, welcome to the Trials. Venture into Overworld to attain your true Potential. Henceforth, all your actions will be measured and weighed, and you will be rewarded or penalized accordingly.

Accumulate experience and accomplish deeds of greatness and you shall be rewarded with gifts of knowledge. Fail to do so, and you will find the Trials unforgiving.

Checking status...
Induction: completed.
Initiation: outstanding.
Enter a gate to complete your player configuration and become a full player. Current designation: Inductee, a player of level zero and rank zero. Experience, Attributes, and Disciplines locked.

Evaluating Potentials...
Your Might is mediocre. Your Craft is gifted. Your Resilience is exceptional. Your Magic is extraordinary.

I lowered my hand and pushed it experimentally through the translucent text hovering before me.

"What is it?" I needed confirmation—even if it was from an orc—that I wasn't going mad, that what I was seeing was real.

"That is your welcome to the Trials.," said the shaman with a grunt. After a sidelong glance at the orcs behind him, he lowered his voice. "Now, accept the oath."

"What?" I asked, not understanding. But it became horridly clear when another message opened a moment later.

Contract initiated: Shaman Kagan Firespawn has offered to take you under his wing as his slave. Accepting the contract shall bind you in perpetuity to the shaman's service. In return, the shaman offers you a master's protection.

As a slave, your free will shall be leashed. If you disobey your master, attempt to abdicate your oath, or earn his wrath, you shall be punished by debilitating negative Traits.

Do you accept Kagan Firespawn's contract of service?

"No!" I snarled. The text disappeared, and I turned a frosty glare upon the shaman.

"Don't be a fool, human!" Kagan cast another nervous glance behind him.

What is he so worried about?

"I will be a better master than you could hope to find in the Orcish Federation. Accept the oath!"

The message window appeared anew, again asking me to pledge my soul to the vile creature. "No," I refused, louder this time. "Never." I shook my head. Never would I pledge myself to one of these monsters.

Yarl stepped forward. "Shaman, is everything all right? What is taking so long?" His eyes narrowed at the sight of the golden disk in my hand, now free of runes. "What are you doing, Kagan?" he growled, his voice heavy with menace.

Kagan snatched the blank Trials Key from my hand and hurriedly shuffled back. "Nothing," he muttered. "Let's get going."

The shaman's denials only confirmed Yarl's suspicions. "Halt, Shaman!" he ordered. Striding forward, he shoved his ugly face into Kagan's. "I am not the fool you think me, Kagan. You've bonded the human to your service, haven't you?"

Caught up in their feud, the two forgot about me. I glanced at the box less than a foot away. Setting aside the strangeness of the Trials and the changes it had wrought in me, I focused on the present. *Here's my chance.* I inched my hand toward the crate.

"What? No!" Kagan, realizing his earlier error, did not back down from Yarl's challenge. Leaning toward the pack leader, the shaman breathed heavily into his face. "Don't seek to question me, Yarl. Don't forget your place!"

My hand grazed the edge of the crate. Carefully, without taking my eyes off the two arguing orcs, I searched out one of the grenades within.

"It is you who has forgotten your place, Kagan! You have no right to take on slaves. Nor is it your place to keep my men waiting for hours while you enact your foolish gambit. Were your earlier words even true? Was the human too unfit to travel the gate? Or just too far gone to make his pledge to you?"

Kagan's face drained of color, but he said nothing.

My hand found an explosive and withdrew it. None of the orcs paid me the least bit of attention. Under the misconception that the shaman had already bound me to his service, they appeared confident of my inability to harm them. Indeed, they were deaf to anything but the drama playing out between their leaders. Even the artillery fire raining from the sky failed to draw more than a passing glance.

Yarl took the shaman's silence as confirmation of guilt. "You took a foolish risk, Shaman, and for what? To further your power by binding the human to yourself. I will make sure the warlord's commanders hear of this when we return!"

I cradled the grenade in my hand as I mentally ran through my plan. Pull the firing pin. Toss it back in the crate. Then run. Honestly, the running bit was optional.

It was unlikely I would escape the explosion, and I didn't really care whether I did. My purpose, my only purpose, was to kill

Mom's murderers. If I died doing it, then so be it. Turning back to the orcs, I waited for my moment.

"You don't know what you're talking about, Yarl," snarled the shaman, but even I could hear the lie in his words.

Yarl laughed. "We shall see, Kagan. We shall see."

It was time. With a bloodthirsty grin, I pulled the pin and tossed the grenade. It was a perfect throw; the explosive landed squarely in the box.

I took off running.

Well... more of an unsteady lurch than a run, but the orcs were slow to respond. The first had just begun to turn my way when I reached the fire shield's boundary.

Staggering through, I limped another three steps before diving to the ground. Behind me, orcs shouted orders as they began to give chase.

Too late!

With an earthshattering roar, the grenade detonated. A ripple of concussive blasts followed as the other grenades exploded.

In my mind, another kind of blast erupted as a flood of Trials messages scrolled across my dazed vision.

Kagan Firespawn, a level 201 Veteran player, has died.
Yarl Sharptooth, a level 130 Seasoned player, has died.
An unknown orc, a level 104 Seasoned player, has died.
An unknown orc, a level 108 Seasoned player, has died.
An unknown orc, a level 105 Seasoned player, has died.
You have gained 0 experience, and advanced 0 levels.

Anomalous results detected. Analyzing events for irregularities...

Players identified...

Non-combatants counted...

Location established...

Fatalities confirmed...

Battle results verified. Anomalies found: 1. Jameson Sinclair has not achieved full player designation. Recalculating player achievements...

You have killed your first player while an Inductee. For this achievement, you have been awarded an epic Trait.

You have killed your first Seasoned player while an Inductee. For this achievement, you have been awarded a legendary Trait.

You have killed your first Veteran player while an Inductee. For this achievement, you have been awarded a mythic Trait.

You are the only player to have slain five Seasoned players while an Inductee. For this achievement, you have been awarded a unique Trait. Your rewards can be claimed during your Induction.

Your reprisals against the representatives of the Orcish Federation and the swift revenge you enacted have earned you the Feat: Orcsbane, rank 3, Mortal Foe.

Feats scale with time and according to your actions. At rank 3, Orcsbane provides you with the *orc hunter*, *burning brightly*, *revulsion*, and *repurpose* Techniques.

Orc hunter: You are aware of any orc that ventures within nine feet of you.

Burning brightly: Reveals your presence to any orc that approaches within nine feet.

Revulsion: You cannot use any goods crafted by orcs.

Repurpose: You may temporarily subvert orcish structures to your own ends.

CHAPTER EIGHT

12 MAY: 5 DAYS TO EARTH'S DESTRUCTION

> *"The humans' technology is strange and admittedly powerful, yet it will benefit them little on Overworld. Given their technology's nature, the Trials will not allow it to function. Without the aid of their Earth-forged weapons, the humans are weak and ripe for conquest. We should prepare for immediate invasion once the Arkon Shield falls."*
> —Lilith Smoke, fiendish spymaster.

Ignoring the Trials' messages, I rolled over and stared at the sky, surprised I was still alive.

It was done.

I had avenged Mom's death. Nothing else mattered. I was done with Overworld, the Trials, *and* the blasted invaders. My purpose was complete, and now I could rest.

Gazing into the endless blue emptiness above, I found myself wondering at the color of Overworld's sky, and then dismissed the errant thought in irritation. *I'll never see it.* A heavy silence had fallen over everything; even the shelling had stopped.

I turned to stare at the spot where Mom had died. The area was scorched. Like the orcs, Mom's remains had been incinerated by the cataclysmic heat of the explosions.

Goodbye, Mom. I'm sorry I couldn't save you. I hope you find peace, wherever you are.

As I stared miserably at the burned ground and floating ash, I noticed with surprise that the charred earth was neatly contained within a circle. The boundary of the shaman's fire shield, I guessed.

I owed my survival to Kagan's shield as much as to my half-hearted attempt to run. It had contained the explosions' wrath as completely as it had repelled the earlier mortar fire. I frowned. But if the shield was impermeable from both directions, how had I been able to move through it?

I shrugged away the mystery. It didn't matter. Someone else could figure it out. I returned to my contemplation of the sky.

My phone rang.

I ignored it at first, my mind shutting down at the realization that it was not Mom, and never would be again. But when it kept ringing, I pulled it from my pocket and stared at the caller ID. It was Eric. I considered cutting the call. My purpose was done. I had my revenge. What reason could I have for continuing?

But Eric deserved better from me. I answered the call.

"Jamie. Thank God! Are you all right! What am I saying? Of course, you're not! I'm sorry. I saw—"

"Eric," I said slowly, interrupting his rapid-fire flow of words. "Why are you still here? Shouldn't you be in Overworld?"

"You're right, I should be, but we ran into unexpected delays. But none of that is important. I saw what happened to your Mom. Jamie, I am so sorry. I can't imagine what you must be feeling right now."

"What do you mean you saw?" I asked, my thoughts still sluggish. *Is Eric here?* I glanced around.

Eric fell momentarily silent. "Jamie, are you injured?" Concern laced his tone. "You don't sound okay."

I laughed hollowly. "No, Eric. I am not all right. My Ma is dead."

"I know, man. I'm sorry," he murmured.

I shoved down the upswell of grief at the sympathy in Eric's voice. "Where are you?" I asked, changing the topic.

"In my apartment, watching you on the news."

"On the news?" I repeated, bewildered.

"That's right. The whole world saw you kill those five orcs. The Internet is exploding in celebration. You've just shown everyone those bastards aren't invincible. I'm proud of you, man."

I bit back another grim laugh. Eric didn't deserve my mockery. "It doesn't matter," I said. "Earth is doomed. Humanity too, probably. But save yourself, Eric. Go to Overworld and build a new life for yourself and Emma."

"We plan to. We were just above to leave." He paused. "What about you?"

I shook my head. "My fight is done. Mom is gone, and I've avenged her death. There's no reason for me to go on."

Eric felt silent. Down the phone line, I heard nothing but heavy breathing... but only for a second. A moment later, the line erupted with hissing, as Emma and Eric whispered in the background. Then Eric returned. "Jamie are you still there?"

I almost smiled. Where else would I be? "I'm here, bud."

"Don't give up, my friend. Please."

"I don't know how to go on, Eric."

"I know." He paused, and even without being able to see him I knew my friend well enough to know he was biting his lip, pondering his next words. "But there are more orcs, you know."

I lifted the cell and stared at it for a second, before returning it to my ear. "What do you mean?" I asked slowly.

"Those five orcs you killed, they aren't the ones really responsible for your Mom's death," Eric muttered. "That's Duskar and the entire Orcish Federation. If you want justice for your Mom, kill them all."

I fell silent as I chewed on Eric's words. They were crazy— ludicrous, even. To declare war on the entire Orcish Federation? A nation even the other Overworlders feared? I chuckled hoarsely. Only Eric would suggest something so outrageous. Or have faith that I could accomplish such a feat.

But he had a point.

Had I *really* avenged Mom? Yarl and Kagan were only the instruments of her death. Those *truly* responsible were Duskar and his warlords. The seeds of doubt Eric had planted flowered into raging discontent.

I had not done enough.

Rage coiled in the pit of my stomach. My friend was right. I had more orcs to kill. And while that remained true, I could not lie down and die.

I heaved myself upright. "Eric, my friend, you're a real son of a bitch, you know that?"

Eric chuckled. "Someone's got to beat you straight," he said, trying to hide the palpable relief in his voice. "What are you going to do now?"

"I'm going to enter the gate." I stumbled to my feet. "Thanks."

"My pleasure, Jamie."

"And Eric?"

"Yeah?"

"Make sure you get your ass there too."

"Will do, bud. Will do."

* * *

I limped forward, the silence around me complete. It was still morning, I noted absently. None of the townsfolk who had fled the orcs had returned. To my left, in the far distance, I made out some watching figures. *The militia,* I thought, waving. No one waved back.

I shrugged and continued on. As I walked, thoughts of Mom intruded, but I shoved them aside. I couldn't think of her. Not now.

To keep my mind occupied and to distract myself from the grief that sat heavy on my heart, I focused on the Trials and its recent flood of messages.

Receiving messages from the Trials directly through my mind was astonishing enough. But what those messages said was almost too spectacular to believe.

I had been generously rewarded for my defeat of the orcs. *Rewards like that can't be normal,* I thought. Had I received so many because I was still an Inductee, or because I had slain enemies so far above my level? Whatever the reason, I doubted my victory here was a feat I could replicate.

On Overworld, I would not have the advantage of human technology. There, I would have to rely only on medieval arms and the strength of my own limbs.

And magic, I reminded myself. *Do not forget magic.*

I opened the first set of messages again. The Trials had judged my Magic Potential as extraordinary, and even through the overwhelming fog of my grief, I felt a twinge of curiosity.

My Magic Potential had made Kagan take foolish risks. *Just how unusual is it?* I wondered. More importantly, how would it serve me on my crusade? Because that was what I was embarking on: a crusade to purge Overworld of Duskar's kind. It was a cause I would not give up on, not until they were all dead... or I was.

I cackled—not entire sanely. *Baby steps, Jamie. Baby steps.*

I was nearly at the gate. A very red gate. I took a second to study it, sure more orcs were waiting for me on the other side.

Or not *me*, particularly, but any human fool enough to place themselves in enemy hands. I wasn't going to do that. I had learned my lesson.

Revenge was best served cold.

I would take my war to the orcs when I was ready, and not before. As long as I had any say in the matter, anyhow.

No, it was not suicidal intent that spurred me to approach the orc gate, but rather the Orcsbane Feat—in particular, one of its Techniques. I called up its description again.

Repurpose: You may temporarily subvert orcish structures to your own ends.

Could I divert the orc gate, as the *repurpose* Technique suggested? I shrugged. *Only one way to find out.*

Stopping before the gate, I marveled at the artifact's immensity. The gate arched high overhead, many times my height. The structure's rim sparkled with alien inscriptions, and its depths swirled with the reddish shimmer of a magical field.

Here goes nothing. I placed one hand tentatively against the gate's metal surface. The metal vibrated faintly and was warm to the touch.

Now what? I held my hand against the gate for an interminable stretch of time. Nothing happened.

I knew from the countless televised broadcasts that I simply had to step inside the shimmering magical curtain to enter Overworld, but I wasn't willing to do that yet—not without confirmation that I could actually *repurpose* the structure.

How do I subvert the gate? I scratched my head with my other hand. As if triggered by the thought, I felt tendrils of energy reach out from me to the artifact and a new message from the Trials open within my mind.

This is gate forty-six between Overworld and the human planet, Earth. The current owner is the Orcish Federation, and the allowed destinations are any orcish settlement in the newly formed Human Dominion.

You have activated *repurpose*. Do you wish to take temporary control of this gate? Doing so will allow you to change the portal's destination to any neutral location in the Human Dominion.

Ah, it's that simple, is it? All right, then, here goes nothing. I mentally confirmed my intention to the Trials.

A second later, I screamed.

My mind felt like it was being torn apart, an unimaginable force battering it. I gasped, my knees collapsing under me. I would have fallen entirely, if my right hand had not remained fastened to the gate, as if it was glued there.

What is going on? I thought before agony lanced my mind, destroying all thought. An image of the gate, pulsing scarlet, as if bathed in blood, sprang into my mind's eye.

The pain reached a crescendo, as my mind was brutally torn open and a conduit was forged between my brain and the gate. How I knew this to be true, I could not say, but I understood it to be the case.

I knew what I had to do next.

Thrusting coils of my will forward, I sent my consciousness racing across the conduit to the gate, blasting away the shimmering red weaves of magic wrapped around it. Slowly at first, then faster, the crimson haze around the gate disappeared. Soon, I would have control of the artifact.

Then I felt the presence of another.

The gate's creator, I realized instinctively. The conduit I had forged had temporarily bridged our minds. His thoughts, which I could now sense, roiled with surprise before transforming into rage and fury.

The gate's owner rushed to stop me, to maintain control of his creation, but he was too late. The last of the red weaves dissipated, and possession was transferred to me.

"Who are you?" thundered the orc, his voice reverberating through my mind. He was another shaman, one far beyond Kagan in power. I shuddered. This was not someone I was ready to face.

A second later, he answered his own question, somehow divining the answer from my own thoughts. *"A human! How?"*

I fled. I could not afford to reveal myself to one like him, not yet. Retracing my steps, I sent my consciousness scurrying across the conduit, back to the safety of my body.

"STOP!" bellowed the shaman.

The strength of his mental command was petrifying, but I didn't succumb to his wrath. I fled, and the shaman followed, pursuing me across the link that bridged our minds.

"Don't think you can escape, human," he threatened. *"I know you now. I will find you. If not today, then another day."*

Reaching the safety of my self, I thrust my consciousness back into my skull and frantically willed my mind closed. The echoes of the shaman's wrathful voice faded as I sealed my mind shut and dropped back into the "real" world.

I sagged down, both hands braced on the floor, head bent, heaving in lungsful of air. I had escaped. But how much had the shaman seen? How much of myself had I inadvertently revealed? Had he divined as much of me as I had of him?

He was high shaman Orgtul. *Orgtul Silverbane.*

I rolled his name around my mouth, adding it to my list of targets. I staggered back to my feet.

Stepping back from the gate, I studied it anew. "Repurposing" it hadn't been that easy after all. I chuckled with grim humor as I again laid a hand to the artifact's rim.

You have successfully repurposed gate forty-six. You will retain control of the gate for thirty minutes, after which ownership will revert to the Orcish Federation.

The shimmering red veil was gone, replaced with a soothing gray. The slap of feet on concrete pulled my attention to my left. Turning, I saw militia soldiers running toward me, waving frantically to attract my attention.

I didn't allow myself to be distracted. My purpose was to kill orcs, and the orcs were in Overworld. It was there I had to go. Let them follow if they wanted.

Stepping forward, I entered the artifact.

You have entered gate forty-six. Beginning transfer to Overworld...

...

...

... transfer interrupted.

Your Initiation is incomplete. Entry into Overworld is not permitted. Redirecting Inductee to Wyrm Island. Transfer resumed and will be completed in 5 seconds.

4...

3...

2...

1...

Chapter Nine

12 May: 5 days to Earth's destruction

"The humans show an uncanny aptitude for magic. Enslaving them will serve us well."
—Orgtul Silverbane.

From one step to the next, I left one world and entered another. The transition was seamless, without the slightest misstep in my footing.

I peered around.

Earth's azure sky and concrete buildings had vanished. Replacing them was a wide beach of pristine sand under a storm-wracked gray sky. Green waves rolled in from the ocean and foamed over rocks scattered along the shore. *Mom would have loved it here,* I couldn't help thinking.

Despite the contrast the beach made from my hometown, there was nothing alien about the landscape. The beach could have been any one of a number of locations on Earth. I looked left and right, and along the shore. All directions appeared empty of life. I was alone.

I swung around to see what lay behind me, and then jerked back in alarm.

Standing patiently less than three feet away—and so very still that I would have assumed her a statue, if not for her lively, curious gaze—was an... entity.

"Welcome, human, to Wyrm Island," said the strange creature. "I am Aurora, your designated guide for Induction into Overworld."

"Uh, hello." I surreptitiously studied this fascinating figure.

Aurora was uniformly purple, from her bare toes to the tips of the long hair that fell to her waist. Sprouting from her back, as still and unmoving as the rest of her, was a pair of feathered wings. Whatever—or whoever—Aurora was, she was clearly not from Earth. But at least, she appeared humanoid.

"W-what are you?"

"I am forbidden from answering an Inductee's questions," Aurora responded primly.

The petite purple figure—half my height—flapped her wings and rose gently aloft until she was at eye level with me. "Now, follow me," she ordered. Turning about, she zipped along the ground toward the island's interior.

I rubbed my chin, perplexed by her behavior. "Wait!" I called, but Aurora didn't stop. She moved so fast I would soon lose sight of her over the sand dune she was headed to. "Damn it all!" I swore, and hurried after her at the fastest hobble I could manage.

As predicted, the purple woman soon disappeared from view, but with no other choice, I limped on in the direction I had last seen her. Reaching the hilltop over which Aurora had vanished, I noticed her waiting at the bottom, her foot tapping impatiently.

Next to her was another gate, nearly identical to the one I had entered on Earth, except that this one was the same startling shade of purple as my guide. In the far distance, I could see where the dunes ended and the ocean began again. The island was far smaller than I had thought.

"Well hurry up," called Aurora, interrupting my inspection of the surroundings. "Don't just stand there—we are on a time limit, you know."

"Huh? Where are we? What is this place?" I asked as I slipped down the loose sand of the beach dune to her side.

"In twenty-seven minutes, the gate you entered will revert to orcish control," Aurora said, steadfastly ignoring all my questions. "If you have not completed your Initiation before then, you will be forced out to a destination of its owner's choosing."

I gulped. I definitely did not want that. But my guide's response left me puzzled. It implied I was still within the gate. Frowning, I looked around. Was this not Overworld?

Before I could frame more questions, Aurora continued. "Our first order of business is to determine whether you will retain your current form on entering Overworld or whether you will choose an entirely new one—a clean slate with none of your existing blemishes." The purple woman glanced at my hobbled foot, making her meaning clear.

I blinked, momentarily speechless with shock. *I could be free of my crippled foot?* Never in my wildest dreams had I contemplated being whole again. The wiki pages I studied had mentioned starting the Trials with a clean slate, but I had not grasped what that meant.

Joy, sharp and bittersweet, flooded through me. I'd never expected Overworld to free me of the handicap that had plagued my adult life. Yet it was tainted by sadness. *If only Mom was here to witness this moment.*

I quickly bottled up my conflicting emotions. *Sort them later, Jamie. Stay focused in the now. Think about the choices you must make here.* After a deep sigh to settle myself, I opened my mouth to answer.

Aurora waggled a purple finger in front of my face, interrupting me. "I advise you to review the information in the Trials windows before you answer, and to carefully study the consequences of both choices."

At my guide's words, two translucent, purple-shaded windows unfurled and floated on unseen currents before my eyes. As Aurora suggested, I studied each intently.

You have the choice between the forms Clean Slate and Made-on-Earth. In either form, your Potentials will remain the same.

In the Clean Slate form, your body will be refashioned to remove both negative and positive effects, including those of aging. Your Attributes, Traits, Feats, and Disciplines will be reset. In their stead, you will be provided with the same basic starting combination as other new players. This includes twelve Attributes Marks, ten Discipline Tokens, one common Trait, and one uncommon Trait.

In the Made-on-Earth form, you will carry over your expertise, strengths, and weaknesses developed during your time on Earth. These include the lore Discipline, the scribe Discipline, the Crippled Trait, the Quick Learner Trait, the Orcsbane Feat, and your four newly acquired Traits.

My heart sank when I saw the Trials information. Starting with a Clean Slate wasn't an option. If I chose it, I would lose the achievements earned from slaying the five orcs.

Seeing the dawning realization on my face, Aurora confirmed my suspicions. "If you choose to enter Overworld with a Clean Slate, you will lose your existing Traits and Feats. Twenty-six minutes remaining."

I didn't hesitate. It was really no choice at all. "I will enter Overworld as I am."

"Very well," Aurora said. "Your decision has been recorded." With a wave of her hand, my guide banished the two windows before me. "Next, you must select the Traits you earned through your recent actions.

"The six categories range from rank one to six. Rank-one Traits, or 'common Traits', are the least powerful and most easily attained. Likewise, mythic or rank-six Traits are the rarest and nearly impossible to attain.

"To begin, choose your epic Trait from the options available to humans."

Another translucent window opened. For a second, I stared at the listed Traits in bemusement, struck by the strangeness of what I was doing, but I brushed aside my doubts. Events had proved beyond doubt that Overworld and the Trials were all too real.

Breathing deeply, I settled my mind and scanned the list. There were hundreds of Traits, and not nearly enough time to consider them all. I couldn't afford to dally. If I did, I would lose control of the gate. I repressed a shiver. That was not something I wanted to risk.

Skimming the list, I read only the titles and not the detailed descriptions of each Trait. There simply wasn't time for that, and

I had already determined my strategy. My priority was finding a Trait to disguise my Potentials.

Kagan had perceived my Potentials too easily. His reaction suggested that my Magic Potential was rare. How rare? I couldn't be certain, but if I walked around Overworld with my Potential open to *analyze*, I would be too tempting a prize.

It took longer than I hoped, but I finally spotted two Traits that fit my criteria.

Trait: Mimicked Core. Rank: 4, epic. This Trait grants a player the *mimic* Technique. It obfuscates a player's Potentials. The deception will be immune to all forms of detection.

Trait: Master of Disguise. Rank: 4, epic. This Trait grants a player the *chameleon* Technique. It allows a player to hide both their Potentials and identity. Foes of sufficiently high level will be able to sense the deception but will not be able to penetrate the player's disguise.

I deliberated between the two. On one hand, Mimicked Core provided the most comprehensive protection. Master of Disguise, on the other hand, allowed me to hide more of myself. The trait description suggested it would allow me to hide even my name from other players.

"Twenty minutes remaining," said Aurora.

Damn it, this is taking too long! "I choose Mimicked Core," I replied, sticking with my original intent and not allowing the added benefits of the Master of Disguise Trait to sway me. *Better to have an undetectable disguise.*

"Noted. Next, choose your legendary Trait from the list of those available to humans."

Another window opened up before me. I rapidly ran my eyes over the list. Less than halfway down, I stopped. Two Traits caught my eye. Given their nature, I felt further study of the list was unnecessary.

Trait: Twice as Skilled. Rank: 5, legendary. This Trait doubles the Discipline Tokens a player is awarded every level. The effect of this Trait is not retroactive.

Trait: Twice as Talented. Rank: 5, legendary. This Trait doubles the Attribute Marks a player is awarded every level. The effect of this Trait is not retroactive.

Considering I was still at level zero, I would derive benefit from either Trait. But which to choose? *Disciplines or Attributes*, I mused. Having more of either would significantly improve my power.

My study of the Trials Infopedia on Earth led me to the conclusion that Disciplines were more important, despite each Attribute affecting multiple Disciplines. With more Disciplines, I would have access to additional Techniques, which could be the difference between survival and defeat.

"I choose Twice as Skilled."

"Your choice has been recorded. Next, choose your mythic Trait from the ones available to humans."

This time, the list of Traits was not as extensive, only half as long as the list of legendary Traits. As I perused the Traits, Aurora's choice of words played over and over again in the back of my mind.

For the third time she had worded her instruction as "available to humans." Did that mean other races had a different selection of Traits to choose from?

Each mythic Trait was suited to a particular style of play, so what would mine be? Given my Potentials, there was little doubt I would invest heavily in the magic Disciplines and Attributes, which would leave me weaker and less dexterous than other players. *The proverbial glass cannon. Should I shore up my weaknesses or double down on my strengths?*

Shore up my weaknesses, I decided. If Kagan's reaction was anything to go by, my Magic Potential didn't need further boosts. Yet with my crippled foot and lackluster Might, I would easy pickings if I was caught without access to magic. I needed to choose either a Trait that gave me an escape option or one that increased my survivability.

I scanned the list again, shortlisting two Traits.

Trait: Ghost. Rank: 6, mythic. This Trait grants a player the *ghostwalker* Technique, which allows them to disperse their body and wander as an invisible spirit for thirty seconds, after which their body will be rematerialized. While in spirit form, the player cannot interact with the world, and they may pass through solid objects.

The Technique's casting time is fast. Due to the damage inflicted by the ability on a player's spirit, it may only be used once a day.

Trait: Spirit's Invincibility. Rank: 6, mythic. This Trait grants a player the *invincible* Technique, which allows them to manifest their spirit as a shield against all forms of damage for thirty seconds.

The Technique's casting time is very fast, but it may only be used once a day.

I chewed on the inside of my lip as I read the Traits' descriptions. I wished I could have both. *Ghostwalker* was definitely the best escape option, since it would allow me to cleanly avoid difficult situations and to enter barred or locked areas.

But *invincible* would grant me immunity and could be used defensively *and* offensively. It also appeared faster-acting. In the end, that fact helped me decide. In an emergency, speed of execution would matter. "I choose Spirit's Invincibility," I said, quietening my doubts.

"Noted. Lastly, choose your unique Trait. Unique Traits are unranked and rarely awarded aside from very special circumstances. Every unique Trait is just that: unique. Only a single player may possess that particular Trait."

Aurora fell silent, momentary doubt clouding her face. "Until now, no player has *ever* been granted a choice when it comes to the unique Trait they acquire. The system has always determined the appropriate reward."

She fixed me with hard-eyed stare. "For your accomplishment of defeating five Seasoned players while still an Inductee, the Trials, in its wisdom, has seen fit to grant you the honor of choosing a unique Trait. Choose carefully, human. You have fifteen minutes left."

The little purple woman looked like there was much more she wanted to add, but she bit her lip, holding the words in. Her explanation was the most expansive she had provided thus far. If I was not already aware of the importance of my choice, her words would have alerted me.

This, I knew, was my true reward. And this choice was not one I could get wrong.

Chapter Ten

12 May: 5 days to Earth's destruction

> *"We cannot ignore the facts. The Elders were here, on this planet, Earth. We must know why."*
> —Arustolyx, gnomish archaeologist.

I exhaled a calming breath as the open purple windows disappeared, replaced by a single golden one.

Thousands of Traits scrolled through the window.

I gulped. How was I expected to read all that in fifteen minutes? I turned to Aurora in panic. "Is there any way to sort the list?"

My "guide" ignored me and stared steadfastly ahead. Growling softly to myself, I got to work scanning the titles.

There were so many, all with longwinded names like "raider of the hidden most depths of the world," "holder of the sacred iron-tooth totem," "hoarder of all things shiny and small," "first conqueror of the underside catacombs," "valiant champion for the free rights of murkers," and so on.

Some titles were so arcane I couldn't even guess what bonuses the Trait granted. I mean, what possible benefits could "twirling rainbow under a midnight sky" grant? Yet I dared not stop to read the descriptions, not with so many to get through.

"Ten minutes remaining," said Aurora.

I looked up from the list for a moment to scowl at her indifferent face. But retorting would only waste time I didn't have. Turning back to the golden window, I forced myself to skim faster through the endless, nonsensical jargon.

My eyes burned with the strain of focusing as hundreds of names scrolled past—most barely pinging on my conscious thoughts at all.

I couldn't recall words I had sighted scant seconds before. . I was scanning the list that rapidly and in a manner that was, perhaps, wholly inefficient.

But, trusting my instincts, I let my gaze rove over the list, waiting for my unconscious mind to spark at the right combination of words. What those would be, I had no idea. Surely *something* in the thousands of names would pique my interest.

"Five minutes," cautioned Aurora.

I pressed on, inwardly beginning to despair. Perhaps, I was going about this all wrong. Perhaps the smarter choice was to forgo the list entirely, and pick random Traits to inspect in detail. But it was too late for that now. I was nearly out of time.

"Three minutes remaining."

The text in the gold window swam as the prolonged strain on my eyes took its toll. Unshed tears collected at their corners. I let the tears stream down my face and kept going.

It is no use. I have failed. I have chosen the wrong tack.

But just as I began to reconcile myself to selecting at random, my eyes stopped moving—seizing on two short words.

I rubbed my waterlogged eyes and leaned forward, peering intently at the Trait's title. I had not been mistaken. I had read the words correctly.

"Dragon's Gift," the title read.

So short, so succinct, so unlike the elaborate, verbose names of the other unique Traits. I stared at it, transfixed.

"Two minutes," Aurora remarked.

Not taking my eyes off the Trait, I willed the golden window to expand and show the Trait's full description.

Trait: Dragon's Gift. Rank: unique. Grants the player access to the dragon magic Discipline.

I leaned back and closed my eyes. This was the one. *This* was the Trait I needed. Never mind that its description was uninspiring and gave almost no hint of the benefits it provided, I knew with bone-deep certainty that this was the Trait I had to choose.

Overworld's Elders were dragons, I recalled, remembering the passage about the Trials' creators. And this Trait would give me access to their magic.

"One minute," said Aurora.

I turned to face her. Despite her stated impartiality, she was beginning to look distressed. I smiled reassuringly. "I choose Dragon's Gift."

Aurora's eyes widened, and for a moment she was at a loss for words. Then, obviously remembering the passage of time, she said in a half-strangled voice, "So recorded. You have forty-five seconds left! Quickly, through the portal! You will have to choose one of the neutral locations as your destination before the transition can be completed. Remember, you only have a few seconds before you lose control of the gate! Now go!"

I went.

As fast as my crippled foot would allow, I hurried to the purple gate. Just before I entered the gate, I heard Aurora shout, "We will see each other again, Jameson Sinclair. When you have levelled up, enter one of the dragon temples on Overworld. You will find me there. Goodbye... and good luck!"

I lifted a hand in acknowledgement and stepped into the gate.

You have exited Wyrm Island. Initiation: completed. Current designation: Initiate. Resuming transfer to Overworld...

...

...

... transfer interrupted.

You have not selected a destination. Redirecting player to waystation 23,424. Location: Human Dominion void. Select a neutral location to resume your transfer. Gate forty-six will revert to orcish control in thirty-five seconds.

I stepped out into a world of gray emptiness.

Whipping my head back and forth, I looked around. There was nothing to see except billowing mist.

What now?

Before my worry could transform into full-blown panic, a translucent map crystalized in the space before me. "Come on, hurry up," I whispered, wondering how much time I had left.

After a full five seconds, the map's manifestation completed. My eyes raced over the magical construct—a map of the Human Dominion in Overworld. I had no idea how large an area it covered, but humanity's new territory appeared sizable. On the Dominion's eastern border was a region marked boldly in red and labeled "the Orcish Federation."

So, our Dominion had been placed next to that of our Patron, the orcs. My gaze flicked to our other borders, but the other territories lying adjacent to the Human Dominion were grayed out—as was the greater part of the Orcish Federation, I realized. Only the orcs' territories that bordered our Dominion were shown on the map.

There was no time to scrutinize the map in more detail. I had to select a destination—fast. I scanned the pulsing gray icons scattered throughout the Human Dominion, assuming they were the neutral locations I was permitted to transition to. All of them were unhelpfully labeled "unclaimed" or "unnamed."

Damn it! Where are the gnomish cities? Or even the elvish ones? My plan was to enter one of the gnomes' cities, or choose a location close to one. Yet with no gnomish cities appearing on the map, there was no way I could be certain of doing that now. It would take even longer to join up with Eric than I hoped.

Out of time, and with no other choice, I turned my attention to a gray icon on the far west of the Human Dominion, about as far as you could get from the Orcish Federation. I would need time before I was ready to face the orcs again; the distance between my selected location and the orcs' territory might just give me that.

Gathering my thoughts, I willed myself to my chosen location, a nondescript settlement on the banks of a river.

The map disappeared, and the billowing mist spun furiously until it transformed into a raging tornado with me at its center. I closed my eyes and ducked my head against the whipping wind. A second later, I felt myself tugged downward, spiraling out of the depths of nowhere, and hopefully into Overworld.

You have selected location seventy-eight as your destination. Exiting waystation 23,424. Resuming transfer to Overworld. Transfer will be completed in 5 seconds.

4...
3...
2...
1...

Chapter Eleven

391 DAYS UNTIL THE ARKON SHIELD FALLS
5 DAYS TO EARTH'S DESTRUCTION

> *"No matter what your Potentials, without Traits and Feats, you'll never amount to anything more than an average player. Accumulate as many of them as you can, as quick as you can."*
> —Anonymous Veteran.

Straight out of the gate, I stumbled and yelped in shock. I sprawled forward, my nose burying itself into the green grass underfoot.

Ooof, that hurts.!

This transition through the gate was far less seamless than the ones before it. Lifting my head from the ground, I spat out the loose dirt and grass clinging to my lips before heaving myself upright into a sitting position. Around me I heard cries of alarm and shouts of dismay—human voices—but with my vision obscured by ominously flashing alerts, I couldn't make out much of my surroundings.

I read the messages swiftly.

Transfer completed. Jameson (Jamie) Sinclair, welcome to Overworld. You have entered location seventy-eight, presently unclaimed and unnamed. Participate in the Trials and become all you can be. Remember, true strength is grounded in experience.

You are now a level 1 Neophyte. Health pool unlocked. Stamina pool unlocked. New Techniques downloaded: *analyze*, *mimic*, *magesight*, **and** *invincible*. **You have acquired Tokens and Marks. Visit a dragon temple to use them.**

You have been blessed with *newcomer*. **This buff rapidly accelerates the learning rate of your Neophyte Disciplines and Attributes during your first day on Overworld.**

Overworld, Book 1 of the Dragon Mage Saga

Flash alert: To all players entering the Human Dominion.

As a new region, the Human Dominion will remain protected by an Arkon Shield for one Overworld year—400 days. Days remaining: 391.

Until the Arkon Shield falls, all races except humans and orcs are confined to the sponsored cities. Orcs, as the Patron of humanity, are permitted to patrol the Human Dominion but are forbidden from exploiting the territory's resources.

Report any infractions at a dragon temple. Punishment will be swift and merciless.

I was finally in Overworld, and the clock had already started ticking on humanity. *I have much to do.*

I acknowledged the Trials' warning and waved it away.

More shouts drew my attention. Something was happening, and I needed to figure out what.

"Tara, come look! We've got another one!" a voice cried behind me.

I looked over my shoulder. There was no gate behind me. Its ninety-foot-high structure was entirely absent. Wherever the portal had deposited me, the trip was one way. *There is no going back now.*

A blond-haired youth loomed above me, dancing impatiently from foot to foot. He was fresh-faced, and without even a hint of facial hair. *Still a teen.* His tattered leather clothes were little more than rags, and he clutched a long stabbing spear.

A blur of motion on my right distracted me from further study of the teenager. Swinging back around, I saw dozens of figures—all human and dressed similarly to the youth—charging in a ragged line toward an incoming flood of creatures.

The sight stopped me in my tracks. The humans were fighting frogs—upright, bipedal frogs, armored and bearing weapons of their own.

"What the—?" I exclaimed, unconsciously scooting away, even though the battling parties were a few hundred feet away.

Where the hell am I?

Swiveling left and right, I took in my surroundings. It did not resemble a settlement of any kind. I was in a wide-open field of grass and upturned soil. Other than a purple, block-shaped monstrosity to my right, I saw no buildings. To the east—assuming the sun rose in that direction in Overworld—was a distant tree line. Closer by was a tented camp. I spent little time looking at it, however. My attention was riveted to what was happening in the other direction.

Several hundred yards to the west, the grassy plain angled steeply downward, hiding whatever lay beyond. The toad-men—*what else to call them?*—were emerging from there.

They bounded up the slope and threw themselves against the ragged line of humans defending the purple building. Surging back and forth, and hollering war cries, the men tried to hold them at bay. Everyone except me and the youth was attacking or defending.

This is a battlefield.

What was I doing here? Had something gone wrong with the transfer?

A grim chuckle pulled my attention back to the teenager at my side. "Not what you were expecting, eh? Don't worry, your reaction is no different from the hundreds of other newbs on arrival. Tara will explain everything when she gets here. She is today's designated induction officer." He smiled sardonically. "A fine mood it has put her in, too."

I blinked, not knowing what to say. "What are those creatures?"

"Murluks," said the youth, his amusement fading. He spat to the side. "Savage little buggers."

The slap of running feet approaching closer halted further conversation. A young woman—just as fresh-faced as the teen—jogged up to his side.

Her hair was midnight-black, and her eyes were a startling green. She was dressed identically to the youth but was armed with a short spear and shield instead. "Hansen, what do we have here?" she asked, the tone of command unmistakable in her voice.

The absurdity of one so young possessing such authority jumpstarted my brain. *Of course! These are players.* Ones who apparently started with a Clean Slate.

Hansen and the woman were probably both much older than they appeared. The woman scowled down at me. Whatever she saw, it did not please her.

"Fresh meat," answered Hansen, with a grin I didn't trust. Gesturing toward me, he said, "Tara, meet the new fish." He turned to me. "New fish, meet Tara." He hefted his spear. "Now that the introductions are out of the way, he is all yours. I'm off to join my unit." Finishing in a rush, he dashed away.

Tara's head whipped toward his retreating figure. "Hansen! Wait, you bastard!"

Hansen didn't wait; if anything, he ran harder, straight toward the battling lines.

Tara turned back to me and ground her teeth before muttering, "Damn you, Hansen. I don't have the time for this." Only then did she address me. Making no apology for her behavior, she asked bluntly, "What's your name, boy?"

"I'm Jamie." I replied evenly, although I was bristling at her tone.

The green-eyed woman squinted at me. "Well, what are you doing just sitting there? Get up, we have to move!"

I considered ignoring her order. I wasn't happy with my treatment, but the shrieks of pain and roars of rage that continued unabated, reminded me that a very real life-and-death struggle was occurring nearby. Now was not the time for foolish games.

Sighing, I pushed myself to my feet, tottering only slightly.

Tara's brows drew together as she noticed my difficulty. "What's wrong with your foot?"

Before I could respond, she divined the answer for herself and her gaze jerked up to meet mine. Whatever she saw in my face confirmed her suspicions. Her eyes widened in disbelief. "You didn't choose a Clean Slate, did you?"

I winced inwardly at her tone but only nodded mutely in response.

For a second, Tara was shocked speechless, but she recovered quickly. "Damn young idiots," she muttered, glowering at me. "You all think this is some sort of game. Jamie, listen closely. I don't know what foolish notion made you enter this place like that"—she gestured to my foot with her spear—"but you're stuck that way now. If you want to survive beyond today, you will do exactly as I say. Understood?"

"I do." And I did. As much as I wanted to defiantly throw Tara's words back at her, common sense made me hold my tongue and swallow my pride.

I was just minutes into my new life, and I had *no* idea what was going on. If I was going to survive, I needed Tara and these people.

And she knew it.

She studied my face for a long minute. Satisfied with what she saw there, she nodded curtly. "Good. Follow me."

I limped over to her side. Tara winced on seeing how much my foot hampered my movement. She shook her head again but didn't say anything. The moment I reached her, she began striding away, although her pace was noticeably slower than when she'd first approached.

For that she had my gratitude. Regardless of what she thought of me, this grim woman did not seem like she would abandon me.

Ignoring the clamor of the battle, Tara pointed to a pile of junk heaped in front of the purple building, which appeared to be our destination. "Our first order of business is to get you a weapon and some armor. Not that we have much in the way of either." She gestured dismissively to her own gear. "After that, we join the defending line. Got it?"

I nodded mutely again.

"You can ask any questions as we go."

"What's that?" I jerked my chin toward the marbled purple building, so incongruous amid the otherwise rustic setting of grass and trees.

Tara followed the direction of my gaze. "That's the dragon temple. It is what makes location seventy-eight a potential settlement. If we lose the temple, we can't level up or establish a base here." She pointed to the loosely strung line of men between the murluks and the temple. "That's why we defend it at all costs."

Ah, I have transitioned to the right location after all.

I considered Tara's words. From researching the wiki, I knew the importance of the dragon temples.

Leveling was how players advanced and got stronger in the Trials. After gaining a level, players were rewarded with Tokens and Marks, which could only be spent at a building like the one ahead. Without access to a temple, players in Overworld couldn't grow more powerful.

Well, that wasn't completely true.

The wiki made it clear that players could still develop themselves outside of a temple; however, *naturally* acquiring the same knowledge and enhancements that were *instantly* gifted by the temple could take months or years—at least for anything beyond the Neophyte rank.

What the advancement process in the temples entailed, I still wasn't sure. But the temples were crucial. If this one was lost, the players in the region would have no way of benefiting from their earned Marks and Tokens—unless, of course, they survived the journey to the next closest temple.

"What are the requirements for your settlement?" I asked.

Settlements were not arbitrarily designated in Overworld. Unlike on Earth, locations in the Trials had to meet a host of prerequisites to qualify as a settlement. Meeting the criteria resulted in benefits for the residents, so I was curious to learn what these people required to establish theirs.

"Securing the area, for one," Tara said, shooting me a puzzled glance.

My question probably isn't a typical newbie one, I thought wryly.

"But it is more complex than that," she continued. "We can discuss it later, assuming we survive today's attack."

We reached the jumble of discarded weapons and leather pieces. "Do you have any martial skills?" asked Tara.

I shook my head.

Her face tightened, but she refrained from commenting. "Then grab whichever leather wraps fit and throw them on. I'll find you a spear. It's the easiest weapon to use."

I glanced down at myself before moving to do as Tara ordered. I had transitioned into Overworld wearing only brown cotton pants, a shirt, and soft leather shoes that didn't feel like they would last long. I glanced at Tara's feet. Her shoes looked nearly in tatters too. I sighed. Good gear was clearly in short supply.

I bent down and rifled through the rags. They smelled awful and looked suspiciously like the same equipment the frog creatures were wearing.

Though I was no expert tailor, I could tell their workmanship was crude. The leather armor was little more than half-cured hides haphazardly stitched together.

Returning with a second spear in hand, Tara noticed my disdain. "They may not look like much, but the leather will stop a murluk's thrust from skewering you through." She paused. "Assuming they strike the right place. Just try not to get stabbed through any of the gaping holes."

Alrighty, then.

"Now stop wasting time." She threw the spear at my feet. "Get dressed and arm yourself."

"Yes, ma'am," I replied, selecting the vest, leggings, and helm most likely to fit. All of them hung loosely off my frame, but they fit... mostly. When I was ready, Tara began moving again. "Let's go."

I trailed in her wake. We were not making directly for the battling lines, but instead headed for its southern end. To take my mind off what was to come, I asked, "Why are we using murluk gear?"

"Noticed that, did you?"

I shrugged; it had seemed obvious.

"We don't have the right tools for our leatherworkers to fashion our own equipment yet. We've been forced to scavenge from the enemy." Her tone grew contemplative. "In a way, we're lucky the murluks found us or we'd would be even worse equipped than we are now."

I glanced from Tara to the pile of junk we'd just left. It was a few feet high. "How long have you been fending off murluk attacks?"

"Since day one," she replied grimly. "The first two days were the worst. We lost so many." She threw me a hard stare. "Remember, fish, this is no game."

I nodded sharply. I didn't need Tara's reminder. Mom's death had taught me more than I wanted to learn about Overworld's savagery.

The din from the battle rose steadily as we drew closer. Tilting my head to the side, I listened carefully. Most of the noise was coming from *beyond* the murluks and the men battling in front of the dragon temple, and seemingly from whatever the sloping ground hid from view.

I frowned. Looking at the path Tara was taking, I realized we weren't joining the temple's defenders as I had assumed, but that we were instead circling around them.

I opened my mouth to ask where we were going, but before I could voice my question, Tara spoke.

"This is a long spear," she said. "You will stand in the second line of the wall and use your spear to thrust past me at the enemy. Always hold the spear with two hands, like this." She demonstrated. "When you want to strike, thrust straight ahead and lean into the blow with your entire weight. Once you've landed a hit, retract your weapon immediately by pulling it straight back. Don't leave it there or you *will* lose your spear.

"Thrust and pull. Nothing else. Keep your feet planted, and rinse and repeat. No fancy twirls, no slashes, no dodges, and *no* heroic charges at the enemy. Most importantly, keep hold of your spear. Don't ever throw it. Got it?"

"Got it," I said, clenching my spear. My pulse quickened and my heart thumped as Tara's instructions painted a vivid picture of the reality I was stepping into.

"And whatever you do, stay one step behind me. Don't move out of position, not even for a second. If I advance, you advance," she ordered. "When I retreat, you do too."

"Yes, ma'am."

"All right, then. Buckle up, boyo, it's time to do battle."

Chapter Twelve

391 DAYS UNTIL THE ARKON SHIELD FALLS

> *"It is no secret that the Trials permanently accelerate a player's learning rate of Neophyte Disciplines and Attributes beyond what is 'natural.' Yet, with the newcomer buff, the Trials do even more for players on their first day. While the buff is in force, a player can rapidly advance his Disciplines and Attributes to Trainee rank in a mere matter of hours. Don't squander it."*
> —Trials Infopedia.

Just as I thought, we bypassed the line of clashing murluks and humans and reached the western end of the grassy plain. Beyond it was a wide-flowing river, which snaked off into the horizon to the north and south.

"That's where we go." Tara pointed to the river below.

I looked where she gestured. We had stopped on the edge of the river's upper bank. Below us, the ground angled sharply down to the river's lower bank, which was a stretch of gently sloping shore nearly thirty yards wide. Waves slapped back and forth across it, turning the lower bank into treacherous mud.

Running north to south, all along the upper bank, was a line of rubble piled next to a shallow ditch. *Excavations?* I wondered, but only in passing. My attention was focused on the near-deafening clash of weapons and the raging mass of men and murluks on the river's bank.

On the edge of the river, wading through the frothing black waters, hundreds of men bellowed and pushed back against a flood of murluks emerging from the river's watery depths. The creatures, still wet and dripping, flung themselves with reckless abandon at the human defenders.

This is the true battle, I realized, staring down at the chaotic scene. By comparison, the fight near the temple was just a skirmish. I swallowed sudden nerves. *And Tara means to take me down there.*

While I watched, thousands of bare-footed, slurping murluks slapped through the mud to beat against the thinly stretched defensive line of men. The human wall bowed and shifted, but it did not break. Rallying to the bellows of their captains, the fighters surged forward and drove the murluks back.

The men did not pursue their frog-like foes into deeper water. Instead, they snapped their line back into shape and reformed the wall along the river's edge. There, they waited for the murluks' next charge... which was already building.

Although hundreds of murluks had been cut down by the defenders' maneuvers, more were surfacing to take the place of their fallen. *So many.* I stared in horror at the revitalized horde. *How are the soldiers holding them back?*

If what Tara said was true, humans had been battling the murluks here since day one. My gaze slid to the woman by my side. *How have Tara's people held them at bay for nine days?*

While I was staring agog at the spectacle, Tara had apparently been assessing the battle. "The line appears weak on the right. They may not survive another charge."

The motion of two dozen men at the foot of the upper bank caught my attention. They had not been involved in the previous clash between murluks and men. Rested and fresh, they moved to take up position in the human wall.

Tara gestured to the fighters. "John's unit," she said by way of explanation. "Reinforcing the right flank, and just in time too." She nodded her approval. "Smart soldier. Come on, let's join them."

Tara leaped down the upper bank, heedless of the danger posed by the steep slope. Despite the desperate clash of weapons, Tara appeared at ease, showing not even the slightest hint of nerves at joining the battle.

The same could not be said of me.

I eyed Tara's sure-footed dance down the slope and bit back a spurt of envy. Even if I wanted to, I could never match her pace.

Tentatively, I tested the soundness of the bank with my good leg. The hard-packed earth did not shift under my weight.

I can manage this. Stepping onto the slope, I followed in Tara's footsteps.

As I struggled down the upper bank, I kept a tight rein on my thoughts. What we were venturing into was nothing like my previous—and only—combat experience.

I had been forced into the fight with the orcs. In that encounter, I had reacted instinctively and had little time to think.

This was different.

This time, I was walking willingly into conflict—even knowing I was abysmally unprepared. My heart pounded and my tongue stuck to the roof of my mouth. *Why am I doing this?*

I wasn't ready. I knew it. Tara knew it. So why was she leading me into battle? *Because they need every man they can get. Their—our?—cause is that dire.*

As much as the thought of the fight scared me, I couldn't shirk from it. Doing so would destroy what little trust I had earned from Tara. And for all the woman's brusque manner, she had treated me fairly, far better than I had a right to expect. If I ran now, I would be branded a coward or worse.

Despite my fear, I had to shoulder my responsibility and play my part. Wiping my sweaty palms dry, I limped resolutely in Tara's shadow.

At the bottom of the upper bank, Tara glanced back. Seeing that I followed in her wake, she nodded. "Good man." Despite myself, I straightened, standing taller under her gaze.

"Tara!" a voice called. It was full of good cheer, out of place on the blood-soaked bank. "Have you come to join us? I thought you'd have left this misbegotten place already!"

Turning, I saw that the speaker was a tall, red-haired man at the fore of the reinforcements. Despite the grimness of the battlefield, he looked as relaxed as Tara.

"Not on your life, John!" she yelled back with friendly wave.

Still chuckling, John peered beyond Tara to me. "Who've you got there?"

"New fish. I'll look after him."

John's face scrunched up, his mask of joviality briefly slipping when his gaze dropped to my crippled foot. "You sure?" He shook his head. "Of course, you're sure. You're Tara. You're *always* sure!" He guffawed again, laughing at his own joke.

"Damn right, John," Tara replied.

My gaze was drawn to John's unit. Some of his men clenched their weapons with the same white-knuckled grip I did. I realized that the pair's friendly banter was not only for the benefit of John's men. I glanced at Tara. Unlike John, she betrayed no sign of hidden tension. *Does she truly feel no fear?*

Further conversation broke off as John and his men raced the remaining distance to the line, slipping into the many gaps in its formation.

Gaps left by their fallen comrades.

I swallowed, averting my eyes from the dead soldiers, abandoned in the churned-up muck. With the murluks readying for another charge, I knew Tara's people did not have time to see to the fallen. Yet the dead's vacant eyes reproached me as I limped past them, through the mud. Lifting my gaze, I saw that beyond the human wall the murluks had pooled into new groups.

Are they about to charge?

Tara stopped three feet away from the defenders and clamped her hand on my shoulder. "Remember everything I told you, and you will be fine."

Not trusting myself to say anything, I nodded mutely and followed her into the line, the men on either side making way for us. Tara, a step in front, was on my left. On my right was a freckled, ginger-haired youth. He nodded at me. "I'm Michael."

"Jamie," I said, licking my lips to moisten them before replying.

Michael glanced beyond me to Tara. "First battle?" he asked sympathetically.

"Yep."

"Don't worry, Tara will take care of you. She's one of our best fighters. Word of advice, though. She has probably forgotten to mention this, but don't neglect your Techniques." Michael leaned in close. "That woman has a supernatural knack for battle. I swear she doesn't even make use of her Trials-gained abilities. Not so for us lesser mortals. I wouldn't have survived as long as I have without them."

Michael's warning was timely. In the chaos of my arrival and the rush to battle, I had forgotten about my Techniques. I smiled gratefully. "Thanks."

"No problem, friend." He turned his attention back to the murluks.

I shot a glance at the creatures myself. They had not yet begun their advance. I had time yet, so I willed open the Trials core in my mind and recalled the messages stored within. As it had on Earth, a translucent window edged in gold unfurled in my mind and words spilled out.

I inspected the Trials alerts.

Disappointingly, none of my Disciplines and Attributes had changed from what Aurora had shown me on Wyrm Island.

I would have to wait until I levelled up and visited the dragon temple to acquire further magical skills. But in the meantime, I would have to make do with the few usable Techniques I had.

Reviewing them, I realized with a start that I knew how to use them already. The knowledge was instinctive, deeply ingrained. Not pausing to marvel at the minor miracle, I prepared to cast *mimic*.

Fool that I was, I hadn't thought to use it yet. But in a throng of humans, all deep in the throes of battle, the chance of anyone bothering to *analyze* me was negligible.

I opened my *magesight*. Reaching for the magic at the center of my being, I tapped into its core and looked upon the world through the lens of magic. It was the first time I had performed such a feat, yet it felt as natural as breathing.

Turning my gaze on myself, I studied the flowing lines of my spirit and found I understood its design. Taken all together, the threads of intricately interwoven spirit that formed my being mapped out the core of who I was—and my Potentials.

I knew that players didn't see this intricate weave of spirit when they applied *analyze*. Most did not have the *magesight* needed, and those who did weren't likely to have the necessary knowledge to understand the complicated twists and swirls of spirit.

For most players, the Trials interpreted a target's spirit weave and reported the results. But now, courtesy of the Mimicked Core Trait, I had the knowledge not only to understand my own spirit threads but also to alter them—superficially, of course, but enough to confound another player's *analyze*.

Reaching out with my mind, I plucked the first filament of spirit and shifted it to where it needed to be. I worked swiftly from there; in just a few seconds my task was completed and my Magic Potential disguised.

It did not take long for the Trials to confirm the changes.

***Mimic* activated. Your extraordinary Magic Potential has been masked and will be seen by others as meager.**

I nodded, satisfied with the results. I couldn't conceal my Potential entirely. If I did, I'd have a hard time explaining how I was able to cast spells. With my Potential revealed as meager, although still noteworthy, the strength of my magic would be hidden.

Or so I hoped.

Out of curiosity, I turned my *magesight* to the nearest murluk. Its being was a chaotic whirl of spirit, but, disappointingly, I couldn't fathom its hidden meaning.

I closed my *magesight*. Each being's spirit weave was unique, requiring its own store of knowledge or careful study to decode. In time, perhaps I could gain the skill, but for now, just like any other player, I would have to rely on *analyze* to understand my foes.

Drawing on my will, I reached out and cast *analyze* on the murluk.

The target is a level 12 river murluk. It has no Magic, meager Might, is gifted with Resilience, and has low Craft.

Knowledge of the murluk filled me as I willed away the message. In an eyeblink, I understood more about the murluk than about most creatures on Earth. My mouth dropped open in astonishment.

The information the Trials provided penetrated and my mouth worked again. For a different reason entirely.

Fear.

The murluk's level was far above mine. The creature likely needed a single hit to kill me!

What am I doing here again?

"Relax, champion." Tara must have sensed my agitation. "Just remember to drive your spear forward and pull it back. Don't worry about anything else."

"But those creatures are more than ten levels higher than me!" I protested.

"You are a... trifle less prepared than my regular recruits," admitted Tara. "Most of them manage to get in some basic training and visit the temple before facing the murluks." She held my gaze. "But you can get through this."

I stared at her in disbelief. A *little* less prepared? *Who is she kidding—*

My thoughts ground to a halt as, with loud, slurping cries and darting tongues, the first of the murluks hopped forward in attack.

The battle was about to begin.

※ ※ ※

My mind went blank and my eyes lost their focus, mesmerized by the mud-spattered, blue-skinned toads with their black alien eyes and their darting pink tongues.

Tara swatted me—hard—snapping my world back into focus. "Get it together, fish," she ordered.

I shook my head to clear it and wrapped both my hands around my spear. Tara crouched low behind her shield, the spear in her right arm at the ready.

I hadn't realized earlier, but she was barely over five feet tall. At six foot, I towered over the diminutive fighter, which would make my job of stabbing from behind her in the second row much simpler.

I breathed easier. *I can do this.* Setting my stance as best I could, I waited.

The murluk line crashed against the human wall in a fury of sound and a flurry of thrusting spears. Ignoring my chattering teeth, I fixed my eyes on Tara and waited for her to move first.

A murluk emerged from the horde with a suddenness that nearly caused me to fall back in surprise. Only Tara's stillness kept me in position.

The warrior thrust his spear at my companion. With enviable calm, Tara flung up her shield and parried away the murluk's strike. Then, in a blur of movement, she slashed out and sliced open the murluk's torso.

Her success fueled my courage.

Despite the dread thickening my limbs, I forced myself into motion. Stepping forward, I jabbed downward at the much shorter murluk, aiming for its throat. I missed, grazing his face instead.

"Good job! Now pull back!" shouted Tara. I withdrew my spear. Tara stepped into the gap and punched through the murluk with a second thrust. The creature fell lifelessly to the mud.

Another took his place.

The second murluk was more cautious. He feinted, then thrust his spear half-heartedly at Tara's legs.

Instead of dodging backward, as the murluk probably expected, Tara leapt forward and slammed her wooden shield down on the spear, trapping it.

After a second's hesitation, I jabbed my spear forward again. Tara, following through on her first attack, struck out as well.

Her blow tore through the murluk's unprotected armpit, while mine merely scratched his arm.

The murluk hung on somehow, alive but mortally injured. Tara did not relent. Rushing forward, she bashed its face in with her shield and stabbed it in the torso with her spear.

With a final gasp, the murluk fell dead.

In the sudden respite, I remembered to breathe again, sucking in a deep lungful of air. In a matter of seconds, Tara and I had killed two murluks... well, Tara had done all the work, but I had helped. More importantly, I'd survived the exchange.

Then something extraordinary happened.

My head buzzed, and knowledge that I knew was not mine seeped into my consciousness. I corrected my grip on the spear, instinctively shifting my hands to where they needed to be.

That's better, I thought, feeling the weapon balance easier in my hand. After that, the Trials' message came as no surprise.

Your combat experience has advanced your skill with spears to level 1.

With adrenaline surging and my blood singing, I felt revitalized and I itched to advance. Elsewhere, the line bowed backward where others were not doing as well.

"Back!" Tara barked, retreating herself. Obediently, I stepped into line with her.

Noticing our retreat and probably hoping to catch us off guard, a murluk leaped forward and stabbed at Tara. Casually—almost lazily—she parried away the blow. Even more impressively, she did not strike out again but instead stepped back into the security of our line.

There, she waited.

The murluk, smarter than his fellows, realized that his quarry was far too wily. He faded back into the horde in search of easier prey. Another, less cautious murluk took his place.

Tara repeated the same precise motions—parry and counterattack. Falling in line with her easy rhythm, I followed her blows and together we skewered our third foe with twin strikes.

As the third murluk fell, a flurry of Trials messages scrolled through my vision.

> **You have gained in experience and are now a level 2 Neophyte.**
> **Your skill with spears has advanced to level 2.**
> **Your strength has increased to level 2.**

The last message was the most surprising. Following on its heels, one of the almost-forgotten runes from my Induction rose out of my subconscious—where it had been patiently waiting all this time—and delved into my body.

I clenched my jaw as the magic worked into my muscles. Raising my hand, I stared at it, once again flummoxed by the Trials' magic.

My body looked the same, but I could feel the difference. I was stronger. I glanced at my dragging foot. *Could the Trials heal it too? And if it can do that, what else can it do?* My mind exploded with the possibilities.

Movement from the corner of my eye broke the spell. A murluk was advancing. Dismissing the Trials' notices, I hefted my spear and got back to work.

CHAPTER THIRTEEN

391 DAYS UNTIL THE ARKON SHIELD FALLS

> "*Magesight is a Technique granted by the Trials to all players with Magic Potential. It is the foundation of both magic and sorcery, and without it, any would-be mage is blind. Truly, without the gift of magesight, magic itself is not be possible.*"
> —Cale Ames, elven spellweaver.

I don't know how long Tara and I spent killing.

The bodies around her kept piling up, and protected by her warrior prowess, I was untouchable.

But, eventually, the bloodbath took its toll. My arms began to burn, and the spear felt like lead in my hands. Despite my exhaustion, I persisted, following Tara's every lead. Step forward. Step back. Lunge. Withdraw.

Until there were no more foes to kill.

I staggered, suddenly dizzy in the stillness that follows battle. I would have fallen if not for Tara's steadying hand on my arm. "Whoa there, fish. Don't you fall now. Not when you've been doing so well."

I wiped the dripping sweat from my brow. "What happened?" I gasped, leaning on my spear for support.

"We've beaten this wave. The murluks are falling back to regroup."

"It's over? We've won?" I bent forward, panting for air.

Tara laughed. "No, fish. Not by a longshot. There are more waves coming." She tapped my shoulder, forcing me to look up. "You did well, Jamie," she murmured. "Far better than I expected. But sit and rest before you collapse. We have just minutes before the next assault."

I sagged gratefully to the ground, not caring about the mud that spattered my face and arms.

"Michael!" Tara called over her shoulder.

The ginger-haired warrior appeared next to her, looking no worse for the day's efforts. "Tara?"

"You got jerky? Our budding warrior here looks like he's about to die of exhaustion. Give him some."

"Yes, ma'am." Michael pulled a packet out from inside his armor and handed it to me. "Eat," he said, "it will make you feel better."

Obediently, I ate.

Tara and Michael were right. After a few mouthfuls of jerky, I felt somewhat restored and began assessing the situation with renewed interest. The river bank was strewn with skewered murluks. I grinned as I noticed the sizable pile in front of us.

Up and down the line, soldiers were kicking the corpses back into the river, the bodies floating away in the bloodied current.

When my gaze swung to the right, the grin slipped off my face. The rest of the line had not fared as well as we had.

More gaps—*many* more gaps—had appeared. I swallowed. I had been fortunate. Unlike most, I had a guardian angel. Without Tara, I never would have survived as I long as I did; of that, I had no doubt.

"How have you endured this long if every fight is this hard?" I asked.

Tara turned away from inspecting the murluk lines to stare at me.

I pointed to the dozens of fallen soldiers. "If you've been taking that many causalities every wave, how have any of you survived for over a week?" Running the cold, hard numbers through my head, by even the most conservative calculations, the human forces here should have died out long ago.

Tara pursed her lips. "You think too much, fish." I continued to stare at her, refusing to let the matter go, and she sighed. "To be honest, we'd all be dead already if not for new recruits like you replenishing our numbers every day."

"So, we're what... cannon fodder?" I studied the dead with new eyes, aghast at the implications. Were they all 'fresh meat' like me?

"No!" said Tara fiercely. "Not that. Never that. On their first day here, all new players are paired with one of our old hands, just like you were with me. It's our job to keep the new fishes alive and teach them all we can."

She sighed, then added reluctantly, "But there aren't enough experienced fighters and there are too many new players. Tomorrow, you'll be left to sink or swim on your own merit. If you survive your second day, the next, and the next after that, you'll graduate to an old hand yourself and will pass on your experience to others. Do you understand?"

"Is that why you pushed me into battle so quickly?"

Tara grimaced. "Partly. There are no exceptions to the pairing rules." She indicated my crippled foot. "Regardless of the circumstances. There are too many new players to baby anyone. No one will mentor you tomorrow, so make the most of your first day."

I mulled over her words. As strange as it seemed, Tara had driven me into battle out of pity. I glanced down at my hobbled foot. What she had left unsaid was that my limp would make surviving without help difficult—if not impossible.

"You said partly. What's the rest of the reason?"

"The *newcomer* blessing," Tara admitted. "It accelerates your learning far beyond the norm. And battle, we have learned the hard way, is the fastest way to improve a player. When you combine the two—combat and blessing—the growth a soldier can see in their first day is phenomenal." She shrugged. "So, we push new arrivals into battle—those who are willing, anyway. It's counterintuitive I know, but it works."

I nodded slowly. It was a brutal system, but looking around at the mud-and-gore-spattered battlefield, I could understand the need. "Then I only have your protection for the rest of the day?"

"Correct. Today, you must put all your efforts into getting as strong as you can. How many levels did you gain in that wave?"

Her words reminded me of the many unread notices awaiting my attention. After the first few messages at the start of the battle, I had automatically dismissed further alerts. In the chaos of battle, I had no time to spare for updates or for the occasional spurts of knowledge and changes relating to the Trials.

Reaching into the Trials core that lay dormant in my mind, I recalled the messages and scrutinized each.

> **You have gained in experience and are now a level 4 Neophyte.**
> **Your skill with spears has advanced to level 5.**
> **Your strength and constitution have increased to level 3.**
> **Your vigor has increased to level 2.**

My stats, while nowhere near impressive, were much better. At least I now felt less outmatched by the murluks. "Three levels," I told Tara. "I'm level four now."

"Not bad. Just remember, *newcomer* only applies to Neophyte Disciplines and Attributes—those below level ten. Once you attain the Trainee rank, your progress will slow dramatically. Do your best to reach level ten today in as many Disciplines and Attributes as you can."

"Got it." I rose to my feet with newfound determination. Knowing what tomorrow would bring, I realised that I would have to rely less on Tara's protection and fend more for myself.

The slap of hopping feet pulled my attention back to the river. The murluks were charging again.

"Right, back in line!" Tara ordered.

I took my place behind her just as our first opponent appeared. Tara parried, then thrusted. Following her attack, I jabbed out. The murluk fell dead, and the next took its place.

Tara stepped forward. I advanced with her, but this time I did not wait for her to initiate. Lunging past my mentor, I used my longer reach to bury my spear into the murluk's midriff before he could launch an attack.

The creature staggered back, rocked off-balance. Tara exploited the opening I had created. Dancing forward, she skewered the hapless murluk.

As the murluk fell, Tara smiled back at me in approval. "Think you can do that again?"

I nodded, elated by our success. That time, I had played more than a token role in the battle. That time, I had helped her cut down our foe quicker.

"All right, then let's do it again."

Advancing, she searched for our next victim. A murluk rushed past, attempting to flank one of our companions on the line. I jabbed my spear at its legs, tripping it up.

Before the luckless creature could heave itself back to its feet, Tara slammed her spear through its back, killing it instantly. Pulling her weapon out in a spurt of blood, she turned a wry smile upon me. "Let's not get too creative just yet, fish. Keep it simple."

I accepted her rebuke with good grace, and we moved on to hunt down more murluks.

We made a good team. Each time, I initiated combat and fouled the murluks' attacks with my longer reach. Afterward, Tara stepped in and finished our prey with a single, lethal strike. The murluks, for all their superior numbers, were defenseless in the face of our coordinated attacks.

My crippled foot, despite my concerns, did not hamper me as much as I had feared. Tara had been right. The long spear was an easy weapon, and in the thick mud of the lower bank, the attacks I employed required neither complex footwork nor speed.

As my awareness of the battle expanded, I realized that teamwork and discipline differentiated the two forces. Glancing along our defensive line, I saw that where the murluks fought individually—often getting in each other's way—the human warriors moved as a cohesive force. This, more than anything, drove our success.

But, eventually, the weight of the murluks' numbers began to tell. Forty yards to our left, the defensive line started to cave.

"Tara! To me, quickly!" shouted John. "We must reinforce the center or the battle is lost."

Tara whipped around, focusing her green eyes in the direction John had pointed. "Damn it!" she muttered, the muscles in her jaw pulling tight. She swung back to me, throwing a quick assessing glance at my leg before resting her gaze on my face. "Sorry, Jamie, I have to go. Will you be—"

"Go!" I said, cutting her off with a lopsided smile. "I'll be fine."

I hoped.

Tara threw me a sharp nod and took off sprinting south along the back of the line toward the hotspot. "Stay alive, fish. I'll be back," she called before disappearing out of earshot.

I turned back to the battle. None of the murluks were advancing toward me just yet. Tara and I had done so well at killing the creatures that an empty spot had opened up in front of us. I licked suddenly dry lips. With Tara gone, I was certain that would not last. Sooner or later, one of the creatures would spot me alone and vulnerable.

"Why did you let her go, Jamie?" I muttered to myself, gripped with a rush of anxiety. "That was foolish. How are you going to survive now?"

A few feet to my right, Michael fought with his unit. On my left, more human warriors battled. Although bracketed by my fellows on both sides, I felt alone, unsure

I did not know how to fight with either group of men. Untrained and crippled as I was, I doubted they would welcome me into their ranks.

None of them were Tara.

It took a special skill, I realized, to do what Tara had done, to train an unskilled raw recruit and simultaneously integrate his attacks with your own. My appreciation for my mentor's efforts grew.

But now I was without her. Now I had to defend myself.

I took a cautious step back, waiting, knowing my limits. I stood little chance against a murluk on my own. Until Tara returned, I would fight defensively, and only when forced.

It was not long before a murluk spotted me, marking me as easy prey. Loping forward, he shoved his spear—almost lazily—toward me.

I swayed away and thrust back, clipping the creature's shoulder.

The murluk hopped away, slurping angrily before advancing with renewed vigor.

I tightened my grip on my weapon… and waited.

The creature jabbed at my torso. I tried to dodge, but with my crippled foot, I was too slow. The murluk's spear skidded off my armor and scored a line of fire along my side. I gasped but ignored the pain. The spear had failed to penetrate my leather vest, although it still knocked the wind out of me.

I staggered backward and managed to keep my feet, but the murluk did not let up. He launched another attack, thrusting at my face. I swayed, barely avoiding a skewering.

He stabbed again, aiming for my heart. Angling my spear upward, I parried away the blow, my teeth clenched with the effort. Although half my size, the murluk was much stronger. It took every ounce of my strength to push aside his blade.

I realized I had to change tactics. The murluk was the better fighter, so the longer our exchange went on, the more likely I was to die. I had to take to a risk.

Charging forward, I jabbed my elbow down into the shorter murluk's face. He staggered back—mostly from shock—but before the creature could recover, I shoved my spear between his legs and twisted, tripping him up.

He fell back with a surprised slurp.

I didn't let up. Closing the distance to my downed foe, I straddled his body, pinning him under my weight.

I felt him writhe beneath me. He was too strong to hold for long. In panic, I raised my spear high and plunged it down. The murluk shrieked and tried to batter me away, but I fended off his blows and jabbed into him repeatedly.

Spurting blood clouded my vision. Ignoring the crimson haze, I stabbed my spear down once more. The murluk's motions slowed.

I didn't stop.

I thrust again and again, blindly burying my weapon into his torso. Gore and guts stained my hands, face, and neck. But I didn't stop. I couldn't. I had to ensure he was dead. It was him or me. I couldn't die here.

Ruthlessly, I let fury consume me. The murluk was not just my enemy, he was an agent of the Trials. Like the orcs, he was every bit as responsible for my Mom's death and for the deaths of all the humans on this battlefield. He had to die. With a tortured cry, I forced my spear down again.

The murluk stopped moving. *Is he dead?* I couldn't be certain. But I couldn't let up. I had to—

Burning agony rippled across my back. Like a splash of cold river water, clarity returned, banishing my cruel mix of rage, grief, and hysteria. Shocked back to my senses, I stared at my hands in horror.

What was I doing?

A blow broke my reverie. I arched my back in surprise as a second murluk attacked from behind. The creature's spear had sliced through my armor, and now my own blood drenched me as well.

Abandoning my weapon—still stuck in my dead foe—I rolled away, and by happenstance more than by skill, I dodged my attacker's next strike.

After wiping away the muck obscuring my vision, I looked up to see the murluk's advance. My breath quickened. I was in trouble. There was no way I could get to my feet in time. Choosing an unconventional tactic once more, I rolled—this time toward the murluk.

Caught off guard, the creature was slow to react. He thrust downward but missed. I bowled him over and tried to push myself upright. Hampered by my foot, I wasn't quick enough, and the murluk beat me in the race to get up. *Damn it!* I stared at the creature bearing down on me.

It was time to cast *invincible*.

Opening my *magesight*, I began to manifest my spirit.

A spear blossomed out of the murluk's torso. Startled, I dropped my spellcasting.

A smiling Michael appeared from behind the slumped-over corpse. "Looked like you needed a hand."

"Thanks," I gasped. Clambering to my feet, I snatched up the dead murluk's spear.

Michael clasped a hand to my shoulder. "Come on, let's get back in line. Things are about to get much worse."

I followed Michael's gaze. The murluks on the northern end of the line had pulled back and were regathering not thirty yards ahead of us. Their numbers were being reinforced by more of their fellows that emerged from the river.

I glanced down the line. The creatures had not pulled back everywhere. The southern flank was being pressed hard, and matters in the center still looked bleak. All was swirling chaos there.

Even with Tara and John's men, it didn't look certain they would hold the line. I swallowed. We would get no help from there, not yet.

We would have to repel the next attack on our own.

Chapter Fourteen

391 DAYS UNTIL THE ARKON SHIELD FALLS

> *"Overworld is too dangerous for the humans to survive on their own. Let them come to us with caps in hand. Or perish through their own folly."*
> —Unknown royal advisor.

I limped after Michael and re-joined the line.

While we waited for the next attack, I rolled up my leather vest to inspect the jagged wound in my lower back. The spear hadn't penetrated deep, and the bleeding had slowed. I breathed easier. It seemed I would live.

Yet the wound still throbbed each time I moved. In the first few moments after the attack, fear and adrenaline had masked the pain, but now... I wondered whether I could still fight. Watching the gathering murluks, I felt my expression harden. There was no choice.

It was fight or run. And I would not flee.

I turned my focus inward and checked my player progress in the Trials core. During the last murluk wave, my body had undergone further enhancements, and I had gained more knowledge. Calling up the Trials alerts, I reviewed the changes.

> **You have gained in experience and are now a level 6 Neophyte.**
> **Your agility has increased to level 3.**
> **Your strength has increased to level 4.**
> **Your skill using light armor has advanced to level 1.**
> **Your skill with spears has advanced to level 7.**

I was stronger, faster, tougher, and I had become more adept with my weapon. At any other time, the changes would have astounded me. But now? Now I despaired. I still hadn't learned enough to survive the next wave.

I leaned on my spear and bowed my head. *When will this battle end?* All I had done since coming to Overworld was fight or wait to fight. *Is every day on this world going to be like this?* Earth seemed a long way away.

"Get ready," shouted Michael.

I looked up. The murluks had begun their advance.

Grimacing at the pain of moving, I brought my spear up and held it ready for the oncoming horde.

So many. This time, neither I nor the other soldiers on this section of the line had Tara to protect us.

"Can we hold them?" I asked Michael.

"Forget the bigger picture, fish. Just keep your position in the wall." But the tremble in his hands belied his words.

He doesn't think we're going to survive.

I peered along the lines of men on the right flank. Dispirited gazes. Weary stances. Drooping weapons. *How many will die in the next few minutes?*

Too many.

Returning my gaze to the murluks, I contemplated a crazy idea. *If I am going to die here, what do I have to lose?* I bit my lip. *Nothing.*

Shrugging, I charged.

Well, it was more of a fast hop, really, a not-so-funny parody of a murluk's gait, but it was the fastest I could manage. The system thought so too.

Your agility has increased to level 4.

I chuckled darkly at the Trials' message.

"Jamie, get back here! What do you think you are doing, you stupid fish?" Michael growled from behind me.

I ignored him, my eyes fixed on the fast-approaching murluks. I fancied I could their eyes widening, amazed at the sight of a lone human charging them.

I grinned. Almost knee deep in the river, I stopped. I had advanced far enough away from our lines. Planting my feet in the muddy river-bottom, I crouched low and held my spear ready. Waiting.

I only have to keep my feet, I reminded myself.

The murluks drew closer. Tens of spears were hefted in the air, ready to impale the foolish human in their path. Watching the creatures through narrowed eyes, I waited. Until... at the last second...

Now, I thought and cast *invincible*.

Opening my *magesight*, I called on my spirit. Energy erupted out of my inner being and wove through my body, both inside and out. In a split second, my physical form was overlaid with a second one of impermeable spirit invisible to normal sight although it glowed a radiant silver in my *magesight*.

***Invincible* activated. You are immune to all damage for 30 seconds.**

Spears hurtled toward me. I itched to raise my weapon in defense, but I bit back the instinct, letting the wall of spears land unhindered.

It was much harder to do than I thought.

I squeezed my eyes shut at the moment of impact. The *ping* of sharpened metal clanging off my spirit form's hardened shell was music to my ears. I smiled. *It worked!* I had believed it would, but that was vastly different from knowing.

My eyes flew open.

Murluks were converging on me from all sides. I dug my feet deeper into the mud and waited for the momentum of their charge to be expended. I knew the greatest danger—in the next thirty seconds at least—was being knocked down and trampled by the crush of bodies above. But the frog creatures weighed little, and their charge had little speed behind it.

I held my ground more easily than expected. Once the weight pressing against me eased, I raised my head. *Now let's see how much damage I can do,* I thought, as I hit back at the murluks.

My spear slid smoothly into the throat of my nearest foe. I leaned into the blow, ignoring the repeated jabs that bounced harmlessly off me. With a wet gurgle, the murluk died. Wrenching back my weapon, I sought bared flesh again.

Murluks swirled around me. Converging on their trapped quarry, they struck at me from all sides, not understanding why their attacks were failing.

My ploy was proving more successful than I'd hoped.

I had expected some of the murluks would be lured away from the human lines by my presence in their midst. What I had not anticipated was for *all of them* to abort their attack and fall on me instead.

Seeing that I held the murluks' attention, the commanders of the northern section of the human lines responded to the opportunity I had created. I heard a voice shout, "To me! Charge! Strike them down from behind!"

I hoped Michael and his fellows on the flank would heed the call; if they didn't, I'd be dead soon. But I had no control over their actions. I had to focus on my own. I had to do what I could to ensure I survived.

Narrowing my focus, I concentrated on inflicting as much hurt on the murluks as I could. Thrust and pull. Rinse and repeat. Over and over again, I jabbed down at the much shorter creatures, with no care for defense.

My foolish gambit was not without its benefits. While I fought, a constant stream of Trials messages scrolled through my vision.

You have gained in experience and are now a level 8 Neophyte.
Your constitution and strength have increased to level 5.
Your vigor has increased to level 4.
Your skill using light armor has advanced to level 6.
Your skill with spears has advanced to level 8.

I grinned wryly. Facing hundred-to-one odds—and surviving—was a good way to gain experience on Overworld. *Walk away from this alive, and at least I'll be stronger for the experience.*

A formless roar made me lift my head. It was the human fighters crashing into the murluks around me.

Finally, I thought. *Invincible* wasn't going to last much longer. Even so, I wasn't sure the right flank's charge would be enough to save me.

It was always a gamble. I returned to my bloody work, reaping as grim a harvest as I could. My arms moving mechanically, I slaughtered indiscriminately.

As the spearmen's attacks began to bear fruit, the pressure on me eased. The human fighters had half-circled the murluks and were dealing death quickly and efficiently. *I might yet survive.*

Then my aura of *invincibility* faded.

The blows raining down no longer bounced off. I jerked fitfully as blades bit into me, assaulted by fresh waves of pain. In a handful of seconds, my health plummeted. I was still alive, but that wouldn't hold true for much longer.

Hunkering down and waving my spear defensively, I gave up attacking altogether.

More murluk blows battered me, although more sporadically now. The weight of humans pressing against the creatures from their rear was too great for them to ignore. They swung to face their attackers.

I began to dodge, parry, and weave in earnest, desperately trying to stay alive long enough for help to get through. But in the end, it wasn't my actions that saved me, or even the human fighters straining to reach me.

It was the murluks themselves.

The battle had reached its tipping point, and the creatures had had enough. Throwing down their weapons, they turned and fled, diving beneath the waves to take refuge in the depths.

I fell gasping to my knees. *I'll be damned! I survived.* Swaying gave way to exhaustion and encroaching darkness, and then I fell face first into the mud.

* * *

Where am I? Waves slapped against my side as my consciousness returned. *Still on the river shore.*

Water splashed my face. I groaned.

"You hear that?"

I didn't recognize the voice. More water was thrown on my face. I sputtered feebly and tried to roll to escape whoever tormented me, but I couldn't move. I was too weak.

"Is he alive?" the voice asked again.

"Of course he's alive, you idiot. Do you think dead men cough?"

I kept my eyes closed. *Dear God, I'm tired.* My body ached everywhere, and I could smell the blood soaking my clothes and armor. I was certain I bled from a dozen cuts or more. *Leave me alone,* I wanted to scream, but I couldn't get the words out. *Let me sleep.*

I had no idea how I had kept fighting through my injuries, but now my body was shackled with pain. *Am I dying?* I was too exhausted to care, wanting to escape it all. *I'm sorry, Mom. I tried.*

"Who knows *what* he is! You saw what he did? Can men do that?" continued the first voice.

"Shut up, Sten. He's just a kid. A *human* kid. Any fool can see that."

"But you saw—"

"Enough!" growled the second voice, the whip of authority unmistakable in his voice. "One more word out of you and you'll be on latrine duty for the rest of the week."

I blew out an irritated breath. *Why couldn't these fools just leave me be?*

"You hear that?" Sten muttered. "He's making strange noises again. We shouldn't be so close."

The other man ignored him.

"Who is this fellow, Michael?" he whispered. I sensed he was kneeling beside me. "You seemed to know him."

"I don't know, Sarge." Michael was bent over me too. "Just some kid I met before the battle. Crippled. I felt sorry for him."

Before the sergeant could reply, a disturbance drew their attention.

"What's going on here, Lloyd?" demanded Tara. I felt the shadows of the two men fall over me as they rose and turned to face her.

"It's your fish, Tara," Michael answered in the sergeant's stead.

"*My* fish?" Tara asked. She dropped down by my side. "What happened?" she growled.

I winced. Even knocking on death's door, I could sense she was displeased.

"I don't know," Lloyd answered. "You saw the disturbance on our flank, when the murluks aborted their charge?"

"Yeah, that's why I'm here. Whose fool idea was that? And which unit did we sacrifice to make it happen? For your sake, I hope that wasn't your idea, Lloyd. Because if it was, the old lady will have your head."

Lloyd shook his head. "It was your boy here."

"What?"

"He charged out of our lines and lured the murluks to him." Lloyd paused, as if unable to believe his words. "He held their attention for what must have been close on a minute. *And* he lived to tell the tale."

"Impossible!" snapped Tara.

"What the cap'n says is true, Tara. We all saw it," Michael said.

Tara fell silent for a moment. "Are you telling me," she said, her voice scathing, "that this untrained boy, who can no more run than I can fly and who didn't know one end of a spear from the other an hour ago, held the murluks at bay all on his own? For a full minute?" She laughed. "What do you two take me for?"

"It's true, Tara," Michael repeated stubbornly.

I sighed. I was both alive and awake. It didn't seem like I was going to go peacefully to my rest anytime soon, and it was past time I entered the conversation.

Before Tara's bites off their heads.

The pair had saved my life, after all, and they didn't deserve a chewing out from Tara for that. Forcing my eyes open, I blinked rapidly until Tara and the two men swam into focus.

"It's true, Tara," I croaked.

Tara's hawk-eyed green stare swung my way. "Jamie, you're awake!" She frowned, realizing what I'd said. "What do you mean it's true?"

I waved her closer, and she leaned down over me, her face right up to mine. "I have a Technique," I whispered so that only she could hear. "*Invincible*. It makes me impervious to damage. It's why I didn't start with a Clean Slate. Don't tell anyone."

Tara stared at me, her face expressionless. "Why didn't you use it earlier?" she whispered.

"Couldn't. It can only be used once a day, and it only lasts thirty seconds."

"Okay," she said, leaning back. "We'll talk more later. Rest now. Our medic is on the way." She squeezed my arm. "Oh, and thank you. You quite possibly saved us all today." After patting my arm once more, Tara stood up. "Sergeant Lloyd, have someone bring him food. Michael, see what's keeping the medic."

Both men ran off to do her bidding. I tried to speak again, but Tara shushed me. Relieved that I was finally being allowed to rest, I tried to let myself fade into darkness. But now that I had opened my eyes, sleep eluded me.

After a frustrated minute, I gave up on the idea altogether. Straining with the effort, I raised my head and took stock of my surroundings. I saw that I had been dragged a few yards away from the lapping water but was still on the river's lower banks. I craned my head in both directions, but didn't catch sight of any murluks.

Thank God the battle is over, I thought, letting my head fall back. To distract myself from the pain spiking through my body, I turned my focus inwards to the Trials core. Another pile of messages had gathered. I scanned through them.

You have gained in experience and are now a level 9 Neophyte. Your vigor and agility have increased to level 5.

Your strength has increased to level 6.

Your constitution has increased to level 10 and reached rank 2, Trainee.

Your skills with spears and light armor have advanced to level 10 and reached rank 2, Trainee.

Alert: Trainee-ranked Attributes and Disciplines do not benefit from the *newcomer* buff or the accelerated learning rates applied at the Neophyte rank.

The learning rate of your Attribute: constitution, and your Disciplines: spears, and light armor, have decreased.

Not bad for an hour's work. I already felt more capable of facing Overworld's challenges. *I still have no magic, though. If I am going to—*

I flinched as my side throbbed from an errant twitch. Dismissing the Trials messages, I turned to my injuries, casting *analyze* upon myself.

Your health pool is at 24% of maximum.

I chuckled. I wasn't nearly as far gone as I'd thought. While my health was low, and my wounds numerous, my condition appeared stable.

It seemed I was going to live.

Sergeant Lloyd returned. "Here, kid, eat this," he said, dropping down next to me. "It will restore your stamina. Until Nic bandages you up, I'm afraid this is the best we can do for you."

Lloyd looked as fresh-faced as Tara and Michael, but if his words were anything to go by, he was no eighteen-year-old boy. *I will have to stop judging people's ages by their faces.* For all I knew, Lloyd was in his sixties.

But I said none of that. "Thanks," I rasped, taking the offered stick of dried meat and beginning to chew. I felt the food's restorative effects immediately as my stamina began inching upwards.

A little later, Michael returned with another man. Unlike the others he was not dressed in armor, and he carried a hefty leather bag strapped across his back. "What do we have here, Tara?" he asked.

"New recruit who needs bandaging. Doesn't seem like he has suffered any serious injuries. Just exhaustion."

The stranger bent over me. "Hi there. I'm Nicholas, and what passes for a medic on this world. Can I take a look at your wounds?"

"Sure, Doc," I replied. "I'm Jamie."

"I can't claim to be a doctor, at least not anymore." Nicholas absently began to inspect me. "I wish my old skills were still useful, but without our technology, they aren't of much value here. Like everyone, I'm learning the Overworld way of doing things."

I nodded, understanding what he meant.

Nicholas finished his inspection, then sat back. "Your condition isn't too dire. You're weak from blood loss and exhaustion, which we can treat easily enough. Your wounds themselves aren't severe. The slash across your back is the worst, but even that is superficial." Rifling through his bag, he pulled out some homemade bandages and a greenish paste.

"How long do you need, Nic?" Tara asked.

"Twenty minutes, tops," promised Nicholas. "I'll have him up and walking after that. Then he is all yours."

Chapter Fifteen

391 DAYS UNTIL THE ARKON SHIELD FALLS

> *"The runes of the Elders are just one of the many mysteries of the Trials we hope to uncover. Although we know beyond doubt that the runes are how players are enhanced, not even our best minds have been able to duplicate their effect."*
> —Taura Biaxal, svartalfar mystic.

Your health pool has increased to 63%.

It took Nicholas just fifteen minutes to stitch and bandage my wounds. The medic applied a liberal dose of green paste to each cut before closing them up. The paste, he claimed, would speed up my healing and prevent infection.

I nodded my thanks to the healer, who hurried off as soon as he was done. No doubt other patients needed his attention.

"How are you feeling?" My mentor was waiting for me with folded arms and a tapping foot. Everyone but Tara had left—some to haul off dead bodies, some to stand guard, and others to tend to chores I could only guess at. I still knew nothing of this place, except that it was run with something akin to military precision. And that Tara was near the top of the command structure.

"Much better," I replied, holding out my arm. With Tara's help, I staggered to my feet. The medic had worked wonders. I was pain-free and no longer bleeding, yet my wounds tingled with a unpleasant numbness, and my limbs felt leaden.

"It'll pass," Tara said when she saw my befuddled look. "Once the salve has done its work, your head will clear, and your limbs will return to normal."

I glanced at her. "What's in the paste?"

"I'm not sure, and I am not certain Nic knows either. It was something he and the other healers learned to make early on." She shrugged. "Whatever it is, it works. In an hour, your wounds will no longer trouble you. Until then, you'll be weak. Can you walk?"

I looked down at myself. My clothes were an unholy mess, and dried blood caked my arms, hair, and face. *I must look awful.* But I felt no twinge of pain as I took a tentative step. "I can walk," I answered.

"Good," Tara said. "Here, lean on my arm. We have to go see the old lady now. She will want to know more about this Technique of yours."

"The old lady?"

"The one in charge here," Tara replied, as we made our way back up river bank. She shot me a glance. "You will do well to tell her everything."

That was not happening—not until I knew what was going on here and how much I could trust this 'old lady.' Tara, though, had earned the right to know more.

"I haven't told *you* everything, Tara," I said.

She threw me a wry look. "Somehow I didn't think you had. Ready to tell me now?"

I nodded. "I have magic," I admitted.

Tara froze mid-step. "What!" she exploded, dropping my arm and swinging around to face me.

Abruptly robbed of her support, I swayed, momentarily at a loss to reply. A pair of soldiers, hauling murluk corpses, stopped to stare at us, but at Tara's glare, they hurried away.

She waited for them to go. "If you have magic," she said, biting off each word, "why did you not use it?"

"Because I don't have *any* magic," I said carelessly.

Tara's brows lowered ominously.

"Spells. I mean I don't have any *spells*," I corrected hastily. "I have Magic Potential, but not the skill to use it yet."

Tara stared at me for a moment, eyes narrowed, as he scrutinized me. A strange tingling suffused my body. She was using *analyze* on me, I realized.

Wondering why I had not done so earlier, I cast *analyze* on her in turn.

The target is Tara Madison, a level 32 human player. She has no Magic, has exceptional Might, is gifted with Resilience, and has meager Craft.

Her level was not as high as I'd expected, given the ease with which she dispatched the murluks.

"Meager magical Potential," Tara murmured. "Not as much as could be hoped for, but a darn sight better than anyone else around here." Tara pinned me with her gaze again. "Why did you not tell me earlier, before the battle?"

I considered her for a moment. *How much truth do I owe her?*

"Because I wasn't sure I could trust you," I said finally.

Tara scowled, clearly finding my answer inadequate. "You could have been killed, you idiot!" she exclaimed. "Don't you realize what a precious resource you are? As a potential mage, you're far too valuable to risk in battle. You should have told me!"

"Don't mistake me for one of your recruits, Tara," I muttered. "I followed you into battle because I was willing to do my part. I appreciate everything you've done for me, but I am *not* under your command." I paused to ensure my words had sunk in. "I am my own player," I continued. "With my own goals. Don't forget that."

Tara met my gaze without blinking, her spine stiff with anger. After a drawn-out moment, she expelled a heavy sigh. "You're right," she said, shoulders sagging. "I apologize. My words were uncalled for. It's just that... survival here has been harder than any of us expected. We are barely clinging on as it is."

She sighed again. "We can't go on as we have for much longer. Something has to change, or everything we've built here will be destroyed." She glanced at me again. "I'm sorry I overreacted. I saw only the cost to our people if you died."

I said nothing for a long while, mostly because I wasn't sure what to say. I sympathized with their plight, but my stupid heroics had almost killed me. There must be thousands of humans in this settlement by now, all fighting for its survival. Yet, who among them had killed an orc?

Only me.

That moment on the shore, when I was at death's door, had reminded me of my priorities. Vengeance came first. I couldn't let myself forget that again. Ever.

But I also knew I needed Tara and her people.

I could not survive Overworld alone. Not yet. There was too much I had to learn of the Trials, humanity's place in this world, and my magic. For the foreseeable future, my place was here... in location seventy-eight.

"Tara," I said quietly. "I am grateful for what you did for me today. I know I wouldn't have survived without you. For as long as I remain in the settlement, you can count on my help. I can promise at least that much."

Tara scrutinized my face, perhaps my pledge wasn't as unconditional as she hoped, but she didn't pursue the matter further. "Thank you, Jamie," she said simply. She placed her arm under mine, and we resumed our journey.

Still thinking about magic and what it would mean, I added, "Don't place too much hope in me, Tara. We don't know enough of Overworld's magic yet. It... I... might not be the solution to all your problems."

"You're right," Tara said. She glanced at me. "I won't betray your trust, Jamie. I will keep your *invincible* Technique a secret if you wish, but I urge you to tell the old lady. You can trust her."

I considered Tara's words. I had used the Technique in front of dozens of soldiers. People were bound to speculate and to eventually figure it out. It didn't make sense to keep it a secret. "All right. I'll tell her."

Tara smiled. "Thank you."

When we reached the top of the upper bank, Tara let go of my arm. I hadn't had much chance to study the area earlier, so I took a long look around.

Directly in front of me was the dragon temple, and behind it was a huddle of tents, enough to house a few hundred people. Farther east, beyond the tented camp, was a forest. To the left and right was open grassland, although in the far north I spotted the hazy outline of what could be hills.

I glanced at the sky. It was as blue as Earth's, with a large yellow sun shining brighter than Sol.

"Where are we going?" I asked Tara.

"There," she replied, gesturing to the mass of tents in front of us. "The old lady will be in the command tent."

I nodded, as if that made sense to me. "What do you call this place?" I looked at her curiously. "You can't just be calling it location seventy-eight."

Tara shrugged. "We haven't formally named the settlement yet. Mostly, we refer to it as the Outpost."

As we resumed walking, I looked around inquisitively. Less than a few yards from the edge of the upper bank, I spotted the shallow ditch we had crossed earlier. Inspecting it carefully, I realized it was the foundation of a wall. A trench had been dug along the length of the upper bank, and fallen poles were placed at regular intervals within it.

Noticing the direction of my gaze, Tara answered my unspoken query. "We've been trying to fortify the Outpost for days, but every time we make progress with its construction, the murluks destroy our work. It's why we've taken to meeting the creatures at the river's edge, not on the upper bank. If we can hold them at bay for a few days, our crafters might have time to complete the wall."

"I've been meaning to ask about the murluks," I said, as we resumed walking. "Why do they attack?"

Tara chuckled. "Your guess is as good as mine. They've assaulted us since day one. They seem determined to kill us off. We haven't been able to learn as much about them as we'd like. We do know they are territorial. They consider this stretch of river—both shores—theirs."

"Have your people tried reasoning with them? The murluks are intelligent, right? They must be if they bear arms and wear armor."

"You would think so," Tara said with a grimace. "But as far as we can tell they possess only rudimentary intelligence—an animal cunning of sorts. No one has been able to detect any speech patterns in the noises they make, nor have we found a means of communicating with them. All attempts at negotiations have failed—disastrously."

"Huh," I grunted. I had not seen mention of the murluks in my study of the Trials Infopedia, so I was no more informed than Tara. "Have you encountered others, besides the murluks?"

"Too many for my liking," she replied grimly. "All hostile. I'm not sure whether it's the same across the whole Dominion, but you can't go a day in any direction without being set upon by a monster wanting to kill you or eat you."

"So, your people haven't explored much?"

Tara shook her head. "What with the constant murluk attacks and other dangers, the old lady decided to keep our forces nearby until we complete fortifications. The only ones who leave the camp are the foragers and hunters. With game so plentiful, even they never have to go beyond a few miles."

So, anything could be out there.

I had more questions to ask about the old lady, the Outpost's organizational structure, and Tara's place in it, but just then we reached the camp. As we passed the first tent, I sensed a charged heaviness to the air. *What—?*

Before I could delve further into the sudden strangeness, energy suffused me. From one moment to the next, I went from feeling drained to feeling buoyant and envigored. I limped with a new spring in my step, and my pace quickened.

What in the world?

Unsurprisingly, a Trials alert followed in the wake of the startling changes.

You have been blessed by an unknown player's aura: *commander's own*. While you remain within its field of effect, your Might and Resilience are increased.

You have been blessed by an unknown player's aura: *inspiring*. While you remain within its field of effect, your health and stamina regeneration rates are increased.

"Buffs," I murmured to myself.

Tara smiled knowingly at me. "That's the old lady's doing," she said. "Nice, aren't they?"

I nodded absently as I studied the area. We stood at the edge of the tented camp. The encampment was larger than it had appeared from a distance and likely sheltered thousands. The tents themselves were roughshod and primitive, constructed from boiled leather hides that had been poorly cut and sewn together.

The heaviness I'd sensed in the air was still prevalent. Some instinct made me open my *magesight*. As it unfurled, my vision exploded with rippling lines of energy. I bit back a startled yelp. *Magesight* revealed the entire camp to be covered by luminous filaments that crisscrossed in a dizzying maze.

The threads interconnected every human in the camp. Looking down on myself, I saw that the energy field had fused with my own being; in slow drips, its energy fed and revitalized me.

It is a mesh of spirit, I realized. *No, not one, but two meshes,* I corrected myself. Following the twin weaves of spirit back their source, I saw that they rippled outward from a tent that was twice as large as the surrounding ones and located in the center of the camp. *That must be where the old lady is.*

I opened my mouth to question Tara further, but before I could, she yanked my arm. "Come on, quit dawdling."

Wordlessly, I let her steer me toward the command tent, my mind still entranced by the delicate mesh overlying the camp. *Is this what magic looks like?* Following hard on that thought came another: *if Tara's old lady already has magic, why do they need me?*

We came to a stop in front of the large tent. Given Tara's impatience to get us here, I expected her to barge inside. But instead, she shifted from foot to foot, studying the closed tent flap. I eyed her askance. She was stalling, I realized. *Why is she suddenly worried?*

"Before we go in, remember to be polite," Tara said finally. She refused to meet my gaze. "The old lady can be a trifle... intimidating at times." Not waiting for my response, she ducked inside.

I stared at the open tent flap, alarmed more by Tara's display of nerves than by her ominous warning. *What am I walking into?* Whatever it was, it couldn't be worse than facing orcs or battling murluks.

With a shrug, I bent down and followed on Tara's heels.

CHAPTER SIXTEEN

391 DAYS UNTIL THE ARKON SHIELD FALLS

> *"Sorcery is magic of the spirit and is fueled by spirit itself. Even those with no Potential for magic may harness it."*
> —Trials Infopedia.

The inside of the tent was brightly lit with torches. In its center was a log table. I frowned at its crude construction, all hacked-off logs bound with sinew and gut. *Can the Outpost's crafters do no better?*

Three people clustered around the table, one of whom I knew instantly was the old lady.

Unlike the other two, she was, well... *old.*

Her hair was iron gray, her posture erect, and her face seamed with age. Her eyes were closed, her hands were clasped behind her back as she listened to two younger colleagues, both as fresh-faced as everyone else in the camp.

Tara cleared her throat.

The old lady's eyelids snapped open. Piercing blue eyes flicked from Tara to me—frank, direct, and coolly assessing.

"Tara," she greeted. Her voice was warm and welcoming, at odds with her military bearing. "I didn't expect you back so soon, and with a guest, no less." Only the barest hint of a pause betrayed her surprise at my presence.

"I'm sorry, ma'am. But this couldn't wait. You've heard about what happened?"

"Marcus has just finished filling me in." She shook her head. "You should have summoned me earlier, Tara," she chided.

Tara bowed her head, accepting the rebuke without dissent. "I'm sorry, ma'am, but the battle turned so swiftly. There wasn't time."

The old lady nodded. "Marcus said the same." She pursed her lips. "It seems I can no longer afford to stay away from these skirmishes. The murluks are getting bolder." She set the matter aside with a shrug. "But I hear events turned out all right in the end. How did our northern flank manage to push back the attack?"

Tara pivoted, angling her body to point toward me. "This is Jamie Sinclair, a new player and the one responsible. He shows promise."

The Outpost leader quirked one eyebrow in surprise. "A new player," she mused. "And crippled to boot." Her words were flat and unemotional, a simple statement of fact that carried no hint of derision. Remarkably, they were also devoid of the pity most people unconsciously voiced with the word 'cripple.'

I had been studying the old lady ever since I entered the tent, and I hadn't seen her cast a single glance at my foot. Yet, somehow, she had astutely divined my disability. The Outpost's leader was dangerously observant. *I will have to be careful around her.*

The tent was silent, and I realized that the others were waiting for me to speak. "Good day, ma'am," I said. "As Tara mentioned, I am Jamie Sinclair, and I'm still very new to Overworld. I entered this morning."

"Interesting," replied the old lady. "Only a few hours in this world, yet somehow you have not only garnered Captain Tara's respect"—I shot Tara a surprised glance. *She's a captain?*—"which is no small feat, but you also managed to repel a murluk attack. And you're already level nine. Impressive, Mister Sinclair. Very impressive."

I started. *How does she know my level?* I had not sensed her *analyze* me, as I had with Tara earlier. *Had* she analyzed me? I wasn't sure. I was almost afraid to try the Technique on her.

"Just Jamie, ma'am," I replied, attempting a disarming grin. "I'm too young to be anyone's mister."

The old lady smiled, as if in appreciation of my effort. "Well, Jamie, I am Commander Jolin Silbright, but most just call me 'the old lady,' for obvious reasons." She gestured to the blond man next to her. "This is Captain Marcus, and this"—she pointed to the black-haired giant next to him—"is Captain Petrov."

Marcus was a slim, dapper looking fellow who looked less a captain than an office clerk, while Petrov was a solidly built man whose height easily topped seven feet. Both men nodded curtly in greeting, their gazes curious.

The commander braced her arms on the table and leaned forward intently. "Now, tell me, young man, how did you stop the murluks?" she asked, her voice stripped of any affability.

I met her gaze. "I have a Technique called *invincible.* It makes me immune to damage for thirty seconds."

"Ah," said the commander. Other than that interjection, Jolin displayed no reaction to my revelation. "How often can you use the Technique?"

"Only once a day."

She nodded, eying me shrewdly. "I assume that was the Trait that made you enter Overworld without a Clean Slate?"

"It was." I had been prepared for the question, so I managed to keep my face blank, concealing the half-truth behind my words.

"I see." The commander leaned back. "A useful Trait, but ultimately not one of much tactical significance."

I didn't dispute the commander's assessment, although I disagreed. Let her draw her own conclusions.

"Well, if that is all, I wish you good luck, young man," said Jolin. "We need every able man and woman to fight for humanity's cause. I trust you will join us in our efforts. Tara will fill you in on the details." The dismissal in her words was clear.

"There is more, ma'am," added Tara.

The commander turned in her direction, one brow arched in query.

"He has magic." Both captains stiffened in response to Tara's words, but again the commander betrayed no hint of surprise.

"Well, then," Jolin said. "Petrov, fetch Tara and Jamie some stools. It seems we are in for a much longer conversation."

※ ※ ※

Petrov left the tent silently.

I cast surreptitious glances at the others. Tara folded her arms and fell into something akin to parade rest, content to await her fellow captain's return. The commander and Marcus, ignoring me, bent their heads over the table and studied something I couldn't see.

I pursed my lips as I studied the commander. *Is she a mage?* I still wasn't sure what to make of her—other than that she appeared both formidable and unflappable.

Deciding to learn more about the people I had fallen in with, I cast *analyze* upon Marcus and the commander.

The target is Marcus Smithson, a level 28 human player. He has no Magic, meager Might, and is gifted with both Resilience and Craft.

The target is Jolin Silbright, a level 49 human player. She has no Magic, mediocre Might, exceptional Resilience, and is gifted with Craft.

Marcus appeared oblivious to my probing. But, despite my care, the old lady's sharp look made it clear she sensed what I was doing.

I ducked my head, shying away from her gaze while I tried to make sense of the Trials' feedback. Jolin had no magic. *That makes no sense.* I frowned. *How did she cast the two auras, then?*

Her level was disconcerting too, much higher than Marcus's or Tara's. *How has she achieved that?* And her age... why had she chosen to enter Overworld in her elderly body? Could she also have Traits from her old life that she wanted to retain? Did that explain her auras too?

Perhaps it's like my trait-given Techniques. I knew that both *invincible* and *mimic* did not draw from my magic—the mana residing within me—but were powered by pure spirit.

Was that the answer? In my *magesight*, Jolin's auras resembled a mesh of spirit. *Are the buffs surrounding the commander an extension of her spirit?*

I was debating using my *magesight* to study Jolin again, when Petrov returned, lugging a log stool under each arm.

The five of us took our seats around the table. Without preamble, the commander resumed the conversation—or was it an interrogation?

"Now, then, tell me about your magic," said Jolin. "What can you do?"

I studied her impassive face. She seemed to have no doubt that I would answer. I shrugged. "I don't have any magic... yet. Only Potential. I haven't visited the dragon temple. I joined the battle as soon as I arrived."

"You entered the fight as a level one virgin?" asked Marcus, his voice heavy with disbelief. "Without even basic training?"

"There was no time," replied Tara with a shrug. "He arrived during the attack. I was sure I could protect him."

Marcus snorted. "That was foolish."

"It was my call," she replied coolly. I noticed that she did not tell him she had been unaware of my Magic Potential until *after* the battle.

Ignoring her subordinates, the commander kept her gaze fixed on me. "And just how did you come to arrive here, Jamie?"

"Ma'am?"

"Location seventy-eight is only reachable through the elven gate at New Springs, and then only to those who refuse the elves' 'generous' offer of pseudo-citizenship. But you are not from New Springs, are you, Jamie?"

I struggled to keep my face scrubbed clean of expression. How had she figured out I wasn't from her town? Her intuition was scary. I realized I would be hard pressed to keep secrets from her.

"I'm not," I replied, choosing to be honest instead of attempting a deception that would likely fail.

Petrov, Marcus, and even Tara frowned at my response. The commander, however, only nodded. "Will you tell us where you are from, and how you got here?"

The direction of the old lady's questioning was worrying, and I had to stop myself from biting my lip. What did she know? Or guess? "Not just yet," I replied, with a shake of my head.

A knowing glint appeared in the commander's eyes, and I realized she had anticipated my response.

"Well then, Jamie, what do *you* want?" Jolin asked.

"Ma'am?" I frowned in confusion. *Where is she going with this?*

"You are clearly an intelligent young man. One who is mistrustful—probably with good cause—and determined to keep his own counsel. But you also have something we desperately need: magic. I suspect you are not the type to be swayed by moving speeches, nor do you appear inclined to join our cause in the long term."

How had she figured that out already? I felt like I was ten steps behind the commander.

Leaning forward on the table, Jolin steepled her fingers. "I don't have time to beat around the bush. So, I'll ask you again: what do you want in exchange for your aid?"

I stared at the commander, somehow stopping my jaw from dropping open. Nothing about this conversation was going the way I had foreseen. I had expected the old lady's reaction to be similar to Tara's, and for her to browbeat me into joining them. What I had not anticipated was a blunt attempt to *buy* my services.

And I was insulted.

I would never stoop so low to demand payment from those desperately in need. "I don't want anything," I replied, scowling. "I will help freely and without payment for as long as I am here. But," I said, meeting the commander's gaze squarely, "I will not join your organization." I jutted my chin at her captains. "Nor will I put myself under the command of your… officers."

A small smile played at the corners of the commander's mouth. "Thank you, Jamie," she murmured. "Your terms are acceptable and most generous. You will not be forced to join us." She sat back and spread her hands on the table, palms out. "But I do have a condition of my own."

I jerked my head for her to go on, still furious but willing to hear her out.

"You are valuable—" Seeing my annoyed look, she held out a hand to still my protest. "Hear me out, please. As a mage, you are important, not just to our budding colony here, but to humanity as a whole. Your worth cannot be overestimated. While you remain with us, you must be protected. Do you agree?"

I mulled her words over. It was not an unreasonable request. "I agree."

"Excellent." She smiled genially and gestured to the giant, who loomed large over the table. "Petrov will serve as your bodyguard."

I glanced at the big man. He had remained tight-lipped throughout the meeting. Even now, he did no more than grunt in acknowledgment of the commander's orders. While I had no cause to dislike the man, I didn't know him. "I prefer Tara," I said, surprising even myself with my words.

The commander's eyes narrowed near imperceptibly. Her gaze darted between Tara and me. "Of course," she said with a negligent wave. "As you will. Tara will serve as your protector."

CHAPTER SEVENTEEN

391 DAYS UNTIL THE ARKON SHIELD FALLS

"Mana is a living, breathing thing. Anger it at your peril."
—Cale Ames, elven spellweaver.

We were ushered out surprisingly quickly after that. Well... I was. The commander kept Tara back a little longer. Routine orders, Jolin had explained.

While I waited for Tara, I reflected on my meeting with the old lady. I had expected to be interrogated about my magic and abilities, and to be provided with unsolicited 'advice.' But while the commander's keen interest in my magic was undisguised, she hadn't shown the slightest inclination toward directing my magical development.

Jolin had pronounced herself confident in my ability to make such decisions on my own. With an airy wave of her hand, she had summarily dismissed me, citing more pressing matters that awaited her attention.

I had left the tent in a daze.

Jolin Silbright, whatever else she may be, was undoubtedly a formidable leader—and she was not an enemy I wanted. She'd seemed to know things she shouldn't, and she kept knocking me off balance with the tack she'd taken.

Standing outside the tent, lost in reflection over the encounter, I found myself wondering if I hadn't been manipulated after all. Jolin had read me so well during the conversation. Why then, at the end, had she chosen an approach that would infuriate me?

Was it a calculated move on her part? Had the commander maneuvered me into volunteering for free?

My brows lowered in consternation. What made Jolin's tactics even more impressive, was that even suspecting what she had done, I couldn't find it within myself to feel outraged. Because I wanted to help.

The longer I thought about it, the more certain I was that the old lady had read me like an open book. She had tailored her approach to match my disposition.

How did she do it?

I shivered involuntarily. Tara had been right. The commander *was* intimidating.

"Jamie?" Tara asked as she ducked out of the tent.

"Hmm?" I turned to look at her. She was watching me curiously. "Sorry, I was lost in thought."

Tara chuckled. "The commander does tend to have that effect on people. Come on, let's get you organized." She strode away.

I cast her a sidelong glance when I caught up. Her demeanor was unchanged. I breathed a sigh of relief. I had been half-afraid Tara would have been offended by what was, in effect, a demotion. Yet, being assigned as my bodyguard didn't bother her.

I turned my attention to our direction, and noticed that Tara was cutting west through the camp. "Where are we going?"

"Well, I figured you'd want to acquire some magic. Our first destination is the dragon temple." She glanced at me. "Unless you'd rather find a place to camp before that?"

"No, you're right. The temple first." I fell silent, studying the tented city around us. It couldn't have been later than noon, but only a few people wandered about. Everyone seemed to be hurrying to one chore or the other. "Where is everyone?"

"Most fighters are in the practice yard, either training themselves or instructing new recruits. The civilians—I suppose that's what you'd call them, although I'm not sure the term fits anyone in this world—will be out gathering or practicing their craft." She grimaced. "To the extent that they can, anyhow."

"I've been meaning to ask... why is everything so...?" I paused and gestured to the shoddy tents, poorly fashioned benches, and our own basic equipment.

"Crude?" Tara supplied helpfully.

I nodded. I had refrained from saying the word 'primitive' myself, not wanting to insult Tara or her people's efforts.

Tara yanked out her short stabbing spear. My spear lay abandoned on the lower bank, too unwieldy to lug around. I figured I'd be provided with another if we had to fight again.

Tara held up the spear for my inspection. "You see that?" She pointed to the polished, sharpened metal at its tip.

I nodded, uncertain where she was going with this.

"This spearhead, and the others like it, are our only source of metal. We have no knives, tools, swords, or metal of any other kind. Without metal-forged tools, it's damned hard to craft anything. Even chopping down the trees in the forest is a bloody chore."

"Ah." I was taken aback. I hadn't fully considered the consequences of Earth's refugees not being able to bring anything to the new world—not even the clothes on their backs.

When I had entered a neutral location, I hadn't been certain what to expect, but I had assumed—naively it seemed—that the Trials would ensure *all* players had access to the bare essentials. This didn't appear to be the case.

I stared around with new eyes. Other than the dragon temple, the Trials had provided nothing in the way of aid for the humans arriving at location seventy-eight. There wasn't even a gate to travel to another location.

The primitive outpost made sense now. *The commander and her people started with nothing,* I realized. *Given that, what they've achieve is impressive. Astounding, really.*

"I suppose players in the sponsored cities have it easier," I said wistfully.

Tara snorted. "Sure, but only if you're willing to sell your humanity for the privilege."

"What do you mean?" I asked, surprised by the derision in her tone.

Tara eyed me. "You haven't met any of the 'Sponsors,' have you?"

"No," I admitted. "Just the orcs." At my slip, an image of Mom—headless, with dead eyes—flashed through my mind. I squashed the memory, ruthlessly ignoring the accompanying upswelling of grief.

Tara's lips parted in surprise at my words. She tilted her head and studied me silently, as if seeing me with new eyes. "When did you—" She broke off abruptly.

I sighed.

"I'm sorry, Jamie. I shouldn't pry. The old lady told me to let you keep your secrets."

So that's why she kept you behind. What other instructions did she give you?

When I said nothing, Tara continued, "The 'Patrons' *are* the worst, but the Sponsors are little better. The elves sent a delegation into New Springs after their gate activated there. Their representatives were full of honeyed words and promises, of how they would help humanity, of how we could be allies, and of how, together, we could change Overworld. But there was just one small catch.

"In exchange for their shelter and aid, the elves wanted any humans that entered their sponsored cities to pledge a year's service in return. The pledge would grant the Elven Protectorate the rights to all dungeons, mines, and other resources discovered by their human *citizens*."

"Really?" I was shocked. "I never heard of anything like that on the news."

"You wouldn't have. The way I heard tell, the elves negotiated an agreement with our government to keep their terms secret from Earth's population." She kicked at a loose rock. "Damn politicians probably sold us down the river to pave their way into Overworld."

I shook my head, not to deny Tara's words, but in disbelief. Surely not even Earth's leaders were corrupt enough to sell our rights in the new world?

"What about the gnomes?" I asked, thinking about Eric and Emma. "Have they demanded the same... concessions?"

"I don't know," Tara admitted, "but I wouldn't be surprised if they had similar agreements in place."

The conversation lapsed after that, both of us lost in our own thoughts. Eventually I asked, "So, everyone here rejected the elves' offer?"

Tara nodded. "Technically, yes, but not all for the same reasons. Some choose location seventy-eight because they couldn't stomach the offer, others wanted to escape the authorities, and yet others came for a fresh start. Some though," she snarled, "chose it because they wanted a 'hard start.' Damn gamers."

I winced. Tara clearly had a poor opinion of gamers. Diplomatically, I chose not to reveal my gaming background and changed the topic. "Then you're not all from one organization? At the battle by the river, everyone worked so well together, as if you had been fighting as a unit for years. I thought perhaps you were all military or ex-military."

Tara's brows jerked up in surprise. "I suppose the commander's talk of captains gave you that idea?"

I nodded.

"Well, you're wrong. We all came here as individuals. Forging ourselves into something resembling a military force—that came later." Tara's eyes grew misty with memory. "The first day here was chaos. People running and screaming in all directions."

She grimaced. "And dying too—by the dozens, on the very steps of the dragon temple itself. Monsters were drawn from everywhere, attracted by the promise of easy prey. I was one of the first to arrive. The first day the gates opened, in fact. And just like the thousands of others who came through that day, I was scared and disoriented."

Tara's voice grew soft. "We all would have died, if not for the old lady. When she came through, things changed. She transformed a motley bunch of individuals—without food, weapons, or armor—into a fledging force."

Tara spread her arms wide. "Everything you see here is the work of the commander. She created our organization, as you call it. Drew up a hierarchy, appointed officers—some with military training, many without. Formed procedures, routines, and checklists. Defined our priorities and, most importantly, gave us purpose and hope." Tara looked me squarely in the eye, her face serious. "We owe her everything. Without her, you would have found a barren wasteland when you came through the gate."

I nodded noncommittally, acknowledging but not necessarily agreeing with Tara's underlying message: that I, too, should be grateful for the commander and do what she asked. *They are a paramilitary organization, even if they didn't start that way.*

It was clear that the old lady ruled, but as noble as her agenda was, it was not mine. I had my own mission. I knew without a doubt that if I joined the commander's outfit, her goals would supplant mine.

"Who *is* the commander?" I asked. "What's her story?"

Tara grinned, breaking the solemnity of the moment. "That's something everyone asks eventually. The short answer is, no one knows. Most of us believe she was in the military at some point in her career. But she hasn't seen fit to share her rank with any of us."

"And her age?"

"You mean why didn't she enter Overworld in a new body?"

I nodded.

"The same reason you didn't: to retain her Traits from Earth. The auras you felt earlier are the least of the benefits she can provide to the troops. Wait until you see her in battle. Her active boosts are something to behold."

"Buffs," I said, absently correcting Tara while my mind picked over the puzzle that was the commander. It was one thing to enter Overworld with your earthly body when you were young and healthy—or relatively so—but to do it when you were as old as Jolin Silbright? That was either foolishness or a remarkable bit of self-sacrifice.

And somehow, I didn't think the commander was foolish.

"What?" asked Tara.

"Uhm, the benefits and bonuses that the commander's Techniques grant, they're called 'buffs.'"

"Oh. Sure."

I turned to my companion, cocking my head. "What about you, Tara? How old are you?"

"You really want to know?" Tara's eyes twinkled.

I nodded. I knew she was older than me. Given how she carried herself, I guessed she was probably in her fifties.

"Twenty-two."

"*Twenty-two?*" I nearly choked over the words. "You can't possibly be—"

The rest of what I was about to say was lost as I tripped over my feet and landed face-first in the dust next to the steps of the dragon temple.

We had arrived at our destination.

Chapter Eighteen

391 days until the Arkon Shield falls

> *"We know even less of sorcery than we do of magic. It is a potent tool, some would say, even more useful than magic, but its uses are limited by how deeply its spells draw from the spirit."*
> —Taura Biaxal, svartalfar mystic.

I picked myself up slowly, pretending to dust myself off to hide my embarrassment. Tara wasn't buying it though. Throwing back her head, she roared with laughter.

"Okay," I said, red-faced. "You've had your fun now."

"I'm sorry, Jamie, but your expression... it was priceless." Tara's mirth faded at last.

I didn't dare ask if she had been joking about her age. She couldn't be younger than me, could she? But I was sure that if I broached the matter again, I would have her rolling on the floor with laughter.

Taking pity on me, Tara returned to the matter at hand. She pointed to the top of the carved purple steps. "The entrance to the temple is up this stairway."

I followed the direction of her arm. The The temple was a Greek-style marble building painted in swirling shades of purple. It dominated the landscape, and was likely visible from miles away. "It must draw a lot of attention," I said.

Tara nodded. "The commander believes that is by design, to keep players on their toes, so to speak. It certainly seems to attract the local wildlife."

I began limping up the staircase. After a few steps, I noticed that Tara was not following. "You're not coming?" I asked, looking back at her over my shoulder.

Tara shook her head. "Even if we both enter the temple at the same time, we'll find ourselves in different locations. The temple doors are portals, of sorts. I'll wait here. Take your time." She paused, then added, "You know you shouldn't invest in anything still at the Neophyte rank, right?"

"Yeah, I do," I replied. Conventional wisdom held that Neophyte-ranked Disciplines and Attributes shouldn't be increased with Tokens and Marks. Until a player reached level ten, the learning rate of Disciplines and Attributes was many times faster than the norm. So much so that a player—unaided by the temples—could advance to the Trainee rank in a matter of days. With my *newcomer* buff still in effect, my Neophyte learning rate was further accelerated.

Unfortunately, without even a basic grasp of magic, there was no way I could train it on my own. I would be forced to invest at least some Tokens in my magic.

"See you soon," I said in farewell to Tara. Climbing the remaining stairs, I pushed open the doors and entered the temple.

* * *

A Trials message unfurled the moment I crossed the temple's threshold.

You have exited location seventy-eight.

I was back on Wyrm Island. This time, I was at its center, a few feet away from the gate I had exited through the last time. Standing next to me, was Aurora.

"Welcome back, human," said the purple woman. "I see you managed to stay out of orcish hands." She looked me up and down. "And level nine already. Well done. I suppose you are here to use your Tokens and Marks?"

"What *are* you?" I asked, ignoring her question.

Aurora did not deign to reply. She crossed her arms and glowered at me.

Her response was not unexpected, but I had thought it worth a try. There was one more thing I could attempt. I drew on my will and cast *analyze* on the purple woman.

Analyze **failed. Your skill is insufficient.**

Aaargh, I thought with a grimace.

"That was rude!" Aurora snapped. "Next time, mind your manners, or you will regret it."

I scratched my head, curious as to how she could punish me, but I was not willing to test her wrath. I bowed. "I apologize, Aurora. You are correct. I am here to acquire new knowledge."

"Hmpf." Aurora appeared not the least bit mollified. With a wave of her arm, a translucent purple window opened in front of me. "These are the Disciplines you may choose from. You have ninety Tokens available."

A familiar list of Disciplines appeared before me. This was an area of the Trials I had spent most of my time researching. Regardless, I combed through the list to make sure there were no untoward surprises.

The Disciplines on offer were identical to the ones described in the Trials Infopedia—with the exception of the dragon magic Discipline, of course. That had most definitely *not* been mentioned in the wiki.

I had already decided on my leveling strategy before entering the temple, but there were a few things I wanted to confirm first. "Can I please see the Traits and Disciplines I earned from my life on Earth? *Before* my Induction."

Wordlessly, Aurora waved her hand, and a new window unfurled.

The knowledge you have carried over from Earth into the Trials includes the lore and scribe Disciplines, and the Quick Learner and Crippled Traits. Your skill as a scribe is at level 6. Your skill in lore is at level 8.

Trait: Quick Learner. Rank: 2, uncommon.

After a lifetime spent studying, you are able to grasp new concepts and assimilate knowledge rapidly. This Trait increases the rate at which your Disciplines advance through natural learning.

Trait: Crippled. Rank: 2, uncommon.

Your left foot is hobbled as a result of an unfortunate accident during your youth. This Trait impairs your movement, halving the benefits you receive from the agility Attribute. This effect is a permanent status effect that cannot be removed by ordinary spells.

I swallowed painfully as I read the effect of my crippling. *It is what I thought. With my handicap, I'll never amount to much as a warrior.* Magic was my only hope of exceling in the Trials.

Banishing further doubts, I turned back to Aurora and made my first choice. "Aurora, please increase my skill in the life magic and dragon magic Disciplines to nine."

"Noted. Your new knowledge will be instilled in your mind once you exit Wyrm Island. You have seventy-two Tokens remaining."

I had thought long on how, even at my low level, I could assist the Outpost with magic. I suspected that the damage a Neophyte mage could inflict with spells would be negligible, compared to an army of spearmen. Sadly, until I levelled up, I believed my offensive potential would be limited.

It was behind the lines that I thought I would be of most benefit. After seeing the primitive healing methods Nicholas had used, there was a good chance I could help save more lives at the Outpost with healing magic—or life magic as the Trials named it.

Dragon magic was a wild card. I hadn't the least idea what it was capable of. Given its uniqueness, however, there was no way I could ignore the Discipline. I *had* to learn everything I could about it.

Unfortunately, unlike knowledge acquired through natural learning, the Trials' gifts were limited by a player's level. Until I leveled up more, I would not be able to further advance my skill in dragon and life magic with Tokens.

Briefly, I toyed with the notion of maximizing my skill in one or more of the other magical Disciplines as well, but I decided to stick with my original plan. "Aurora, please increase my skill in the fire, earth, water, air, and death magic Disciplines to one."

"Noted. You have sixty-seven Tokens remaining."

There were other non-combat Disciplines I wanted to learn, but it didn't make sense to acquire any of them now. First, I would try training them naturally; only after reaching the Trainee rank would I return to the dragon temple for further understanding. For now, I was satisfied with my choices. "I am done with my Discipline selections. Thank you, Aurora."

"Very wise," she replied. "Do you wish to use any of your Marks at this time?"

"No, thank you." Constitution was the only Attribute I would consider raising right now, but Attributes, like Discipline purchases, were limited by a player's level. At the moment, my constitution exceeded my level.

"Very good, then we are finished," said Aurora, pleased to be done with me again. "Enter the gate, and the changes to your body and mind will be made."

I turned away and headed toward the gate, but not before waving irreverently at the purple woman, which had her scowling anew. I smiled at her expression. But my humor faded quickly as I considered what came next.

I still had no spells.

The dragon temples only gifted players with foundational understanding of a particular Discipline. They did not grant them knowledge of the Discipline's many specialized abilities: Techniques. Understanding how to channel life magic didn't mean I knew how to cast a healing spell. I would have to learn that separately.

From the wiki, I knew the usual way for players to acquire Techniques—including spells—was through lorebooks and trainers. Knowledge of the rarer Techniques were closely guarded in the Dominions, although the more commonplace Techniques were available for purchase—at least in the cities. Location seventy-eight, of course, had no wizard trainers to tutor me.

I will have to create my own spells.

Daunting as the prospect sounded, spell creation was not difficult for common, low-ranked spells, or so the wiki claimed. The higher a player's magic skill, the better their chances of discovering a spellform from the related Discipline. To improve my chances of formulating dragon and life magic spells, I had maximized my skill in both Disciplines.

Another factor in my favor was the information I had gathered from the Trials Infopedia. My research meant that I already knew of—even if only in the least technical sense—the most popular low-ranked spells from the standard magic Disciplines. It should be no great hardship to rediscover them. Or so I hoped.

But when it came to dragon magic, I was on my own. I had no knowledge to fall back on, nor did I have the least idea whether I was capable of creating dragon magic spells. Or even whether any of spells would be useful, especially at my low rank. Discovering dragon magic spells, I suspected, would require diligent practice and experimentation.

I sighed as I reached the gate. I still had a lot of work before me. With a final wave to Aurora, I stepped through the portal.

You have exited Wyrm Island. Modification request detected. Initiating update procedure.
Changes analyzed...
Alterations verified...
Updates approved...
Downloading new knowledge...
...
...
Download complete. Transfer to Overworld resumed.

*　*　*

I stepped back out of the temple with new knowledge swimming in my head and Trials' notices obscuring my vision. I ignored the messages, preoccupied by something else entirely.

I was different.

No, that wasn't right. I was the same, but some previously disconnected part of me was no longer absent. Connections had snapped into place between me and my mana. I could feel it. Flicking open my *magesight*, I studied myself anew.

An enigmatic smile stole across my face as I observed the wellspring of potential at the center of my being. It was my magic—the means by which I could exert my will upon the world, and change it. It was both power and promise mixed into one.

The means by which I will exact my vengeance.

My smile broadened into a grin. *At last,* I breathed. *At last I have what I need.* I returned to my study of the magic at my core. Slow-moving channels of mana extended outward into my body. They had not been there before my visit to the temple. Or, if they had, I hadn't the understanding to identify them.

Now, though, knowledge of magic—the essence of it, and the weft and weave of its crafting—was mine to use. I closed my *magesight*. Limping back down the temple steps, I finally turned my attention to the Trials alerts hovering for attention.

You have entered location seventy-eight.

Your skill in dragon and life magic has advanced to level 9. Mana pool unlocked.

Your skill in air, death, earth, fire, and water magic has advanced to level 1.

You are the first player to have learned dragon magic. For this achievement, you have been awarded dragon lore.

Lore note: Dragon magic is a universal skill. Unlike other magic Disciplines, which are governed by a single Attribute, dragon magic is affected by all Potentials. Spells from the Discipline may draw from any combination of Attributes and Potentials.

A groan escaped me as I read, and then reread, the lore note. *Damn it! Why does dragon magic have to require every Potential?* It destroyed all my carefully laid plans for Attribute enhancement. And what did this unexpected twist mean for the Discipline itself?

If the power of my dragon magic spellcasting relied on my poor Might Potential, then arguably—despite its uniqueness—my dragon magic would be weaker than other, purely magic Disciplines. I bit my lip. Had I made a mistake in choosing the Trait?

"What's happened?" Tara sounded worried. "Did something go wrong?"

I glanced up. I had reached the bottom of the stairway, where Tara danced impatiently from foot to foot. I couldn't tell her about my dragon magic, of course. It was too dangerous a secret to share.

"I just realized I don't have any spells," I lied, keeping a straight face.

"Oh, that," said Tara, understanding dawning. "Don't worry about it. We had similar problems with our martial Techniques. Spend some time experimenting with your magic and you'll be sure to discover one or two spells at least. It won't take long, I promise."

"Ah... all right," I replied, trying to stop my face my burning with shame. I didn't like lying to her, but I had no choice.

"What magic Disciplines did you learn?" Tara asked, as we set off.

"Life magic and... fire magic."

Her eyes shone. "Excellent!" she exclaimed. "The medics will be overjoyed when they hear that. Let's get you settled down somewhere quiet to practice. The sooner you figure out a healing spell, the better."

We were making a beeline towards the tented camp, I saw. I glanced up. The sun was still high in the sky. "Will the murluks attack again today?"

Tara shook her head. "The creatures only attack just after dawn. We've not had a single assault in the afternoons." She tugged at my sleeve. "Move it," she said, almost affectionately, as she hurried me along.

She's in a good mood, I thought. My own excitement had been spoiled by the revelation about my dragon magic, though. I couldn't just ignore the Trials information either. If I wanted my dragon spells to be viable, I needed to alter my planned approach and advance my physical Attributes, too.

I sighed. "No, Tara. Magic training can wait." I didn't require much to practice magic, just a quiet spot and time. I could just as well attempt spellcrafting at night. Right now, while the sun was still up, there was other training I needed. Especially with my *newcomer* buff still active. "Let's go to the training grounds. Its time you took me through my paces."

CHAPTER NINETEEN

391 DAYS UNTIL THE ARKON SHIELD FALLS

> *"Magic is a manifestation of the caster's will through the use of mana, but very few possess mana. Only those with Magic Potential are so gifted."*
> —Trials Infopedia.

Tara laughed.

"Don't worry, Jamie," she said. "No one is going to make you hold a position in the wall anymore. You're too important. Forget about weapon training." She pulled at me again, not changing course.

I slipped out of her grasp. "I'm serious, Tara," I insisted.

Her steps slowed, and her amusement faded. "Why?" she demanded.

"I'm just a Neophyte," I replied. "My spells are still weak. I can't wholly depend on them just yet. I need to be able to defend myself when I'm without magic." It was true, but it was not the real reason for my request. I had to raise as many of my physical Attributes as possible to Trainee rank. Any martial skills I gained in the process would be a bonus.

Tara snorted. "You aren't destined to be a grunt, Jamie. And there will always be others around—like me—to see you don't come to harm."

I opened my mouth to reply, but Tara held up her hand, stilling my objections. "Now, I know every boy dreams of being a mighty warrior, but that's not you, Jamie. You're meant to be a mage. *Our* mage. Now, enough time wasting. Let's get you to work." She turned around and began heading toward the tents again.

I stared at Tara's receding back. She was completely ignoring my agreement with the commander, acting less like a bodyguard and more like my chaperone.

"I should have gone with, Petrov," I grumbled. Tara might think she knew what was best for me, but she was wrong.

"No!" I yelled, not budging from where I stood.

Tara jerked to a halt and swung to face me. "This isn't a bloody game, fish," she growled. "Quit this foolishness. We need your magic. Desperately. You must spend every waking moment training it!"

"No."

"You goddamn idiot." Tara stomped back to me. "Don't you get it?" She shoved her face inches from mine. "You're *crippled*. Even with all the training in the world, you won't be able to hold off the monsters of Overworld. Not with a spear, nor with any other weapon."

I swallowed, feeling my face redden. But I refused to back down. Folding my arms, I held her gaze. "Be that as it may, Tara," I said slowly, "I insist. Take me to the training grounds." I paused. "Or I'll find someone else who will."

For a drawn-out moment, Tara said nothing. Then her expression blanked, and she threw up her hands. "Have it your way, fish," she ground out. "Follow me." Brushing past me, she strode south, fury radiating off her in waves.

I silently followed on her heels.

I had no doubt I was going to regret forcing Tara to train me, but even if I wanted to, I knew I couldn't ignore my physical conditioning. I would just have to bear the consequences of her anger.

※ ※ ※

We reached the practice yard with Tara muttering under her breath and me moving at a fast limp to keep up. Hidden by a fold in the land, the training ground was south of the temple and the tented camp. As we drew up, I saw hundreds of young men and women sparring, running laps, marching to order, and some even firing arrows at distant targets.

East of the practice yard was a separate demarcated area lit with dozens of campfires. I had seen the smoke earlier, but I hadn't yet had a chance to question Tara about it. Fewer people were gathered around the campfires than on the training ground, but they were just as industrious.

"Are those the crafters?" I asked.

Tara scowled at me, although she still answered. "Yes. With none of our fortifications erected yet, the safest place for them to work is near the training ground."

I nodded. "Where do we go, then?" I asked, staring at the busy field.

Tara glanced at me, her eyes still hard. "How is the wound on your back?" she asked abruptly.

My brows flew up. I had clean forgotten about the injury, and I couldn't recall the last time I had experienced a twinge from it. Tentatively, I twisted my torso. No pull of pain accompanied the movement. The time I had spent in the presence of the old lady must have sped up their recovery. "Fully healed," I replied in surprise.

"Good. Follow me." She strode into the chaos of the training ground. Ignoring the friendly calls of her fellows, Tara made straight for the fighting circles in the middle.

Curious looks and loud whispers followed me as I limped in Tara's wake. I could not help but overhear many of the soldiers' remarks. Clearly, I had garnered a bit of fame in the Outpost already. My crippled foot made me immediately recognizable, and speculation was rife on how I had survived my brash charge on the murluks earlier today.

But nowhere did I hear the slightest mention of magic. To my relief, it seemed that the commander had not shared that news with her people yet. As it was, the attention I attracted was already enough to make me uncomfortable.

Tara entered an empty sparring ring marked by no more than two concentric circles cut in the dirt. She stopped at the far end of the ring and turned about to face me. A curious crowd of soldiers formed around the edges. Ignoring the many watching eyes, she asked, "All right, fish, where do you want to begin?"

Her expression was pointedly neutral, but it had not escaped my notice that since our little spat outside the temple, I had been demoted from 'Jamie' to 'fish.' *She's still angry, then.* "What do you advise?" I asked carefully.

Her eyes narrowed. "*Now* you want my advice," she muttered, too low for the gathering spectators to hear. Raising her voice again, she asked, "What are your lowest might and resilience Attributes?"

I gazed inward and queried the Trials core. "Perception, followed by willpower."

"Perception, anticipation, and intuition are one and the same." Tara sounded like she was giving a lecture. "To train perception, you must anticipate your opponent's moves. The better you do this, the faster you will train the Attribute. Do you understand?"

I nodded.

"Willpower is a measure of your ability to withstand pain, to persevere, and to push on despite the odds or how much you hurt. To advance it, you must experience pain. Understood?"

I nodded again.

"Good. We will train both."

I winced. *Now why does that sound ominous?*

Tara padded to the side of the sparring circle and pulled out a spear. "Since you're familiar with a spear, we will continue your training with it. What is your spear Discipline at?"

"It's at the Trainee rank."

Tara's eyebrows shot up. "It is? That was quick. It will be a waste of *newcomer* to attempt training it further then." She dropped the spear and studied the pile of weapons. After a moment, she picked up a flat plank with a crude leather grip bolted on the inside—a shield—and a heavy log narrowed on one end—a club. "These will do," she pronounced and walked over with both items.

"This will not be pleasant, Jamie," Tara whispered, as she helped me strap on the shield.

Her voice was even and devoid of her earlier anger, which made her warning all the more chilling. I shivered.

"I will not go easy on you," Tara continued. "My advice: forget the spectators, keep going for as long as you can, and remember why you are doing this—whatever that fool notion may be."

I gulped. Suddenly, martial training was not looking like such a good idea. *Too late to back out now.* "All right," I muttered.

She squeezed my hand in a tender, motherly way—which only heightened my anxiety—before walking away. Removing her own weapons, Tara picked out a club and a shield for herself.

Tara retuned to the circle and set her stance. Facing me, she imparted her final instructions. "This will not be like any sparring you may have done back on Earth. The Trials and its system make training infinitely easier on Overworld. Try to copy my stance and match my blows. Don't worry if it doesn't feel right just yet. As we spar, the system will gift you with skills, and your stances and strikes will come more naturally. Ready?"

My mouth dry, I nodded. Despite her slighter build, the casual assurance with which she twirled her club was intimidating.

Why am I doing this again?

"Let's begin."

* * *

On the tail end of her words, Tara dashed forward, her form a blur. I was too shocked to move, let alone block or dodge.

Her shield drove upward, bashing the club from my unresisting hands. At the same moment, her club drove into my shield—deliberately, I suspected—and sent me flying backward. With a heavy thud, I crashed into the dirt.

The crowd brayed with laughter.

Flat on my back, I stared up at the sky. *How did she move so fast?* I barely had time to register her first motion before she had completed her last. Sighing, I picked myself up and swatted away the clinging dirt.

Tara, her face expressionless, kicked my club toward me. "Again," she said.

I grabbed my weapon and limped back into position. Crouching low, I watched her warily. Tara burst forward. I knew she was too quick for me to stop, but I tried anyway, raising my shield to fend off her blow.

It did me little good.

Once more, I flew backward. This time, however, I landed face first. As I lay there with my nose and mouth pressed into the loamy soil, I realized my efforts weren't wholly useless. Something within me felt different. Ignoring the taunts of the spectators, I examined the sensation.

Your skill with shields has advanced to level 1.

The Trials message cued my thoughts in the right direction. My understanding of how to employ a shield had improved. I grasped—just a little better—how to fend off blows, when *not* to meet a hit head on, how to angle a shield to deflect an attack, and when to avoid blocking altogether. *Marvelous*, I thought, examining the new store of knowledge in my mind.

"Again." Tara's command interrupted my musings.

Spitting out loose blades of grass, I heaved myself upright.

Tara gave me no time to recover.

She came in hard and fast. I struck out, hitting nothing but air, as Tara slipped under the blow. She countered, her club thudding into my midriff.

I staggered back, my breath expelled in a rush. Tara followed. Her club snaked out again to bruise my other side. Gritting my teeth against the pain, I retreated, holding my body sideways and raising my shield defensively.

I wanted to rub at my smarting sides, but I stopped myself, unwilling to show weakness in front of onlookers. As hard as Tara had hit, I sensed she'd actually held back. Her blows contained only a fraction of her full strength. I winced at the thought of truly facing her in combat. *It's going to be a long afternoon.*

Tara advanced again, her face devoid of all expression. The warrior struck. I blocked—more by accident than design. She struck again, and then again, raining down blows at an ever-increasing pace.

I stopped one in ten—if that.

Agony gripped my body. I gasped at each fresh wave, helpless to do otherwise. Resolutely, I slid backward and attempted to intercept her attacks.

But Tara's onslaught was unrelenting.

Her strikes were too fast, her blows too numerous for me to deflect. I fell back again, trying to open the space between us.

I was too slow.

Tara closed like an avenging angel. *Pride be damned!* Desperate to avoid further pain, I hopped backward as fast as I could, trying to keep as much weight off my hobbled foot as I could. My movements lacked grace, and no doubt provided rich entertainment for the watching crowd. *What a sight I must look.*

Right on cue, laughter erupted as Tara chased me around the ring. *Damn idiots.* My face flamed. *Amuses them to see a cripple get beat up, does it?*

I lowered my shield, and, roaring in fury, stopped retreating. Abandoning defense altogether, I met Tara head-on, striking back wildly.

It did me no good.

Nor did Tara let me off lightly. She punished me for my rashness—meticulously and systematically. Weaving deftly between my clumsy thwacks, she landed blow after blow with scary precision.

But even through the aches, stings, and throbs that beset my body, I realized Tara was still pulling her blows. Not that it felt that way. Each new hit brought a fresh blossom of pain, and every time her club flew at me, I winced, expecting crushed bones and mangled flesh.

Eventually, Tara's shield bashed me in the face and put an end to my ill-advised attack. I staggered to my knees, and then crumpled to the floor.

"Again!" called Tara.

I rolled onto my back, gasping for breath. *Dear lord, what have I gotten myself into?*

"Stop, Tara!" called someone from the crowd. I craned my neck in the direction it had come from. *Michael.*

"Can't you see he has had enough?"

The crowd had fallen silent. *Probably stunned by my stupidity,* I thought blackly.

"Stay out of this, Michael," Tara replied.

I heaved myself back to my feet, swaying and dazed from Tara's last blow. *Remember why you are doing this,* Tara had said earlier. She didn't know the true horror that had driven me here. I wondered whether she would have given me the same advice if she knew.

All right, Tara. I'll take your advice.

I reached into myself to unseal the deep, dark pit in which I had buried gruesome memories.

Mom's cold, lifeless eyes and bloodied corpse flashed before my eyes. Grief lashed at me, but I refuted it. *Sorrow is no use to me.*

I shoved aside anguish, letting rage replace it. My limbs trembled—not with fear, but with adrenaline and strength. Pain would not stop me. Weakness would not hold me back. Tara could not stand against me.

I will have my revenge.

Clenching my fists, I tightened my grip on my shield and my club. Then, with a bloodcurdling roar, I charged.

* * *

It was not much of a charge.

And it didn't take Tara long to set me down on my rump—none too gently, either.

But I refused to give up.

Time and time again, I stumbled up and set upon Tara. In my near-frenzy, I lost all concept of time and restraint. I threw myself at Tara mindlessly, as a beast would. I beat at her with every ounce of my strength and rage.

Tara must have glimpsed something of the darkness that simmered within me, the black roiling hate that I did my utmost to unleash upon her.

I was lucky that the green-eyed captain was the fighter she was. In my berserker state, I could have hurt her and not realized it—if she given me the slightest chance.

But not once did Tara falter.

Despite everything I threw at her, I failed to land a single blow. Bobbing and weaving, Tara evaded my attacks while her own club wrote lines of black and blue on my body.

It was cathartic.

With every rage-fueled attack I launched, the heaviness within me receded. With every agonizing blow I suffered, the darkness tainting me lessened, even if only a smidgen. Toward the end, I fancied I saw both understanding and pity in Tara's eyes as she let me spend my fury upon her.

* * *

Hours later, I finally collapsed.

Lying flat on my back, I blinked up at the red-tinged twilight. My body was worn out and refused to move further.

Tara's face appeared above mine. "Had enough?" she asked, her voice solemn.

I sighed, and then nodded mutely.

She sat cross-legged next to me. "You feeling any better?"

"Yes." To my surprise, I realized it was true—mostly. I turned to look at her. "Sorry," I added.

Tara just nodded. "Want to tell me about it?"

I swallowed, triggered by the thought. *Was I ready to talk about Mom?* Memories rushed to drown me in grief anew. I squeezed my eyes shut. *No, not yet.* "I can't right now. Maybe in a few days."

Or weeks. Or months.

"Okay," replied Tara with calm acceptance. "You need rest. Let's get you back to camp." She helped me stagger upright. I was too shaky to stand on my own though, and I had to lean on her for support. Looking around, I noticed the training ground was empty. "Where's everyone?" I asked, confused.

Tara rolled her eyes. "Training ended long ago. Even the most sadistic got bored watching you being beaten to a pulp. Everyone's gone to supper. We better hurry ourselves. It's not safe out after dark."

Still a bit perplexed by the passage of time, I missed Tara's next words. "Sorry, what did you say?"

"I asked how did you do?" she repeated.

I stared at her blankly.

"Your Disciplines and Attributes, you idiot. How much have they improved?"

"Oh." I called up the waiting Trials messages.

Your agility, perception, vigor, strength, and willpower have increased to level 10 and reached rank 2, Trainee.

Your skills with clubs and shields have advanced to level 10 and reached rank 2, Trainee.

Amazingly, I had reached Trainee rank in all my might and resilience Attributes.

"I think I'm done with martial training," I said, smiling a toothy, bloody grin.

CHAPTER TWENTY

391 DAYS UNTIL THE ARKON SHIELD FALLS

We had missed the call for supper, and the cooks had already dampened the fires in the crafting yard. In some ways, that was a relief. I wasn't ready yet to face those who had witnessed my berserker rage on the training ground.

Tara helped me back to the tent I had been assigned: one close to hers and to the commander's. Leaving me at the entrance, she hurried off in search of a hot meal for us.

I sank to the ground, too weary to make my way inside. *I'll just rest here until she gets back,* I thought, closing my eyes.

It had been an eventful day. I had gained nine levels, and despite my body's bruised and battered state, I felt altogether healthier, stronger, and quicker. The last time my body had felt so capable was... before the accident.

Since then, I had let myself waste away. There seemed no point trying to regain my form. It had been so much easier to ignore my body and devote my attention to pursuits of the mind—gaming, primarily. I had become rather good at it, too. *Infernally good,* according to my friends. I smiled at the memory.

And yet... it had taken just a day in Overworld to restore my flagging body to its former state. If I could come this far in one day, to what heights could I push my body in the coming weeks and months?

Opening my eyes, I stared down at my stretched-out legs. They looked no different, but I could feel their newly contained power. My gaze drifted to my hobbled foot, turned at an unnatural angle. *Still crippled, though. I won't be running marathons anytime soon, but at least I can hop faster now,* I thought with a chuckle.

Despite everything, I was grateful to the Trials for the changes wrought in my body. *Perhaps Overworld isn't all bad,* I admitted. *And being disabled doesn't mean being helpless.* That was a truth I hadn't been able to acknowledge on Earth. Here, in this unforgiving world, I would have to push my body beyond what it had been capable of even when whole.

"Here you go." Tara came up from behind me and interrupted my musings with two steaming bowls.

"I can't promise it will be the best meal you've ever eaten," she said, handing me one. "But it's filling." She sat down next to me. "Just don't ask what's inside."

I took the bowl eagerly, too hungry to care about its contents. "Thanks."

We both fell silent as we dug in. Tara was right. The taste left much to be desired, but that didn't stop me from gulping down the food.

When I was stuffed, I sat back with a contented sigh. "Ah," I said. "I needed that."

Tara grunted in acknowledgement as she swallowed the last of her dinner. "Be careful not to miss meals on Overworld. Hunger can affect your body in weird ways."

I nodded, realizing how fortunate I was to have met Tara during my first moments in Overworld. She was proving to be an invaluable mentor and... friend. "Thanks for everything today, Tara. I doubt I'd have survived without you."

"Damn right you wouldn't have, fish," she replied with a grin.

Her earlier animosity had vanished, for which I was thankful. However, her grin faded when she set down her bowl. "About earlier..." She hesitated. "I'm sorry. I shouldn't have called you a cripple. It was uncalled for."

"No. I needed to hear it. I can't ignore my impairment or what it means, especially on Overworld." I paused. "I hope you'll forgive me for pushing you to train me."

Tara shook her head. "You were right to, and I was wrong for trying to deny you." She smiled. "Besides, you did better than I expected. Perhaps with more training you'll even be able to hold your own as a fighter one day."

I groaned. "No way am I putting myself through that again."

Tara's smile broadened, but she said nothing. And neither did I. Words felt unnecessary as we sat in companionable silence.

Eventually, Tara got to her feet. "I'll see you in the morning." She hesitated. "Will you be all right tonight?"

I nodded, knowing it was my episode during sparring that had prompted her to ask. "I'll be fine."

I stood too, flinching at the fresh pain my movements inspired. Tara had done no lasting harm, yet I knew I would feel bruised for the next few days.

Tara winced sympathetically. "You'll feel better in the morning."

"I hope so," I muttered.

Tara laughed as she walked away. ""Goodnight, Jamie."

"Night, Tara." I waved goodbye.

* * *

Alone once more, I ducked into my tent, waiting for my eyes to adjust to the dark so I could inspect my new residence.

When the gloom lessened, I saw the tent was mostly bare. A hide pallet stuffed with straw lined one side, and on the other was a wooden pail filled with drinking water. I eyed the bed wistfully. Despite its rustic appearance, it looked invitingly soft. But much as I craved sleep, I couldn't retire just yet.

I still had magic to practice.

My *newcomer* buff was still active, and I needed to train my magic Attributes while it remained in force. Yet weariness hung heavily on me, and I failed to muster any enthusiasm for the task.

Maybe life magic can ease some of my aches. But even the promise of pain relief failed to stir my interest. I sighed. *Time for more drastic measures.*

Limping to the pail, I dunked my head and came back up with a gasp. The water was unpleasantly cold, which served my purpose perfectly. The clinging tendrils of sleep were banished temporarily.

Shaking my hair dry, I sat down cross-legged on the hard earth, as far away from the tempting pallet as I could, just in case. *All right, where to begin?*

All magic was unique to its wielder. Each had a different footprint. My first step was to discover my own magical signature and to attune myself to the mana swirling within me. I couldn't explain how I knew that, but I knew it as well as I knew how to hold a shield or thrust a spear—all gifts of the Trials.

I closed my eyes and looked within myself with *magesight*. Mana—the stuff of magic—flowed lazily through my body and settled in a still, deep pool at my center.

Gathering a small amount, I willed it upward into my mind and studied its composition. I dribbled the mana into my mouth and tasted its velvety sweetness. I formed some in my hands and felt its oily texture. Snorting more of it, I identified its lavender scent. I pulled it through my ears and listened to its joyous gurgle. Finally, I let the mana pool out of me, and observed its swirls of cobalt.

Only then, when I felt certain I understood *my* magic, did I begin manipulating it.

Drawing its swirling essence into shape, I willed the mana to do my bidding, visualizing what I sought from it. *Heal*, I ordered, internally vocalizing the command to give further form to my will.

Obediently, mana streamed out of my center, then stuttered, pooling in confusion before dissipating into the ground.

You have failed to create a spell. Mana lost.

I hadn't really expected to succeed on my first attempt, yet I couldn't stop a sigh of disappointment. I considered the remnants of the failed spell that still glowed in my *magesight*.

Given no further direction than my order to heal, my mana had chosen a shape and form of its own volition. I knew from the wiki that using magic was not akin to employing a tool.

Magic was a living thing. Mana sometimes followed not the will of its wielder, but its own path. If the wiki was to be trusted, magic had a mind of its own, albeit a crude and primitive one. Studying the form and shape of the spellcasting that hovered in my *magesight*, I could believe it.

In an attempt to fulfil my will, my magic had formed a complex lattice, far beyond anything my simple order to heal had directed. While the spellform appeared off-kilter, it was *nearly* correct; or so my Trials-gifted understanding of life magic led me to believe.

Narrowing my focus, I traced each weft and weave of the spell, trying to identify its points of weakness. Some filaments of mana were more out of place than others. In my mind's eye, I adjusted the structure.

I had little idea whether the changes would improve or worsen the design, but given my lack of more definitive information, spellcrafting by trial and error was the only approach available to me.

When satisfied with my changes, I drew on my mana again and willed the altered spellform into being.

The spell fizzled.

But even in my failure, I had learned something. After scrutinizing the spell construct, I saw where I had gone wrong. Gathering my will, I began anew.

And failed again.

Ten attempts later, I finally succeeded as mana darted out of my body and coated my hands in a subdued blue-white glow.

You have spellcrafted a touch-based healing spell, from the Discipline of life magic. The name assigned to this spell is *lay hands*. Its casting time is fast and its rank is common.

Your channeling and spellpower have increased to level 2. Spell rating unlocked.

I did it! I grinned. *I can't believe I actually did it!*

Holding up my glowing hands, I stared at them, transfixed. Even witnessing the evidence of my magic, I was incredulous. *I am a mage now,* I marveled. *Only a fledgling one, but a mage nevertheless.*

Once I'd had my fill of self-indulgence, I touched my mana-infused hands to my left shoulder. Spelled tendrils of energy seeped into my body. Repairing torn muscles and restoring bruised skin, they left a soothing balm in their wake.

The pain in my battered shoulder vanished.

Tentatively, I flexed my arm. No twinges accompanied the motion. I grinned in delight. *Incredible!* I recast *lay hands* multiple times—until its spellform was indelibly etched in my mind, all my bruises had faded, and the last of my aches were banished.

When I was done, the mana pool at my core had drained to half. But I didn't care. Finally, I was free of pain. The repeated spellcasting had other benefits too. My magic Attributes had increased.

Your channeling and spellpower have increased to level 3.

So far so good, I thought, dismissing the Trials alert. *Now for the hard part.*

It was time to attempt a dragon spell creation.

Scratching my head, I pondered how to go about the task. My life magic spellcrafting had been, if not easy, at least not a complete shot in the dark. I had already known the *lay hands* spell existed and the basic mechanism of its operation. But I had no starting point for dragon magic spellcrafting.

What did I know about dragon magic? Almost nothing. While the Trials had gifted me with some knowledge of the Discipline, the information was sketchier than I would have liked. I had only a vague concept of what dragon magic truly was, and little idea of what it could accomplish.

So, what I know of dragon magic is not worth writing home about, and it's not going to help with my spellcrafting, but what do I know of dragons? What are they synonymous with?

Fire. Flying. Scales. Claws. Size. Strength.

I pursed my lips, considering the concepts I had come up with. Of the six, fire was the one I was most familiar with and likely the easiest to try manifesting with a spell. Closing my eyes, I began.

Drawing out my mana, I pictured fire as I imagined a dragon would breathe it: a churning vortex of flame, a broiling inferno, a destructive jet of heat and light. I willed the fire into being, visualizing it flaring out of my mouth. *Burn!* I commanded.

My mana surged up and out of me in response to my will. With frenzied purpose, it began to form a spell construct. But, a moment later, with the spellform only half-realized, the magical structure collapsed, and the mana seeped back into my body.

You have failed to create a spell. Mana lost.

Aargh! Black disappointment filled me as I stared at the stark emptiness in my *magesight*. This time, I didn't even have a basic spellform to tweak and experiment on.

No help for it, but to try again. Varying the projection in my mind, I willed fire into being once more.

* * *

Twenty failed attempts later, I was close to quitting.

No matter how much I altered the images in my mind, my mana refused to form the crudest of spellforms. Either my magic had no understanding of the concept of a dragon's fire, or what I visualized was at odds with how it *should* be done.

Either way, I began to think the task was impossible. And now my mana pool was nearly drained. Halting my efforts, I took a moment to reflect on my labors.

Something felt off.

In every failed attempt, mana had raced to do my bidding. But each time the magic had collapsed in on itself, dissolving partway into forming a spell construct. Though it had not looked as if the mana was confused about its purpose—on the contrary, my magic had appeared eager to fulfil its given task—but for whatever reason, it had been unable to.

Almost as if some essential ingredient is absent.

I rested my head in my hands while I thought. *What am I missing?* I went over what I knew of dragon magic. It wasn't much. A handful of facts on the form and texture of fire, the all-encompassing nature of dragon magic, and the uniqueness of the beings that had invented it.

Yet, as I picked through my meager store of dragon knowledge, a memory of the earlier lore note I had received from the Trials kept intruding.

Ceding to my intuition, I recalled the message.

Lore note: Dragon magic is a universal skill. Unlike other magic Disciplines, which are governed by a single Attribute, dragon magic is affected by all Potentials. Spells from the Discipline may draw from any combination of Attributes and Potentials.

"A universal skill," I murmured, chewing my lip. I had wondered at the wording, but I hadn't known what to make of it. I still didn't. But taking in the entire Discipline description, I began to have an inkling...

Do dragon spells require more than mana? If the Discipline drew from all Potentials, it made sense that they might. *Could that be the difference?* I wondered as an idea took shape. *It's worth a try at least.*

Inhaling deeply, I began anew. I visualized a dragon's fire in as much detail as I could, but I did not immediately will it into being. Holding the shape of fire in my mind, I fed mana into the image until it was full to bursting.

Still, I didn't release the spell, seeking further fuel for the magic. Following some half-understood instinct, I drew on my being and pushed threads of spirit into the spell.

Spirit refused to heed my call.

It was not that the weaves of spirit did not answer to my will; they did. Fine filaments separated from the greater weave of my being and flowed into my mind, as directed. Yet they balked at entering the spellform.

Goddamn. I had been sure spirit was the missing ingredient. I released its weaves to fall back into my being but kept the shape of fire fixed and infused with mana in my mind.

I drummed the fingers of one hand against my leg. *If not spirit, then what?*

In frustration, and for want of better ideas, I poured all of myself into the spell that I could think of. Flesh, bone, blood—

Pain jolted through me.

The mana in me was burning. In shock, I nearly dropped the spellform. Ignoring the agony suffusing my body, I studied the spell construct I held in my mind in fascination. Where before, the mana threading its form had been a cool cobalt, it now shone a luminous gold.

I realized the flows of mana had been ignited—by my blood! *The missing ingredient was blood!*

The pain vanished. Still transfixed by the beauty of the spellform, I barely noticed. Sure now of what I had to do, I fed more of my blood into the spell.

Mana and blood mixed, transforming the spellform into a raging maelstrom that fought to escape my grasp. Belatedly, I realized the spell might be beyond my skill to cast. *What happens if I lose control?* I wondered with sudden unease.

Setting aside doubt, I struggled to retain my grasp on the volatile spellform. Sweat beaded my brow as my will was stretched to its limit. Despite the fire's raging, I held firm and maintained control.

Finally, it subsided, leashed to my will. I heaved a sigh of relief. *Now to see whether all this effort was for naught.* Gently, I coaxed the fiery torrent out through my hands.

A flood of Trials notices shouted for attention; I ignored them, my attention captured by something else entirely.

My hands had burst into flame.

Startled by their brightness, I jerked my head away and nearly toppled backward. *Goddamn, I am on fire!* I scrambled to my feet and rushed out of the tent in panic.

I wasn't thinking. Fear had overruled my senses. The only thought in my mind was that I was burning and needed help.

The pail, you idiot! Use the water from the pail!

Two steps out of the tent, I froze—conflicted between searching for help and dashing back into the tent. Then another thought intruded.

There's no pain.

Befuddled, I stared at my hands. The flames still licked eagerly at them, but my skin was undamaged. I took a cautious sniff. There was no smell of charring. I turned my hands over and studied them anew. The flames were doing me no harm. *I am immune to my own fire!*

What I had done started to sink in. I had cast a dragon spell! I laughed, partly in relief at my survival—my experiment had been more dangerous than expected—and partly in delight at my success.

My laugh echoed shockingly loud in the silent camp. Taken aback, I spun about to see if anyone was watching.

I was alone. Above me, the stars shone brightly, and the moon—foreign and unfamiliar—was high in the sky. Time had flown far quicker than I had imagined, and night had fallen fully.

My blood was still singing with fire too. *Burning away.* I examined my hands again with my *magesight*. The spell was still active. Every second, more of my mana and life flowed into the spellform to fuel its flames.

My glee faded. The spell was still draining my magic and life. Quenching the fire with a flick of my will, I opened the Trials alerts to try to make sense of what was going on.

You have spellcrafted a touch-based spell from the Discipline of dragon magic. The name assigned to this spell is *flare*. Flare is a persistent spell and while active drains all three of the caster's energy pools: mana, stamina, and health. Its casting time is very fast and its rank is common.

You are the first player to have spellcrafted the dragon spell *flare*. For this achievement, you have been awarded dragon lore and two Marks.

You have gained in experience and are now a level 10, Trainee. You have reached player rank 2. Player leveling rate decreased.

Lore note: Dragon magic is unique among the magic Disciplines. Where spells from the other magic schools are imbued only with mana, dragon spells are infused with the caster's own lifeblood. Lifeblood contains a portion of both the player's stamina *and* life.

This significantly increases the cost and danger of dragon magic, but it also makes spells from the Discipline three times more powerful than their counterparts.

Flare is the simplest of dragon magic spells. It is a bright, uncontrolled burst of flame that burns with the intense heat of dragonfire. All dragons are born knowing the spell, giving even the smallest of hatchlings the means to defend themselves. Yet the spell should be used cautiously. Many a hatchling has gone to their death after draining away their own lifeblood through the use of *flare*.

I read and reread the Trials alerts, the lore note in particular. While I was pleased to have reached player rank two, the other messages perturbed me. Dragon magic was both powerful and dangerous. *I'll have to be careful how I use it.*

I ducked back into my tent. I still had some mana remaining. Before I bedded down for the night, I intended on expending it all and reaping whatever benefits I still could from *newcomer*. Yet, even as I began channeling life magic again, I couldn't help dwelling further on the troubling implications of the Trials' messages.

CHAPTER TWENTY-ONE

390 DAYS UNTIL THE ARKON SHIELD FALLS
4 DAYS TO EARTH'S DESTRUCTION

> "Many believe dragonfire to be myth and not fact. Yet the snippets of lore and text the Elders left behind are rife with mention of it. Dragonfire is as real as the Elders."
> —Arustolyx, gnomish archaeologist.

Despite my exhaustion, sleep did not come easily. When it did, it brought nightmares—horrifying images of headless corpses and rivers awash with blood. After waking up screaming for the third time, I gave up on sleep altogether.

What I wouldn't do for a cup of coffee. But other than the pail of water, there was nothing to drink.

Slaking my thirst with half the pail's contents, I dunked my head in the rest. Rubbing my swollen, red-rimmed eyes, I ducked out of my tent and into the brisk night. The sky was lightening, and dawn was not far off. The rest of the camp still slept, giving me a moment to think.

I sat down cross-legged outside my tent and considered my plans for the new day.

My training last night had finished well. I had my raised my magic Attributes and my skill in both the life and dragon magic Disciplines. *I even managed not to set the tent on fire,* I thought wryly.

Control over the *flare* dragon spell had proved difficult. Dragonfire craved blazing free and wild—guzzling my mana, stamina, and health in the process. In hindsight, I was fortunate my spellpower was low when I'd begun. Otherwise, I would have surely set everything nearby ablaze, or been consumed from within.

Yet the spell could be controlled.

By throttling the mana and lifeblood I infused in *flare's* spellform, I had reduced the resulting flames and the spell's energy drain. It made for an interesting dynamic, although one that might be tricky to control in battle. But by the end of my training, I had improved my control to the extent that I felt comfortable employing the spell in combat.

Opening the Trials core in my mind, I reviewed my other gains from last night.

Your skill in dragon and life magic has advanced to level 10 and reached rank 2, Trainee.

Your channeling and spellpower have increased to level 5.

I made progress, I thought with a pleased smile. But despite my improvements, I was concerned about what *flare* meant for my future growth.

If all dragon spells consumed life, stamina, and mana, I would have to split my Attribute advancements between Resilience, Might, *and* Magic Potentials, whereas I had originally intended using the Marks I earned solely on magic Attributes.

In particular, I would have to invest in both vigor and constitution. The first influenced the size of my stamina pool, and the second determined my health pool. But I simply did not have enough Marks for such widespread investment.

Of course, I could just avoid dragon magic altogether, use it sparingly, or not attempt to maximize the benefits I derived from the Discipline.

But that would be a mistake.

I could not ignore the lore note. If dragon spells were three times stronger than the spells from other magic Disciplines, it would give me an edge when facing stronger, more numerous enemies.

"I need more Marks," I muttered, stating the obvious. But how to get them? The Trials had awarded me two Marks for discovering the *flare* spell. If it did that for every dragon spell I discovered, it might add up to a tidy sum... but how many new spells could I create?

Not nearly enough for the Attributes I want—no, need.

If I was going to have my revenge on the orcs, I had to push the limits of what I could gain from the Trials; even then, I had few illusions that destroying the Orcish Federation would be easy.

If only I had earned *two* mythic Traits from slaying Mom's killers, then I could have—

Wait a minute.

I stilled as a half-remembered thought surfaced. There had been a piece of text in the wiki that had made mention of acquiring Traits. It struck me as odd at the time, because unlike everything else in the wiki—which was meticulously laid out and unambiguous—that particular passage had been hidden in an unrelated section of text.

I hadn't paid the passage much attention, thinking it a mistake. But now, recalling what Tara had said about the Sponsors and the pledges they required of humans, I wondered.

The text in question referred to dungeons—an important resource in Overworld. Seeded with large numbers of hostile creatures, they were a quick and reliable means of gaining experience and leveling—probably because the Trials replaced slain creatures over time. How, was anybody's guess. But there was no doubting that players entering a dungeon could expect to find it populated with a wealth of enemies.

All of that meant a settlement that controlled a dungeon had an assured means of advancing its players. None of this was a secret though, and while it made dungeons nearly as vital as mines, it did not make them extraordinary.

Yet the strange passage in the wiki had alluded to dungeons yielding *even more*. It had suggested that after a dungeon was cleared for the first time, the responsible players would be gifted with Traits.

I hadn't placed much stock in the information. The potential for such a mechanic to create imbalanced players was too obvious, and I could see no reason why the Trials would reward players like that.

But... the Trials was not fair. Indeed, it seemed to eschew fairness altogether. I could not forget that.

If dungeons that were cleared for the first time granted Traits, then their value was *incalculable*, which would explain why the elves had demanded the pledges that they had from humanity.

From what Tara had said, human citizens in the elven cities were prevented from even *entering* a dungeon. And why would any Sponsor bother forbidding that? Dungeons respawned, after all. *Unless.* I pursed my lips.

Unless dungeons do *grant Traits.*

I nodded to myself. The more I thought on it, the more convinced I was that I was right. I could see it now.

When the Arkon Shield dropped, a swarm of high-level teams from the other Dominions would invade, seeking to be the first to claim the new dungeons. I scowled. And the orcs—*our Patrons*—had a head start on the others.

I suspected that the orcs—the only ones with a free run of the Human Dominion during the isolation period—would use the year to secure every dungeon they found. They'd do that both to prevent any upstart human from robbing them of their prize and, of course, to save the rewards for themselves.

Before this point, I hadn't understood why the other races would go to all the trouble of becoming Patrons and Sponsors. But if it gave them a leg up on their rivals in the race to get to new Traits? Then yes, it would make sense—a frightening amount of sense.

But the Trials hadn't left humanity completely exposed either. The Arkon Shield gave us some breathing room. And the dungeons gave us a chance. If human players claimed the dungeons' first-clearance Traits, we could at least tilt the odds a bit more in humanity's favor, if not level the playing field altogether.

We only had a year, though.

I knew then what my focus had to be in the coming months: find and clear as many dungeons as possible.

But I was being overly optimistic. Dungeon-hunting was a task for tomorrow. I chuckled. *More likely it will be weeks before I can set off in search of a dungeon,* I thought with a wry smile. Dungeons were notoriously challenging, and I was by no means ready—yet.

Before I could attempt one, I needed to get stronger. A large part of that I could achieve by helping to secure location seventy-eight. Not to mention that once the settlement was established, it would provide me with a safe base of operations, including food, supplies, and equipment.

My magic, I knew, could be the key to securing the Outpost. I chewed my lip worriedly. This brought me back to the problem of my Attributes. In the near future, there was little I could do to gain more Marks. Until I increased my Attributes and expanded my energy reserves, I would have to use my spells sparingly.

I eyed the messages in my Trials core again. My resilience and might Attributes couldn't be further enhanced without increasing my player level. But my magic Attributes still had a way to go.

I had yet to figure out a way to advance elemental resistance, but I couldn't train spellpower without using mana, which I refused to do at the moment. With a full day ahead of me, my mana was too precious to burn away in training.

One of the harsh realities of Overworld was that, short of sleep, there was no way to regenerate mana, or none that the wiki hinted at.

There was no such thing as a mana regeneration Discipline, and food helped less than it did with stamina. It was a mage's biggest weakness. It also gave warriors a viable strategy for defeating spellcasters.

If I can't train spellpower, what about channeling?

I rubbed my chin. Perhaps it could be trained without actual spellcasting. My *newcomer* buff hadn't expired yet. I glanced up at the sky. I had perhaps an hour to dawn. *Time enough to get in some more training.*

Closing my eyes, I began to mediate, channeling mana up from the deep pool at my center and into my mind before letting it fall back again, then repeating the entire process. One endless loop. Up and down. Up and down. Up and down...

* * *

My snore broke off and my eyes snapped open as Tara shook me again.

For a second, I didn't know where I was. I blinked, and the camp snapped into focus. The sun was shining now, and people were up and about. I had fallen asleep.

"Hey, you there, fish?" Tara snapped her fingers in front of my face.

I turned toward her.

"You slept here all night?" she asked.

I yawned. "No, I came out an hour before dawn," I mumbled absently while I considered the two Trials messages hovering before me.

Your channeling has increased to level 10 and reached rank 2, Trainee.

Your *newcomer* buff has expired.

I sighed in relief. I had managed to advance my channeling after all.

"Something the matter?" Tara frowned.

"No," I replied, deciding not to elaborate. "Where to now?"

"Breakfast first. Then we head to the river. Here, arm yourself with these." She handed me a club and a shield.

I raised my eyebrows at her questioningly.

"You'll be better able to protect yourself with a club and shield than a long spear. Right now, it's more important for you to stay alive than to kill murluks."

My lips turned down, but I knew Tara was right. While I hadn't fared too badly on the spear wall yesterday, there had been some hair-raising moments.

"Will the murluks attack today?" I asked while I examined the weapons.

Tara shrugged. "They have every day so far. I expect today will be no different." Her eyes narrowed, as if she couldn't contain her curiosity. "Did you manage to learn any spells?"

I smiled. "You'll see."

* * *

Tara hurried me through the crafting yard for breakfast. The area was packed with hundreds of spearmen, all in a similar rush. In passing, someone shoved a bowl of porridge—at least that was what I thought it was—into my hands.

I looked for a place to sit.

"No time," Tara said, seeing me stop. She was gulping down the contents of her bowl as she walked. "We eat on the move," she mumbled through another mouthful.

I looked at her askance but nodded agreeably. Limping in her shadow, I scooped up the gruel while studying the yard with interest.

Smaller campfires for cooking and larger fire pits with skins and haunches smoking over them dotted the space. But the area was too crowded with fighters for me to spot any of the crafters.

We cleared the crowds and reached the edge of the crafting yard. Tara dropped her empty bowl to the ground. "Leave yours too," she ordered. "One of the cooks will collect them later."

She is in a hurry. After slurping down the last of my breakfast, I discarded my own bowl and followed her west toward the river.

"How's your body?" Tara asked, as we made our way through the empty training grounds. "Still sore?"

"Much better." I smiled.

"Told you you'd feel better in the morning. But don't forget to stretch before the battle."

"Yes, ma'am."

As we neared the edge of the upper riverbank, I spotted dozens of men and women working in the ditch we had crossed yesterday. "What are they doing?" I asked in surprise.

"The foundations for the fortifications were completed yesterday," replied Tara. "This morning, the crafters are erecting the wall itself."

Her face creased with worry. "We're running out of time, Jamie. The constant battles are taking their toll, and the number of new recruits from Earth has fallen off sharply." Her tone was grim. "We aren't replenishing our ranks fast enough. If we don't finish the construction soon..." She shook her head in denial. "From now on, the crafters will work while we fight."

I stared aghast at the unarmored crafters in the trenches. "But if we get overrun on the river, they'll be defenseless!" I exclaimed.

"They will have to bear the risk." Tara's hard, unflinching green gaze met mine. "It is up to us to ensure it doesn't come to that, Jamie."

I nodded slowly, studying the crafters as we approached. None of them glanced our way. Intent on their labors, they were oblivious to all else. I swallowed. If the murluks breached the spearmen's line, the crafters would not survive long.

Reaching the trench, we picked our way across one of the many logs bridging the dug-out ditch. All along the upper bank, spearmen hurried to the river over similarly placed logs.

I glanced over the bank's edge and saw that over a hundred fighters had already gathered on the shores of the lower bank. The Outpost's spearmen, armed and ready, sat in a line formation two rows deep as they waited for the murluks to appear.

Behind the double line, which swelled as more troops streamed down the riverbank, was a neatly formed square; at its center was a familiar white-haired figure.

My eyebrows rose. "What is she doing here?"

Tara glanced in the direction I indicated. "The old lady will command today's battle. We lost too many yesterday, and we can't afford for our defenses to falter, especially today. Not with the craftsmen exposed." Her gaze darted to mine. "Besides," she added, amusement coloring her voice, "the old lady is eager—as we all are—to see your magic in action."

I rubbed my chin and fought off a grimace. Even I didn't know what to expect from my magic. I hoped the commander wasn't placing too much stock in it. Something else was puzzling me, too. "Why wasn't the commander here yesterday?"

Tara sighed. "Holding the murluks at the river is important, but protecting the dragon temple is more crucial. The temple isn't indestructible. On our second day here, it was almost destroyed.

"While the entire population of the Outpost was embroiled in a pitched battle with the murluks, a pack of ogres trampled our camp and attacked the temple from the east. Fortunately, a new arrival through the gate warned us of what was transpiring. We managed to save the temple before it crumbled away entirely."

I frowned. "I didn't see any damage yesterday. It looked new."

Tara shrugged. "Whatever magic created the dragon temples also repairs them. As long as a temple hasn't been completely destroyed, it will restore itself—or so I'm told. Our temple was unusable for nearly a full day while it reconstructed itself. Since then, the old lady usually holds herself in reserve in the camp or at the temple itself."

I turned over Tara's words in my mind as I slipped down the upper bank. Matters in the settlement were more desperate than I'd imagined. *And it will only get worse. Once the gate to Earth closes, the Outpost will get no more reinforcements. What will become of the settlement then?*

I shook my head. The commander and her people were racing against the clock just as much as I was. Tara was right. If they didn't secure the Outpost soon, location seventy-eight was doomed.

If the other neutral locations were struggling this much too, what did it mean for humanity? Given the difficulties faced by the Outpost, I began to question whether humanity could establish an independent colony anywhere in the Dominion—a Dominion that was supposedly ours.

What will become of us then?

Would humanity, as a free, independent people vanish? Would we exist only as subjects—slaves or citizens—of our Patrons and Sponsors? It was an unsettling thought, one that redoubled my determination to help Tara's people establish the settlement.

Before I move on, as inevitably, I must.

Arriving on the lower bank's muddy stretches, Tara strode directly toward the commander and the rear-guard. "All right, gentlemen," the old lady was saying as we approached, "you have your orders. Let's be about it. And remember, we need every man. Make sure no one takes foolish risks today."

Petrov spotted our approach. With a jab of his chin in our direction, he alerted the commander to our presence. Jolin turned around. "Tara," she greeted. "I trust you know your orders already?" The old lady's gaze darted to me. "Keep our mage alive."

Startled exclamations rose from those men close enough to overhear. Soon, a furious ripple of whispers rolled through the ranks. I stifled a groan. The commander, it seemed, was no longer keeping my status a secret.

"Yes, ma'am," replied Tara with a snapped-off salute.

The old lady's gaze rested on me. She had to be conscious of the keen interest her words had sparked, yet her face betrayed no awareness. "Good morning, Jamie," Jolin said affably. "I heard you had quite an afternoon yesterday."

I shrugged, trying to match her nonchalance. I knew what she was doing, and I didn't appreciate it. The commander was using me to give her troops hope. Which was all well and good for them and for her, but less so for me.

I could feel the pressure of the soldiers' stares. *They are not my responsibility,* I told myself firmly. *It is not up to me to save them all.*

"Just training," I answered, struggling to appear unaffected by the dozens of eyes following me. It was not easy.

Jolin raised one eyebrow, although she didn't comment further on the subject. "We have another difficult battle today. Will you be able to offer us any assistance?" she asked, with seeming indifference.

I wanted to answer no, yet under the crushing weight of the soldiers' expectations, I felt myself saying something else entirely.

"I can."

I knew immediately that it was a foolish thing to say. My magic was untried and untested. My plan had been to try a few minor spells, nothing flashy. Nothing risky. Nothing that would attract too much attention to myself.

Only that is no longer the case, is it? You and your big mouth. Now these men expect you to save them. What possessed you, Jamie?

But I knew why I didn't deny the commander. Tara's words flashed into my mind: *"They will have to bear the risk."* The image of the defenseless crafters in the trenches accompanied it, as did the hungry hope in the eyes of the soldiers looking on.

I sighed and elaborated further. "I have a spell that should hurt the murluks badly."

A momentary look of surprise flitted across the commander's face—so quick I wouldn't have noticed if I hadn't been watching for it. She scrutinized me carefully, and her own expression grew grave, like she'd somehow divined the direction of my thoughts. "What do you need?"

"Only someone to guard my back. Tara can do that well enough."

"Nothing else?" asked the commander, one eyebrow raised in polite disbelief.

I hesitated. "Space, maybe."

"Space?"

I nodded. "I am not sure how well I can control the magic."

The commander frowned. "You will not injure my men." It was not a request.

I bowed my head, receiving her message loud and clear.

"Where do you want to take up position?" she asked.

I looked over the rows of spearmen sitting in the mud. The battle line stretched a few hundred yards in both directions already. "On the north flank," I answered, choosing it for no reason other than that I had been there yesterday.

A shout rang out from the south, drawing our attention. The water had begun to froth and bubble. As I watched, a bulbous head broke the river's surface.

The murluks had arrived.

"Well," said the commander, "you'd best be on your way. The battle is about to begin."

I nodded sharply. Swinging about, I shuffled to the right end of the spear line, dragging my crippled foot behind me.

"Jamie?" called the commander.

I stopped and turned around to face her.

"Good luck."

"You too, ma'am," I said, before limping off again.

Chapter Twenty-Two

390 DAYS UNTIL THE ARKON SHIELD FALLS

The morning stillness was shattered as, all along the line, sergeants and captains shouted orders and spearmen jumped to their feet.

The water's frothing intensified as more murluks surfaced. A lot more! Soon, the entire river was carpeted in living blue. The horde made no move to advance, however, content to wait until their numbers built.

"Bloody hell!" Tara eyed the enemy.

I looked at her in concern. "What's wrong?"

"There's a damn sight more today than yesterday." Tara's eyes never left the amassing enemy as she kept pace beside me. "Or any other day," she added after a moment's reflection.

I swallowed and quickened my pace, wondering if *we* would survive today's confrontation.

Despite our renewed urgency, Tara and I were still out of position—racing along the back of the human line—when the murluks swept forward in a tide of angry slurps and bobbing spears.

"Hurry, Jamie!" Tara urged.

But I was already going as fast as I could. For the umpteenth time, I cursed my foot and the circumstances that had led to its damage.

We were still dozens of yards from the northern end of the line when the tide of blue crashed into the spearmen braced to meet them. Unconsciously, Tara and I had both skidded to a halt to watch the moment of impact.

The murluks outnumbered the thin wall of humans many times over. It seemed impossible for the soldiers to weather the flood. Heart in my throat, I watched the horde break against the spearmen.

Orders were yelled, and as one, shields were braced and spears lowered. Then, with a tremendous roar that contained as much fear as it did fury, weapons were thrust out.

The line bowed, but it did not buckle. Men fell, but did not falter. No one ran. No one broke. Unflinchingly, the spearmen faced their enemy and held. Relief whipped through me as, unbelievably, the murluks were halted.

But not without cost.

In places, the spear wall was already in tatters. Reinforcements were racing to plug the gaping holes. Tara unclipped her shield and drew out her spear as she made to join the line.

I flung out a hand to clutch her arm. "No, Tara. Let's stick to the plan. Help me and you will better help them." *I hope.*

She looked torn. Her desire to race to her companions' aid was naked on her face, but equally visible was her hope.

Hope that my magic could do the impossible.

I kept my face impassive, letting no hint of doubt cloud my expression. *How did I end up in this situation?* I wondered. I was gambling far too much—everything, really—on the slim chance that my untried magic could work miracles. I *knew* it wasn't smart, but I was already committed. I couldn't let Tara or the Outpost's residents down.

Whatever Tara saw in my face, it convinced her. She wrapped her arm around mine and yanked. "Come on, then," she said. "Let's go get it done."

I let her pull me along. No matter how graceless the maneuver, or how embarrassing it was being dragged by the short-statured captain, I did not attempt to hinder her efforts. Haste was more important than dignity.

We reached the northern edge of the spear wall. At my request, we moved beyond, until the closest of the battling humans and murluks were more than two dozen yards south of us. "This is far enough, I think," I said.

Tara dropped my arm and readied her weapons. "What now?" Her eyes skipped left, to the lines of struggling men. I could see she was eager to join them.

I left my own shield and club in place across my back. If things went as planned, I would not need them. "We need to go beyond the line—"

I broke off as a slew of Trials alerts flooded my vision.

"Ignore that," ordered the captain, her impatience growing. "It is just the old lady casting her auras. Finish what you were about to say."

With difficulty, I dragged my eyes away from the Trials messages and dismissed them. Jolin had an impressive number of buffs at her disposal. It gave me new confidence. Boosted by the commander, the spearmen's own strength would be doubled, if not tripled.

This battle isn't lost yet.

I turned back to Tara. "We need to advance beyond our lines, right up to the water's edge, and then close on the murluks from the north—"

"What?" Tara's tone held both disbelief and outrage. "Are you mad? You want us to flank the murluks? You and me, all on our lonesome? What are you thinking!"

"Tara, listen—"

She paid me no attention. Her ire growing, she spoke over me. "The moment we're spotted, the creatures will swarm all over us. We will be overwhelmed in no time! Not even your *invincible* will save you. And don't be hoping for rescue from the fighters. The commander won't let the spearmen break formation." Tara glowered at me as she paused for breath.

"*Trust* me, Tara," I begged. If I didn't convince her now, I'd lose her. "I don't intend for us to be overwhelmed. Once I cast my spell, I'm pretty sure the murluks won't stay to face us."

"*Pretty sure?*" Tara's words dripped with sarcasm.

"Unfortunate choice of words," I replied hastily.

She still didn't look convinced.

"I will do this alone if I have to," I added.

Tara's brows drew down as she scowled, her doubt warring with her duty. The commander *had* ordered her to guard me. Finally reaching a decision, she grabbed my arm and hauled me toward the river.

"Don't disappoint me, Jamie," Tara growled. "If this madcap plan of yours gets more of our people slain, I will kill you myself."

I stayed silent, but inwardly I agreed with this fierce green-eyed warrior. If my plan failed, I would let her.

As we hurried to the river's edge, I cast an anxious gaze south. The human line had not crumpled yet. Despite the preposterous weight of numbers bearing down on them, they stood firm.

There is still time. I ran my eyes over the nearest murluks. Fully engaged in their battle against the spearmen, none of the creatures had spotted us yet.

That would change soon.

We made it to the water's edge without mishap. I waded a few steps into the river before swinging southward. Knee-deep in the sloshing waves, I took a moment to prepare myself.

The northern edge of the murluk horde was less than thirty yards away, and the creatures were recklessly throwing themselves against the spearmen. Curiously, the murluks made no attempt to encircle or flank their foes. They surely had the numbers to do it. Not only that, but with the river to conceal their movements, they could easily pull off the maneuver.

But such cunning was beyond them. Brute force was the only tactic the creatures understood.

They are primitive, I told myself, hoping to assuage my jangling nerves. My entire plan—such as it was—hinged on the murluks' lack of guile. I was hoping, perhaps foolishly, that the creatures shared the instinctive fear of fire common to most beasts.

I paused, struck by a sudden and worrying thought. *Surely the commander must have tried using fire against the murluks already? Idiot! Why didn't you consider that earlier?*

It was on the tip of my tongue to ask Tara, when I glimpsed her expression. Her patience was wearing thin. If I gave her further reason to doubt the soundness of my plan, I suspected she would drag me away.

Nothing for it, then.

"Right, let's advance," I said before Tara could hurry me along again. Following my own command, I shuffled forward through the dense river mud. "Whatever happens, Tara, stay behind me."

"Got it," she replied curtly.

I shaped the spellform of *flare* in my mind as we advanced. Keeping a careful eye on the murluks, I held the spell at the ready but uninfused.

Ten yards from the battling lines, the first of the murluks finally noticed us. Slurping excitedly, eight of the creatures veered away from the spearmen and charged our way.

"Jamie!" Tara yelled a warning.

"I see them." Drawing on my lifeblood and mana, I charged the spell construct in my mind, wincing at the split-second of pain the spell caused as it roared to life, setting my blood alight.

The dragonfire immediately set itself against my will and attempted to spew forth in an uncontrolled burst. With effort, I kept the raging torrent within me at bay and continued my advance, drawing closer to the murluks still.

Confident, bunched together, and betraying not the slightest hint of suspicion, the creatures charged, racing to be the first to get to us.

"Jamie! Do—"

I blocked out Tara's shouting. Narrowing my eyes, I peered intently at my oncoming foes. When the closest was little more than two yards away, I flung up both my arms, palms facing outward, and unleashed my dragonfire.

Impatient to escape my clutches, twin jets of flame roared from my hands and exploded into cones of heat and burning light that incinerated everything within a six-foot radius.

The murluks were caught squarely in my trap. The scorching flames licked at their unprotected skin, transforming the creatures' slurps into shrieks. Betrayed by momentum, even the murluks in the rear fell into the dragonfire's hungry embrace, despite their frantic efforts to flee.

Unbidden, a Trials message popped open in my vision.

Spontaneous *analyze* triggered by your attack. You have uncovered a murluk Trait: Vulnerability to Fire. Your skill in anatomy has advanced to level 1.

"Now isn't the time," I growled. Dismissing the alert, I turned my attention to the burning murluks. All eight writhed in agony. Some rolled in the mud, trying to extinguish the flames, while others attempted to crawl feebly away. They were no threat. Not anymore.

But they aren't dead either.

Hardening my heart against their whimpers, I kept my dragonfire centered on them. It took five seconds—five long seconds, during which I wished I could close my ears just as easily. Five endless seconds before their cries were forever silenced.

When it was done, nothing remained but smoking trails of ash.

Lowering my trembling hands, I stared in horror at the destruction I had unleashed. I thought I'd known what to expect, but I couldn't have been more wrong. *Flare* had burned hotter and brighter than any normal fire. It consumed everything in its path, the dragonfire leaving nothing behind, not even bones.

"Jamie?" Tara's voice quavered with uncertainty—Tara, who had betrayed so little anxiety before.

I turned away from contemplating the smoldering piles of ash and reaching out to her, I began, "Tara—"

She stepped back, her eyes wide and white with alarm.

I quickly dropped my hands, certain it was the gesture she was fearful of. "Don't be scared. I won't hurt you!"

She scowled. "I'm not *afraid*, you fool. It's your eyes!"

"My eyes?" I asked, confused.

"They're gold!" Tara pointed to my face, regaining her composure. "And glowing."

"Oh," I said, not sure what else to say. Focusing my *magesight* inward, I realized my blood was still singing with dragonfire. Even though I had cut off its outward flames, the *flare* spellform remained active within me.

Cutting off the flows of mana and lifeblood, I soothed the fire within me. "Better?" I asked.

"They're back to normal now." Tara leaning forward and gazed searchingly into my eyes. "What was that spell?

"A rare fire magic spell," I replied smoothly, my voice betraying no hitch as I lied. I had been prepared for the question. "I was fortunate to discover it."

Tara grunted. Her eyes flicked beyond me, and I turned to follow her gaze. The battle continued unabated, but my skirmish with the eight murluks had not gone unnoticed.

The scorching flames had attracted dozens more of the creatures. Breaking away from their attack on the spear wall, the murluks gathered in an unruly crowd a few yards away from us.

Yet they did not approach any closer.

Hopping in agitation, they were obviously torn between attacking and fleeing.

I was right: murluks are afraid of fire.

"Advance down the river, eh?" said Tara, looking from me to the murluks. "How long can you keep those flames going?"

"I don't know," I admitted. "Certainly not long enough to cover the length of the spear wall. But I'm hoping that won't be necessary. I expect the murluks will flee when they realize what they're up against."

Tara toed a pile of ash and smiled. "I dare say you're right, fish."

* * *

Moments later, Tara and I were advancing south again.

With much slurping and hissing, the swarming murluks backed away.

That's it. Run. You don't want to face me.

I hoped the threat of dragonfire would be enough to carry the day. But it was not to be.

More of the creatures abandoned their attack on the lines to join the mass of bobbing frog-flesh facing Tara and me. As the murluks barring our way south grew, their retreat slowed.

They find safety in numbers, I realized. *It fuels their courage.* I licked dry lips. At least fifty murluks faced off against us. *Will my dragonfire be enough to stop them?*

"They'll charge soon," I called over my shoulder to Tara. "Ready?"

"Ready," she affirmed, her voice grim.

I raised my arms and prepared to *flare.*

At the gesture, the murluks rushed forward, splashing through the churned-up mud in a mad dash. I didn't wait for them to close. Spreading my arms wide, I unleashed dragonfire. White-hot flames spewed forth, and this time I made no attempt to control them.

I let the fire rage free, watching steely-eyed as the flames fanned out in a semicircle three yards around me—the extent of my spellpower's reach.

At the last instant, courage abandoned the murluks. Or sense prevailed. The ones at the fore tried to halt their reckless dash. But it was too late. The tide could not be stemmed. Inexorably, the creatures fell into the inferno of waiting flames.

Fire rippled through flesh, bubbling hungrily through skin, blood, and bone. In a shockingly short time, the murluk charge crumpled, transformed into swirling ash and charred remains.

Dizziness assailed me. I staggered, toppling to my knees. My pulse beat erratically, and stars danced before my eyes.

I had attempted too much, I realized. *What happened to being careful?* I chided myself.

The spell had consumed a huge chunk of my mana and an even larger portion of my health. My life dangled on a slender thread. Fighting nausea, I deactivated *flare.*

"Jamie! Jamie, are you all right?"

"I'm fine," I lied. "I just need a moment to gather my breath. The murluks?"

"Gone!" Tara announced, with savage satisfaction. She paused. "That was some spell."

I chuckled weakly. "Yeah, it was." Still resting my hands on my knees, I cast *lay hands.* Mana slipped through my fingers, suffusing them with a gentle blue radiance. The spell's light lasted only an instant before my body siphoned away its energy. I sighed, breathing easier as new life flowed through me.

"What was that?" Tara's sharp eyes had not missed the telltale glow that had surrounded my hands.

"A healing spell, *lay hands.* I injured myself when I fell," I lied. To distract her from further questioning, I raised one arm. "Help me up, please."

With Tara's help, I staggered to my feet and surveyed the scene. The battle's fury had not diminished. The murluks still attacked in a frenzy, although their numbers on the northern side had substantially dwindled. More than a few of them had fled after witnessing their companions' fate.

"Things have eased on the right." Tara echoing my thoughts. "That section of the line will hold."

I nodded. Farther south, however, matters were still in doubt. Turning my gaze inward, I studied my reserves of stamina, health, and mana. My mana pool was more than half full, and my health was fully restored.

My stamina was another matter entirely.

Given the disparity between my Might and Magic Potentials, my reserve of stamina was much smaller than my mana. And my flagrant use of dragonfire had drained it to less than a quarter.

I still had enough for a few more uses of *flare*, but I wouldn't be able to pull off another uncontrolled burst. "Let's keep advancing," I said.

"You sure?" Tara scrutinized my face. "Can you keep going?"

"I can," I said. *I must.* "But I can't perform the stunt I just did again," I admitted. "My mana is running low. I should be able to keep casting long enough to scare off the murluks, though."

I couldn't tell Tara my stamina was low; it would invite too many questions. Once more, I was forced to lie.

* * *

We resumed our plod through the mud. None of the remaining murluks turned to face us. Ignoring me, the creatures pitted themselves against the spearmen. But as we closed to within *flare* range, the murluks finally reacted to our presence.

As one, they turned and fled.

Peeling away from the right flank, the creatures dove for the safety of the water. I sighed heavily. Finally, the murluks had learned their lesson.

Ragged cheers rose from the spear wall, where the spearmen raised aloft their weapons in salute. I raised my arm in tentative acknowledgement.

"Keep going, Jamie," Tara said. "There's still more to be done."

She was right. Not all the murluks had abandoned their assault. While our immediate area was free of enemies, the murluks still pressed the attack farther south.

"Right!" I stepped forward again.

Behind me, Tara beckoned a spearman from the lines. A stout red-haired man jogged toward us—the lieutenant, John.

He clamped a meaty hand on my shoulder and squeezed. "Good job, fish." He grinned.

"Thanks," I said, drawing to a stop.

"Keep going, Jamie," Tara urged. "I need a few words with John here. I'll catch up."

With a shrug, I did as she asked, surveying the spear wall as I went. Thousands of murluks swarmed the field, the closest a hundred yards away. All along the center and left, the creatures threatened the human lines, forcing the commander to fully commit her reserves. She and her guards had also joined the line.

The battle was by no means won.

I shifted my attention to the right. Here and there, gaps dotted the line, but by and large, the northern flank remained whole and unengaged.

Why haven't they been redeployed to strengthen the center? My gaze slid to the whispering pair behind me. Was Tara giving John new orders?

Just then, the murluks attacking the center noticed our approach. "Tara!" I yelled in warning.

After a last hurried exchange with John, she rushed to my side. "Ready, Jamie?"

I squinted at the two dozen murluks closing in on us. "These I can handle, but if more of them attack—"

"Don't worry," Tara assured me. "I have a plan. Help is on its way."

I glanced at her quizzically, but had no time to question her as the murluks surged into range. Raising my hands, I shot dragonfire into the nearest murluk. I made no effort to kill it, though; instead turning off the flames after two seconds.

It was enough.

At the appearance of the scorching fire, the murluks deserted and leaped for the river, many still aflame. They submerged themselves, but even the water failed to douse the flames.

I shifted uneasily as the murluks thrashed. *Will the flames burn out eventually? Or eat them alive?*

A sick feeling shuddered in my stomach. It was not a death I would wish on anyone.

Leaving the dying murluks to their fate, I tore my gaze away from the sight and continued my advance. After another few dozen yards, and a second burst of *flare*, I sent even more of the creatures fleeing.

By this time, the commander and her captains, realizing what I was about, adapted their tactics, and the rhythm of the battle changed.

The spearmen, given fresh orders and renewed hope, waited in anticipation of my approach. When I neared, they used the chaos I caused to inflict damage on the fleeing murluks; some even launching their spears at the retreating creatures. Behind me, the north flank curled round, and followed in my wake, ready to provide support.

The tide of the battle had finally turned. It was only a matter of time before the murluks were routed completely. But just as our advance reached the line's center, my stamina ran out.

"Tara," I gasped, hands on knees. "I'm out of mana."

Her reply caught me by surprise. "One moment, Jamie."

I frowned. *What did she mean by that?* Turning, I saw her signal to a spearman behind us. In response, the soldier lifted the makeshift flag he carried and waved it wildly. My frown deepened. What was going on?

A moment later, my *magesight* was nearly blinded as a rippling mass of spirit erupted from the rear of the human lines and spilled over the surrounding spearmen, including me.

You have been blessed by *rejuvenation*. Your health, stamina, and mana have been fully restored.

Shocked, I straightened from my hunched posture, suddenly thrumming with new energy. I felt revitalized. My aches had vanished, and I brimmed with renewed vigor.

And it was not just me. All along the river's banks, our soldiers bounced on their feet, their own tiredness banished.

Amazing, I thought. Blinking to clear my *magesight* of the blinding afterglow, I traced the spirit weaves back to their source—unsurprising, they originated from the old lady.

I swung to stare at Tara.

"What do you think of *that* buff?" she asked, eyes twinkling.

"How is that not magic?" I murmured.

She tilted her head. "Marcus calls it sorcery. Magic of the spirit." She scratched her head. "But he also said it isn't *true* magic, whatever that means." She shrugged. "Regardless, the commander's *rejuvenation* spell has saved us more times than I care to admit."

I nodded. The spell was incredible, and it explained why the commander had entered Overworld in her old skin.

"Sorcery," I mused, considering my own trait-given Techniques. I recalled mention of the subject in the wiki. Sorcery was not considered magic, nor was it a Discipline. Consequentially, I hadn't taken the time to study it.

Now I wished I had.

Putting together what I had seen in my *magesight* and what Tara had just told me, I realized that my *invincible* and *mimic* Techniques were also sorcery.

Clearly, sorcery was powerful, perhaps even more powerful than dragon magic. *Can I learn the* rejuvenation *spell, or other sorcery Techniques?*

I shook my head. The matter demanded further consideration, but now wasn't the time. I had another task to see to. I turned back to the murluks.

Casting *flare* once more, I set to work.

* * *

You have gained in experience and are now a level 12, Trainee. Your spellpower has increased to level 7.

Inhaling, I dismissed the Trials alerts. The battle was over. With myself and the spearmen *rejuvenated*, it did not take long to dispatch the murluks.

I glanced at the sky. The sun had hardly moved position since we had arrived at the river. *It's barely been an hour,* I thought. Yet it felt like days. And while my reserves of stamina and mana were healthy, I was bone-weary.

How many did I kill?

I brushed away the thought. It did not bear reflection. *The murluks are our enemies. Their deaths are necessary.*

A hand clamped down on my back. "Nice work, Jamie," Tara said. "Magic is an even more potent weapon than I suspected. With a dozen more like you, we could vanquish the murluks once and for all."

I offered her a quick—if forced—smile before changing the topic. "Do you know where the healers' tents are? I am sure the medics can use my help."

"Admirable, but not necessary." She shook her head. "Nic and the others will cope. Besides, there aren't likely to be very many injured right now. The commander's ability restores all but the dead. Come," she said, tugging at me, "we should go report. The old lady is sure to want to see you."

I didn't fully agree with Tara's reasoning, but I allowed myself to be led away. Swinging sharply left, Tara headed for the lines of spearmen, who were still in formation in case the murluks returned. The men were jubilant, chanting the commander's name.

From what I gathered, today's victory was one of the quickest in the Outpost's short history. As we waded through the spearmen's ranks, I heard my name called.

I jerked my head, surprised. It seemed that my own role in the battle hadn't gone unnoticed by the men. But it wasn't for accolades that I had done what I had, and despite the role I played in today's victory, the true architect of the Outpost's survival was undoubtedly the commander. It was her plans, her leadership, and her inspiration that had allowed humankind to establish a toehold here. My part was small by comparison.

The commander was still with the reserves, overseeing the battle's aftermath. At our approach, she held out her hands in welcome. "Jamie," she said, her hands trembling slightly, "that was well done. Thank you."

Taken aback at the sight of her, I was momentarily speechless. The commander was a far cry from the Jolin I had met yesterday. Weariness clung to her frail frame, and only Petrov, on whom she leaned heavily, was keeping her upright. In my *magesight*, her spirit hung in tatters. Her battle castings had claimed a heavy toll. Today, there was no disguising Jolin's age. *She looks ancient.*

But despite her appearance, Jolin's eyes shone with fierce determination and her smile radiated gratitude. *She genuinely cares for her people,* I thought, *to sacrifice so much for them.*

I inclined my head. "Just doing my part, ma'am."

She studied my bowed head for a moment. "It is more than that," she said gently. "My men may accord today's victory to me, but I know better. What you've done here, I will not forget. It's given us the respite we so desperately need. And now," she breathed, "we get on with the business of building the settlement."

I looked up at her. "You don't think the murluks will attack again, then?"

She waved a wrinkled hand dismissively. "They might, but the course of any future contest is now almost certain." She paused. "Assuming you stay, of course. You are not leaving us yet, I hope?"

"Not until the settlement is founded," I confirmed, "and the walls built."

She studied my face for a second longer. Satisfied with what she saw there, she added solemnly, "Thank you, Jamie. I—"

Her words broke off as Captain Marcus waved for her attention. "I am sorry, Jamie, other matters demand my time," Jolin said. "We will pick this up later. I have called a conference for this afternoon to decide the settlement's future. You must join us." She glanced behind me. "Tara, make sure he is there."

"Yes, ma'am," Tara replied.

And with that, we were dismissed.

Chapter Twenty-Three

390 DAYS UNTIL THE ARKON SHIELD FALLS

After the battle, Tara and I were left with little to do. My conversation with the old lady had been so brief, I hadn't had a chance to question her about sorcery or dungeons, or even about her intentions regarding the settlement.

What now?

I wondered, chewing at my lip. "Let's go find the medics," I said eventually.

Tara rolled her eyes, but she didn't object. Many of the soldiers called out in greeting or nodded respectfully as we passed. I chuckled, amused at how quickly their attitude toward me had changed.

"What's so funny?" Tara asked.

"Just yesterday," I said, gesturing with my chin at the men, "they were laughing at the crippled boy being beaten by the big bad captain. Today, they applaud."

Tara stopped and swung about to face me. None of the shared amusement I'd expected to see on her face was present. "You do them a disservice, Jamie," she said, her tone serious. "They jeered at you yesterday, true. But not for your crippled foot. They ridiculed themselves, or rather, the memory of themselves. They experienced the same drubbing you got at my hands."

Tara held my gaze, making sure I understood her meaning. "You may not have noticed it, but by yesterday evening you had earned their respect. None of them expected a new fish to last that long." She threw me a hard look. "Much less a crippled one."

I lowered my eyes, accepting Tara's rebuke. Her words shamed me. "I'm sorry," I said quietly. "Sometimes I am too cynical."

Tara laughed. "And perhaps a touch unforgiving."

"That too," I said, smiling with her.

We fell into a companionable silence for the rest of the way along the river shore. Scaling the upper bank, I saw that three large tents had been pitched next to the training ground. As we approached, a surprised Nicholas greeted us. "Tara, Jamie, what are you two doing here? Not injured, I hope?"

"Nothing of the sort, Nic." Tara pointed to me. "You've seen what he can do?"

"Indeed." Nicholas nodded at me. "And thank you, by the way. Your efforts made my job much easier today."

"He can heal too," said Tara. "That's why we're here."

Nicholas' gazed locked onto mine. "*Magical* healing?" he asked eagerly.

I nodded. "A life magic spell called *lay hands*. Do you need me to do anything?"

Nicholas opened his mouth. Paused. Then closed it again. He sighed. "On most days, the healing tents would be swarming with patients, and I'd given anything for a mage's aid. But today the commander's casting has seen to the injured already."

Nicholas' expression suggested he half-regretted the missed opportunity to witness healing magic. Over his shoulder I caught Tara's I-told-you-so look. Ignoring her, I said, "The commander's spell healed *all* the injuries?"

The medic nodded.

Even with Nicholas' confirmation, I still found it hard to believe. Restoring all allies to full health in a single spellcast was an extraordinary bit of sorcery. I frowned as another thought occurred to me. "Why doesn't she use it every day?"

The medic's eyes flicked briefly to Tara before he answered. "I wish she could. But from what I understand it will be days before she can use *rejuvenation* again."

I nodded, understanding. *Invincible* used nearly my entire spirit to cast. Its long recharge time was, in fact, the time required for my spirit to replenish itself before being used again as a shield. And from what Nicholas said, it seemed that *rejuvenation* must have had an even longer recast time.

Sorcery—as powerful as it is—is not without limitations.

"It was generous of you to offer your aid, though." Nicholas interrupted my musings. "I hope I can I call on you when the need arises?"

"Of course, Doc," I replied absently.

"Thank you," he said. "Now I must go. Duty calls." He clasped my arm in farewell and rushed off.

"Well, where to now?" Tara asked me once we were alone again.

I was wondering the same thing. I rubbed my face in thought. "The temple," I answered at last. "Then how about we go hunting? It's about time I saw what lies beyond the settlement."

* * *

Tara, much to my surprise, readily agreed.

I had expected her to be fiercely opposed to the notion of leaving the Outpost, so I had all my arguments well in hand. Her easy capitulation left me slightly perplexed.

"Right, we're here," Tara said, as we stopped at the entrance of the temple. "You go in and do what you have to while I see to our preparations."

"Preparations?" I asked, confused.

Tara waved aside my question. "Don't worry about it. If I'm not back by the time you're done, wait here. Don't you go wandering without me, understand?"

I nodded agreeably and Tara hurried away. *What is she up to?* I wondered as I watched her dash off. Shrugging away the mystery—Tara would do what she wanted—I limped up the steps to the temple.

* * *

You have entered Wyrm Island.

"What? You're back?" asked Aurora. "*Already?*"

I turned around to face the purple woman. She hovered in the air, her scowling face inches from mine and her wings fluttering.

I opened my mouth to reply, but before I could, Aurora spoke again. "Don't you know I have better things to do than pander to your needs?"

I didn't know that, actually. But I wasn't going to tell her that. *What does Aurora do between my temple visits? Does she even exist outside the temple?* Her words and manner certainly suggested she was more than just a construct of the Trials.

Stepping back, I bowed, my face a mask of contrition. "Apologies, Aurora," I murmured. "I will endeavor to bother you as little as possible in future."

My manner did little to mollify the purple woman. "What do you want?" she snapped.

Straightening from my bow, I said, "I'm here to acquire knowledge and enhance my Attributes."

"I know *that*," she retorted. "Which ones?"

I decided not to try my guide's patience furthers. "Please advance my dragon magic, life magic, constitution, vigor, and channeling to twelve."

I had only gained three levels since my last visit, and while I was accumulating a tidy sum of Marks and Tokens, I was not prepared to expand my repertoire of Disciplines yet. Changes made in the temple were irreversible. I could not afford to choose wrong.

With that in mind, I had decided only to improve those Attributes and Disciplines that had reached Trainee rank and were essential for spellcasting.

"Done!" Aurora waved one arm. "You have ninety-three Tokens and twenty Marks remaining. What else?"

"That's it," I replied.

Aurora's wings slowed to a stop, and she dropped to the ground. "That's it," she repeated. Her glare intensified. "You mean to tell me," she said, sounding out the words carefully, "you bothered my rest for these paltry changes?"

I winced. *Time to beat a retreat.* "Let me not keep you further, then," I said, swinging around to leave. "Bye, Aurora," I called over my shoulder as I limped back to the gate.

The answering silence was deafening.

✳ ✳ ✳

You have exited Wyrm Island. Your constitution, vigor, and channeling have increased to level 12.

Your skill in dragon and life magic has advanced to level 12.

I stepped out of the temple with a bemused grin. Aurora was as irascible as ever. *Who—and what—is she? Is it just me she dislikes, or everyone? And what do other players think of her?*

I scratched my head. I had not seen any mention of Aurora—or temple guides, for that matter—in the wiki. Which, come to think of it, was strange, especially considering how distinctive the purple woman was. I would have to remember to ask Tara what she thought of her guide.

Looking around, I saw the area around the temple was empty. Tara was still not back. I sat on the steps and pondered my development while I waited.

Despite effecting minimal changes to myself in the temple, I had advanced considerably as a player since I'd entered Overworld. Physically I had matured. I was stronger, quicker, and less vulnerable during combat. Magically, I was no slouch either. Notwithstanding my Neophyte-ranked spellpower, my spell damage was impressive, especially if the battle against the murluks was anything to go by.

Yet I had still a long way to go.

Physical confrontation—particularly up close—remained my biggest weakness. Considering my poor maneuverability and low health, if I wanted to survive long in Overworld, I *had* to stay out of melee range.

I needed a means of ranged attack. *Tonight,* I thought. *Tonight, I will try to create a ranged spell.*

Leaving aside the matter of my combat development, I turned my thoughts to the other aspects of my player growth.

The Trials had a player profile for players to keep track of their advancement and measure their progress. Before now, I hadn't felt the need to use it, but as the repertoire of my Disciplines and Traits expanded, I knew it would become invaluable.

Now, how do I open it?

I smiled. Summoned by thought alone, a window unfurled from the Trials core in my head.

> **You are a player of rank: Trainee, and level: 12.**
> **6% of Magic Potential actualized.**
> **21% of Might Potential actualized.**
> **8% of Resilience Potential actualized.**
> **1% of Craft Potential actualized.**

I tilted my head to the side as I considered how the Trials had summarized my development thus far. It was a strange way to measure a player's progress, yet it was in keeping with the Trials' emphasis on fulfilling one's Potential. And there was a wealth of information hidden beneath those few short lines of text.

Until now, I'd had no hard measure of how far I could advance my Attributes, but now, considering the percentages the Trials had assigned to my progress, I could determine my Potentials accurately and just as importantly: how long it would take to fulfil them.

Performing some rough calculations in my head, I estimated that I needed to advance over two hundred levels before I maximized my crucial Attributes of spellpower, channeling, vigor, and constitution. That was assuming a gain of two Attribute Marks per level, and it did not even consider the investments necessary for defensive Attributes, such as elemental resistance and willpower. While not a priority, I knew I couldn't ignore them entirely.

That's far too long! A familiar frustration welled up inside me. I had to get stronger—faster!—or I wouldn't be ready when it came time to face the orcs again.

Find a dungeon, I told myself. *And soon.* But I also had to help establish the settlement. I sighed. *So much to do.*

I was about to banish the player profile floating in my vision when the Trials data on my Craft Potential caught my attention. My Potential for Craft was nowhere near that of Magic, but nor was it insignificant. Frowning, I considered the crafting Disciplines.

Thus far, I had steadfastly ignored that aspect of the Trials, concentrating instead on my magic and might Disciplines. But at some point, I was going to have to devote time to developing my crafting. I sighed again. Another item for the 'to do' list.

There will be time to consider crafting further in the coming days, I thought. *Right now, my focus has to remain on my combat prowess. Even if—*

Voices interrupted my thoughts. Tara had returned, and she wasn't alone.

Walking alongside her were two men and two women. Michael and John I recognized from the battles at the river. The women, however, were strangers. I inspected Tara's companions carefully.

Both redheads, the women wore their hair tied up and had large bows slung across their backs. The men dragged sleds behind them, empty save for their long spears.

"Jamie," Tara said, "this is Laura and Cassandra, both hunters. And Michael and Lieutenant John you've met already. They will be joining us."

I raised an eyebrow at Tara but chose not to question her decision. I had expected our hunting trip to be less... organized, more a walk through the wilderness than a concerted effort to hunt game. But Tara, it seemed, had other plans.

I limped down the temple steps and exchanged greetings with the four. "What are the sleds for?" I asked.

"To bring back whatever game we find," replied Tara. "We can ill-afford to waste anything. While food may be plentiful right now, that may change at any time."

"Where do we start?" I asked.

Michael, John, and Tara looked to the two hunters for guidance. The women exchanged glances. Studying them more closely, I saw they bore a striking resemblance to each other. Both had elfin features, hazel eyes, and freckled skin. *They're sisters.*

"A herd of elk-like creatures roam plains to the south," said Laura. She pursed her lips, thinking. "The forest to the east has plentiful small game: rabbits, buck, wild pigs. But there are more predators."

John pulled a face. "Gah! Not elk meat again. I've had my fill of that for now." He paused. "Buck sounds delicious."

"And bacon even better," Michael chimed in. He rubbed his hands together. "Let's go east."

Disregarding the pair's comments, I asked, "What's to the north?" I didn't ask what lay to the west, assuming the region across the river belonged to the murluks. I doubted anyone wanted to go *that* way.

"We don't venture there much." Laura's eyes darkened. "Giant spiders infest the hills north of the Outpost. They've killed dozens of our hunters. The commander has declared the area off-limits."

"We should head south," insisted Tara, ignoring Michael's groans. "The six of us together should be able to bring down an elk and fend off any fire lizards we run across."

Fire lizards? I was tempted to ask about them, but I was more interested in the northern hills. "What level are the spiders? And why haven't you rooted them out?"

The sisters exchanged worried looks before shooting glances to Tara. Sighing, Tara waved for the pair to answer me.

"The spiders are around level thirty, those we've seen," said the second sister, Cassandra. "Physically, they're not strong, but they have a paralyzing bite, and they also tend to attack from hiding." She shuddered. "I was on one of the first scouting missions to the hills. Back then, we were less wise to the dangers of Overworld."

She paused, obviously gathering her thoughts. "We were less than an hour into the hills when one of the creatures ambushed us. Until the spider sprang out at us, we were unaware of its presence. When it attacked, we were caught flatfooted. I barely got away, and then only because it chose my partner for its target. He didn't make it." Cassandra fell silent, lost in dark memories.

"As for why we haven't rooted them out," Laura continued, "the spiders' nest is in a warren beneath the hills. In an enclosed, lightless space, the creatures have the upper hand. Any team we sent down there would be butchered. The spiders have never ventured out of the hills, so the captains don't believe them to be an immediate threat to the Outpost." She shrugged. "In the end, the captains decided it would be more trouble than it was worth to clear out the spiders."

I disagreed. I glanced at Tara, who would have been one of the captains in question.

The area had to be made safe, if only so scouts could patrol the region. While the spiders remained, the colony's northern border was unsecured. And I was certain the commander knew it too. *She probably has too much on her plate to deal with them right now.*

"Let's head north," I suggested.

Tara's lips thinned. "That area is off-limits. The commander pronounced it so."

"I'm not under the old lady's command, remember?" Tara glowered at me, but she said nothing. "I'll go alone if I have to," I added, pressing her further.

Tara growled. "Jamie, if you think I am going to let you—"

"I'll go," added John.

"Me too," seconded Michael.

Tara turned her scowl upon the two men, but before she could berate them, John raised his hands. "I'm not questioning the commander's orders, Tara. She had good reason for barring anyone from venturing into the hills." He gestured to me. "But that was before the arrival of our mage."

Tara folded her arms and stared at the lieutenant, unmoved by his words.

John held out his hands, imploring her. "Think, Captain. You saw what Jamie did to the murluks. His fire magic can swing the odds in our favor. We shouldn't ignore the opportunity."

I eyed John. I hadn't heard him address Tara by her title before. Clearly, he had done so deliberately. I glanced at her. While she still looked unhappy, Tara was wavering. John had chosen the correct tack.

"We've never managed to scout out the hills fully." Cassandra weighed in. "With the spiders gone, we might find the resources we so desperately need. Maybe even some ore."

Tara opened her mouth, then closed it again. She sighed, eyeing each of us in turn. "You all want to do this?"

The other four nodded. "We might very well die out there. Are you all prepared for that?"

The others shifted their feet, but no one looked away. "We face death every day on the riverbank," John muttered.

"That's different, and you know it," Tara scoffed. "The menace we'd face in the hills is tenfold more dangerous."

Tenfold? I swallowed. Tara thought it was *that* risky? *It doesn't matter how ill-advised this venture is,* I thought stubbornly. *We have to do it.* Time was of the essence, both for the Outpost and me. We could not afford to play it safe.

"Nowhere is free of danger on Overworld, Tara," I said. "Not yet. If we want to carve out a haven for humanity, we have to take risks. Repeatedly."

She stared at me. If we had been alone, I suspect my words would have earned me an earful. But with the other four already on my side, Tara relented. "All right," she said finally. "But if things become too dangerous, we retreat. No debates. No arguments. Agreed?"

We all nodded.

CHAPTER TWENTY-FOUR

390 DAYS UNTIL THE ARKON SHIELD FALLS

It was a two-hour hike to the northern foothills. The sisters, although believing the intervening region to be safe, jogged ahead to scout it out.

Once they disappeared over the horizon, Tara turned to the rest of us. "Let's get moving. We have to hurry to make it back in time for the old lady's conference."

I nodded, and the four of us set off north.

We crossed through the settlement's northern outskirts without encountering anyone. Most of the Outpost's activity was concentrated in the west, near the river, or to the east in the camp.

I paused when we reached the Outpost's northern boundary. Little more than an open trench marked it. Work had not yet begun on the wall on this side of the settlement, which made sense. Fortifying the western perimeter against the murluks' attacks had been the commander's priority.

We crossed over into the countryside beyond with little ceremony. The flat, open plains were unexpectedly pleasant. Traveling in single file—at Tara's insistence—we waded through the knee-high grass.

The plains' expanse was spotted with blooms as far as the eye could see. Other than small birds winging through the air, there was no wildlife to speak of.

It is beautiful. Mom would have been happy here. I shooed away the thought. *Beauty can be dangerous too,* I reminded myself. *Who knows what lies beneath?*

On guard against being lulled into a false security, I scanned the horizon, but as time passed and no threat presented itself, I relaxed. Deciding to trust the two sisters to forewarn us, I turned my attention inward. *Time to give further consideration to my magic.*

The Trials Infopedia had insisted that all magic Disciplines could be self-taught, without the aid of spellbooks or trainers, albeit with great difficulty. Given the situation with the murluks, I hadn't risked trying to do so with dragon and life magic.

But if I could train the other magic Disciplines on my own—to Trainee rank at least—it would save me Tokens.

Reaching within myself, I drew mana into my mind and shaped it into a rudimentary construct of fire, or what I thought was the spellform of fire. With my fire magic Discipline only at level one, my understanding of it was crude at best.

I started with fire magic, for obvious reasons. I hoped that its similarity to dragon magic would make training the Discipline easier. I willed the spellform into being, but it refused to materialize.

It's not quite right, I thought. *Let's try this.*

Time sped by as I toyed, twisted, and turned the mana construct, letting instinct and intuition guide me.

At one point, I sensed Tara addressing me. For a split-second, I tore my attention away from the intriguing puzzle in my mind and let awareness of my surroundings seep back. But as we were neither in danger nor at the foothills, I waved off her question and returned to my study of the magic within me.

When the pieces in my mind finally slipped into place, and my rudimentary understanding of fire expanded, the concepts I had struggled with suddenly seemed so simple and self-explanatory that I was left wondering why they had taken me so long to grasp.

Your skill in fire magic has advanced to level 2.

I smiled, pleased by my achievement. *Now to do it again.*

I started to dive back into the depths of my mind, when I felt Tara shaking me with unnecessary violence. "Jamie, goddamn it, wake up!"

Shocked out of my trance, I surfaced back into the present and looked around. A series of hills rose a few yards in front of me. Marching into the distance in ever-increasing heights, the hilltops became the sheer rockfaces and jagged peaks of a mountain that edged the horizon.

"Oh," I said in surprise. "We're here."

Tara smacked the back of my head. Hard. "We've been *here* for the last twenty minutes, you idiot! We had all but given up on you waking and we were about to head back to the Outpost. Are you all right?" Her eyes were strained with worry.

I blinked. "Twenty minutes? Really? Sorry, I was training," I said as contritely as I could. Reaching up, I rubbed the back of my head. It hurt.

"Training?" Tara narrowed her eyes.

"My magic," I said, not elaborating further. "But I am ready to continue." I looked behind me. The others were sitting down, resting while they waited for us to finish. "We can go on now."

"You sure you're okay to continue?"

"I'm fine." I waving off Tara's concern. Stepping forward, I led the way into the hills.

* * *

Tara did not let me stay in the lead, of course. But my gesture served its purpose. A few minutes later, the six of us were deep into the hills.

In stark constant to the green and vibrant plains, the hills were dusty shale and rock. Sparse, uniformly brown vegetation clung to the unwelcoming soil.

We moved cautiously through the rolling hills. Made wary by Cassandra's tale, all six of us were on guard. When a roar shook the air, I jumped.

The others froze.

"Mountain lion," murmured Laura.

"Will it attack?" I asked.

"Unlikely," she responded. "It's no match for the six of us."

"How far to the spiders' warren?" asked Tara.

Cassandra pointed north. "Maybe thirty minutes that way. But I can't be sure. We were never able to get close enough to pinpoint its exact location." She paused. "We should ready ourselves for an ambush."

"Everyone, weapons in hand and eyes sharp," Tara ordered. "From here on, we move in formation. No one break ranks." Her eyes settled on me as she added, "For *any* reason."

I nodded. The others drew their weapons. Michael and John wielded long spears, Tara had her stabbing spear and shield, and the two hunters gripped their longbows. I strapped on my shield, but left my club holstered and kept my right hand free for casting.

We resumed our advance with Tara in front, the hunters and me protected in the center, and John and Michael bringing up the rear. With the possibility of an ambush high, the hills loomed even more ominously to my mind. Behind every boulder and in every shadowed slope, I imagined enemies. I rubbed my sweaty palms dry. Where would the attack come from?

If Cassandra is right, we must almost be at the warren's entrance, I thought, beginning to believe we would reach it without mishap.

A slight shift in the sand to my right caught my eye. *What was that?* I wondered. But I didn't look, hesitant to take my eyes off the hills leaning down balefully.

We were in a particularly narrow pass between the hills. Despite the sun overhead, the overlooking slopes cast long shadows across the ground. It was an ideal spot for an ambush. Like the others, I anxiously scanned the surroundings, studying every cranny for hidden enemies.

But the ground underfoot was safe. *Wasn't it?*

The sand twitched again. no longer able to ignore the movement, I darted a quick look at the ground, feeling my eyes widen as realization struck. "Watch out—"

My cry came too late.

From either side of us, two blurred shapes burst out of the ground and leaped onto the party in a shower of dirt. S*piders!*

I despaired. Despite our care, we had been caught off guard.

Michael managed a half-strangled cry before he disappeared beneath the giant arachnid attacking from the left. John was quicker, managing to raise his spear in time for the leaping monster to skewer itself.

I swung left, rushing to Michael's aid. A spider the size of a large dog was stabbing its razor-sharp limbs down on the fallen spearman. Before it could turn my way, I slapped my hand onto one prickly leg and unleashed *flare.*

The raging inferno boiled out of me, consuming the creature. It shrieked as its brown skin turned an angry red at the point of contact. To my immense relief, none of the flames spread out from the creature to endanger Michael, who lay helpless on the ground.

Behind me, the three women yelled as they converged on the second spider. Pinned by John, it made for an easier target. But before I could see how the others were faring, my foe dug its other limbs out of Michael and struck at me.

I tried to dodge, but I was hampered by my need to keep my right hand clasped onto the spider and was unable to duck away.

The forest of hairy limbs descended on me, each sharper than a murluk spear. I clenched my jaw to cut off the shriek that threatened to erupt as the attacks bit through my armor and into my torso.

Aaargh! I rode the pain, refusing to let go of the leg I had trapped. I bashed at the spider with my shield, then ducked my head behind it as the spider retaliated.

I rode the second wave of attacks better, using my shield to fend off the spider's legs while I continued to pour ravenous dragonfire directly into its body.

I could already tell my dragonfire was not as effective against the spiders as it had been with the murluks. A murluk would have been ash by now. The spider, though, was very much alive.

But I was already committed. I dared not loosen my grip on the monster. Doing that would expose Michael to *flare.* I couldn't control it well enough to be certain it wouldn't burn him, not when he lay so close.

The spider battered me with its limbs for a third time, and although I foiled half its attacks, those that got through shredded my armor with laughable ease. Grim-faced, I ignored the rivulets of red spreading across my torso and held on.

As I had hoped, the white-hot fury of my dragonfire eventually proved too much for my foe to endure. *No you don't,* I thought as it turned to flee. I wasn't going to let it go that easily. I tightened my grip on its leg and hung on.

The spider yanked its leg, desperate to free itself. I smiled a bloody grin and wrapped my left arm around it as well. The creature had already lost. It just didn't know it yet.

The spider grew frantic, and in its panic, it dragged me a few feet across the ground. But with both of my hands wrapped around its leg, escape was impossible.

It only took a few more seconds.

Inevitably, the spider collapsed in on itself, and its life drained away. A Trials message floated into view.

You have gained in experience and are now a level 13 Trainee.

I rolled onto my back and cackled, the sound more than a little disturbing. For a moment, it was all I could do to lie still while my chest heaved and I gasped for breath.

I was a mess. *Again.* My health was dangerously low, and my armor was blood-covered and cut to ribbons.

A cut-off cry from nearby made me lift my head. The others were still battling the second spider, which was pinned on the end of John's spear. While it struggled to escape, Tara danced around its waving limbs and struck at will.

Firing arrows at point-blank range, Laura and Cassandra were doing their fair share of damage, while John maneuvered his long spear to pin the spider, so it couldn't escape.

They have matters in hand, I thought. Summoning my mana once again, I cast *lay hands* on myself. Under the spell's touch, my wounds closed over. I rose to my feet, unsteady from the blood loss but otherwise hale. I limped over to Michael.

The spearman lay unmoving. For a moment, I feared the worst. But his chest moved up and down. He was alive. I sighed in relief and inspected his body.

Despite his comatose state, Michael had sustained minimal damage. *Unlike me,* I thought, chuckling. I had come far too close to dying.

On his neck, Michael bore twin puncture wounds. *He's been paralyzed.* Setting my hands to his torso, I healed Michael's injuries. *Lay hands* failed to remove the paralyzing effect of the spider's bite, however.

I scratched my head worriedly. Would Michael be alright? Had the spider's toxins done more than paralyze him?

"Jamie, are you okay?" asked Tara, running up to me.

I turned around to face her. "Yeah." I gestured at my blood-streaked body and tattered armor. "It looks worse than it is." It did now, anyway.

"I'm sorry," she said. "I shouldn't have left you to tackle that spider alone. When I saw you take hold of it... and after how you handled the murluks... I thought—I thought..."

"It's all right, Tara," I said, stopping her flow of words. "You made the right call. I got the better of the damned thing... eventually." Beyond Tara, I spied the carcass of the second spider and John limping over to join us. "Need healing?"

The big man smiled. "Please."

I set my hands on the lieutenant and healed him. *His* injuries weren't bad either. It seemed I had borne the brunt of the damage. *You're not a damn tank, Jamie,* I berated myself.

If I wasn't more careful in future, I'd kill myself with *flare*.

Now, wouldn't that be funny.

* * *

Much to everyone's relief, Michael recovered from the spider bite, though his face remained as pale as a sheet. The paralysis had locked his limbs in place but left his mind unaffected. He had seen and heard everything.

I lay on my back, recuperating, while the others inspected the two corpses. The spider I had burned hadn't turned to ash like the murluks had. The murluks' vulnerability to fire had probably magnified the damage they sustained.

John and Tara had flipped one of the corpses on its back. The spider weighed little. Laura and Cassandra were inspecting the corpse, running their hands over its limbs and scrutinizing its skin. They even went so far as to sniff the darn creature.

I scratched my stubble, bemused. *What are they up to?* Curious, I rose to my feet and joined them. "What are you doing, Cassandra?"

The redhead flicked her eyes away for an instant from the spider to glance at me. "Call me Cass," she said. "We're inspecting it, with *anatomy*."

Anatomy was a combat Discipline that advanced *analyze* and increased the degree of information it provided, including a creature's strength and weaknesses. It could supposedly reveal an enemy's vulnerabilities in real-time during combat. How? I was unsure. "Doesn't the spider have to be alive to use the skill?"

"No." She rocked back on her haunches. "In fact, it's easier to apply this way. My skill in the Discipline is still too low for success to be certain on living enemies."

"Find anything?" asked Tara.

"It has a paralyzing bite." Laura forced open the spider's jaws and gestured to two protruding mandibles. "But we already knew that. The bite does minimal damage, and the paralysis wears off after about a minute. But the effect is intensified with repeated bites. It's how the spiders kill their prey, I imagine."

Beside me, I felt Michael shudder. I sympathized. Being eaten alive would *not* be a good way to go.

Laura rubbed her hands across the creature's patterned torso. "The skin is tough and resistant to piercing, but its bones are light. Crushing weapons will be most effective against them."

I unsheathed my club. "Like this?"

At Laura's nod, I handed the weapon to Tara. She would make better use of it than I could.

Tara nodded gratefully. "Anything useful we can harvest from the creatures?" she asked the hunters.

"Some silk in this one's spinnerets," Cassandra answered. "The skin will be useful too."

"Good. Load the bodies onto the sled," Tara ordered.

Michael and John saw to it. Joining them, I used *analyze* on the dead spiders.

The target is a level 30 brown spider scout. It has no Magic, meager Resilience, is gifted with Might, and has low Craft.

The spider's meager Resilience explained its low health and why I'd been able to kill it, even though it was beyond my level.

Staring at the corpse, I began inspecting it as I had seen the sisters do.

You have uncovered a brown spider Technique: *paralyzing bite*. Your skill in anatomy has advanced to level 2.

It worked, I thought happily. I would be sure to inspect all of my slain foes in future.

"Jamie! Stop playing with the bodies," Tara grumbled. "Let's get moving. Everyone, make sure you watch the damn ground. Let's not fall for the same trick twice."

Chapter Twenty-Five

390 DAYS UNTIL THE ARKON SHIELD FALLS

Cassandra was spot-on about the location of the warren's entrance. After traveling a few dozen yards farther, we halted at the base of another hill.

A large hole had been dug out in the ground, and judging by the cobwebs stretched across its width, it was unmistakably the entrance to the spiders' warren. Eight feet tall and about three feet wide, it was large enough for us to walk through upright—and suspiciously unguarded.

"You really want to go in there?" Tara asked.

"I do," I said firmly. "The spiders are physically weak. And we know how to kill them now." I gestured to the club she held in hand.

Tara eyed me doubtfully, although she didn't contradict my words. Laura rejoined us, bearing an armful of small branches she had left to scavenge. We would need light inside. With a burst of *flare,* I lit each of the torches.

Then, without further discussion, we filed into the warren. It was dank, dark, and moldy. Cobwebs draped the sloping tunnels, cementing my conviction we were in the right place.

But surprisingly, even after we had advanced a few yards into the warren, no spiders burst out of its depths to defend their home. I had expected be assaulted the moment we entered. Yet in the first twenty yards, we encountered no opposition.

What's going on? I wondered. *Something about this doesn't feel right.*

Presently, the entrance tunnel, which so far had been unerringly straight with neither twists nor detours, opened into a large cavern, ten yards in diameter.

As we spread out across it, I spotted three more exits descending deeper into the warren.

If we are going to be ambushed, it will be here, I thought. "Be careful—"

I broke off as a flood of Trials messages filled my vision.

You have discovered a lair. Your skill in lore has advanced to level 9. Name: Brown Spider Warren. Age: Infancy, less than thirty days old. Designation: Unclaimed. To claim this lair, defeat all its guardians.

Warning: You have entered the Brown Spider Warren with a party of six. The maximum party size for this lair is five. Reduce your party. Time remaining before the warren is destroyed: 2 minutes.

"A lair," I breathed in awe.

The others were also studying the messages that appeared before them, their expressions confused.

"What is a lair?" muttered Tara.

"A lair," I explained, rereading the Trials messages with avid interest, "is like a dungeon, but differs in two notable ways. Firstly, they usually contain only a single species, and secondly, they can be claimed, whereas a dungeon cannot be."

Silence greeted my words.

I closed the Trials message and faced the others. They were all staring at me.

"How do you know all that?" asked Tara finally.

"I read the Trials Infopedia."

"Infopedia?" asked John.

I glanced across the five. "None of you are gamers, are you?"

Their blank looks were answer enough. Clearly, they didn't even know about the wiki's existence. But now was not the time to explain. We had to get organized.

"I'll tell you later. The important thing is that one of us needs to leave."

"No." Tara shook her head. "This is more than we bargained for. We *all* need to leave. We'll reassess matters after we've reported to the commander." She swung away, heading for the entrance.

"Wait, Tara," I ordered.

She turned around, surprised by my tone.

"I don't think you understand what this discovery means. A lair can be an incredible resource for the Outpost. If we claim it, the creatures spawned here belong to the settlement."

Tara stepped back toward me. "You mean they will be... domesticated?"

"Something like that," I replied. "It will take work to mature the lair, but any spiders born in the warren will be allied with the settlement. And," I continued, seeing she was beginning to be swayed, "the longer this lair is unclaimed, the stronger it will grow. At the moment, it's still young. Now is our best chance of claiming it."

Tara bit her lip and considered my words. It didn't take her long to decide. "Cass," she ordered, "head back to the Outpost. Report directly to the old lady. Tell her what we found and what Jamie has surmised." She glanced at me. "And make sure Captain Marcus is present when you do."

I looked questioningly at her.

Tara's lips curled down. "Like you, Marcus is a gamer. He will make sure the commander understands the importance of your words."

Nodding agreeably, I swung back to study our surroundings. We could not stay in the cavern for long. It was too open, and we would be overrun if the spiders assaulted us here. *But which way do we go?*

As Cass hurried out of the warren, another Trials message dropped open in my sight.

You party has been reduced to five. Lair run will begin in 30 seconds.

I frowned as I read the message.

The countdown timer sounded ominous. While my knowledge had impressed the others, I had told them the sum of what I knew about lairs.

The little I knew pointed to the Trials exerting some control over a lair's creatures. Why else hadn't the spiders attacked us when we entered the warren?

How the Trials achieved dominance over a lair's inhabitants, I had no idea, but its latest message supported the notion. I couldn't be certain what the Trials meant by a 'lair run,' or by the countdown timer, but if I had to guess... I'd say we were about to be attacked.

"Tara," I called. "When that timer runs out, I expect the spiders will swarm up those three tunnels from deeper in the warren."

"What numbers can we expect?" she asked, clearly believing in my expertise to be greater than it was.

"I don't know," I admitted. "But the lair is still in its infancy. Probably not too many."

Tara, thankfully, did not question my vague response. "Let's back up into the tunnel we entered from," she ordered. "Michael, John, plant the torches somewhere in the cavern. We're going to need the light. Laura, you're in the rear. Shoot over our heads when they come. John, you're with me in the front—"

"No, Tara," I said. "I have to be up front to use *flare*."

She hesitated for a beat. "John and Michael, you two behind us. Just like in the spear wall, stab over us into the spiders. Try to pin them in place with your spears."

A chorus of "yes, ma'am" followed Tara's orders, and we fell into formation, retreating to where the entrance-tunnel fed into the cavern.

Tara and I took up position just inside the tunnel mouth. The narrow opening would reduce how many spiders we faced at any one time. Fastening my shield to my left arm, I braced myself against Tara, who stood on my right and watched the cavern's other openings.

My prediction proved correct.

As soon as the timer hit zero, a stream of brown swarmed up into the cavern. In the blur of shapes, I couldn't make out their numbers. Not waiting for Tara's orders, I infused my mana with lifeblood and cast *flare* into the scurrying forms as they reached the mouth of our tunnel.

Dragonfire exploded outward, drenching nearly the entire tunnel.

The spiders were caught unprepared.

Limbs and torsos caught aflame, and eyeballs popped in the sizzling heat. Shrieking in fright, the creatures wheeled and clambered all over one another in their haste to escape. As quickly as the tide of brown had surged forward, it rolled back.

Eager to put an end to the spiders' menace, I stepped forward, my palms facing outward with flames pouring out.

A hand gripped me, holding me back. "Wait," instructed Tara. "Don't be foolish. We will be overrun if we advance into the cavern. Let them come to us."

She was right. I stepped back into formation and let the flames of my dragonfire die down. Turning back to our foes, I saw that they had retreated to the far end of the cavern. Dancing along the cavern's rim, they chittered angrily amongst themselves.

"I make out ten," Tara said.

"Me too," confirmed John.

I nodded, agreeing with their assessment. There were more spiders than I'd expected. *This could get messy. Perhaps we should have retreated.* It was too late for that now though. I was sure the lair creatures wouldn't let us go.

The spiders all sported burns of some sort, but none looked incapacitated. I grimaced. My opening attack hadn't reduced the threat in any meaningful way, and while the creatures appeared afraid to attack again, they also seemed unwilling to let our intrusion go unanswered.

"Laura," Tara called over her shoulder, "see if you can hit one. Let's provoke the blighters into attacking again."

"I'll try," said Laura doubtfully. "But the way they're weaving about..."

"Give it your best shot," Tara said. "Jamie, keep yourself ready."

I nodded curtly and reformed the construct of dragonfire in my mind.

An arrow sped over my head and crashed into the cavern's far wall, failing to hit any targets. But despite the miss, Laura's attack spurred the spiders into motion... just not in the way we expected.

Instead of charging forward in one formless mass, the spiders split into four vectors of brown. Two raced along the left wall, two along the right, two sped straight across the cavern, and the other four... well, the other four leaped onto the cavern roof and surged toward us *upside down*.

My eyes widened and I gulped, realizing now why the dimensions of the warren were so odd. Of course spiders didn't travel along the ground—the creatures were equally comfortable traversing the walls and roof of the warren.

But despite our foes' unconventional approach, I reacted quickly. "I'll handle the ones on the roof!" I shouted. "Keep the others at bay!" Casting *flare*, I turned my hand upward.

Dragonfire blazed eagerly from my hands. Strained almost to the limit of my reach, the flames licked the tunnel roof. The incoming spiders attempted to dodge, but their numbers hampered their efforts.

In a confusing zigzag of motion that failed to steer them clear of the flames path, all four spiders on the roof fell prey to my dragonfire. Well before they reached me or Tara, the creatures lost their perch and fell in a burning mess.

My hands tracked their motion, hoping to catch not just the original four with dragonfire, but the other six that had in the meantime converged on the party.

The spiders proved more cunning than anticipated. As their burning fellows fell to the ground, the other six scattered and scaled the tunnel walls on either side.

I screamed in silent frustration.

I couldn't target the spiders on the right wall with *flare* without endangering Tara. Given no other choice, I directed my flames to the left wall and the four still writhing on the ground. The rest of the party would have to deal with the three spiders clinging to the right wall.

Dragonfire roared out and scorched rock and spider alike. The three racing along the left wall tried to evade the inferno, but there was nowhere for them to hide, so the only way to run was back. And it already appeared too late for that.

Trapped squarely within the flames, the spiders caught alight. Near instantly, the sensitive hairs that allowed the creatures to cling to walls, burned to nothingness. The three skittered desperately for purchase, but their fall was inevitable. In a tangled heap, they joined their burning fellows.

I extended both arms and focused my dragonfire on the seven curled-up spiders. Some tried to advance once more, but the damage they sustained was too heavy. With the fate of my enemies certain, I glanced to my right to see how the others fared.

They were holding three spiders at bay—barely.

The creatures seemed wary of the spearmen's weapons. Dancing along the walls, the spiders feinted forward in attack, but a jab of John's spear was enough to send them scuttling back.

The reach of Michael and John's spears served to keep the spiders off the roof and walls, but it did not stop them from rushing Tara. As I watched—helpless to intervene—one of the spiders leaped at the captain while the other two menaced her from the ground.

Alive to the danger, she bashed the creature away with her shield.

Before the dazed spider could recover, Michael surged forward and pinned the beast with his spear, affording Tara the opportunity to lay into it with her club. But with both Michael and Tara momentarily occupied, the other two spiders saw their chance to strike.

With a running leap, both creatures launched themselves through the air.

At me.

In horror, I watched them hurtling toward me. I could not turn my dragonfire upon them without releasing the other seven from the flames or hurting Tara.

Tara's head whipped up, sensing the spiders' motion. Her club flashed out. She was a fraction too slow though, and the spiders passed by her unharmed.

John, standing tall, thrust downward with his long spear, skewering one of the creatures. Relief surged through me, but that still left the other.

At the last moment, just as the remaining spider crashed into me, I cut off *flare* and attempted to fend off my attacker with my right arm.

It was not enough.

The nimble creature skittered over my arm too fast to follow. Before I could do anything else, the dog-sized spider wrapped its legs around my shoulders and bit down.

I froze.

In an instant, icy numbness suffused my body and I couldn't move. My left hand, still extended, was locked in position. My right hand was unresponsive too. Despite the paralysis, I could still feel everything. My eyes stared wide, fixed on the seven charred spiders, still alive, but too feeble to be a threat.

I am helpless, I despaired.

I swayed as the monster wrapped itself around my neck and dug its claws into me. Pinpricks of pain assailed me. *This is bad.*

A roar split the air. *John,* I thought. Next, a shadow flicked across my vision. *A thrust spear?*

Finally, Tara's club came hurtling down on the spider—and on me. Pain blossomed across my right shoulder, and it felt as my bones had been crushed.

I didn't begrudge Tara the injury though. *As long as she gets the damned spider off me, I don't care.* The weight on my back lifted as the spider leaped off. Unbalanced by the motion, I toppled backward.

Cool hands on my back slowed my fall. *Laura.*

Gratitude swelled up in me.

My companions had rescued me.

* * *

I was a helpless spectator to the rest of the battle, but that didn't concern me much as the others made short work of the remaining spiders.

By the time my paralysis wore off, all ten spiders were dead, and I had gained another level.

You have gained in experience and are now a level 14 Trainee.

I gasped and breathed in deeply as I regained control of my body. "That was not pleasant," I muttered.

My companions looked up from their labors. Michael and John were piling the corpses together while Tara and Laura kept watch.

"You okay?" Michael walked over to lend me a helping hand up.

"Yeah, thanks," I said, as I cast *lay hands* on myself. Once again, I was the only one who had taken meaningful damage. *This is becoming tiresome, Jamie.*

I limped over to Tara and Laura.

Tara's gaze swept over me, making sure I was alright. "We go on?" she asked, her face betraying no hint of her own feelings on the matter.

I was surprised—not by the question, but that Tara was leaving the decision to me. I hesitated before answering, "Yes. This lair is young. The spiders we killed must be the bulk of its inhabitants. There can't be many left."

Could there?

Tara nodded, her face still expressionless. "Which way?" She pointed to the three exits.

I gazed at the tunnels in question. The two on either end were smaller than the one in the middle. "We check all three," I answered, "but let's leave the largest for last."

We set off in a single file down the left tunnel. In short order, the tunnel shrank even further, forcing us to duck our heads and walk bent over.

It left us vulnerable, but at least the spiders could only come at us one at a time. *Unless more of the damn creatures are buried underfoot,* I thought sourly. To guard against possibility, Tara took the lead, jabbing her spear into the ground as we went.

In the end, no attack came. The seemingly unfinished side tunnel ended abruptly twenty yards in. Relieved not to be forced to fight at such close quarters, we backed out and explored the right tunnel.

It too was empty. It stopped short in a wall of bare soil just a few yards in. More than anything, the unfinished tunnels were evidence of how young the lair was. *Ten spiders in a warren only days old,* I thought, chewing on my lip. *What will a fully matured lair look like? And what will it take to claim such a lair?*

We returned to the cavern and prepared ourselves, knowing that whatever still occupied the warren awaited us in the main tunnel.

* * *

Five minutes into the main tunnel, we encountered our first branch. A smaller passage opened out on the left.

"Wait up," said Tara as she drew to a halt near the opening. She tilted her head to the side. "You hear that?"

Quietening my breathing, I listened. A low-pitched hum emanated from the tunnel.

"What is that?" John whispered.

Frowning, I strained my ears. The noise was familiar. Almost like... chittering.

"More spiders," Laura said, echoing my own thoughts. The others dropped their hands to their weapons, and I readied *flare*. For a drawn-out moment, we waited.

When, after nearly a minute, the expected attack did not materialize, I let the spellform dissipate. The chittering continued unabated.

"We have to go in," I said.

Tara glanced to me.

"If whatever is in there hasn't attacked yet, it isn't likely to. We can't wait here all day."

"All right, but just you and me," Tara said. She turned to the others. "You three stay here. If anything comes up the tunnel, shout. If whatever is in this side passage is too much for us to handle, we'll run straight back. Be ready."

The others nodded, and we set off.

The side passage carried on straight for less than five yards before bending sharply to the right. Hearing Tara's sharp intake of breath as she rounded the corner, I hurried to join her but was stopped short—just as she had been—by the sight that greeted me.

The tunnel opened into another small chamber, which was filled with dozens of hanging cocoons. Below them, scores of spiderlings, feeding hungrily on whatever lay within.

It's a nursery, I realized.

Standing in the center, its forelegs raised in warning, was a single adult spider. It was guarding the young—which explained why it hadn't attacked yet.

Tara glanced at me, the question on her mind clear in her expression.

To be sure of what we were facing—and what had to be done—I picked one of the helpless-looking spiderlings and cast *analyze* upon it.

The target is a level 2 brown spiderling. It has no Magic, meager Resilience, is gifted with Might, and has low Craft.

"We have to burn them out," I said grimly. "If we don't, we can't claim the lair." I pointed to the spiderlings. "They may not look like much now, but in days or weeks they will be fully grown."

Tara nodded. "How do we do it?"

"Get behind me," I said. After Tara moved into position, I flung the torch I carried into the room.

The flaming stick fell among the webbed cocoons and set them alight. Though the fire spread neither fast enough nor hot enough to burn the room's occupants, the spiderlings didn't know that. In a flood of brown, they fled the only way they could—directly toward us and my waiting dragonfire.

It was over in seconds.

The spiderlings crisped into near nothingness almost instantaneously. Only their guardian—the sole adult spider—put up any sort of fight, but even it failed to reach me through the scorching flames.

When the deed was done, more than two hundred small carcasses littered the ground.

You have gained in experience and are now a level 15 Trainee.

In disgust, I dismissed the Trials message. The spiders were hostile, yet the killing I had done in this room left a foul taste in my mouth.

Without a backward glance, I swung around and left. Wordlessly, Tara followed on my heels.

The others sensed our mood when we rejoined them, and silently fell into position. As we ventured deeper into the lair, I hoped that whatever else we encountered was nothing like the nursery.

Chapter Twenty-Six

390 DAYS UNTIL THE ARKON SHIELD FALLS

I got my wish, but not in the way I hoped.

Ten minutes after leaving the nursery, the five of us were stretched out flat on a ledge, staring down at our last obstacle to claiming the warren.

The central tunnel had continued its arrowlike path for another hundred yards before abruptly ending on a ledge overlooking an enormous cavern. Its gaping, empty space dwarfed the other chambers we had entered. Flat on our stomachs, it had taken minutes to carefully worm our way to the edge.

Our caution was not unwarranted.

The single occupant of the cavern was a creature from our worst nightmares—a mammoth spider.

I cast *analyze* on the monster a second time, hoping I had misinterpreted its information the first time.

The target is a level 50 brown spider queen. It has meager Magic, mediocre Resilience, exceptional Might, and low Craft.

The sleeping queen seemed unaware of us staring down on her from above. She was as large as a house—if not bigger. Each hairy brown limb was twice as large as me, and her flat torso could have accommodated all of us comfortably.

She looked impossible to defeat.

We must find a way. Somehow.

The warren couldn't be secured without the queen's death, and it was crucial that we claimed it—for more than just the Outpost's sake.

Everything I had told Tara earlier was true: if the warren stayed unclaimed, it would get stronger, and the population of brown spiders in the region would multiply.

Yet it also hadn't been the *whole* truth.

Claiming the lair, would also yield other benefits. A lair wasn't a dungeon, but I was betting—or hoping—that the Trials would reward us with Traits for being the first to clear the warren.

I couldn't walk away, no matter how difficult the task appeared. *This is what you wanted*, I told myself. *This is what you need to get stronger.* I had to take the risk. We had to face the queen in battle. *But how do we kill her?*

No matter how desperately I wished to slay the creature, it would do me no good if I could not come up with a viable plan. My thoughts raced.

Tara tapped me on the shoulder. Silently, she motioned me and the others back.

I grimaced, not wanting to go, but we couldn't talk here. An idea had already started to take shape in my mind. It was a madcap plan, to be sure, yet I was certain it could be made workable.

Tara led us back up the main tunnel, all the way to the nursery. "Okay, people, what the hell *was* that?"

Although she addressed the question to the party, it was to me she looked.

"That," I said slowly, "was the lair boss."

Her forehead furrowed. "Boss?"

"The final obstacle to us claiming the warren," I said, trying to explain the queen's nature in the best possible light. I paused, then added reluctantly, "The queen will be more difficult to overcome than the rest of the lair put together."

Tara snorted. "As if I couldn't tell that already." She shook her head. "Right, pack it in, people. It's time to get moving. We've come as far as we can." She began striding up the tunnel. "Let's report what we've found to the old lady."

The others followed her.

I didn't move. "Tara, wait," I called.

She turned around. Clearly reading my intentions from my face, she said through thinned lips, "I don't care what you say. There is no way we are fighting that thing."

I was silent for a long moment. "I think there's a way to kill her."

Laura laughed, but her amusement faded when no one else joined in. "He *is* kidding, isn't he?" she whispered to Michael.

He chuckled. "Somehow, I don't think so. He's batshit crazy, that one."

I winced at the spearman's description of me but didn't take my eyes off Tara.

The captain likewise ignored the two. "No." She folded her arms across her chest.

"Hear me out first," I pleaded.

"Did you not see it has magic?"

"I did. But I'm sure we can handle it."

Her foot began tapping. "Whatever hairbrained scheme you have up your sleeve, Jamie, I don't want to hear it. I will not let whatever madness drives you endanger all our lives. We—"

"I don't need help," I said abruptly, cutting off her tirade.

Tara's mouth closed with a snap.

"I will tackle the queen on my own." It would make things more difficult—nearly impossible, if I was being honest—but Tara appeared adamant in her refusal, and I would not walk away.

"And how are you going to do that, lad?" John chuckled. "That beastie there will swallow you in three bites or less."

I faced the lieutenant. "You're forgetting how I held back the murluks the first day, John. Thirty seconds," I said, staring at Tara. "For thirty seconds, I can ignore everything the queen will throw at me. That is time enough to kill her."

A hush fell over my companions, and when it was broken, it was by John, not Tara. "You seriously think you can do this?" he asked.

"Yes," I said, letting no hint of doubt weaken my voice. "I'm not suicidal," I added a moment later.

John guffawed. "Oh, but you are, my lad. You are. No man in his right mind would attempt what you're contemplating. But..." He shook his head. "If you really want to do this, all right."

Tara switched her glare from me to John. The big man folded his arms and did not back down.

"The boy has proven himself thrice over," he said quietly. "If he thinks he can do this, I believe him."

Tara's mouth worked soundlessly, like she wanted to dispute the lieutenant's words. Remarkably, she gave way to his level gaze. "Fine." She swung around on me. "But I want to hear your plan before we begin."

* * *

I spent the next two hours recovering and eating. Even though my mana pool had been about half-full, I didn't fancy taking any unnecessary chances.

"I am *not* suicidal," I muttered. Despite the impossibility of the task, I truly believed the spider queen could be slain. Yet... I worried about her magic—not that I could tell Tara that.

The only other magic user I had seen in action was the orc shaman back on Earth. If the queen's magic was anything like his, I was surely doomed.

Don't think like that, I admonished myself. I couldn't afford to let pessimism affect my thinking. If the battle looked unwinnable, I would retreat. Large as she was, there was no way the queen could pursue us once we escaped her cavern.

As long as I make the decision to retreat early enough, I will be fine, I assured myself. Gazing inward, I checked my reserves of energy. My stamina was fully restored and my mana was three-quarters full. *Right, time to do this.*

"I'm ready," I said, standing up.

The others looked up from where they waited. Each clasped my hand in encouragement. "Good luck, fish," Michael said, handing me his spear.

I nodded my thanks, and then turned to Tara, who looked like she had something to say.

"Are you sure about this, Jamie?" Her green eyes shone with concern, and her face was solemn.

"I have to do this," I said. "For the Outpost."

And Mom.

She weighed my words. Then, satisfied, swung around wordlessly and led the others a few paces off.

I watched them for a moment before turning to face the ledge. This was it. Stretching out flat on the tunnel floor, with the spear in my right hand, I crawled the last few yards to the ledge.

The plan called for the others to hang back for a minute before following. They had strict orders not to interfere until then. I could only hope they'd listen.

As I reached the edge, a Trials message floated into view.

Your skill in sneaking has advanced to level 1.

How nice, another Discipline. I smiled wryly. Moving with deliberate care, I peered down into the cavern. The queen squatted in the same position we had last seen her.

I exhaled in relief. *Good. No need to change the plan.* Rising silently to my feet, I took a few controlled breaths to clear my head. I was ready. Lifting the long spear, I held it over my head in a two-handed grip.

Then I leaped.

I plummeted straight down. Widening my eyes to stop them snapping shut from the air rushing by, I fixed them on my target.

Mid-fall, I activated *invincible*.

Near instantly, weaves erupted outward and a second skin of spirit shrouded my body. I waited a heartbeat longer. Then, almost at the end of my ten-foot-long plunge, I drove the spear downward.

As planned, its point made contact first.

Given impetus by gravity, the long spear plunged deep into the spider queen's thorax. With an audible crack, the tip broke through the monster's protective exoskeleton and kept going until more than half its length was lodged in the gargantuan creature.

A second later, I crashed into the spider queen's ridged back. I bounced, and if not for my white-knuckled grip on the spear's shaft, would have been flung off altogether. But I had been prepared for the violent impact and hung on. Barely.

An angry scream tore through the chamber.

Invincible did nothing to stop the sound from penetrating, and I fought the impulse to slap my hands over my ears.

The wisdom of that decision showed itself a moment later, when the behemoth under me erupted into life. Kicking her legs into motion, the spider queen spun about in a mad blur as she searched for her attacker.

My body was flung aloft.

Again, the spear anchored me and stopped me being tossed aside by the agitated queen's twirling. Grimly determined, I tightened my grip and prepared to ride out the storm. But after a few seconds, when the monster did not stop her crazed motion, I began to worry.

"Goddamn," I growled between gritted teeth, "when is she going to stop?"

With shocking abruptness, the spider queen stilled.

As soft as my voice had been, she had heard me. Realizing I had only a short window to implement the next stage of my plan, I yanked out the spear.

It drew free easily... until the spearpoint caught on the cracked edge of the queen's exoskeleton. Growling in frustration, I tugged at the weapon again. Any moment now, I expected the queen to burst into motion.

Fortune was finally with me. On my second pull, the spear wrenched free. I gasped in relief—then, without hesitation, I plunged my right hand into the queen. Ignoring the slime of the creature's innards, I shoved my arm as far as it would go, right up to my shoulder.

The monster beneath me trembled, about to spin into action again. Pressing my body flat against her back, I wrapped my left arm around one of the deep ridges lining her thorax.

Then, spreadeagled in position, I cast *flare*.

Predictably, that set the queen off. Her shriek shook the cavern as she beast roared into motion. This time, she dashed headfirst into the nearest cavern wall.

She's figured out where I am.

In a shower of loose rock and earth-shaking tremors, we made impact with the cavern wall. I winced as my left arm lost purchase and I was flung about. But my right hand was clasped firmly in place, and dragonfire continued to pour from it into the queen.

Anxiously, I checked my health, nearly crowing in exultation as I noticed it remained full.

I was right!

Invincible really did protect me from everything, including the health drain of *flare,* even though I was the source of the damage. The Technique was cannibalizing my own spirit to replenish my lost lifeblood. I had been right to place my trust in it.

Up until this point, I hadn't been certain it would actually work, but now I had a real chance of succeeding.

The queen reoriented herself. In the momentary respite, I refastened my left hand around her body. She set off again, charging toward the opposite wall.

Trying to dislodge me.

Once more, we slammed with bone-crushing force into hard rock. Again, I held on.

Despite the dizzying changes of direction and nausea-inducing deacceleration, I was pleased by the tactics the monster had chosen. The queen may not have realized it, but with her repeated attempts at bulldozing she was harming only herself.

I was protected by *invincible*. She not. And ever so slowly—more through her own efforts than mine—the queen's health drained away.

The colossus spun about and charged once more. I braced myself for impact with the far wall, but two steps into her headlong rush, the spider queen surprised me. She shot out threads from the spinnerets in her abdomen and anchored them to the cavern roof. Retracting the cord of glittering silk, she hoisted herself aloft.

On the way up, I glimpsed the party staring up from the ledge, awe and fear in their eyes.

They shouldn't be there, I thought. *Not yet. Why aren't they following the plan?*

Further thoughts of the party fled as the queen began her mad dance once more. Running upside down along the roof, she circled dizzily. Once. Twice. Her attempts left me rattled and shaken, but tenaciously I clung on.

You won't get rid of me like this!

As if in response to my thought, the fine hairs coating the queen's body retracted.

I frowned. *What are you up to now?*

The spider queen stilled. Then dropped.

Clever, I thought, realizing what she was attempting. It wouldn't work, of course. But the beast didn't know that.

We plunged to the cavern floor, landing in another bone-jarring collision. Darkness followed as the queen's weight crashed down on me. If not for *invincible*, the impact surely would have been fatal.

Instead, I was alive and still pouring dragonfire into the crazed creature while she tried to kill me. I flicked my eyes inwards and queried my Trials core. I still had more than ten seconds left on *invincible*. The spider queen had to be close to death by now.

This was a much easier fight than I expected. I smiled in satisfaction. *Soon it will be over.*

A moment ticked by, then another, and still the queen did not move.

Sickening dread coiled in the pit of my stomach as an unwelcome thought intruded. *She's trying to suffocate me.* What happens if I'm stuck under her when *invincible* runs out?

The queen moved, and relief gushed through me. *The fall probably dazed her.* Surging upward, she regained her feet. In preparation of her next wild maneuver, no doubt.

I didn't care. Whatever she did now wouldn't change the course of the battle. I had survived the worst the beast could throw at me.

This fight is won.

A moment later, the monster proved how wrong I was.

The queen didn't fly into motion as I'd expected. Instead, she remained locked in stillness while motes of dancing green rose from within her. Starting at her feet, they rippled upward and suffused her entire being.

I gulped. The queen had called upon her magic.

It did not take me long to figure out the intent of her spellcasting. As I watched, the many cuts and abrasions covering the monster's body began to close over.

Damn it, she is healing herself.

In my *magesight*, what had started as a slow dribble turned into a raging torrent as more emerald motes spun out of the beast and rushed to the source of her injuries. *Some sort of rapid regeneration.* Would it heal her fully?

If it did, this battle was lost.

I queried my Trials core again. I had only seconds left on *invincible*.

Time to cut my losses and flee? I glanced up. The safety of the ledge was too far away. With my foot slowing me down, I'd never make it.

All right, Jamie, you're going to have to see this through.

The queen broke charged into action again. To my immense relief, the motion signaled the end of her spell, and the dancing motes vanished.

But instead of spinning again, as I'd anticipated, the monster's limbs began to tremble and heave, thrusting large clods of dirt upward. She was digging, I realized.

Why is she digging?

Stuck in the middle of the spider's back, I was blind to her purpose, but I didn't dare leave my position to check.

Whatever she is doing, I can't let her finish.

My gaze darted to where my hands were fastened to her. Dragonfire continued to pour out unbated from both palms.

The queen's healing spell hadn't completely reversed all the damage I had inflicted, especially not where my flames burned the hottest. I could only imagine the damage my right hand—still plunged in the queen's innards—was doing, but the damage from my left hand was clear to see.

Where my dragonfire met the queen's skin, the hardened carapace had turned brittle and cracked.

It looks weak enough to smash through.

I didn't hesitate. Closing my hand into a fist, I smashed down. My arm plunged through more easily than expected.

The queen shuddered.

You felt that!

But she didn't stop digging. With both hands plunged into her body, I hoped *flare* would inflict even greater damage.

She couldn't sustain much more of this, surely. But I failed to convince myself. My niggling worry grew.

The protective spirit shroud around me flickered and died as *invincible* expired. I had been expecting it, but still... The vulnerability of my position grew more real as my health began to drain.

It's either you or me.

The moments ticked by, and the queen's furious scramble in the dirt never ceased. More worryingly, the creature didn't appear any closer to expiring.

I looked up, and with a start saw that we had already sunk below the surface of the cavern's floor.

Just how fast could the queen shovel dirt? And what was the meaning of all this digging? Was she trying to escape?

Dirt fell onto my head. I spat out the gritty grains of sand. The queen's hole was deep enough now that much of the upturned soil slid back in. Ducking my head against the falling shower of brown, I kept pouring flames into her.

As quickly as she'd begun, the queen stopped her frantic excavations. At the sudden silence, I raised my head. The queen was spinning, sending dozens of silk strands out in all directions, to the edges of the hole she had dug, and across.

My brows furrowed. *Cocooning yourself. Why?*

A second later, the entire space above was covered with glistening silver cloth, sagging down from the edges. Then the queen began to pulse.

Now what?

Throbs of blue light emanated from her core and rippled out in a wave.

What the—?

The light reached the boundary of the queen's skin and flowed along it. I glanced down as the blue glow passed beneath my body.

I recoiled in fear. *Another attempt to get rid of me?*

But my panic abated quickly. In the wake of the spell, I remained unaffected.

Yet the queen's skin had changed, hardened.

Whatever spell she was using, it was transforming her. Before my eyes, her dull brown carapace was turning to cold gray stone—a stone that looked disturbingly impervious to fire.

I glanced at my hands, still embedded in the queen. Were her insides turning to stone too? And would the spell make her immune to *flare?*

The urge to flee grew. The spider queen's cunning was greater than I expected.

I've lost, but maybe I can still escape.

Before I could withdraw my hands, the last thing I expected happened.

With a final, forlorn sigh, the queen's body crumpled inward. For a second, I could only stare uncomprehendingly.

Dead?

I couldn't believe it. But that could be the only explanation. Whatever spell the queen had been attempting, she had begun its casting too late. On the brink of disaster, I was victorious.

Pulling my hands out of her corpse, I rose shakily to my feet. Beneath me, the behemoth's lifeless form remained unmoving.

I've done it! It finally sank in. *I've won.*

I opened my mouth to roar out my triumph to the party, and nearly staggered right off as an avalanche of Trials alerts crashed through my vision.

> You have gained in experience and are now a level 18 Trainee. Your spellpower has increased to level 8.

> You are the first human player to have slain a creature champion on your own. Creature champions are monsters that have evolved to assume command of their brethren. For managing this task without the aid of your companions, you have earned the Feat: Lone Slayer, rank 1.
>
> At rank 1, Lone Slayer provides you with the *slayer's boon*, and *tenacious* Techniques.
>
> *Slayer's boon*: When fighting a creature champion on your own, you are blessed with an aura that increases your damage by 2%.
>
> *Tenacious*: When fighting a creature champion on your own, you are blessed with an aura that reduces the damage you take by 2%.

> Your party has vanquished the lair's occupants. Find the lair core and claim ownership of the warren. Your party is the first to have vanquished this lair. For this achievement, you have been awarded the Trait: Spider's Blood.
>
> Trait: Spider's Blood. Rank: 1, common. This Trait increases your resistance to all toxins by 10%.

> Your party is the seventh human party to clear a lair. This achievement has earned you the Feat: Lair Hunter, rank 1.
>
> At rank 1, Lair Hunter provides you with the *lair sense* Technique. *Lair sense* makes you aware of any lair within 10 yards of your location.

Stupefied, I collapsed back down on the queen in shock. *Well, you wanted rewards, Jamie. Now you have them.*

"Three levels, two Feats *and* a Trait," I murmured. It was much more than I'd expected, yet I couldn't help feeling a little disappointed. I had not been given what I had hoped for: a Trait that granted more Attributes.

You can always try finding another dungeon or lair.

I doubled over, overcome by mirth. Not even I was that crazy. My laughter faded as I gave the matter serious thought. *Well... perhaps I am.*

Lying backward, I stared up at the silk-speckled roof, considering the possibilities.

"Jamie! Jamie! Where are you?" shouted Tara.

"Down here with the queen," I called.

Casting *lay hands,* I healed myself before wearily rising again. I couldn't see the others. From the sounds of their voices I could tell they had climbed down the ledge and were in the cavern, but the sagging mass of silk blocked my view. Tentatively, I poked at the cocoon, which at its lowest point hung less than a foot above my head.

"How do we get through this stuff?" John shouted from the edge of the hole. "My spear can't pierce it."

"Give me a second," I said. Stepping gingerly over the queen's corpse, I made my way to the rim of the hole. "Stand back, I'm going to try burning through."

Casting *flare* again, I set my hands to the silk. The coils of silver dissipated immediately. Worried faces peered through the ragged hole.

"Need help?" Tara asked.

"I'll live," I said with a chuckle, grasping the muscular arm John shoved at me. He pulled me out with little effort. "Thanks, John." I dusted away clinging strands of web.

"I can't believe you did it, you bugger," he remarked.

I gave him a lopsided grin. "Me neither."

Tara gazed down the hole. "What was the queen doing, there at the end? We saw blue light streaming outward."

"I'm honestly not sure," I replied. "It was like she was trying to encase herself in a protective shell."

"Doesn't matter now, whatever it was," said John, clapping me on the shoulder. "The lair is ours!"

"Not yet." I shook my head. "We still have to find the lair core."

"This must be it," said Laura from behind.

I turned to see her and Michael walking up to join us. Laura was clutching an egg-shaped object with a luminous blue sheen.

"The moment I touched it, I got a message from the Trials," she said. "It asked if I wanted to claim the lair." She smiled. "But it didn't seem right for me to. That honor belongs to you." She held the lair core out to me.

I glanced at John and Tara. "Go on, take it," Tara said.

Nodding, I took the glowing egg from Laura.

You have acquired a Brown Spider Warren lair core. If unclaimed, the warren and core will be destroyed in 1 hour. Do you wish to claim the lair and become its settlement liaison?

Warning: You are not a resident of any settlement. Lairs can only be owned by a settlement. To retain this lair after claiming it, you must become a settlement resident within 4 days.

I studied the Trials' message quizzically. "Did you receive the warning too?" I asked Laura.

She nodded.

I pursed my lips as I considered the implications. I hadn't known it was necessary to be a resident of a settlement to claim a lair, but that only made the need to establish the Outpost more urgent. And then there was the part about 'settlement liaison.' I turned the core over in my hands, hesitating.

"What's wrong?" asked Tara.

I shoved the core into her hands. "You do it."

She looked at me blankly. "Why?"

I shook my head, not wanting to explain. What I didn't say was that I hadn't made up my mind about becoming a resident of the Outpost. I knew from the Infopedia that residency—like citizenship—was no simple matter.

Becoming a resident bound a player to a settlement *and* its leadership. I didn't know Jolin well enough to be comfortable placing myself under her thumb.

Breaking any binding oath of service in the Trials came at a cost. Joining or leaving settlements was not something to do arbitrarily. There were consequences.

What the consequences would be for the Outpost, I didn't know. Each settlement was different. But it didn't seem wise to take the risk.

Better not to be bound in the first place...

I continued to hold the core out, insistent that Tara take it.

"Fine," she said. Closing her eyes, she interacted with the core.

I watched keenly. Seconds later, the core disappeared from Tara's hands, and she opened her eyes.

"What happened?" I asked.

"It's done," Tara replied. "The core has returned to its place in the lair." She looked at me. "And in four days, if we still haven't formed the Outpost into a settlement, or if the core is found and claimed by another, we'll lose ownership of the lair."

John looked thoughtful. "The commander will have to post a guard here."

I nodded, then noticed Tara was still gazing inward. "Something wrong?"

"I got a new Trait," she said, surprise coloring her voice.

I bit back a spurt of envy. "Oh?"

"Spider Captain," replied Tara, her eyes unseeing as she read the Trait description. "The Trait changes the attitude of *all* brown spiders toward me to neutral—whether of this lair or not."

"Wow," said Michael. "That's useful."

I nodded. It certainly was. And Tara deserved it. I looked down on the queen's corpse and the wealth of silk spun across the hole.

Overworld, Book 1 of the Dragon Mage Saga

"Now," I murmured, "how do we take all this back with us?"

CHAPTER TWENTY-SEVEN

390 DAYS UNTIL THE ARKON SHIELD FALLS
4 DAYS UNTIL THE WARREN IS DESTROYED

Removing the queen's body from the lair was impossible without cutting it up, and none of us had bladed weapons suitable for the task.

After burning free the silk cloth covering the hole, I climbed back down and used *flare* to burn the queen's body into smaller parts. The spell the queen had attempted in her dying moments had dissipated with her death, and while my task was backbreaking, it was not inordinately difficult.

It was gruesome and bloody work, but necessary. The Outpost desperately needed resources. The queen's hardened hide alone was worth the effort, and that wasn't counting the silk and other toxins we harvested from her corpse. By the end, Michael and I were drenched in ichor and gore.

It took hours, but finally we were done. I looked ruefully at my blood-soaked clothes and armor, sure I would never wear any of it again. Our grisly work, however, was not without benefits.

You have uncovered a brown spider queen's Technique: *paralyzing bite*. Your skill in anatomy has advanced to level 3.

You have uncovered a brown spider queen's Technique: *transformation chrysalis*. Your skill in anatomy has advanced to level 4.

You have the discovered a champion core. The special properties of this item are unknown. Your lore skill is insufficient.

Transformation chrysalis? I eyed the Trials message speculatively. So that was what the queen was attempting. But transform into what? I suspected that it was good we never got to find out.

I looked down at the object in my hands. The champion core was no larger than my fist, and after being scrubbed clean, it resembled a large diamond. It looked quite unlike the lair's core. I turned the crystalized object over in my hands. I had seen no mention of champion cores in the wiki. I hadn't even known they existed.

I pursed my lips in thought. While I didn't know what purpose the cores served, I could guess. The Trials had to have a means of controlling lairs and their bosses. Looking at the core, I thought I had figured out how.

An unpleasant thought made me shiver.

Was the Trials core in my head similar too? Could *I* also be controlled by the Trials? I didn't think so. I could see no reason the Trials would want to control players, not after going through all the trouble of giving them such freedom of choice. *But I can't be certain,* I thought, disturbed anew.

Raised voices—lots of them—caught my attention. I stilled, listening intently. Tara, John, and Laura were in the tunnels above, transferring our spoils to the sleds outside. They had company. Friendly company, by the sounds of it.

"This way," I heard Tara say. "They're back here."

"I still can't believe you cleared the lair," replied whoever accompanied her. "They are supposed to be—" The voice broke off and fell into a stunned silence.

"Good God! What is *that*?" asked another.

Looking up, I saw a blond head appear over the hole. It was Captain Marcus. I smiled. The commander had finally sent help.

* * *

Marcus had two dozen players with him and, thankfully, many more sleds. There was no way we could have transported everything we'd harvested from the warren back to the Outpost without them.

We got all the sleds loaded and moving before nightfall. Four men—miserable about drawing the short straw—were left behind to guard the lair.

I couldn't help but feel sorry for them. They would be the first players from the Outpost to spend a night outside the camp, and were clearly afraid. But Marcus and Tara were certain the men would be safe within the lair, and I couldn't argue with the need to guard the area.

After scraping off the worst of the filth and grime covering my armor, I took a last long look at the queen's cavern. It turned out that the queen had not been lying idle all the time she was in the cavern. She had been laying eggs.

In small, neatly dug shafts beneath the place the queen had occupied, Laura had found thousands of glistening, pale-yellow orbs.

Many were still unbroken. Marcus and I agreed it was best to leave them undisturbed, in the hope that once the settlement's claim to the warren was cemented, the newborn spiders would be friendly, or, better yet, allies.

* * *

The journey back to the Outpost felt much longer than the one to reach the lair.

Marcus just would not stop talking.

The blond captain was an enthusiastic gamer who had entered Overworld early on. Although he had known of the existence of the Trials Infopedia, Marcus hadn't taken the time to study it. Choosing to be a pioneer, he had faith that his ability as a 'pro gamer'—his term, not mine—would help him figure things out as he went along.

To his credit, he had since come to regret that decision. After arriving on Overworld, he'd sought out and interrogated all those who had read the Infopedia.

In this case, me.

Marcus believed he had struck gold in me. No one else in the Outpost had studied the wiki to the extent I had. During our two-hour trip back to camp, the captain did his best to wring every useful piece of information from me.

I was happy to share what I knew, but his questions grew tiresome. Finally, as we crossed the open trenches of the Outpost, I pleaded exhaustion and fled.

The others were splitting up, each heading to their own tent or chores. My gaze rested on Laura. I had not forgotten my wider plans, and the hunters were the most suited to aid me.

"Laura, hold up a sec," I called before she disappeared. She paused in her steps and swung around to face me. I limped to her side. "I meant to ask you earlier but didn't get a chance: how much of the surrounding area have you hunters scouted?"

"To the east and south, we have explored everything within a day's journey. To the north, our scouting ended at the foothills. No one has been foolish enough to attempt crossing the river to the west yet." She gave me a quizzical look. "Why?"

"The proximity of the warren to the Outpost has made me question the positioning of the gate exit locations. Perhaps they aren't random after all. Perhaps each is carefully chosen by the Trials and the area around appropriately seeded. If we found one resource nearby, there may be others too."

Laura nodded, following my reasoning. "What are you looking for?"

"An obelisk," I answered promptly. "Made of obsidian, about twenty feet tall, and covered in glowing runes. It should be impossible to miss."

"It certainly sounds that way," Laura agreed. "What is it?"

"The entrance to a dungeon." Most dungeons in Overworld were supposed to be clearly marked and easy to find, deliberately. There were hidden ones, disguised in the far reaches of the Dominions, but I couldn't expect to find any of those yet.

"Hmm," said Laura. "I won't pretend to know what that is, and I haven't come across anything like you've described myself, but..." She looked away, frowning in thought. "I remember one of the other scouts mentioning an artifact like that." Laura turned back to me. "Let me ask around."

"Thanks. Please, let me know the moment you find out anything. It's important."

She nodded agreeably before striding off.

Tara caught up to me. Watching Laura's departing figure, she asked, "What was that about?"

I shrugged. "A hunch. There may be other resources nearby that we can exploit. I've asked her to find out what she can."

Tara stared at me. "Our experience in the warren was bad enough. Please tell me you're not hoping to find another lair?"

I remained silent. A dungeon, I imagined, would be an even harder challenge. But I didn't think it was the time to tell Tara that.

Her expression twisted, seeming to take my silence to mean she had guessed right. But she let the matter lie, just shaking her head at my folly before turning to other concerns. "Anyhow, I came to tell you the commander's conference starts in an hour." She wrinkled her nose. "You should clean up before then. I'll have someone bring fresh clothes to your tent."

"Oh?" I said. "I thought we would have missed it. Wasn't it supposed to have happened in the afternoon?" The skies had darkened, and night had fallen.

"The old lady postponed it when Cass brought news of our find." She fixed me with a mock glare. "You've already delayed the meeting once. Try not to be late the second time."

* * *

Before heading to my tent, I stopped by the temple.

The day's venture had been wildly profitable. Aside from the spoils, Traits, and Feats I had earned, I had advanced six player levels—far more than expected.

My speedy return would not please Aurora, but there was no helping that. I maintained my earlier conservative approach, spending my Marks and Tokens only where essential. It kept my time in the temple to a minimum, although that didn't lessen Aurora's ire as much as I'd hoped.

As I limped out of the temple, I read and dismissed the Trials message confirming my changes.

Your constitution, vigor, and channeling have increased to level 18.
Your skill in dragon and life magic has advanced to level 18.
Marks remaining: 14. Tokens remaining: 141.

I frowned. Keeping three different Attributes maxed was fast draining my surplus of Marks.

I had to find another source of Marks soon, not only to keep my health, mana, and constitution increasing, but also to invest in my other, much-ignored Attributes.

A problem for another day, I told myself as I entered the camp.

Inside my tent, I bathed quickly. Tara, bless her, had managed to get a tub hauled in. It was cold, but still a luxury. After changing into new clothes, I hurried to the commander's tent.

I was still late.

Outside, Tara was tapping her foot impatiently. "Finally! I was just about to send someone looking for you. Come on in. They're waiting."

She ducked inside and I followed her without protest.

The tent was crowded. Besides Jolin, Petrov, and Marcus, four others were crammed in: two men and two women. The strangers did not wear armor, which I took to mean they were non-combatants—crafters.

The commander's gaze flicked our way. "Good, we're all here now. Tara, Jamie, take a seat please. I will spare us all the introductions. We have much to go through tonight." Her eyes met mine briefly. "Doubly so, after Jamie's latest adventure."

In the midst of taking my seat, I paused. Jolin's glance had been indecipherable. Yet there was a hint of something—*concern perhaps?*—in her scrutiny. I shot a look at Tara, wondering what she had reported to the old lady. *Probably everything.*

"Before we dive into the details," the commander continued, "Petrov, please present your report on the state of our defenses."

"Yes, ma'am." Petrov's voice was a dull rumble. "Our forces stand at one thousand, two hundred and sixty-five. Two hundred and thirty-two are experienced fighters above level twenty, about six hundred are new fish below level ten, and the remainder fall somewhere in between."

I winced at the numbers. Half of the commander's fighting force were raw recruits. For those ratios to hold true, the Outpost's daily losses had to be high.

"How many new arrivals today?" asked one of the male crafters.

Petrov consulted his notes. "Eighty-two that survived."

A blond crafter gasped. "Why so few?" she asked. "That's a sharp drop. Were our losses from this morning's battle that bad?"

Petrov shook his head. "The reverse, actually," he said, darting a look in my direction. "Thanks to our mage, the murluks barely scratched us today."

"Why the drop?" asked a brown-haired man, his tone tinged with worry. "And what do we do about it? Without a steady supply of recruits from Earth, we're doomed. We all know that."

The other crafters nodded in agreement.

Petrov opened his mouth to reply, but the commander waved him to silence. "The number of new players entering from Earth has been dropping," she said, fielding the question herself. "We have known that for some time." Her expression turned grim. "I expect recruits to drop even further over the next few days. There is nothing we can do to control who enters the gate and when. We must assume the worst." She met each of her subordinate's eyes in turn. "I expect all of you to plan accordingly."

Silence fell in the wake of Jolin's pronouncement. The commander let it draw out for a moment before continuing, "Thank, you, Petrov. Marcus, proceed with your report please."

The slim, neatly attired gamer stood up. "Our complement of hunters and scouts stands at sixty-five." His lips thinned. "We lost four more in the forest today. As near as the recovery teams could tell, both pairs were killed by a quadrupedal predator. This is the third loss we've suffered from these predators in the forest in as many days." He paused. "But no one has caught sight of the beast yet."

No one living, he meant. I rubbed at the goosebumps that formed on my arms. *The forest sounds even worse than the foothills.* I was glad my party had headed north today.

Marcus' eyes roved over the assembled men and women. "Once more, please urge your people to volunteer for scout duty. I know many are afraid to venture beyond the safety of the camp, but we need more scouts." Marcus was openly pleading with his fellows now, the desperation in his voice undisguised.

The others shifted uncomfortably and looked away. "Please," he begged, "we can't secure the region otherwise."

Jolin placed a hand on his arm, and the captain inhaled to calm himself. "On a more promising note," he continued, "the foothills to the north have been cleared." He nodded at Tara and me. "I'm sure Tara will have more to add on that." He sat back down.

"Thank you, Marcus," the commander said. "The scouting situation is grave. Please heed Marcus' call, people." Jolin turned to the first of the crafters. "Soren, your report, please."

A sturdily built brunette man, with large calloused hands, stood up and began without preamble, "Work on the palisade is progressing steadily." He nodded to the three captains. "With the soldiers stopping the murluks from destroying our earthworks, construction on the west-facing wall has advanced smoothly. I expect the first phase of the riverside palisade to be completed tomorrow."

A sigh of relief ran through the tent.

"Phase one?" I whispered, leaning closer to Tara.

"Erecting the wooden fence," Tara whispered back. "On their own, the walls should be enough to keep the murluks out, but the commander wants the walls to be more than a deterrent. She wants our men to patrol atop them, and she wants guard towers, fortified gates, murder holes, and the like. For all that to happen, the walls need to be reinforced. That's the second phase: adding brickwork."

I nodded thoughtfully. The old lady was thinking ahead. If she managed to implement her vision, I imagined the Outpost would become a formidable settlement indeed. Realizing that Soren was still speaking, I turned my attention back to him.

"... but progress on other sections of the wall is not going as well. While the trenchwork is complete, we don't have enough timber to surround the entire settlement."

Soren sat down. Not waiting for the commander's go-ahead, the other male crafter leaped to his feet. "I sympathize with Soren's concerns, I really do," he said. "But you all know the conditions we're working in. Until my people get better saws, axes, shovels, and so on, logging cannot proceed any faster. My men are working as fast as they can, but we need better tools!" He slumped down in a huff, crossing his arms over his chest.

"Thank you, Albert." The commander's voice was even, neither rising in response to the crafter's challenge nor ignoring it. "We understand the limitations your men are working under. The soldiers are likewise incapacitated. Your people are to be commended for their efforts thus far."

Albert grunted in acknowledgement, and Jolin turned to one of the women. "Melissa, what is the progress from our smiths?"

"Slow." The woman sighed. "We're still struggling to get the forge going. Until we do, we can't create any of the tools we need."

"So still no luck melting the murluk spearheads?" Marcus asked.

Melissa shook her head. "None. We've tried everything. But my people haven't given up. We're still trying."

Jolin's lips tightened. It was the most concern I had seen her display in the meeting so far. "See that your people keep at it, Melissa," she said softly. "We need those tools."

Melissa ducked her head. "Yes, ma'am."

Jolin turned to the last woman. "Beth, we'll skip your report for today. Things are progressing well on the food front, at least."

Beth nodded, and the old lady turned her attention to the room at large, letting her eyes rest on each of her subordinates in turn. "So, now you all know our woes," Jolin said. "I know it's tough, people. I know there are challenges, some seeming impossible." Her eyes hardened. "But no more excuses. We are running out of time. If we don't want what we've built here to slip through our fingers, we *must* find solutions. Get creative, people."

Albert shot to his feet, his mouth open to protest.

"Sit down, Albert," Jolin said. Her tone was mild, but there was no mistaking the steel behind it.

Albert sat, his face reddening.

"Now," continued the commander, "I believe we have one additional deadline. Tara, will you?"

"Yes, ma'am," Tara said, rising up. "Through Jamie's efforts, we've cleared the warren of brown spiders in the foothills. The Trials have classified the warren as a lair, which Jamie and Marcus tell me is a good thing. Once we've bound the lair to the Outpost, the tame spiders birthed in it will be ours to command."

A murmur of surprise rippled through the room.

"There is a catch," Tara said. "To retain ownership of the lair, we must establish the Outpost as a settlement within four days."

"Impossible!" Albert exploded, but at glance from the commander he shrank back in his seat.

"The lair is an invaluable resource," said the commander. "And it has fallen into our lap thanks to the good work of Jamie, Tara, and their team. We dare not lose it. We *will* make that timeline."

This time, no one protested the impossibility of the task. "What do we need to establish the settlement, Marcus?" Jolin asked.

Marcus began ticking off points on his fingers. "One: a population greater than one thousand. As of today, with combatants and non-combatants, we are sitting at just under two thousand. We meet that requirement comfortably."

"Good," replied the old lady. "Next."

"Two: a guard complement of one hundred at the Trainee rank. Another requirement we easily fulfil. Three: food stores sufficient for one week. Also, check. Fourth and most problematically: controlling access into and out of the settlement."

"Which means finishing the palisade," said the commander.

"Which means finishing the wall," agreed Marcus.

Jolin closed her eyes in thought. A moment later, she opened them. "Logging is now our top priority," she announced. "Albert, Melissa, drop everything else. I want you two to go away tonight and come up with a plan."

Albert opened his mouth, but Jolin held up her hand. "I am not finished. Albert, you may conscript whoever you need from the other crafters. Beth's people, especially, can be spared right now. Melissa's too."

"I still want a few people working on the forge," Melissa spoke up.

"Yes, but no more than a handful." The commander turned back to the logger. "Will that suffice, Albert?"

Albert's eyes narrowed. "What about the soldiers? Can I draw from their ranks too?"

Jolin shook her head. "No, you cannot. The murluks remain a threat. Until the wall is up, the spearmen are our sole defense. I will not weaken our forces on the river."

She made no mention of me, I noticed.

Albert scowled and muttered under his breath, but he didn't argue.

Satisfied with his response, Jolin added, "Very well, that's settled. Albert, Melissa, I expect to hear your plan tomorrow. Understood?"

They looked visibly unhappy, but they knew better than to protest. Reluctantly, they nodded their agreement.

"Good, then you are all dismissed. Jamie, stay awhile please."

* * *

Jolin waited for the others to leave before turning to me.

"You keep surprising me," she said, waggling a finger at me. "Tara told me of your fight against the queen. I must say, I'm impressed and... disturbed. Once again, you've accomplished a seeming impossibility. Thank you."

I shrugged, uncomfortable with the praise. "Just doing what needs doing, ma'am."

She smiled. "Oh, but I think it's more than that." She withdrew something from her pocket and held it out to me. "Do you know what purpose this serves?"

I looked at the object. It was the champion core from the spider queen. "No. I do have a few guesses, though. Nothing certain just yet. But whatever the core's purpose, I am sure it is both valuable and important."

"Marcus said the same," mused the old lady. She set the core on the table. After walking to the tent opening, she stared out into the night. "I doubt I'll ever understand how this world works, Jamie. How beasts like that spider queen can exist, or what that stone is, or even how humanity landed up here." She shook her head. "It's all beyond me." The commander swung around and held my gaze. "But it is not beyond you."

"You do yourself a disservice, ma'am. I may understand aspects of this world better from my... uh, gaming experiences... but you have done all right. More than all right, to be honest. All these people would be lost without you. They need you."

The commander smiled. "Thank you for that, Jamie. And you are right, they do need me. For now. But only for now. Their future will be in the hands of people like you, Jamie. People like Marcus. People who understand this world better."

"That is not a burden I wish to bear, ma'am," I said softly.

Sadness shone through the commander's eyes. "It is not a matter of choice, Jamie. You will learn that one day."

I knew where this conversation was leading, and I knew what Jolin wanted. I stayed stubbornly silent. What she wanted wasn't in me to give. I had my own mission. Someone else would have to protect the Outpost.

"You know what I am going to ask of you, don't you?"

"I can't stay, ma'am."

Her eyes narrowed. "That is not true, Jamie." Her voice thickened with disappointment. "You can. But you won't." Sighing, she turned away. "Go. You're dismissed. And take the core with you. It's yours by right."

I shuffled uncomfortably, shocked by her abrupt dismissal and unaccountably ashamed.

She asks too much! I struggled to hold to my anger, but my heart wasn't in it.

Saying nothing, I grabbed the core and made my escape.

CHAPTER TWENTY-EIGHT

390 DAYS UNTIL THE ARKON SHIELD FALLS

I ducked into my tent, my emotions in turmoil. For a long time, I sat alone in the darkness, staring at nothing.

I had been elated by our successes today. I'd felt that I had accomplished something good, both for my cause and for the people here. And while the conference had underscored how desperate the Outpost's situation was, it hadn't detracted from what and the others and I had achieved.

The commander, though... her words had spoiled all that. In her eyes, I was obstinate. Willful. Wayward. But I wasn't. *Was I?*

I knew what Jolin wanted. She'd have me bind myself to the Outpost and sacrifice myself—as she had—for the people here. But I couldn't. I had my own cause. An *important* cause. I couldn't take up hers.

"Who does she think she is?" I growled. "Why can't she be satisfied with what I'm willing to give?" I had promised to stay until the settlement was established. It was still a promise I intended to keep. But after that?

I would leave. I had to.

How dare she try to shame me into staying. I had made it clear from the beginning that I wouldn't join the Outpost. Her people were not my responsibility. Leaving didn't equate to abandoning them. They were not mine to begin with. Their fate was not my burden to bear. It was unfair of Jolin to ask that of me.

But was it?

What's the right choice here? To stay and build the Outpost into something more, into a new home for humanity? Or to seek vengeance?

Is vengeance ever the right choice?

I rubbed my face with my hands, feeling my purpose waver. In spite of myself, I felt swayed by the commander and her demands.

It was a seductive proposition—to join the Outpost, put down roots. To grow the settlement with Jolin, Tara...

No. I couldn't let myself forget why I was here. "Vengeance," I whispered. "I live only for vengeance."

Yet even to my ears, my conviction was weak. Bowing my head, I rocked back and forth, as memories of my last moments on Earth resurfaced. Mom's death, perfectly preserved in the deepest recesses of my psyche, replayed in my mind.

Tears wet my face as I relived the moment. *Oh, Mom, I miss you.* Then the grief burned away, and horror dug its claws into me once more. Hate flooded me. Rage consumed me. And finally, my thirst was rekindled. Thirst for orc blood.

I remembered now. I remembered who I was. *Why* I was.

I sealed away the horrific memories, burying them deep once more. They had served their purpose. Clarity had returned.

I knew what I had to do.

I could do good in the Outpost. I could get strong, do right by the commander and her people. Especially now, when they were beset on all sides. But after that? Once the settlement was established, they wouldn't need me.

And I wouldn't need them.

Staying indefinitely would only hold me back. The right course would be to leave. I was certain of it.

I pursued vengeance, but it wasn't just revenge I craved. My hatred had purpose. A purpose that advanced humanity's cause. The orcs were mankind's enemy. They had to be opposed or what little remained of humanity would be under their boots.

Taking the battle to the orcs might not be the right thing for the Outpost now—but it was the right thing to do. I had to believe that. This settlement, however strong, could not stand against the tide of orcs that would one day descend.

My purpose wasn't to protect, but to avenge.

For Mom. For all of us.

* * *

"Jamie! Are you in there?"

My eyes flew open at the sound of Tara's voice. I groaned and sat upright. What time was it? Light streamed in through the tent. *Morning, by the looks of it.*

"Jamie?"

"I'm here," I rasped. I licked my chapped lips. "Coming," I called, louder this time. Laboring upright, I limped out of the tent, shielding my eyes from the morning sun.

"You don't look so good," said Tara, hands on hips, "but come on. We're already late."

"Late?" I asked, still befuddled by sleep. "What for?"

"The murluk attack."

My mind snapped into focus. "Right, let's go."

We silently made our way out of the camp. The doubts I had wrestled with last night still clouded my thoughts, and I felt little desire to engage in conversation.

As we neared the river, I nearly stopped short. Along the top of the upper bank, large tree-trunk beams had been implanted in the earthworks. Soren had been right last night, I mused. They had made good progress.

But the palisade was still incomplete, and gaps still dotted its length. If we didn't hold back the murluks today, all their work would go to waste.

We slipped through the half-built palisade and, standing on the edge of the upper bank, surveyed the scene below. Spearmen were neatly arrayed along the shore, with Jolin at their back. Catching sight of her, bitterness swelled within me.

I swallowed it back. Now was not the time.

"Strange," murmured Tara. She squinted up at the sun. "They're late." Not waiting for my response, she leapt down the bank, stopping when she saw I hadn't moved. "Hurry, Jamie," she called.

I didn't look at her. I was recalling last night's conference: Petrov's report, Soren's troubles, and Melissa's failures. There was so much to be done to secure the settlement. *Three more days*, I mused. It was not nearly enough time.

My eyes moved from the incomplete wall to the lines of spearmen. More than a thousand soldiers—the bulk of the Outpost's manpower—were bogged down here, defending the river. The murluks were a distraction, I realized. All these men could be better used elsewhere.

I didn't agree with everything Jolin had said last night, but she was right about one thing: the time for half-measures had passed. Coming to a decision, I stepped forward.

"Tara," I called as I slid down the bank. "Have the commander pull the spearmen back all the way to the top of the upper bank." Reaching Tara's side, I outlined the rest of my plan.

"That's a damned fool idea," she said, throwing up her hands in disgust. "But I'm tired of telling you no. Go pitch your idea to the old lady. She can be the one to deny you this time."

"You're going to have to explain it to her."

"What?" she asked. "Why?"

"The murluks might appear at any moment. I have to get to the shoreline." While that was true, it wasn't the real reason I sent her in my stead. I didn't feel up to facing the commander just yet.

I limped past a staring Tara. "Go, Tara," I snapped.

She went.

* * *

Ten minutes later, I was sitting cross-legged in the mud and gently lapping waves of the river. I was the only human along the entire expanse of the lower banks.

I had feared the commander would deny my request or the murluks would attack before the spearmen could reposition. But neither of those things occurred.

Jolin shifted her men with such speed that I wondered whether she had known what I would do all along. But that was impossible. The idea hadn't even occurred to me until a few minutes ago.

Now, alone on the shore, I wondered whether we had gone to all this trouble for naught. The murluks had still not shown up.

Are they even going to attack today?

My plan was simple. I was bait. It had worked the first day, when I saved the right flank, and I hoped it would work today on a much larger scale. This time, I had dragonfire to call upon, and I wouldn't need the spearmen to rescue me.

It was a reckless plan. But no more foolish than attacking the spider queen, I thought with a wry smile. And the commander had agreed to it. So, it had to have *some* merit.

A splash pulled my attention back to the river. The first murluk had surfaced, and many more followed behind him. I got to my feet.

When they saw me alone on the shore, the murluks paused., but they didn't hop forward eagerly as I'd expected. They appeared tentative... almost afraid. Crowding within the safety of deep water, they slurped hesitantly at one another.

I frowned. Did they remember yesterday's battle? Had it made them wary? It was certainly possible. After all, they were smart enough to construct primitive weapons and armor.

What do we really know of the creatures? Why do they only attack in the morning? For that matter, why do they attack at all? And where do they come from?

I shook my head. All good questions, but meaningless right now. I couldn't let the battle be drawn out. One way or the other, I had to end it quickly. Wading a few steps into the river, I raised my hands and prepared to *flare*.

Although they were well out of my reach, the murluks shrank back. *Ah!* I halted my spellcasting. *So they do remember.* Many of the creatures dove back into the river, and for a second I dared to hope it meant an end to the day's hostilities.

But not all the murluks fled.

For every two that retreated, one surged forward. Perhaps, they were emboldened by the fact that I was unaccompanied. My pulse quickened. A thousand murluks—if not more—converged on me.

My palms grew sweaty. Even expecting such numbers, I was hard-pressed not to flee. *The numbers don't matter,* I told myself. *You're ready.*

And I was.

Holding my nerve, I backstepped out of the river onto firm ground. The first wave of murluks closed to within a few yards. I lowered my hands and let them approach unmolested.

It was hard.

The temptation to *flare,* to burn away my attackers, was nearly too great to ignore, but I held to my plan.

Now that the murluks had made up their minds to attack, I didn't want to scare them off too early. First, I had to draw in as many as possible. The murluks reached me. Before their spears touched me, I cast *invincible.*

Then I threw a punch.

Though it was weak and poorly directed, the blow landed, even as *invincible* turned away the murluk's resultant spear jab.

Your skill in unarmed combat has advanced to level 1.

I grinned at the Trials message, my tension draining away. With fresh confidence, I threw another punch, ignoring the forest of murluk spears thrust my way.

Alone and without magic, I was a tempting target. More murluks leaped toward me—jabbing, thrusting, and pulling. Under the weight of their numbers, I toppled over. But even buried under a horde of blue, I was not worried.

It was part of my plan, after all.

Instead, I fixated on my Trials core. When the timer on *invincible* hit fifteen seconds, I acted.

Through my hands, which I had been careful to keep facing outward, I cast *flare.* The murluks recoiled, but they were packed too tightly to dodge the flames.

They burned. In ones and twos, and then in dozens.

As the weight crushing me eased, I spread my arms wider, incinerating hundreds.

Too late, the murluks realized they had been baited. Those that could, fled, reversing the tide of creatures flowing from the river.

I jumped to my feet and followed. Shoes squelching through mud, bone, and charred remains, I limped after the murluks. My peripheral vision revealed that none of the creatures had advanced beyond me to the ranks of spearmen on the upper bank.

But although the murluk attack had been thwarted, I did not let up with *flare*. The more creatures I slaughtered, the more today's disaster would be burned into their psyche. *Hopefully, it will forestall future attacks.*

I pursued the creatures right to the water's edge, casting *flare* to the very limit of my reach. Murluks, slid, fell, and shrieked in agony as they struggled to escape.

I did not relent.

Mercilessly, I burned every creature in reach, leaving ash drifting in my wake. A minute later, my task was complete.

All the murluks had fled. A hush fell over the river. Turning, I saw the lines of spearmen gaping in stunned silence from above.

I began limping back to them.

The commander raised her hand, and the air resounded with a roar as the spearmen cheered my victory.

CHAPTER TWENTY-NINE

389 DAYS UNTIL THE ARKON SHIELD FALLS
3 DAYS TO EARTH'S DESTRUCTION
3 DAYS UNTIL THE WARREN IS DESTROYED

Tara met me on the lower riverbank. "Good job, Jamie," she said quietly.

I nodded, not breaking stride. I was trying hard not to think of the slaughter. Once again, the Trials had rewarded me, and I had gained another level from the death I had dealt.

You have gained in experience and are now a level 19 Trainee.

"The old lady wants to see you," Tara said.

Involuntarily, I glanced at the upper slope of the riverbank. Jolin and her guard were nowhere in sight, and the spearmen were dispersing, some heading to the training ground while others, jogging in formation, headed east. I hoped that meant the commander had sent them to aid the loggers.

"Later." I waved away Tara's words. I knew it hadn't been a request, but I didn't care. "That crafter from yesterday's conference," I said. "I want to go see her."

"Who? Melissa?"

"Yes, that's right."

Tara said nothing for so long that I thought she would refuse. "This way," she replied eventually.

We climbed the riverbank in silence, lost in our own thoughts. Today's battle had finished even quicker than yesterday's. I could scarce believe it was less than an hour since I had descended to the river.

As we neared our destination, Tara finally spoke up. "Why do you want to see Melissa?"

I didn't answer. I didn't think Tara would understand. My excursion to the crafting yard was partly an excuse to hide from the commander and from her soldiers' adulation. The tribute the spearmen had paid me at the end of the battle had caught me by surprise. Their praise was heartfelt, and it had felt good to hear it, but it also made me feel guilty.

Today, the spearmen had lost none of their comrades. My magic had spared them. But when I left, they would start dying again. I knew I couldn't save them all, even if I stayed. It didn't stop me from feeling responsible, though.

Was that what Jolin intended? Had she ordered her troops to salute me, knowing it would make me feel this way?

Escaping the commander's manipulations wasn't the only reason I wanted to see the crafters. There was something else I had in mind.

The crafting yard was mostly deserted. Those who were present were already hard at work when we stepped into the yard.

Tara led me to the center of the camp, where I spotted Melissa and two other men near a misshapen clay oven.

No, not an oven, I realized, remembering Melissa's words from the conference. *A furnace.*

One of the men, wearing oversized hide gloves, used two wooden poles to pull out a clay pot and set it on a table.

The three huddled over the contents, inspecting them.

"Damn it," growled Melissa. "We've failed again."

"Maybe we need more coal," said one of them men.

"It ain't the coal." The other spat to the side in disgust. "It's the blasted furnace. It's not good enough."

The first man scratched his head. "What else is there left to try?" His companions didn't answer, all three falling silent as they pondered their options

I examined the furnace as we drew closer. It was a simple conical construction of clay and mud. A chimney belched black smoke out of the top. Unlike everything else in the Outpost, the furnace looked well-fashioned, if rudimentary.

Melissa looked up and caught sight of us. "Tara," she said, surprise clear in her voice. "What are you doing here?" Her face fell. "Is there trouble at the river?"

"No," Tara replied. "Nothing like that." She jerked one thumb toward me. "He wanted to see you."

Melissa's gaze swung to me, her face uncertain. "Jamie, isn't it? The mage?"

The two men studied me curiously at Melissa's words.

"That's right," I said. "I heard what you said in the conference yesterday, and I thought maybe I could help."

Melissa looked taken aback. "With making the tools?"

Before I could answer, the second of the two men barked out, "What? You're a blacksmith too?"

"Hush, Anton." Melissa cast a chiding glance at the man.

When she turned back to me, I nodded. "Yes actually, with making tools." I glanced at Anton. "I'm not a blacksmith, but I may be able to help."

Melissa's eyebrows rose. "Explain," she said.

"If I understand correctly, you're having trouble reforging the murluk spear tips, right?"

Melissa nodded. "Yes. Whatever metal they're made of is beyond our furnace's ability to melt."

"I can help with that—I think."

"How?" she asked.

"Magical fire."

Anton snorted. "Look here, lad. No open flame can melt these here spear tips. My furnace is hot enough to melt steel. If that ain't done the job, your fire ain't gonna do squat either."

"Maybe." I shrugged. "But it can't hurt to try."

Melissa glanced at Tara, who caught the look and nodded.

"Very well, Jamie," said Melissa. "It's worth a shot."

"You can't be serious!" protested Anton.

"Quiet, Anton," snapped Melissa. "Let the boy try. At this point, we've nothing to lose."

Anton muttered imprecations under his breath, but didn't object further. Folding his arms, the blacksmith watched as I joined them at the table and peered into the clay bowl.

Inside were two murluk spearheads, blackened and soot stained, but otherwise none the worse from their time in the furnace.

"Will you set the bowl down on the floor, please?" I asked the first man, whom I assumed to be Anton's assistant. Without comment, he used his poles to place the bowl on the ground.

Falling to my knees, I bent over the bowl, while the others—even the scowling Anton—leaned close to watch. I glanced up at them. "Everyone may want to take a step back. This might not go as planned."

They fell back hurriedly.

All right. I stared into the bowl again. *Here goes nothing.* I reached within myself and charged the spellform of *flare* with mana and lifeblood. Then, doing my best to focus the inferno within me, I attempted casting *flare* through the single finger I pointed at the bowl.

I failed.

Flames burst from my entire hand and enveloped the bowl, its contents, and the ground underfoot. "Damn it," I muttered.

I'd thought my control of *flare* was better than that. But done was done. I let the flames rage for a few seconds before cutting off the flow of mana and lifeblood and peering at the result of my handiwork.

Urgh.

The grass and soil were scorched. The clay bowl had disintegrated. And the spearheads' precious metal—the whole point of this bloody exercise—had vanished into the ground.

"Sorry," I said, glancing over my shoulder at the others. "I hoped to do better."

"Ha! I knew it!" Anton strode forward triumphantly. "I told ya you wouldn't—" He stopped in stunned silence as he caught sight of the shattered bowl and the traces of metal soaking the ground. "Bloody hell!" he exclaimed.

Melissa's eyes grew wide too as she noticed the spearheads were gone. "You've done it!" she breathed.

"Well, not exactly," I pointed out, "I may have melted the spearheads, but the metal has been lost."

"Unimportant," she pronounced. "We can devise a means to trap the metal.

"Perhaps we can try using rocks," said the assistant, his voice pitching higher with eagerness.

"Or a thicker vessel," grunted Anton. He rubbed his chin thoughtfully. "Much thicker." His scowl had vanished entirely, I noticed.

"So, we can make this work?" I asked Melissa, bemused by their reactions.

"Definitely, young man," she said. "Definitely."

* * *

It was not as easy as the three crafters made it out to be.

Into pot after pot, I cast *flare*. One and all, they crumbled, shattered, or cracked. Eventually, the blacksmiths stopped filling the vessels with spearheads, and we focused solely on creating a suitable container.

It took longer than expected, but finally, we achieved a workable solution: a monstrous slab of clay and rock able to withstand the five-second burn necessary to melt the spearheads.

"Well done, laddie!" Anton thumped me heavily on the back as he inspected the metallic liquid floating in the indentation at the slab's center. "We've finally done it!"

Anton, it turned out, had been an amateur blacksmith on Earth. Being unable to apply his skills on Overworld had upset him greatly. But now that I had proven my usefulness, it seemed I was destined to become his new best friend.

"Thanks," I said, giving the man a wan smile. "Give me a second to rest before we continue."

I sat and wolfed down the food the crafters brought for me. Tara had long since grown bored with our repeated failures and had gone to see to her own much-neglected duties.

Anton's assistant—whose name was Jeremy—was inspecting the slab of clay and rock. His brows were furrowed as his fingers traced its surface.

He looks concerned, I thought. "What is it, Jeremy?" I asked between mouthfuls.

"Hairline cracks in the clay." He glanced from me to Anton. I doubt the slab will last more than three or four attempts."

Anton bustled over, and together the two men scrutinized its surface. Eventually, the blacksmith straightened. "You're right, Jeremy. I'll ask Melissa to get the others started on a second one."

It had taken the crafters hours to make the slab. My gaze stole to the heap of discarded spearheads on my left. The pile was still growing, as junior crafters bought in bags more of the stuff from wherever they had been stored. Accumulated from over a week of fighting, the spearheads made a tidy pile.

I tried to calculate how long it would take to melt them all. If the crafters had to make a new slab after every five attempts, the answer was simple: *too long.*

I couldn't afford to spend days melting spearheads. I closed my eyes, mustering my will. I knew what needed to be done. The smiths had done their best in creating the slab, but the solution was not a bigger, better one.

Its time I refined my control. If I could narrowly focus *flare*, I could spare the mold its scorching flames.

In battle, I hadn't needed to regulate the flow of my dragonfire. Time and again, I had unleashed its flames unchecked, trying to do as much damage as possible.

Yet it was *possible* to focus the flames. I knew that. I had done so already—albeit on a small scale—by varying the span of flames released through my hands.

But the degree of control necessary to concentrate my dragonfire into a finger-wide jet of flame was beyond me. I had been trying all morning without success.

Now, though, faced with the possibility of days spent melting spearheads, I was determined to succeed. With a heartfelt sigh, I rose to my feet. This crafting business was almost more exhausting than fighting.

Seeing me back on my feet, Anton asked, "Feeling better, lad?"

I nodded. "What's next?"

"Now that we've proven the concept," said Anton, rubbing his hands in glee, "we can begin the *real* work and start forging equipment. The others have prepared the molds already. If you are ready, we can begin."

I wiped my mouth free of crumbs. "All right, let's get to work."

Anton and his fellows had thought long and hard about what needed to be created and in what order. With minimal fuss, they cut a channel in the slab so the melted metal could flow into the chosen mold.

The tool they had chosen first was not at all what I'd expected.

You have created a basic blacksmith's hammer. The special properties of this item are unknown. Your lore skill is insufficient.

Your skill in blacksmithing has advanced to level 1.

Your artistry and industriousness have increased to level 2.

For all the hammer's simplicity, the crafters who witnessed its creation cheered as loudly as the spearmen after our victory at the river.

Anton grabbed my hand and pumped it vigorously. "Thank you, my boy," he said, tears shining in his eyes. "Thank you."

I smiled and patted his shoulder awkwardly.

From there, things proceeded apace. We crafted tongs, shears, knives—plenty of knives—axes, needles, and hammers.

With every crafting, I applied my will and did my utmost to suppress the dragonfire spewing from me. And although I could discern no improvement, I persisted. The morning wore on, and when we broke for lunch, I collapsed in a heap, physically and mentally exhausted. All my reserves of energy were in the red, but I had been ignoring them, focusing instead on the task at hand.

While I munched mechanically through my bowl of food, I watched Anton and Jeremy circle the latest slab. Both men were scratching their heads.

"What is it?" I called.

It's nothing," Anton said. "Just strange, that's all." He fell silent.

"What's strange?" I prompted.

Anton pointed to the clay block. "This here slab has lasted six meltings so far, and it's still going strong." He barked a laugh. "Jeremy and I are trying to figure out what we did right in its making."

I paused between mouthfuls. "Did you say it has lasted longer?" I hadn't noticed. Over the morning's work, my world had narrowed to the simple task of creating dragonfire. I had been so fully immersed in refining and observing my spellcasting through my *magesight* that I had blocked out awareness of everything else. I had even lost sight of the items we had created.

Jeremy was nodding. "Yep. In fact, the last few molds have *all* lasted longer than the original ones." He shrugged. "But we don't know why."

I mulled over his words. *Could it be me?* I wondered. Was my control of *flare* improving?

* * *

Shortly after lunch, any doubts I harbored that my efforts at control were failing, vanished. Mid-crafting, I paused as a wall of floating text covered my vision.

You have spellcrafted a touch-based spell, from the Discipline of dragon magic. The name assigned to this spell is *restrained flare*. **Restrained flare is a persistent spell that produces less dragonfire than** *flare,* **but at a lower energy cost. Its casting time is fast and its rank is common.**

You are the first player to have spellcrafted the dragon spell *restrained flare*. For this achievement, you have been awarded dragon lore and two Marks.

Lore note: *Restrained flare* is a common dragon magic spell. It produces a jet of flame whose intensity and span can be controlled by the caster.

The spell demands precision, and it is one that any hatchling wishing to tame the dragonfire within themselves must learn. With this spell, the wise hatchling recognizes that dragonfire is not only destructive but that it also has an incredible potential to create.

I smiled foolishly at the Trials alert. I had done it. Studying the spellform of *restrained flare* with my *magesight*, I realized it was not so much a new spell as the evolution of an existing spell, brought about by the continuous application of will and my attempts to leash the raging fire within me.

That led me to wonder: could I evolve *flare* further? If so, what benefits would it yield? I would have to think further on the matter.

"You all right, lad?" asked Anton, seeing my frozen expression. "Something's happened?

"Something has," I admitted. "But nothing bad." I turned to the blacksmith's assistant. "Jeremy, will you bring one of the clay pots we started with originally? I want to try something."

"You sure?" he asked, eyeing me doubtfully.

I nodded.

Anton frowned. "What are you up to now?"

"You'll see," I said, smiling.

Jeremy placed a clay bowl with two spearheads on the slab. I bent over the vessel and pointed one finger at its contents. Then, constructing the spellform of *restrained flare* in my mind, I released a fine jet of flame directly at the spearheads.

"Wow," said Jeremy as he beheld the bar of white gold that leaped from my hand into the bowl. "What is that?"

Anton caught on quicker than his assistant. "You've learned a new spell, haven't you, lad?"

I nodded, not looking away from the bowl. My smile widened as the spearheads melted without damaging the clay bowl. "Now," I said to the two men, "our work can proceed much faster."

*　*　*

By day's end, all of the spearheads had been melted and *every* crafter in the Outpost had been provided with the tools of their trade.

The spearheads had not produced nearly enough metal to forge weapons for the fighters, but neither I nor the crafters had questioned the need to prioritize tools over weapons. The tools were crucial to the settlement's survival, and, at this stage, better weapons were not.

All in all, it had been an exhausting but satisfying day of work. And while my efforts had done little to advance my combat prowess, they had yielded other benefits.

Your skill in blacksmithing and lore has advanced to level 10 and reached rank 2, Trainee.

Your spellpower, artistry, and industriousness have increased to level 10 and reached rank 2, Trainee.

It was surprising that even without *newcomer*, my blacksmithing Discipline and craft Attributes had advanced so rapidly, but they had only been at the Neophyte rank, and we had forged hundreds of items today.

"Lad," said Anton, walking up to me just as the sun was setting. "You've done great work here today. I can't begin to thank you enough."

"No thanks necessary. I am just glad I was able to help."

"That's mighty generous of ye, boy. But we all thought you deserved something for your efforts." The blacksmith held out an object.

Solemnly, I took the proffered item.

You have acquired a basic metal dagger. The special properties of this weapon are unknown. Your lore skill is insufficient.

It was a simple knife, one of the last we had created. Its blade was affixed to a comfortable wooden handle and it had been placed in an unadorned leather sheath.

"Thank you, Anton," I said with a small bow.

"You're welcome. And don't be a stranger. You need anything, you come see me. Take care, Jamie," Anton said in farewell before walking away.

* * *

I made my way back to my tent, my feet stumbling and head drooping. The crafting had claimed its toll. I was as weary as I had ever been. I chuckled. Exhaustion was my constant state of existence these days.

I splashed water across my face and ate the supper left for me by some kind soul.

Then I got to work again.

Sitting cross-legged on my pallet, I began channeling mana. Given the business of the last two days, I hadn't had time to create a ranged spell. I couldn't put it off any longer.

I called up the construct for *flare* and studied the spell within my mind. *How do I modify it to create a ranged variant?* I wondered. My success with *restrained flare* had given me a few ideas for evolving *flare* in other ways, and despite my tiredness, I was eager to try them.

I prodded at the spell construct in my mind, modifying the design and shape until I was satisfied with its new form. Then, pointing my hand at the unoffending pail, I infused the spellform and released the casting.

You have failed to create a spell.

I sighed and began anew.

*   *   *

Hours later, I gave up.

No matter how many variants of the *flare* I had tried, no matter how much or how little lifeblood I infused, no matter the will I exerted in propelling dragonfire further than a few yards, I failed to create a projectile spell.

I had tweaked and retweaked the spell construct. I had refined and perfected its spellform until I felt the spell vibrate in faultless harmony with itself. My projectile spell design was flawless. I was sure of it.

Yet some vital ingredient was missing.

I drummed my fingers restlessly. *Perhaps my skill is too low. Or perhaps I am just too tired to see the flaws in my design.* Whatever the case, further experimentation would not yield better results.

I would sleep on it. Maybe in the morning, I would figure out what I was missing. Unable to keep my eyes open any longer, I collapsed onto my pallet.

Chapter Thirty

388 DAYS UNTIL THE ARKON SHIELD FALLS
2 DAYS TO EARTH'S DESTRUCTION
2 DAYS UNTIL THE WARREN IS DESTROYED

"Jamie? Jamie, wake up. I have to talk to you."

I groaned and rolled over, but Tara didn't let me go back to sleep. She tugged at my shoulder again.

I blinked open my eyes and stared blearily at the dark shape leaning over me. I knew it was Tara, yet I couldn't make out any of her features. My gaze slid to the open tent flap. No light streamed through. What was Tara doing here so early?

"Eh?" I croaked, the best I could manage given my groggy state.

Tara sat back on her heels and handed me a cup of water.

Sitting up, I gulped it down gratefully. "What time is it?" I squinted at her.

"An hour before dawn. I wanted to tell you I'm sorry," she added after a hesitant pause.

I blinked. "Tara, you're going to have to be more specific than that. My brain is still waking up," I said with a smile.

My quip failed to raise an answering grin.

"I knew something was driving you, Jamie," Tara continued, her face grave. "But I hadn't realized how dark a tragedy you had suffered, or how raw the wound must still be. I'm sorry for some of the things I said to you... they must have hurt."

My smile faded. "Tara," I said carefully, "what are you talking about?"

She met my eyes, her own filled with pity. "Some of the new recruits that came through yesterday brought news of a 'crazed cripple' who had managed to kill an orc hunting party." Her voice grew heavy. "Apparently, the whole world watched as he took revenge on them for... for killing his mother. When I heard the story, I knew it had to have been you." She smiled sadly. "After all, you *are* the only crazed cripple I know."

My face froze as Tara's words hammered into my brain. From the depths of my mind, the specter of Mom's death rose up again. My mouth opened, then closed soundlessly. Images flashed before my eyes in torturous detail. It felt real, *too real*. I gasped. Clutching at my arms, I bent forward and tried to escape the scenes playing out in my head.

Tara waited patiently, watching me with an expression that was more open than it had ever been before. Her hands reached out and hovered halfway, a wordless offer to share the burden of my grief.

I rocked back. I couldn't deal with her pity, not now. "And you had to wake me before dawn to tell me this?" I lashed out, even though I knew she didn't deserve it.

Tara's eyes bored into mine. Inwardly, I shrank back, already regretting my words. I almost blurted out an apology, but that would mean mentioning Mom and dragging up memories best forgotten. Not ready for that yet, I stayed silent.

"No," Tara replied, her voice cold as she withdrew her hands. "I came this early because I have been reassigned. The loggers were attacked in the woods yesterday. The commander wants their protection detail increased. She has put me in charge. My company is about to move out. I thought it best to speak to you before I left." She rose to her feet. "But you're right, I should not have bothered you with this so early. Good day, Jamie." She spun on her heel to leave.

"Wait, Tara," I called, stopping her before she left. She halted, but she didn't turn around.

"Who else knows?"

"The commander," she said, her back stiff. "Possibly the other captains, too. I'm not sure."

My head fell. *Everyone.*

Tara waited a heartbeat for me to go on, but caught up in my misery, I barely noticed.

Then she left, and I was alone.

* * *

I tried to go back to sleep after that, but, unsurprisingly, it proved elusive. My emotions were a jumbled mess, circling in on themselves like sharks. Despite my best efforts, I couldn't rid my thoughts of Mom and... of Tara.

"Enough, Jamie," I growled. I stomped out of my tent and sank down on the cool ground. It was still dark, and most of the camp's inhabitants were asleep. On the eastern side of the camp, movement stirred. It had to be Tara and the loggers, getting an early start.

I jerked my head around. I didn't want to think about Tara. For want of something to occupy my thoughts, I turned my mind to spellcasting.

I called up the spellform of the dragonfire projectile spell I had conceived last night and inspected its design again. I could no more find fault with it today than I could last night. Then again, my mind wasn't particularly clear this morning either.

In disgust, I banished the spellform and began training my magic. Picking the air magic Discipline at random, I drew mana into my mind and shaped a rudimentary construct of air.

I followed the training philosophy I had applied during the journey into the foothills, falling into a light trance while I experimented with the form and shape of air.

An hour later, as the first rays of the rising sun touched my face, I opened my eyes. The training had done me some good. My racing thoughts had quietened.

I inhaled deeply and checked the Trials alert awaiting my attention.

Your skill in air magic has advanced to level 4.

Not bad. I dismissed the message. After rising to my feet, I limped westward to the river.

To my surprise, the spearmen were not gathered on the lower riverbanks. Studying the skyline, I realized why.

The wooden palisade had been completed—or at least its western section had—and the spearmen were gathered inside its boundary.

After I reached the wall, I pushed through the ranks of waiting spearmen. Morale was high among the soldiers. They chatted and laughed in a jovial manner. Yesterday's success, or the wall's completion, had raised their spirits.

Spotting Lieutenant John and Captain Petrov, I strode over to join them. They stood before the only open section in the riverside wall. Given the size of the open area, I assumed a gate would be installed there soon.

"John," I greeted him, as I drew closer. "Any sign of the murluks yet?"

"No." He scratched his head in confusion. "They're late again."

I nodded. It was a good sign. "The spearmen will meet them here?"

"That's the plan," agreed John. He gestured to the break in the wall in front of us. "We were hoping to funnel the creatures through this space. Assuming the buggers can't breach the palisade itself, we should be able to hold them at bay here easily enough." His gaze slid toward me. "Unless you were planning on doing your whole solo act down at the shore again?"

"I actually was," I admitted. "But it doesn't look like I'll be needed here today, even if murluks do show up."

"The men will feel better with your presence," John assured me.

I stared out of the open gate. The river remained quiescent. No splashes marred its surface. *Will the murluks show up today?* I wondered.

Frowning, I sat down to train my air magic further while I waited.

* * *

Your skill in air magic has advanced to level 6.

The murluks did not come, and I gave up waiting for them after an hour.

"Looks like they are a no show. I'm going to see if I can make myself useful elsewhere. Will you send someone to fetch me if I am needed, John?"

"Sure thing, Jamie," he replied.

Where to now?

The murluks' non-appearance was a double-edged sword. On the one hand, it freed up the soldiers to help out elsewhere, but on the other, it robbed the Outpost of its only source of metal.

What if the murluks don't return? I wondered. *What then?* The settlement would need to find a source of ore, I gathered, and the mountains beyond the northern foothills were the most likely place to find it.

Marcus, I recalled, was in charge of the scouts, so I asked a passing crafter to direct me to him and hurried to find the blond captain.

Outside the scout captain's tents, I found two familiar faces.

"Jamie!" exclaimed Laura. "What are you doing here?"

"Hi, Laura, Cass. I came to see to Marcus. Is he in there?"

"Yes, we're just waiting to see him ourselves," replied Cass.

"Ah all right. How are you two doing?"

The pair exchanged glances. "Well we haven't had any adventures as exciting as our trip through the warren, if that's what you're asking," replied Cass with a laugh.

"It was an altogether boring day yesterday," agreed Laura. "Which was fine by me." She eyed me thoughtfully. "We heard you created quite the stir."

I shrugged. By my own measure, I hadn't done much, only what was necessary.

As if sensing my discomfort, Laura moved the conversation on. "Oh, I found out more about those obelisks you were looking for."

"The dungeons?" I asked, my eyes lighting up. "Tell me," I demanded.

"What's this about dungeons?" Marcus appeared at the entrance of his tent and studied the three of us with interest.

"Morning, Marcus," I said, turning to the captain. "I asked Laura to find out if any of the scouts had encountered any obelisks," I explained. "The Trials mark the entrance to dungeons with them."

Marcus' eyes gleamed. "Ah," he said. I could tell the thought of dungeons excited him too. But a moment later, he frowned. "You should have come to me," he said reproachfully. "I receive all the scout reports, you know."

I spread my hand in apology and turned back to Laura. "Did you find one?"

"Well, not me," she said. "Another of the scouts did. She spotted the obelisk in a forest clearing nearly a day's journey east of the Outpost. You can't miss it."

"I remember that report now." Marcus stroked his chin. "Gemma found the object about four days ago. A twenty-foot-high structure. No one knew what it was or why it was standing in an empty forest clearing." He frowned. "She said it was covered with red inscriptions."

"Red?" I asked, deflating. "You sure the writing was red?"

"Yep," replied Laura. "I spoke to Gemma yesterday myself. The whole structure was covered in scarlet runes pulsing so ominously that the poor girl was afraid to approach too closely."

"Why the long face?" asked Marcus, observing my reaction.

I sighed. "Because red runes mean the dungeon is only suitable for Veteran players, players above level two hundred. For us to enter the dungeon now would be suicide." Seeing the amused looks, the two women directed my way, I scowled. "Even for me," I muttered.

"Pity." Marcus sounded wistful. "It would have been nice to go on a dungeon dive." He shook his head regretfully. "But enough daydreaming. What did you want to see me about?"

I glanced at the two sisters. They had been waiting first.

"We'll wait," said Cass amiably. "You go ahead."

Nodding my thanks, I followed Marcus into his tent.

"We need to find ore," I said without preamble.

Halfway through taking a seat, Marcus paused. "I agree. Do you know where we can find some?"

"No, but searching the mountains to the north is our best chance."

Marcus shook his head. "It's not that I don't agree with you, but the mountains are too far. We can't send our scouts more than a day's journey away. The wilds are too dangerous for them to camp overnight. I won't ask that of them, not until they—and we—are stronger."

I frowned. Marcus had a point. "What about the spider warren?"

"What about it?"

"It's a few hours north of here, and you already have men stationed there, right? If you base your scouts at the warren, could they get to the mountains and back in a day?"

"I hadn't thought of that," Marcus murmured. He rubbed his forehead, giving the matter some thought. "It could work," he pronounced eventually. "Thanks, Jamie. I'll speak to the commander today. I'm sure she will agree."

"Excellent," I said, preparing to leave. "Well, that's all I wanted to see you about."

"Jamie?" Marcus said, causing me to pause and turn back around.

The scout captain shifted uncomfortably. "I'm sorry to hear about your Mom. What those bastards did to her was more than cruel. I just wanted to say... I understand."

A mask of neutrality dropped over my face. Nodding curtly, I ducked out of the tent.

* * *

In need of solitude, I headed back to my tent, deciding to spend the rest of the afternoon training my magic. That way I would escape any further unwanted sympathizers.

I didn't want to talk about, or even think about, the events from my last day on Earth, but with the story floating around the camp, I knew everyone was going to want to offer their sympathies.

Why can't they see I don't want to talk about it?

Head bowed and eyes downcast, I hurried to solitude. I had almost reached the sanctuary my tent offered when the clatter of spears and the thump of marching feet attracted my attention.

I jerked my head up in alarm.

A company of soldiers was jogging past me, heading east through the camp. Their faces were grim, and they appeared in a hurry. *Something is wrong,* I thought. Scanning the spearmen's faces, I recognized one.

"Michael!" I waved to attract his attention. "What's going on?"

"The loggers," he yelled back, though he didn't slow down or drop out of formation. "A message just came in. They're under heavy attack and have taken casualties. We've been ordered to reinforce their guard company."

"What sort of attack?" I shouted as the column passed by and the distance between us widened.

Michael shrugged apologetically, too far away to continue the conversation, but I took his gesture to mean he didn't know.

My gaze tracked the disappearing soldiers as I considered what to do. The spearmen were traveling too fast for me to keep up. I glanced at the commander's tent. I could ask the old lady what was going on.

Or I could ignore it all and take refuge in my tent.

Damn it! The Outpost needed those tree trunks. And Tara was in the forest with the loggers. *She could be in trouble.*

Growling in frustration, I spun away from my tent and set off after the spearmen.

Chapter Thirty-One

388 DAYS UNTIL THE ARKON SHIELD FALLS

Of course, I stood no chance of catching the soldiers.

I could only follow in their footsteps and hope that disaster hadn't already overtaken the spearmen or the loggers by the time I got to wherever they were going. Reaching the Outpost's eastern trench line, I found it unguarded and crossed without fuss.

I knew I should have informed the commander of my plans and asked for an escort—or at least told someone where I was heading. But I didn't feel like explaining myself or risking further talk of Mom.

Moving at the fastest pace my crippled foot would allow, I hobbled along. The spearmen's tracks were easy to read. They cut east through the grassy plains on a direct path to the smudge of forest on the horizon.

Ten minutes out of the camp, I belatedly thought to take stock of my equipment. I had no provisions, and except for the knife sheathed at my belt, I was unarmed. Fool that I was, I hadn't even thought to retrieve my club and shield before setting off. But it was too late to turn back now. After an hour's lonely trek, which was thankfully uneventful, I reached the edge of the forest.

I paused to consider its wooded depths before venturing within. Oak, redwood, ash, and pine trees arched high overhead and cast long shadows across the leaf-scattered forest floor. At ground level, the foliage was sparse, with only the odd bush to hamper passage.

I couldn't help but marvel at the familiarity of the vegetation. Had the trees existed in Overworld before the gates to Earth had opened? Or had they been transplanted here during the creation of the Human Dominion? It was a reminder that much of Overworld remained a mystery to me.

I bent down and inspected the ground. Deep marks scored the soft soil beneath, probably from the logs Soren and his men had dragged back to the settlement. The trail led farther east, into the forest.

At least finding the loggers will be easy.

But studying the looming giants, I suddenly questioned how safe the woods were. Amid the trees, my visibility would be much reduced, and since I was alone, I would be easy prey. *You should have thought of that earlier, Jamie.* I chuckled.

Shrugging off my doubts, I advanced cautiously. The trail continued eastward for another hundred yards before veering south. Keeping my ears strained and my head swiveling from side to side, I followed the tracks.

Around me, the dank air was eerily silent. Not even bird calls disturbed the stillness. *Is it always this quiet? Or is it a sign of a lurking predator?*

The forest had me on edge. I tightened my grip on my blade. Even though my knife skills were non-existent, I felt safer holding the weapon. I kept my magic prepared, too, ready to unleash *flare* at a moment's notice.

Ten minutes later, I passed the first hacked-off tree. Then another. But still the forest remained sleeping around me, with neither the sound of chopping nor the cries of battle disturbing the air.

I frowned. *Where is everyone?*

I quickened my pace. I had to be nearing the logging camp. Any moment now—

I smashed face-first into the ground as a heavy weight descended on my back. For just a moment, I felt a hot, slavering breath on my face before pain whitened my world.

Iron jaws clamped down on my neck, and a second later fangs carved out a chunk of my flesh. I tried to roll over, but my attacker had pinned me down.

The pain was brutal. I screamed soundlessly, loamy earth filling my mouth and muffling my cry.

I struggled to think. To breathe. To act.

My arms were trapped beneath me, which made both *flare* and my knife useless. Frantically, I tried to free one of my hands. It was no use. They were wedged tight.

My attacker bit down again.

I arched my head up in pain, the tendons of my neck straining. *Aargh, that hurts.* Tears streamed down my face, and death loomed closer.

I knew I was going to die here unless I did something.

I don't need my hands to flare.

On the brink of calling on *invincible,* the thought floated into my mind like an epiphany. *Of course.* Changing tack abruptly, I cast *flare.*

White-hot dragonfire, thirsting for blood, roared out of my back and through the open wound of my mauled neck.

My attacker's growl transformed into a surprised yelp. A second later, the crushing weight on my back disappeared.

I stopped casting *flare* and rolled over, frantic to see again and find my foe. The motion scorched my back with new agony. I gritted my teeth against the pain. My armor was the cause, I realized. The leather had melted and its burnt sinews bit through my skin.

My throbbing neck was little better. Though the flames had cauterized the wound, my neck felt vulnerable. But I didn't have time to tend to myself.

I had to kill my attacker.

Remaining in my prone position, I let my gaze rove over the surroundings and jump from tree to tree.

Nothing.

No branches rustled. No leaves stirred. No blurred motion caught my attention. Where had my foe gone? And how had it disappeared so—

Between one blink and the next, I was under attack again.

Weight pressed down on me and a dark shape blotted out the sun. I had a split second to recognize slitted eyes, a snarling muzzle, and fangs—lots of fangs—before the beast's gaping maw snapped downward.

But this time, I was ready.

Before the predator clamped its jaws around my head, I cast *flare* into its belly.

The creature—*wolf?*—whined. My dragonfire-wreathed hands flew up to grasp the beast and hold it prisoner while I poured flames into its torso.

But in an eyeblink, my foe disappeared.

This time, I had been watching the beast when it happened. The creature had not leaped off. One moment it had been there and the next it was gone.

Some form of teleportation?

My head swiveled back and forth as I tried to keep watch on all approaches at once. Images of my attacker flicked through my mind. It was definitely lupine. And my fire had hurt it. How bad, I couldn't tell, but *flare* had left scorch marks along its sides. *I smelled singed fur, so I had to have—*

My headlong thoughts paused.

There had been no burns on the beast's muzzle, and there should have been if it was the creature that had initially attacked me.

So, I have at least two attackers.

Even worse, if the beasts really *could* teleport, scanning the surroundings would make no difference. I would not see the next attack before it arrived. A tremor of fear gripped me.

Abruptly, I dropped the spellform of *flare* and, summoning life magic, cast *lay hands*. I knew it was a risk, but so was leaving my wounds unattended.

Soothing waves of healing rippled through my back and neck, but I had no time to enjoy the relief from pain. Two four-footed figures—almost as if summoned by the spell's luminous blue glow—blinked into existence two yards away on either side of me.

I had no idea why the beasts had chosen not to materialize on top of me again, but I was grateful. It gave me the time I needed to prepare. Dropping the weaves of *lay hands,* I readied *flare's* spellform.

The beasts leaped. I flared.

Twin howls of agony tore through the forest as dragonfire met hounds. Mid-leap, the pair disappeared, vanishing from the flames' depth. My heart pounded. Despite my success in fending off the attack, I knew I was in trouble.

Neither of the beasts had borne any burns. Either they could heal themselves... or I had four attackers.

I'm being stalked by a pack of teleporters!

I swallowed my fear. If I was going to survive the encounter, I had to change the dynamic. Sitting up, I searched for somewhere I could hold the pack at bay, but the terrain was the same in every direction: an endless march of trees.

I drew my knife. I knew it was silly—why did I need the knife when I had *flare?*—but I kept it in hand anyway. Scooting backward, I braced my back against the nearest trunk and held myself ready.

The beasts kept me waiting.

I scanned the area. There was no sign of the pack, but I didn't doubt they were nearby. To relieve the tension that coiled tighter and tighter within me, I opened my *magesight.* Perhaps where my physical sight failed, my magical one would succeed.

My *magesight* was stubbornly empty. Disappointed, I made to close it, but I paused when a shadow flickered past my view.

Slowly, I rotated my head. I hadn't been mistaken. My stalkers were visible as pools of darkness in my *magesight,* circling menacingly around me. They lurked behind the trees, just out of physical sight.

Clever beasts.

The pack's constant motion prevented me from determining their number, but just knowing where they lurked helped immensely, and I felt some of my fear subside.

Given the space to think, I considered the circumstances that had brought me here. *Where are the loggers? Where are Tara, Michael, and the rest of the spearmen? They can't be far away.*

I wondered whether I should abandon my position and go in search of the Outpost company, but I suspected that moving would make me even more vulnerable. Perhaps that was what the beasts were waiting for: for me to expose myself.

"Help!" I shouted. "Is anyone there?" If I was stuck here, there was no harm in trying to attract the loggers' attention to my position. Maybe someone would hear me. My voice echoed startlingly loud through the silent forest, but there was no answering cry.

A hound blinked before me, perhaps spurred by my cry and hoping to take advantage of my distraction. But I had been expecting the move.

I cast *flare*, and it blinked away.

"Damn it," I snarled as the creature escaped my flames unscathed.

Another materialized to my left. I flared, and missed again as it blinked away.

A third repeated the maneuver on the right. Predictably, I failed to hit it.

I ground my teeth in frustration. "Goddamn dogs," I swore. The pack was testing me. The pit of my stomach dropped as another, more unpleasant thought, occurred.

Or they are draining my mana? Just how cunning are these beasts?

A fourth blinked in. I waited. The hound tilted its head quizzically at me, its wintry gray eyes boring into me. Then it blinked away.

A second later, a shape hurtled down from the tree above. I flung up my right arm and cast *flare*.

With a yelp, the hound blinked out just before its weight could touch down on me. This time, I recognized the beast. The scorch marks on its muzzle marked it as my first attacker.

So, there are only the four. I felt my rising hope at the possibility. I was not as overmatched as I feared.

The pack returned to circling. But not for long.

A beast blinked into view on my right and barreled toward me. I cast *flare*, but this time, the creature only ducked its head and, with a low growl, kept coming.

Another beast materialized on the left. With my other hand, I cast *flare* directly into it. It, too, was undaunted. The pack was changing its tactics again.

Just as the first two clamped their jaws onto my flaring hands, the third beast dropped from the trees and the fourth appeared at my feet.

They were trying to overwhelm me, and this time, *flare* was not scaring them off. The fourth hound dived for my throat.

Reacting faster than thought, I activated *invincible*.

The hound bounced off. I spat a stream of blood from my mouth and grinned. The tables had turned. I flared harder, pouring flames out of my hands.

Now I've got you, doggies.

All four beasts were trapped in the blazing inferno. Flames boiled off me and licked at the pack clinging to me. Fur was singed, skin melted, and paws charred.

Then, the hound on my left blinked away. It was followed a moment later by the one my chest. Dread curled within me.

They were retreating again.

I couldn't let them escape. I had to kill at least a couple while *invincible* lasted.

I flung myself sideways and grappled with the hound chewing on my right arm. Wrapping my arms around it, I held on for grim life.

The beast at my feet disappeared.

But the one I clung to, whether pained from the dragonfire spewing into it or because I had wrapped myself around its torso, stayed put. Projecting all my fear and rage into the beast, I *flared* until it collapsed into a smoking heap.

Then I lurched to my feet and ran.

* * *

I didn't get far.

My crippled foot, and the pack's ability to teleport, made escape impossible. I wasn't trying to outrun them—not exactly. I had hoped to find the loggers' trail, which I had lost sight of during the initial attack. If I found it, I could cautiously withdraw.

But whether I was searching in the wrong direction or simply failed to see the path, the clock on *invincible* ran down without me finding the loggers' tracks.

With my chest heaving, I drew to a halt and doubled over, hands on my knees, to consider my options. Fleeing without the protection of *invincible* was risky. The hounds could strike at any time.

On the heels of that thought, three pools of darkness slunk into my *magesight*.

They were back.

Can the beasts sense my spells? I wondered. The timing of their return was too coincidental otherwise. *Damn if these dogs aren't smarter than the murluks.*

Continuing the search for the loggers' trail was no longer an option. Forced to admit defeat, I planted my back against another tree, bettering my odds of survival. But even with one of their number dead, the pack showed no sign of abandoning their hunt.

With a weary sigh, I settled myself in to keep watch and prepare for the next attack.

Chapter Thirty-Two

388 DAYS UNTIL THE ARKON SHIELD FALLS

I lost count of the number of assaults I fended off.

The three hounds, scorched and scarred from dragonfire, kept blinking in, testing me with feinting attacks, and then jumping out again. They were more wary, but no less persistent.

Each time, the pack inched closer and closer until I was forced to *flare*. Then they would flee. More often than not, they dodged the flames.

Every so often, they circled me before trying to bait me again. There was no pattern to their assaults. They attacked at random intervals, keeping me on edge, attempting to wear me down. But although I knew what the beasts were playing at, I was helpless to stop them.

Inevitably, I knew I would lose. I tried casting *flare* as little as possible, to conserve my stamina and mana, but I had no illusions that I would triumph.

During one of their many attacks, I took the opportunity to *analyze* the creatures.

The target is a level 32 phase hound. It has meager Magic, is gifted with Might, is gifted with Resilience, and has no Craft.

The results told me little I didn't know nor gave me any clue how to overcome the canines. My best hope, I decided, was to hold out until the Outpost company found me.

While I had lost the loggers' trail, I knew I couldn't have strayed too far from their path. I kept calling out once every five minutes. Someone had to hear me eventually.

But as the day waned, turning morning to afternoon and afternoon to twilight, I began to lose all hope of rescue. The phase hounds were tireless, and I feared they would welcome taking our stand-off into the night. Once darkness concealed their attacks, my end would come quickly.

I stared up at the light of the setting sun filtering through the trees. My time was almost up. *I've waited long enough*, I decided. *No rescue is coming. If I'm to survive the night, it'll be up to me to change my fate.*

For the umpteenth time, I took stock of my resources. I needed to bring my magic to bear, find a way to hurt the creatures while they hung teasingly out of my *flare's* range. But I had been wracking my brains all day for a way and had yet to devise a workable plan.

I glanced at the knife sheathed at my hip. It was my only weapon, yet it was useless. *Perhaps if I threw it...* Bah! And lose it? *If only I had a spear—*

I paused. "A spear," I mused aloud. My gaze flickered from my knife to two nearby saplings. *Can I make one?*

Cautiously, I edged away from the tree at my back to the nearer of the two saplings. I ran my hand along its length. It was thin enough; I judged that I could saw through its base or maybe uproot it entirely.

With one eye on the circling pools of darkness in my *magesight*, I yanked the sapling free. Working quickly, I trimmed off its branches.

When I was done, I had a nine-foot-long pole. But while my new weapon was a goodly length, its wood was too green and wiry, lacking the firmness I needed from a spear.

I grimaced. *It's a damn sight better than nothing, Jamie.* Limping to the next sapling, I repeated my feat.

Then, with two 'spears' at my side, I braced my back against a nearby tree and waited for the next attack.

* * *

"Well, dog, it's about time you fellows showed up." I looked up from the "spear" end I had been sharpening with my knife.

A phase hound had blinked into being five yards in front of me. Its ears pricked forward at the sound of my voice, but it didn't otherwise move from its predatory crouch.

The beasts had learned the limit of my *flare* range and were careful to appear outside it.

In no hurry, I hefted one of the saplings and climbed to my feet. My encounters with the pack had developed a rhythm of their own. I knew the hound facing off against me wouldn't attack until one of its fellows showed up.

Ignoring it, I watched my flanks for the pack's favored tactic. Invariably, the one in front tried to hold my attention while the others, attempting to catch me off guard, rushed in from the left and the right.

The tactic had yet to work, though the pack seemed committed to it. Thankfully, the hounds had not tried rushing me all at once again. If they did, I knew I wouldn't survive. But I had instilled enough fear during the creatures' first failed attempt to make them wary of repeating the tactic.

A second phase hound blinked in on my right. Watching it through narrowed eyes, I raised the sapling spear in readiness. Would it pounce this time or edge nearer?

The beast padded closer and stopped three yards away, just outside *flare* range. I lowered the sapling spear in my arms. Its length was unwieldly, but, with some difficulty, I kept it pointed at my target.

The hound fixed its gaze on me, its eyes not straying the sapling's way.

I smiled grimly. *Good.* Stepping away from the tree, I lunged forward with the spear.

The hound made no attempt to dodge. Its only reaction was a surprised flick of its ears.

My spear tip struck the hound's chest dead center, but instead of piercing the creature, the sapling bent on impact. *Aaargh*, I screamed in silent frustration. My 'weapon' hadn't so much as scratched the hound's coat.

The beast glanced down at the stick poking into its chest. Its mouth opened, and its tongue lolled out.

The bloody thing is laughing at me! I thought in amazement.

Then the dog bounded forward.

I removed my left hand, letting the spear sag, and cast *flare* at the leaping beast. But I struck only air as the beast blinked out.

The second hound, which had been waiting patiently, rushed in. I swung *flare* in its direction, and it blinked away.

The third hound appeared on my left. It didn't attack. Crouching down on all fours, it watched me insolently from well outside of *flare's* range.

With a frustrated snarl, I stopped casting *flare*. I knew the one on my left was waiting for me to turn my dragonfire its way so that it could blink away, but I was tiring of the pack's games. I didn't want to give it that satisfaction.

Instead, I hefted the sapling again and charged. As I thrust forward, I cast *flare*—an act born more from thwarted anger than anything else. At best, I hoped to catch the hound by surprise and to close with the creature while it was distracted.

But as dragonfire rippled from my hands and into the sapling, I felt the spellform in my mind change to something else, seemingly of its own volition. My eyes widened in shock. My magic had never behaved this way before! Caught off guard, I didn't resist as the spellform shifted shape and expanded outward, into the sapling.

Dragonfire raced along the wood's length, and then, to the astonishment of both the hound and me, a bar of liquid gold leaped out of the spear's tip and struck the creature.

The hound howled as a searing beam of dragonfire plunged into its chest. I stumbled to a halt, too stunned to take advantage of the creature's momentary confusion.

A second later, the hound blinked out. I barely noticed. An avalanche of text clouded my vision.

You have spellcrafted a ranged spell, from the Discipline of dragon magic. The name assigned to this spell is *fire ray*. **Fire ray**

is a single-cast spell that must be invoked with the aid of a Focus. Its casting time is very fast and its rank is uncommon.

You are the first player to have spellcrafted the dragon spell *fire ray*. For this achievement, you have been awarded dragon lore and four Marks.

Lore note: *Fire ray* is an uncommon dragon magic spell. It produces a single beam of dragonfire that is powered by the caster's health, mana, and stamina.

Simple touch-based spells are not fully realized in Overworld and only exist while their spellforms remain connected to their caster's mana pool.

Projectile spells are different and are ordinarily too complex to be cast by novice mages. Their spellforms must be tied-off so that the spell can exist even when disconnected from the caster.

The *fire ray* is not a true projectile spell but a variant of a touch-based spell that is transformed into a ranged attack with the aid of a Focus—usually a wizard's staff.

You have cast *fire ray* through an unattuned Focus. A redwood tree sapling has died.

The Trials messages took my breath away. Belatedly, I realized that the spellform my *flare* spell had morphed into was the one I had been practicing last night. The same one that had failed repeatedly.

"A wizard's staff," I muttered. *That's* what I had been missing all along. *But what is a Focus?* I hadn't come across the term before.

I looked at the sapling in my hand. The wood was charred, turned lifeless by the forces it had channeled. Yet, given the dragonfire that rippled through its core, the sapling remaining surprisingly whole. I ran my hand down its length. The wood had dried up. There was no give through its length at all, and the tip had hardened nicely. *It will make a much better weapon now*, I thought.

I turned my gaze outward and scanned the surroundings. The hounds had retreated into the shadows once more. They weren't gone, though. Like me, they were probably contemplating my latest display of magic and what it boded for our contest.

Certain I remained secure—if only temporarily—I cast *analyze* on the weapon in my hand.

The target is a burned redwood staff. This weapon has no special properties and is unattuned.

So, the Trials considered the weapon in my hand a staff, not a spear. I wondered at the repeated reference to attunement. I knew what it meant to attune my mana. But what did it mean to attune a weapon?

Unfortunately, since I had never suspected I'd have magic, I hadn't delved much into the subject of the wizardly arts in the Trials Infopedia. Now, I felt caught out by my ignorance. I would have to find a way to fill the gaps in my understanding. *If I survive the day, of course.*

I recalled that when I had cast *fire ray* earlier, its spellform had extended from my mind into the staff, almost as if the sapling had been part of the spell. Tentatively, I tried to channel mana through the staff, but the weaves refused to enter the wood.

I frowned, but before I could experiment further, the three hounds blinked into existence and formed a semicircle five yards around me.

I dropped into a crouch, staring at the beasts. This was a new tactic. Lowering the staff, I held it horizontally like a spear.

The beasts shied away from wherever the staff pointed, clearly fearful that more dragonfire might erupt from it.

It gave me hope.

Calling upon the spellform of *fire ray*, I attempted to extend it through the staff, but again the weaves refused my command.

Your spell has fizzled. Magic can only be channeled through living objects.

I stared at the Trials alert in frustration. It did not bode well. Warily, I bent down, dropped the burned staff, and picked up the second sapling in its stead. If I had interpreted the Trials message correctly, I would manage only a single cast through it.

But I doubted the hounds knew that.

My movements triggered a response from the pack. In sync, they padded forward to overwhelm me again.

I couldn't allow that to happen.

Tightening my grip on the unburned sapling, I pointed it at the hound on the far left and cast *fire ray*.

A line of dragonfire shot across intervening space. The beast tried to sidestep the burning ray, but it was impossible to miss at this distance, and my beam struck the hound squarely in the muzzle.

The hound yelped and blinked out. The other two chose that moment to pounce.

Half-expecting the move, I was ready. I planted the rear end of my now burned staff into the ground and angled the sharpened end at the closest hound.

The beast realized the danger too late. Before it could teleport away, its own momentum drove the hardened spear tip through its torso.

Your skill with staffs has advanced to level 1.

I dropped the staff, not caring whether the hound blinked away. Since it was skewered, it was no threat. Spinning around, I prepared to fend off the third and last phase hound.

But I was too slow.

The beast, a half-seen blur, crashed into my side and sent me sprawling. In a fury of tooth and claw, it rushed back at me. I rolled, narrowly escaping its snapping jaws.

The first hound rejoined the fray. Teleporting onto me, it pinned me down. I threw up my hands and shielded my neck and face, which did little to protect me, as the hound only shifted its attack lower.

Near simultaneously, the jaws of the two hounds clamped onto my torso and legs. Agony rippled through me. I bit back a scream as one of the hounds buried its muzzle in my insides.

Death loomed near, and the battle's conclusion drew close. One way or another, the contest between the hounds and me would be decided in the next few moments. The time for conserving my mana and lifeblood had passed.

In terrified fury, I cast *flare*—and not just from my hands, but from everywhere. Empowered by the volatile mix of my panic and terror, waves of dragonfire rolled off me. I urged the flames on, fanning them hotter and hotter until I burned so brightly I could barely make out the hounds. Holding nothing back, I spent my lifeblood with no care for the cost.

I either died now, or I won.

Trial alerts popped into my vision, but I banished them as fast as they appeared. Blindly, I grasped the hound on my chest. It writhed, desperate to escape, but I held on tighter. Either it died first, or I did.

Vaguely, I sensed the other hound blink away from the superheated flames streaming off my body. I let it go. There was nothing I could do to stop it.

In seconds, the hound in my grasp disintegrated into ash, and I found myself alone at the center of a white-gold world.

I was dizzy, and my thoughts were sluggish. Stunned, I stared at the flames dancing about me. They wreathed my body from head to toe, flickering in a manner both enticing and hypnotic.

I knew I was dying. And I knew I should quench the fire. But, enchanted by the beautiful flames, I couldn't seem to care.

Why not let it all go? This is as good a way to die as any. Why fight on?

Unbeckoned, Mom's dead, unseeing eyes formed in the flames and bored into mine.

I blinked. My thoughts snapped into clarity. I couldn't let go. Not yet. My fight was not nearly done.

"Not like this," I croaked. With a tortured gasp, I applied my will and quenched the outpouring of mana and lifeblood. The dancing flames simmered, and then died, and the specter of Mom faded.

Thank you, Ma, I whispered in farewell before blacking out.

* * *

I woke up coughing blood and bile.

My skin had been scorched clean, cleansed of everything by the dragonfire. Clothes, armor, hair—all of it had burned away.

My health was dangerously low. I barely clung to life. Everything hurt. *God, it hurt.*

Reality intruded, and I recalled where I was. *The hounds,* I thought. *Where are the hounds?* I had only killed one. Where were the other two?

Glancing upwards, I saw red tinged the sky. That meant I couldn't have been out for long. The beasts could return at any time. *Move, Jamie. Heal yourself. Fear won't keep the wretched creatures away for long.*

I moved with torturous slowness. I pushed myself into a sitting position and braced my back against a tree. Channeling mana, I cast *lay hands*.

Almost immediately, I began to breathe easier. I cast the spell again, and then twice more. Only when my health was fully restored did I turn my attention to the surroundings.

To my surprise, I found I wasn't alone.

The hound that had skewered itself was where I had last left it, and from its faintly moving chest, I realized it was still alive. I grabbed the second discarded redwood staff and hauled myself to my feet.

As I staggered closer, the creature stiffened, sensing my presence. But by now I was certain the hound was helpless, so I drew right up to it without fear.

It lifted its head and snarled a warning.

"Well fought, mutt," I whispered. Raising the sharpened staff high overhead, I drove it into the pinned beast.

You have gained in experience and are now a level 20 Trainee.

I collapsed to my knees next to the corpse. While I regained my breath, I called up the Trials alerts from earlier in the battle.

You have spellcrafted a caster-only spell, from the Discipline of dragon magic. The name assigned to this spell is *living torch*. *Living torch* is a persistent spell that produces three times more dragonfire than *flare*. Its casting time is average and its rank is common.

You are the first player to have spellcrafted the dragon spell *living torch*. For this achievement, you have been awarded dragon lore and two Marks.

Lore note: *Living torch* is a spell of last resort. It produces an uncontrollable inferno that invariably is only quenched when the caster's lifeblood is spent. Across the ages, when faced with grave peril many a dragon—even elder ones—have chosen to immolate themselves through flames of a *living torch* rather than perish at their foe's hands.

"A spell of last resort," I murmured. It had certainly been that. But despite having crafted another spell, it was beyond me to feel much enthusiasm for my latest achievement. It was enough that I knew how I had killed the hounds.

I dismissed the messages and inspected myself. My stamina hovered in the red, and my mana, too, was almost drained.

What now? I mustered the strength to regain my feet. I was lost in the forest, naked, without food or shelter, and night was falling.

"Mage Jamie?"

I looked over my shoulder. A man and a woman stood a few feet away—hunters, by the look of the bows strapped on their backs.

Wide-eyed, they took in the scene.

"You've got to be kidding," I said. "*Now* you find me?" I chuckled, a broken sound that transformed into a hacking cough.

I bent over, overcome by the spate of coughing. Only my grip on the staff that pinned the hound kept me from collapsing entirely. With nearly superhuman effort, I brought myself under control.

The two watched in confusion. "Are you all right, Jamie?" The women shifted nervously from foot to foot, clearly concerned, but she didn't come any closer. *I wouldn't either, if I found a strange, naked, blood-coughing man kneeling over the corpse of a dog.*

"I'm fine." I suppressed a second bout of hysterical laughter that threatened to overcome me. "Well, not quite. Can you help me up?"

The two hurried forward and hauled me to my feet. The woman averted her gaze, and the man offered me his armor. I gratefully accepted it and dressed while the woman left to report to their company. The other hunter, unarmed and now dressed in his underclothes, kept me company. Once dressed, I slumped back down and closed my eyes, stealing what rest I could.

"Here you go, sir." The hunter offered me a piece of jerky.

I laughed. "I'm no 'sir.' Call me Jamie, please." I bit down on the dried meat. It was heavenly.

The hunter bent over the hounds, studying the corpses. Picking up something, he held it out to me. "Is this yours?"

It was my knife. I must have mislaid it during the fight. "Thanks."

"Jamie?"

I swung toward the voice and saw Tara, accompanied by the female hunter and another, vaguely familiar man.

"Yeah it's me," I said with a smile that I'm sure looked ghastly. "Hard to recognize without any hair, right?" I ran my hand over my smooth scalp.

"What happened?" Tara knelt next to me, her face tight with concern. The man loomed over both of us.

"They happened," I gestured to the hounds. "Four of them ambushed me on my way here."

"But what are *you* doing here?" asked the man, frowning.

I recognized his voice from the conference. It was Albert, the head logger. "I heard about the attack and came to help."

"Alone?" asked Tara, her brows furrowing.

I nodded. "I know, I know. I should have brought an escort. It was foolish not to."

Tara's lips thinned, but she didn't say anything further. After rising to her feet, she went to inspect the dead hound.

Albert was still frowning. "The attack happened in the morning," he said. "Why come now?"

I chuckled. "I left the Outpost hours ago, following on the heels of the spearmen sent to reinforce Tara's guard."

Albert's eyes widened. "You've been fighting these things all day?"

I nodded. "It was not pleasant, let me tell you."

Tara rejoined the conversation. "There is only one body here."

"You won't find the second. It left behind only ash." I thrust my chin to the trees to our right. "The corpse of the third is somewhere that way. The last one got away, I'm afraid."

Tara gestured in the direction I pointed, and the two hunters set off to investigate. "So now we know where they went," she murmured.

I tilted my head and looked up at her curiously. "What do you mean?"

Her gaze dropped to me. "The logging camp was attacked by six of these creatures this morning. We lost ten men and women in the assault," she said grimly. "We managed to kill two. The other four ran off. We've been waiting for their next attack ever since."

"Which never came, because you've been holding them off all this time," added Albert, his voice tinged with respect.

I chewed over their words. So there had been six hounds. It was a good thing Tara's people had killed two. I shuddered to think how I would have fared against all six.

"How did you manage to kill them?" I asked, puzzled. over that curious detail. "Every time I got close enough to *flare* into them, they teleported away."

"They can't teleport when restrained." Tara shrugged. "We got lucky figuring that out, but once we did, they fled... to ambush you, it appears."

The hunters returned. "We've found the body, Captain."

"Good," Tara said. "Albert, have your people send over some sleds. We'll load up the bodies and haul them back to camp." Tara leaned down and pulled me up. "Come on, Jamie, let's get you back to camp."

Gratefully, I accepted her help. But once I regained my feet, Tara started to move off.

"Tara, wait..." I grabbed her arm before she could step away. "About this morning," I whispered so that the others wouldn't hear. "I shouldn't have reacted the way I did."

Tara stilled for a moment before patting my arm and gently freeing herself. "We'll talk it about later."

I watched uncertainly as she walked away. It was not the blanket forgiveness I'd hoped for, but it was more than I deserved. I could only pray I hadn't destroyed our friendship altogether.

Tearing my gaze from Tara's departing figure, I turned to the logger. "Albert, would you do me a favor please?"

"Of course." he said.

"Would you have your people gather some young trees for me?" I pointed out the two burned staffs. "Saplings like those, only green and alive."

Although clearly perplexed by the request, the logger agreed. "Sure, Jamie." Stepping closer, he clasped my hand. "Melissa tells me we have you to thank for our new tools?"

I nodded.

"That was good work," Albert said. "You will do well to focus more of your talents that way. Rebuilding our civilization is what will save humanity." He glanced at the dead hound. "Not battling creatures like that." His lips turned down. "Leave that to the fighters."

I freed my hand, struggling not to roll my eyes at Albert. I didn't agree with him, but I wasn't about to get into an argument. With a wave of my arm, I bade him farewell.

Then, following after Tara, I began the long trek back to the Outpost.

CHAPTER THIRTY-THREE

388 DAYS UNTIL THE ARKON SHIELD FALLS

"All living things possess spirit."
—Trials Infopedia.

The loggers and their guard companies caught up with us soon after.

It seemed that when the scouts had caught sight of the strange burning light through the trees, the loggers had already been heading back to the Outpost.

The train of logs, hauled by men with sleds alone, lumbered through the forest, making the trip back much longer than the one going out. I did not mind though. Weary as I was, the pace suited me just fine.

Tara and I didn't get a chance to talk. She most of her time scanning the surroundings for threats or barking orders to the soldiers under her command. Despite Tara's concern though, we reached the Outpost without mishap, rolling into camp well after nightfall. The loggers had stayed out much later than usual to meet their quota of felled timber. And while the Outpost still remained short of the logs it needed for the palisade, Albert was satisfied with the progress they'd made today.

The loggers' new saws and axes had made tree felling much easier, and Albert was convinced his people would meet the commander's deadline, if only marginally.

When we reached the camp, as much as I wanted to, I didn't let myself fall straight into my pallet. My battle with the hounds had shone a glaring light on my deficiencies.

I couldn't afford to be caught so unprepared in future. With a sigh, I sank down and resumed my air magic training.

An interminable time later, I reached my goal for the night.

Your skill in air magic has advanced to level 10 and reached rank 2, Trainee.

I smiled in satisfaction at the message. *Right, that's enough.*

With that thought, I rested my head on my pillow and was soon dead to the world.

* * *

When I finally pried open my eyes the next morning, the sun was already high in the sky. Sitting up on my pallet, I noticed a fresh set of clothes and armor had been set aside for me, along with some food.

By now, the murluk attack had either already happened, or they had failed to show up again, so there was little point hurrying. I took my time with breakfast, savoring each morsel.

When I left my tent, I found the camp mostly deserted. Everyone else was up and about their daily chores.

What to do today, Jamie?

Despite the successes of the last few days, I still had a long list of things to accomplish. I needed to check in on the guards at the river, visit the dragon temple, train my magic further, and find Tara. Then there was the palisade. To meet the deadline, the wall had to be completed by day's end tomorrow.

I chewed my lip, wondering where to begin.

Priority one, I decided, would be to see how the builders were faring. With that in mind, I set off for the crafting yard.

* * *

The builders' yard was buzzing with industrious activity when I got there. Despite my newly shaven look—or because of it?—everyone seemed to recognize me. Friendly greetings and cheerful waves marked my passage through the area.

At the center of the yard, I drew to a halt. Now that I was here, I was unsure where to begin looking for the builders.

"Jamie!"

I turned at the shout. "Melissa," I greeted as the head blacksmith approached. "How are you?"

"Much better now that my people are equipped with the tools of their trade. I didn't get a chance to thank you for that the other day."

I waved off her words. "You, Anton, and Jeremy were as much responsible for our success as me," I said. Before she could contradict me, I went on. "I am actually looking for Albert, or Soren—the head builder."

Melissa smiled wryly at my change of topic. "You're too late. Both left the camp before dawn. Albert and his people are in the forest, and you will find Soren on the north side of the encampment. The builders are working on that section of the wall today."

"Oh," I said, disappointed. Though now that I thought of it, I shouldn't have expected to find the pair here. I had also hoped to speak to Tara, but she was likely guarding the loggers again today. *Perhaps I'll see her tonight.* "Do you know how the work on the palisade is going?"

"Now that his builders have the logs they need, Soren foresees no problems in completing it in time."

"That's great news," I said, relieved. "Thanks for the feedback, Melissa. I just wanted to make sure everything was on track."

As I began to turn away, she stopped me. "Wait, I almost forgot. Albert's people left something for you."

"They did?"

"Yes," she said, a frown marring her face. "It's a handful of green sticks. I thought it was a mistake, but Albert insisted you wanted them." She raised an eyebrow in question.

"I did. I mean, I do," I said with a pleased grin. "Can you show me where they are?"

Melissa led me through the yard to a large table filled with an assortment of items. On the end of the table were three saplings, just as I had requested.

Thank you, Albert.

The saplings were all about two inches thick and between four and six feet in length. I cast *analyze* upon each in turn.

The targets are a rowan, ash, and oak tree sapling. These items have no special properties.

Melissa scratched her head. "I have no idea what you want with them, but they're yours."

"Thank you," I murmured. Laying my hand on the rowan sapling, I channeled mana through it. A second later, a Trials notice opened before me and immediately made me regret my impulsive action.

A rowan tree sapling has died. Your lore skill is too low to attune this Focus.

I frowned at the message. Outwardly the rowan's appearance had not changed, but I could feel that the spark of life that been present inside it was now absent.

Contrary to the Trials alert, I had not been attempting an attunement. Idle curiosity, sparked by my experience casting the *fire ray* spell, had caused me to channel mana through the sapling, nothing more. Yet the Trials had interpreted my actions as an attempt at attunement.

It did not escape my notice that the sapling had been referred to as a 'Focus.' A Focus, I surmised, had to be a living object and it was as much a mage's tool as a hammer was a smith's.

I chewed my lip thoughtfully. Could the process to attune a Focus be similar to the one I had used to attune my mana? But why did I need lore, then? That was unexpected.

"Something wrong?" asked Melissa.

"No," I replied. "Can I take these?"

"Of course, they're yours."

"Thanks," I said. Grabbing the saplings, I began to step away, then stopped. "Oh," I said as I withdrew the knife I had shoved into my pocket for want of a sheath. "Can you get someone to make me a new casing? Th old one was… uhm, destroyed."

Melissa looked wryly at my hairless face. "Yes, I heard about that," she said, taking the knife from me. "I'll have someone bring it over to your tent when it's done." She eyed my armor. "Perhaps some better-fitting armor is in order too."

* * *

Back in my tent, I sat down crossed-legged with the second sapling across my knees. I stilled my breathing and closed my eyes, and then I opened my *magesight*.

Lines of spirit flowed through the sapling. They were nowhere near as complex as the intricate web forming my spirit, but they were nonetheless unmistakable.

Ever so carefully, I attempted the process of attunement, much in the same way as I had attuned my mana.

The sapling, of course, had none of its own mana. But after thinking on the matter I had concluded that the attunement process for a Focus required me to align *its* spirit to *my* mana. That way, the Focus would survive my spellcasting and wouldn't die as the previous saplings had when exposed to my magic.

I gathered my mana and dribbled a little into the sapling—the smallest amount I could manage. I exhaled in relief when it caused no adverse reaction, and then I moved on to the next step. Manipulating the mana I dropped into the wood, I coaxed the sapling to recognize my magic.

The wood's grains shifted minutely in response to my will, but then, a moment later, they snapped back, seemingly rejecting my magic. I watched, dismayed, as the spirit weaves riddling the sapling vanished.

An ash tree sapling has died. Your lore skill is too low to attune this Focus.

My face fell. "Damn!" I muttered. I had felt so close to success.

I considered the Trials message. Again, there was the reference to my lore being insufficient. Lore was not a Discipline I had studied much in the wiki. It wasn't a combat Discipline but rather a crafting one. Yet lore seemed essential for attuning a Focus.

Do all mages need lore... or only those creating their own Focus?

I sighed. If only I still had access to the wiki, I could learn more of the Discipline and consider its merits in greater detail. But I had no choice now.

I ran my hand along the dead sapling's length. I knew I couldn't ignore the Trials alert for a second time, and I had only one sapling left. I could get more of them from the forest, but I suspected that, without increasing my lore, I would keep failing.

I would have to increase the Discipline through the temple, if only for the benefit of creating an attuned staff. I set aside the saplings. Before I visited the temple, I wanted to train at least one other of my magical Disciplines.

I had spent my trip back from the forest last night analyzing my battle with the hounds. Two things had become immediately apparent to me.

One: I was too vulnerable at night. And two: I couldn't always depend on *flare* and *invincible*. The day-long standoff with the hounds had taught me that if I couldn't bring my spells to bear on my foes, I was helpless.

The solution was obvious: I needed a disabling spell, a means to hold my enemies in place while I damaged them. I knew of a basic spell that could do the job, but it was from the Discipline of earth magic.

I closed my eyes and drew up my mana. Manipulating the magic, I shaped a rudimentary representation of earth in my mind. Then while I let intuition guide me, I twisted and turned the mana as I refined my understanding.

I don't know whether it was because I was getting better at magic, or as a result of my past training in the other magic Disciplines, but whatever the reason, I advanced my knowledge of earth magic much faster than I'd expected. After only a few hours of practice, I reached Trainee rank.

Your skill in earth magic has advanced to level 10 and reached rank 2 Trainee.

Wincing at the stiffness in my limbs, I creaked to my feet and ducked out of the tent. The time had come to visit the dragon temple again.

* * *

You have entered Wyrm Island.

Aurora met me in the center of Wyrm Island, next to the gate. Like the previous few times I had been here, she didn't seem happy to see me.

"Human," she said, her voice oozing boredom. "What can I do for you today?"

I bowed, minding my manners as I had been warned to, despite her less-than-courteous demeanor. "I'd like to advance my Disciplines and enhance my Attributes," I replied.

"You have one hundred and sixty-one Tokens and twenty-six Marks available. What Disciplines and Attributes do you wish to train?"

"Dragon magic, life magic, earth magic, air magic, and lore. Please increase them all to twenty." After the temple made the changes, I would have four magic Disciplines to call upon, giving me some much-needed versatility.

"Done. You have one hundred and twenty-seven Tokens remaining," Aurora said. "In which Attributes do you wish to invest your Marks?"

"Vigor, channeling, constitution, and spellpower." Now that I had increased my spellpower to rank two, the limit of what I could expect to achieve with training, I could not easily enhance it further without Marks.

"Noted," Aurora said. "You have ten Marks remaining. Your new knowledge and the changes to your body will be effected once you exit Wyrm Island."

Satisfied with the improvements I had chosen, I waved goodbye to the purple woman and stepped back through the gate.

* * *

You have exited Wyrm Island. Your spellpower, constitution, vigor, and channeling have increased to level 20.

Your skills in dragon, air, earth, lore, and life magic have advanced to level 20.

Stepping out of the dragon temple, I felt the new knowledge settle within me and my body adapt to its new Attributes. A pleased grin broke out across my face. I was getting stronger.

And now it's time to attune my staff.

Limping down the temple steps, I began to hurry toward my tent. That was when a scream cut through the air.

High, shrill, piercing—it was a child's cry.

I froze. What was a child doing here? Turning around, I saw a family of three—two parents and one child—in almost the exact same spot I had appeared on entering Overworld.

Two spearmen hurried toward the trio. They had likely been posted to keep watch for new arrivals. The child, a girl who looked no older than ten, was bawling. Unlike the vast majority of human players, she had entered in her own body. So had her parents. They were both middle-aged, with gray-flecked hair and faces lined with worry.

What were her parents thinking, bringing her to Overworld?

Slowly, I made my way to the trio. The two spearmen were trying to calm the family. The parents appeared just as confused and fearful as their daughter.

"Ma'am, sir, I am Jamie," I said, cutting through the shouting and screaming. "How can I help?"

"Who *are* you?" demanded the father, rounding on me.

I paused. "I am the settlement's mage," I replied. Knowing he would likely scoff, I cast *flare*.

The parents stepped back, afraid, but the girl's screams stopped as I had hoped they would, and her eyes lit up in fascination at the flames wreathing my hand. "Can I touch it?" she asked, reaching out.

I drew my hand back and shook my head. "No, you cannot, kiddo. It's dangerous."

"But I want to," she said crossly.

Smiling, I kneeled down before her and cast *lay hands*. Holding out my glowing, blue-white hands, I said, "Here, you can touch this."

Her hands snapped out immediately, but her father stepped forward to pull her back.

"It's all right," I told him. "There is no danger."

He hesitated, but before he could intervene, his daughter decided the matter. "It tickles!" the girl said as her hand touched mine and the spell faded.

The father relaxed, and I rose to my feet. "You are in Overworld, sir." I addressed the man. "In the Outpost, a location settled entirely by humans." I hesitated, glancing down at his daughter. "Why did you come here?"

"I'm Greg," the man said. "And we had no choice."

"No choice?" I asked, confused.

"I don't know when you left Earth, young man, but things back home have turned grim. Volcanoes, tornadoes, earthquakes, every natural disaster you can think of; they're all happening, all over the world, and all at once. The *only* places on Earth not unstable right now are the gates and their immediate vicinity."

Greg's lips twisted. "People are finally taking the overworlders' words to heart. The exodus has begun in earnest. Millions are fleeing through whichever gate is closest." He shook his head. "I don't know how many will make it. We were more fortunate than most. Our own home was very close to a gate, so we entered it as soon as we could."

I frowned. "Are you from New Springs?" It was the town Tara, the commander, and the other recruits had come from.

Greg shook his head. "No. I am from London. The gates have been—what did that reporter call it?—unlocked. You can choose to exit anywhere in the Human Dominion now."

I pursed my lips. "Why come here though? Why choose location seventy-eight?"

Greg hung his head. "Honestly, we chose at random." He rested a hand on his daughter's shoulder. "Because of Claire here, we underwent our Trials Initiation together." He smiled bitterly. "At least this blasted world had the decency not to separate us from our little girl."

My brows shot up. All *three* had been initiated. Surely the child was too young? "Claire is a player?" I asked.

"Not a full one," answered the mother, her voice quivering. "Or that's what those stone tablets we found in Wyrm Island led us to believe." She clutched at Claire protectively. "Until she becomes an adult, my poor girl is defenseless!"

I was puzzled by the mother's words. *Stone tablets? What's she talking about?* I hadn't seen any items like that during my visits to the island. But before I could question her, Greg spoke up.

"Now that isn't quite true, dear," he said. "Those tablets said Claire can train her Disciplines through natural learning." He paused. "Whatever that means."

I glanced down at the little girl and applied *analyze*. The results were surprising.

The target is Claire Thompson, a level 1 human child and future player. Due to her child status the target's Potentials are hidden, temple access is denied, and experience gains are locked.

I frowned, troubled by the analysis report. I turned to the two spearmen, who had been patiently observing our conversation. "Soldiers, you better take these three to the commander and make sure she hears their story." I hesitated. "Also, tell her that given what's happening on Earth, she can expect more recruits today and tomorrow—many more."

The two nodded and led the family away. Claire waved goodbye and I waved back. Jolin would no doubt reach the same conclusions I had after she heard the family's story, but I wanted to be sure she didn't miss the implications. I only hoped the Outpost could cope with the sudden influx of refugees that was certain to follow.

CHAPTER THIRTY-FOUR

387 DAYS UNTIL THE ARKON SHIELD FALLS
1 DAY TO EARTH'S DESTRUCTION
1 DAY UNTIL THE WARREN IS DESTROYED

Lost deep in thought, I made my way back to my tent. Greg's words kept playing over in my mind. The situation back on Earth, which I hadn't had time to think about over the last few days, now felt altogether too real.

How would Greg's family—and others like his—survive on Overworld?

The Trials did not consider Claire a full player, which meant she couldn't enter a temple or level up. It was a cruel handicap. The poor girl could still be killed or hurt, but at the same time she was barred from the benefits players received—benefits that helped them survive.

Children would have to be sheltered on this world, I realized, even more so than on Earth. But how would we do that when most adults couldn't even protect themselves here?

Unbeckoned, the commander's words whispered through my mind: *'Their future will be in the hands of people like you, Jamie.'* If I joined the Outpost, I could help keep families like Greg's safe.

No, my mind refused the possibility. *I can't stay.*

Thousands of human children must be scattered all over the Human Dominion by now, all in as much danger as little Claire.

I had to at least try to help. And the only way I knew to help Claire and all the other Earth refugees was to get stronger.

I reached my tent and ducked inside. Sitting down cross-legged on my pallet, I pulled the last remaining sapling over my knees and considered it.

For a time, my mind refused to focus, but the troubles of Greg's family, the Outpost, and Earth eventually faded from my consciousness, and with grim determination, I got back to work.

My increased skill in the lore Discipline had furthered my understanding of the Trials and the underlying principles of Overworld. I now knew that all magic was different and that most living things considered foreign magic—in its raw form—to be hostile.

Depending on the complexity of the entity, lifeforms reacted differently when faced with the threat of foreign magic. A person like Tara would instinctively shrug off an attempt to channel magic through her. But the spirit weave of a simpler organism— like the sapling I held—was not robust enough to fight off invasive magic, so it died.

To prevent that instinctive response, I had to encourage the living wood to align itself with my magic. I *had* been on the right track earlier; I had just gone about it wrong.

Opening my *magesight*, I delved into the five-foot-long oak on my knees, studying it intently until I knew its every knot, gnarl, and grain. When I was certain I understood the sapling as fully as I could, I began to attune its nature to mine, carefully introducing my magic's velvet swirls of cobalt blue.

Inch by inch, the living cells in the sapling tasted the droplets of my mana and reformed, sip by sip. The grains of oak kept shifting until, eventually, they aligned perfectly with the channels in my body.

I knew the exact moment it happened. When it did, the sapling transformed from a thing apart into a living extension of myself, as much a vessel of my magic and will as the rest of my body.

You have discovered: *basic attunement*, a Technique from the Discipline of lore. *Basic attunement* is an ability that creates a bond between a Focus and a magic wielder, allowing the mage to cast spells through the attuned Focus. Its casting time is very slow and its rank is common.

You have created an oak wizard's staff. This Focus has no special properties, can only be used by Jameson Sinclair, and has a basic level of attunement.

I stared in amazement at the staff in my hands. The attunement had transformed it. Its previously gnarled, soft, slightly pliable texture was gone. Now it was a smooth, unvarnished length of wood as hard and unyielding as steel. Its color had changed too. The oak's natural brown had darkened to a near-uniform black.

Closing my eyes, I could sense the staff's presence as much as I could any one of my limbs. Tentatively, I raised the staff off my knees and held it horizontally aloft.

Then I cast *flare*.

Dragonfire flowed from my hands and rippled down the Focus, wreathing its entire length in flames without damaging the staff.

Yes! Now this is a proper mage's weapon. I rose to my feet and made my way to the training ground. *Time to improve my skill in the staff Discipline.*

* * *

The training ground was crowded.

Men and women crammed the large space even more than on my previous visits. Had the settlement's fighting force grown that much?

I strolled through the sparring warriors until I spotted a familiar face. "John!" I called to the giant who was shouting instructions to two youths. Judging by their poor form, they had to be day-zero fishes.

John turned, a welcoming smile on his face. "Jamie!" His eyes roved over my hairless features. "I heard about your escapade in the woods. Looks like it was some fight."

"You wouldn't believe half of it," I said with a laugh. "I tell you, I found myself wishing I was facing the spider queen instead."

"That bad, eh?" John tsked sympathetically.

I nodded. "I meant to come by the river earlier. Did the murluks show up today?"

John shook his head. "Nope, no sign of them at all. I reckon you scared them off for good. Good riddance, I say." His eyes drifted to the black staff in my hands. "So, what are you doing here, Jamie?" He gestured to the staff. "And what is *that*?"

"My wizard's staff," I said with a grin.

"A wizard's staff?" John tugged on his beard. "What's that?"

"You'll see," I promised. "Care to spar? I need to train up my staff skills." I glanced at the youths he was training. "Or are you busy?"

John shook his head. "Don't worry about those two. One of the other instructors will see to them." He ushered me to a nearby sparring circle. "Don't cry too badly when I beat you." He grinned broadly. "I won't go as easy on you as Tara did."

* * *

John did beat me. Repeatedly.

But I kept at it, all through lunch and most of the afternoon. I didn't stop, not until my staff skill reached Trainee rank. Training the staff Discipline took many more hours than my magic Disciplines, but when the sun began to set and I limped back to camp, I was satisfied with my progress.

I twirled the staff as I walked. Although my staff lacked the sharpened end and longer reach of John's spear, the black rod had held up well against the bigger man's weapon. The staff packed a hefty blow, and the few times I had landed a hit on John, I could tell he had felt it.

John had snuck in more than his fair share of blows, of course, but despite his friendly threats, he had not beaten me nearly as severely as Tara had in that memorable sparring session. *And,* I reminded myself, *our sparring would have gone very differently if I'd used my magic.*

On the way back to my tent, I stopped by the temple and increased my skill in the staff Discipline to level twenty. Given how much a part of me the staff felt, it would be my weapon of choice from now on.

When I reached my tent, I sat outside in the cool night air. I had to accomplish one more task for the day: spellcrafting the pair of spells I wanted.

The next hour passed in a blur as I experimented with air magic spellforms. One particular spell took longer to create than I'd expected, but after repeatedly pouring mana into my eyes, the magic did more than fizzle out.

You have spellcrafted a caster-only spell, from the Discipline of air magic. The name assigned to this spell is *night vision*. **Its casting time is average and its rank is common.**

I blinked, staring at the sleeping camp with new eyes. The night around me had transformed. Its shadows had disappeared, and, in their stead, the world shone with startling clarity, as if lit by a noonday sun.

I smiled. Now I could see in the dark like any nocturnal predator.

Next, I turned my attention to my earth magic. Juggling spellforms in my mind, I willed the ground beneath me to transform, and in short order, it did.

You have spellcrafted a touch-based disabling spell, from the Discipline of earth magic. The name assigned to this spell is *sinking mud*. **Its casting time is fast and its rank is uncommon.**

I stared down at my body in surprise. I was buried hip deep in mud. The spell had mutated a nine-yard long cone of ground from solid, hardpacked earth to clinging, sticky mud, with me at its center.

Perhaps not the wisest choice to attempt the spell on the ground directly beneath me. I chuckled. Not even being trapped in mud of my own devising was enough to spoil my mood.

It had been a fruitful day all around. I had significantly expanded my repertoire of Disciplines and spells, and I was better equipped to face whatever challenges the Trials threw my way.

Still chuckling, I dragged myself out of the mud and into my tent. I looked forward to whatever the new day brought.

CHAPTER THIRTY-FIVE

386 DAYS UNTIL THE ARKON SHIELD FALLS
THE DAY OF EARTH'S DESTRUCTION

I woke up early, reinvigorated, refreshed, and just a little nervous. Today was the fourth day since we had claimed the spider warren, and today the settlement had to be established to retain the lair. *We will not lose that lair,* I vowed, although I had no reason to believe we wouldn't succeed.

The Outpost's development had been progressing well since the murluk attacks had stopped, and I had advanced significantly too.

I am a proper wizard now, I thought, smiling as I rose from my pallet to face the new day. I almost felt ready to set out in the wider world.

Once the settlement was founded, things would change. The Outpost wouldn't just be a location anymore. The region would be owned territory, belonging to whichever faction the commander joined, or created. The dragon temple would advance and offer further benefits to players.

At least that was what the wiki said.

My smiled faded. But today the gates on Earth would also close. Forever. I still wasn't certain what would become of our home planet and the people left behind. But I could do nothing for them.

I am doing the best I can. I fended off further dark musings. It was too early in the day for pessimism.

Stepping out of my tent, I found a surprise waiting for me: a crate filled with goods. Lying on top of the piled items was my knife, housed in in a new soft-leather sheath.

But that was not all.

Beneath the blade was the new armor Melissa had promised. Smiling, I lifted out the items and used *analyze* on the crafter's gifts.

The target is a set of spider leather armor: a leather vest, leggings, helm, gloves, and boots. Made from the carapace of a brown spider queen, this set is resistant to piercing.

The target is a set of silk clothes: cloak, shirt, and pants. Made from the silk of a brown spider queen, this set improves the wearer's ability to camouflage themself and is extremely durable.

"Well," I breathed, awed by the magnanimity of Melissa's gifts. The crafters had outdone themselves.

The armor, made from supple brown spider hides, was many times better than the crude murluk armor I presently wore. Each piece interlocked seamlessly, as if made with me in mind, offering few vulnerable points for an enemy to target.

The silk clothes were a wonder too. The ankle-length hooded cloak, dyed brown to match the armor, blended into the surroundings as I moved. The gifts were priceless. I would have to thank Melissa when next I saw her.

Equipped in my new gear, I strode from my tent a new man. I left only the gloves unequipped, pocketing them instead. Glancing up, I saw the sky had just begun to lighten. Dawn approached. If I hurried, I could catch the loggers before they left for the day.

I planned on spending the day with Albert's team to ensure nothing went wrong with the last shipment of logs needed to complete the palisade.

And I needed to speak to Tara.

It was past time I mended things between us. I was making my way east through the camp when a cry from behind stopped me.

"Mage Jamie! Mage Jamie, stop!"

I turned around. A soldier I didn't know was sprinted up to me. "Is something wrong?" I asked.

"The commander wants to see you," he panted, as he stumbled to a halt.

I hesitated. I hadn't spoken to the commander since I'd rejected her offer to stay. I sighed. *That is another fence that needs mending.*

But first, I had to speak to Tara. "Tell her I will come see her later," I replied.

"You have to come now." The messenger shook his head. "The commander was insistent."

I frowned. Jolin could wait, but before I could say that, he burst out, "Another mage has arrived!"

My mouth dropped open. "A mage?" I repeated. "A *human* mage?"

He nodded vigorously. "Yes, from Earth. He came through the gate not long ago and he's with the commander right now."

I pinched the bridge of my nose. The news was unexpected, and I honestly wasn't sure what to make of it. "All right then, lead on."

※ ※ ※

The commander's pavilion had expanded since I had last been there. No longer a single tent, it had blossomed into a series of interconnected hubs. The command center—as I decided to dub it—was a hive of activity, with messengers scurrying back and forth.

I studied the scene with bemusement. *When had the Outpost gotten so busy?*

As we drew closer, other changes became apparent. A squad of spearmen guarded the entrance, and the vicinity was cordoned off.

I frowned. *When did the commander start needing protection within the camp?*

The guards immediately recognized me, whether from my gait, lack of hair, or staff and waved us through. *Good,* I thought. *At least, bureaucracy hasn't set in yet.*

Entering the command center, I received my third shock of the morning. The first tent had been configured into an antechamber lined with benches, all of which—even this early in the morning—were full.

"Who are all these people?" I murmured.

The messenger glanced at me. "Recruits waiting to see the commander. They haven't stopped arriving since yesterday. The commander and the captains have been up all night, busy with meet and greets." He leaned in and added in a low whisper, "Some of the new fishes have quite an air about themselves, demanding—can you believe it?—to see the commander as soon as they arrived."

So, I thought, studying the antechamber, *the exodus has begun in earnest.* I ran my gaze over those filling the benches. Nearly all of them wore the same basic clothes I had arrived in days ago. Some bore haughty expressions, and others scowled, but most were confused and afraid.

As I strode through the room, faces turned my way. Some shrank away, others narrowed their eyes in suspicion, and yet others stared enviously at my gear. Self-conscious, I hurried to the next room.

There, each seated at a desk, were Captain Marcus and Petrov. A long queue of people lined up in front of each man.

The two captains looked harried and worn-out. Neither looked to have slept at all. Suddenly, I felt guilty for my own rest.

"Go on in." Marcus looked up and waved me through. "She is waiting." As I passed, he muttered, "And try to contain your temper."

Wondering at his last comment, I stepped into the commander's office. Jolin was seated behind her desk, a much newer, sturdier construction. Standing at her back was a muscular soldier, perhaps a bodyguard, and lounging in the chair across from her was a new fish, marked so by his attire.

The seated stranger's expression held none of the fear or confusion seen on the faces of recruits in the antechamber. Instead, he looked... bored and put-out.

Blond, blue-eyed, and large of frame, he seemed extraordinarily confident and self-assured.

The new mage, I guessed.

I noted with relief that the commander had not undergone a transformation in my absence. Her face bore the same cool, patient expression of calm in the center of the storm.

"Ah, Jamie," the old lady said, "there you are." Neither her voice nor her expression betrayed that we had parted on poor terms the last time we spoke.

"Good morning, ma'am," I replied, taking my cue from her.

"Wow! Cool digs, dude," said the new player, eyeing my equipment.

"Uh... thank you," I replied.

Not acknowledging my reply, the youth's blond head whipped to the commander. "I want a set of those, gran." He paused. "But better."

Gran! I almost choked at the fish's words and tone, but I disguised my reaction behind a cough. The bodyguard behind the commander stirred but didn't otherwise react.

"Of course, Lance," replied the commander, her tone too bland.

My own expression cleared at Jolin's reply. Clearly the old lady was humoring the new fish. *Who does this Lance think he is?* I thought, laughing on the inside.

I shuddered to think what Tara would make of him. Although... on second thought, it might be amusing to watch the two meet.

"Lance, I'd like you to meet Jamie, our resident mage," Jolin said. "Jamie, this is Lance, a mage as well."

Lance's gaze narrowed as he studied me.

Assessing the competition? I wondered. A moment later, a strange ripple passed over me. I was being *analyzed*.

The moment the ripple passed, Lance snorted and turned back to the commander. "I'm twice the mage this cripple is, Gran. Whatever he can do, I promise you I'll do two times better." Turning my way, he shrugged nonchalantly. "No offense, dude."

I stared at Lance, both appalled and fascinated. But before I could respond to his insult, I sensed the commander's eyes on me. I glanced her way.

I don't know whether it was because I was getting better at reading her or whether she was deliberately revealing her thoughts, but I could feel Jolin's sudden tension.

Holding the old lady's gaze, I replied to the mage, "None taken." At my response, the commander relaxed minutely.

"Damn shame about your foot, though," Lance continued, oblivious to the subtle exchange between Jolin and me. "And damn foolish to have kept your old body, man. But I suppose I can't expect noobs like you to know any better. You should have taken the new form, dude."

I fought the urge to sigh. The reason for Marcus' muttered comment was abundantly clear now. Yet I was curious about the new player and his casual dismissal of my Magic Potential.

Just how strong a mage is he? Reaching out, I cast *analyze* on Lance.

The target is Lance Gillian, a level 1 human player. He is gifted in Magic, is gifted with Might, has mediocre Resilience, and has meager Craft.

He had the makings of a decent mage—at least based on his Potential. His attitude, however, left much to be desired.

Lance sensed my *analyze* as clearly as I had his. "Impressive, ain't it?"

"Very," I replied dryly.

Lance turned back to the commander. "With my Magic Potential, things will change around here, I promise you. Just heed my advice, lady, and we'll get along just fine."

Seemingly stumped for a response, the commander said, "Jamie is a gamer too."

Lance swung back to me.

I shot the commander a wry look. *Thanks, ma'am.* I finally had an inkling of why I had been summoned. The new player was clearly a handful, and with his status as a mage, he needed delicate handling. The commander, though, appeared at a loss on how to go about it.

"What games did you play, dude?"

"Oh, a bit of this and that," I replied.

"Ah, a casual player." Lance nodding knowingly. "Not a *real* gamer, then," he said as an aside to the commander. He turned back to me. "But don't worry, I'll show you the ropes. I've studied that damn wiki from end to end. I know this game backward now."

"You studied the Infopedia?" I asked, my interest piqued for the first time. I didn't bother explaining that the Trials wasn't a game. He wouldn't have believed me. But he would learn.

"Yep," said Lance, poorly concealing a yawn. "It's why I delayed my entry into Overworld so long."

Well, well, perhaps there is something to be learned from Lance after all. "That's great!" I said, rubbing my hands together with false enthusiasm. "I look forward to learning at the feet of a master such as yourself!"

From beyond Lance, the commander shot me a glance. *Okay, perhaps I laid it on a bit thick.*

"Sure, man, whatever. I'm happy to show you the ropes," said Lance. "As long as it doesn't hamper my own leveling of course." He yawned again.

"Lance, you look tired," said the commander. She gestured her bodyguard forward. "Jim, please show Lance to his tent so that he can get some rest."

"See you soon, Lance," I said, waving farewell as the mage stepped out.

Turning to the commander, I saw she had bowed her head and was rubbing delicately at her temples. It was the first sign of stress or anxiety I had seen from her.

Lance must have really tried her patience.

"How old is he?" I asked, eliciting a laugh from Jolin.

"I don't know," she said, then snorted. "But too young by far."

"Was I that bad?" I asked. It had been less than five days since I'd arrived on Overworld, but after meeting Lance it felt like a lifetime.

The old lady's face turned serious. "Not by half, Jamie."

I nodded, embarrassed by her praise. "May I?" I pointed to Lance's abandoned seat.

"Please do."

"Things are quite busy out there." I gestured to the antechamber as I sat down.

The commander nodded. "Recruitment has picked up considerably. I expect that today alone we will get several thousand recruits." Her eyes turned distant. "People are panicking back home. Now that Earth is in its final hours, everyone is desperate to escape."

She turned back to me. "Thank you, by the way, for sending that family to me yesterday. I hadn't foreseen children. It adds a new urgency to what we do here."

I nodded, knowing what she meant.

"What do you think of Lance?" she asked.

"You mean besides the obvious? If he really *has* studied the wiki, then he is an invaluable resource. I'd advise setting Marcus on him to extract as much information as possible."

"I'll do that. And what of his Magic Potential?"

"I am afraid Lance will find it much harder on Overworld than he expects," I said. "He will need to be protected."

Had I needed as much protection?

I hesitated before going on. "Don't expect the same from Lance as what I've been able to accomplish. It's not arrogance," I added quickly. "But I have some... unique advantages that I doubt Lance possesses."

The commander smiled. "Jamie, I don't expect *anyone* can accomplish what you have."

I blushed and fell silent. The animosity of our previous exchange had vanished, and while a gulf still lay between the commander's position and mine, I sensed no bitterness in her. To my surprise, I realized that I, too, bore none toward her.

As if sensing the direction of my thoughts, the old lady sighed. "I want to apologize for my words the last time we spoke, Jamie. I was harsher on you than I should have been, especially given what you suffered." She met my eyes, her gaze frank and direct. "What you accomplished back on Earth was commendable. An inspiration, even—to all of us. I wanted to let you know that I understand."

I swallowed painful memories. "But you don't agree with my path."

She didn't look away. "No, I do not," she said softly. "Your place is with us. With the people of this settlement. I won't claim I am not disappointed by your choice, but I will not stop you from carving your own path. And you will always be welcome here."

I bowed my head, trying to hide my emotions. "Thank you for that, ma'am," I said once I had regained my composure. I decided to move the conversation on, not wanting to dwell on the topic of my leaving any further. "What is the progress on the palisade? Will we make today's deadline?"

"Yes, thank God," replied the commander, accepting the change in direction without comment. "Tara and the loggers should be back by midday with the last shipment of wood, which will give Soren and his builders enough time to finish the final sections on the east side."

"Excellent," I said, relieved by the confirmation. "Well in that case, I thought that today I would—"

"Commander! Commander!" A messenger barged into the chamber unannounced.

Jolin looked up calmly. "What is it, Devlin?"

"The murluks, ma'am," replied Devlin. "They're back."

Chapter Thirty-Six

386 DAYS UNTIL THE ARKON SHIELD FALLS

Despite her age, the commander was spryer than I was. Before I could lift myself from my chair, Jolin was out of hers and marching into the antechamber. The scout followed on her heels, filling her in on the details in rapid-fire fashion.

I missed most of what he reported, although what little I heard left me with the impression that the murluk army had swollen considerably. Hurrying in the pair's wake, I found the old lady addressing her captains and other officers.

"Petrov, sound the alarm and marshal the men at the western gate," the commander ordered. "Jim, gather my guard. We move to the gate as soon as they are assembled."

Jolin swung to the waiting messengers. "Inform the head crafters. I want any of their people near the river moved back immediately. I also want Soren's team on standby."

The commander glanced at her scout captain. "Marcus, fetch the new mage, Lance. I want him under my watch during the battle. He is liable to do something foolish otherwise," she muttered.

"Yes, ma'am," replied Marcus.

Throwing the commander quick salutes, the assembled officers dispersed to see to her orders.

Jolin turned my way. "Jamie, can I trust you to do whatever needs doing?"

It was one of the things I admired about the commander. She never attempted to control my magic; instead, she trusted me to fulfil my role. Her confidence made me more determined not to fail.

"Yes, ma'am," I replied, echoing Marcus. "I'll see you on the wall."

I broke away from the commander as more officers converged on her. I noticed unhappily that many of the new fishes, curious about what was going on, had stolen into the room, and I hoped someone would take them in hand. I had no time to take care of it myself. I had to get to the river.

Even at my quickest limp, it took me ten minutes to cross the camp. The Outpost was in chaos, its usual order crumbling with the sudden influx of new recruits. People ran furiously back and forth, getting in each other's way. Already uneasy about the murluks' reappearance, I felt sure the new chaos would not help the forthcoming battle.

When I got to the western palisade, I found that it, too, had not escaped the disorder plaguing the settlement. New fishes wandered aimlessly along the wall, disturbing the armored spearmen, who were trying to form ranks.

"Damn it," I growled. "Why hasn't someone chased those idiots away yet?"

Seething by the time I reached the palisade gate, I barged through the ranks of spearmen arranged in a cordon around it, ignoring their greetings.

The sliding gate, which had been under construction the last time I had seen it, was standing open. John and two officers I didn't recognize, argued animatedly before the gate. The big lieutenant looked worried—scared, even—which made no sense. We were only facing murluks, after all, and whatever the number, murluks were manageable. Especially with both the walls and my magic to tilt the odds in our favor.

Leaving them to it, I ran my gaze along the palisade. Only two elevated platforms—each no more than a few yards wide—had been constructed thus far. They had been placed about fifty yards on either side of gate.

None of the other earthworks planned for the second phase of construction had been built, which explained why the gate was still open. With no walkways on the inside of the palisade, archers could not fire on the enemy from atop the walls. Being unable to man the walls reduced their strategic value to that of a simple barrier. The palisade's *only* purpose in the forthcoming battle would be to funnel the murluks to the relatively narrow opening of the gate, where it was expected they would be easily held at bay.

No one expected the murluks to try scaling the walls with siege towers or ladders; as long as the walls held, the outcome of the battle should be assured.

"As long as the walls hold," I muttered.

Having seen enough, I joined John and the other officers. "Morning, John," I greeted.

The big lieutenant spun around. "I can't tell you how glad I am to see you, Jamie!" the lieutenant's face flooded with relief.
John's response puzzled me. *Why was everyone panicking?* "What's all the fuss about?" I gestured to the state of the camp.

John cleared his throat and pointed to the open gate. "Best you see for yourself," he said, unusually serious.

From where I stood, I couldn't see the river through the gate—the riverbanks sloped too steeply for that. With a bewildered glance at John, I limped through the gate to the edge of the upper bank.

My mouth dropped open in shock at the spectacle below.

Thousands of murluks were gathered along the river, their ranks stretching to the north and south, many rows deep. New lines were forming every minute.

But that was the least distressing part. At the forefront of the murluk army, evenly spaced along the line, were... giants.

Giant frogs! Each looked twelve feet tall and all of them were armed with clubs and shields. Slurping noisily, they bobbed along the line, shoving back any smaller murluks that shifted out of place.

What are those creatures? Reaching out with my will, I used *analyze* on the closest.

The target is a level 29 river murluk overseer. It has no Magic, exceptional Might, is gifted with Resilience, and has low Craft.

"Overseers," I murmured. The description was apt, considering the way they appeared to be maintaining order amongst their smaller brethren. But while the overseers were enormous, given their levels, I judged the threat they posed to be manageable.

I let my eyes slide to the back of the line, where a truly monstrous creature surfaced from the river depths.

I had not looked directly upon the behemoth before this, hoping it was just a figment of my overwrought imagination.

Sadly, that was not the case.

Ignoring the furious churning in my guts, I swiveled to face the river monster.

It was a murluk too—or rather, what a murluk would look like if grown to the size of a tree. Despite being immersed hip-deep in the river, the behemoth towered over its smaller companions, dwarfing the murluk overseers.

That thing has to be at least thirty feet tall!

Wider than a boat, the beast stood in the water as if it owned the river. In hands as thick as tree trunks, the colossal murluk wielded a club bigger than I was. Its face, atop a neck corded with muscle, was contorted in fury. Raising the massive chunk of wood, the gargantuan murluk slammed it down on the river's surface and roared a dull, formless noise that made the ground shake and sent waves smashing into the shore. Even from under the shadow of the gate, I felt the hot stink of the creature's breath—fetid with mud and rot.

Ducking, I shielded my nose and mouth while I waited for the roar to die down. *Bloody hell! Was that roar a challenge? To me?*

I turned back to the behemoth. Sure enough, the creature's bulbous eyes were fixed unerringly on me.

I swallowed. *Alrighty, then.* With trepidation, I cast *analyze* on the monster.

The target is a level 57 river murluk chieftain. It has mediocre Magic, exceptional Might, exceptional Resilience, and low Craft.

The chieftain has magic! That, more than the monster's size, scared me.

I tightened my grip on my staff. How was I going to combat his magic while fighting off an entire murluk army? And where had the chieftain and the overseers come from?

I didn't wonder *why* they had come; that much was obvious. The chieftain was here for me. I was sure of it.

"A goddamn terrible sight isn't?" John said from beside me.

I nodded, my dry mouth unable to form any other reply.

We both studied the murluk horde in silence. "How long have they been gathering?" I asked eventually.

John scratched his head. "Ten minutes, maybe."

I rubbed my chin as I considered John's words. Despite the force the murluks had assembled, they hadn't begun their advance. We had some time yet to prepare ourselves.

I was worried, though.

Now, when it faced its gravest peril, the Outpost was the most disorganized than I had ever seen it.

"Let's get the troops ready," I suggested. "The commander will be here soon, but right now, someone needs to get things under control. Send some soldiers to push back that crowd of gawkers. Have the men march the new fishes to the temple. They can wait out the battle in safety there. And get some men up on the platforms to keep watch on the murluks."

John just grinned at me.

It took me a moment to realize why: I had just ordered him around like a superior officer. I felt my face redden. "Sorry, John, I didn't mean—"

"Nah, it's fine, Jamie. Your orders make sense. I'll see to it." He grinned. "I'm not opposed to following sensible commands, you know. Just don't give me any dumb ones, and we'll be all right," he added with a laugh before jogging back to his men.

I watched John for a moment. He was a good man, and I was thankful he had been on guard here at the gate.

Turning back to the river, I kept watch on the enemy. Murluks were still emerging from the water. I tried to estimate their numbers, but after reaching ten thousand, I stopped. How many soldiers did the Outpost have? A thousand?

Ten-to-one odds—at best.

I winced. Our chances were not good. *But we have the palisade,* I reminded myself. *And the commander. And me.*

The murluks, though, had their overseers... and the chieftain. I turned my attention to the giant murluks. Their number was much easier to determine. All told, there were ten overseers.

The tread of approaching feet interrupted me. The commander and Petrov stopped beside me. Jolin studied the murluks in silence, her face impassive. "Do you know what magic the chieftain has?"

I shook my head. "There's no way to tell. Not until he uses it."

She accepted my answer without comment. "Will you be able to protect our troops from his spells?"

I thought about it for a moment before shaking my head. "I don't think so," I admitted. "I don't have any defensive magic that will work on a scale large enough. My spells are best used offensively." I scrutinized the chieftain. "Perhaps I can keep him too distracted to launch any of his spells."

Jolin tilted her head in consideration. "Then the chieftain is yours to handle."

I bowed my head, accepting the command.

The commander turned to Petrov. "Captain, triple the men in the cordon around the gate, and have the rest of the spearmen arranged in a line along the wall in case the murluks think to scale the palisade. I also want all our hunters summoned and deployed as archers. They will be firing blind over the palisade, but, given the enemy's numbers, they are unlikely to miss."

"Yes, ma'am." Petrov saluted.

"One more thing, Captain," Jolin called, as Petrov marched away.

He swung around, and Jolin continued more quietly, "Have a detail on retrieval duty. Their orders are to strip our dead of weapons and armor and pass them to the new fishes."

The captain studied the commander for a long moment before inclining his head in acceptance. "Yes, ma'am," he replied grimly.

I shivered. If the commander was contemplating using the new fishes, the situation had to be dire. "How many men do we have?" I asked quietly.

"Less than I'd like," replied Jolin. "Tara has two oversized companies under her command at the logging camp. I've sent a runner to call them back, but I fear they will return too late." She paused. "We have nine hundred fighters at our disposal."

I gulped. *The odds are even worse than I thought.* "When do you want me to begin my attack?"

"Wait for the murluks to advance first. The longer we draw this out, the better," she replied. "Given the murluks' penchant for attacking at dawn, I'm certain they don't fare well in the heat of the day. If the battle drags on, I suspect the creatures will retreat."

That sounded promising. I glanced upward. No clouds marred the sky.

"Wow! Will you look at the that!"

The commander and I both swung around. Lance was striding through the gate, a much-aggrieved Marcus in tow.

The mage stopped at the edge of the upper bank. "Talk about power leveling!" He rubbed his hands together in glee. "I can already feel the levels rolling in!"

I rolled my eyes, while, from behind Lance, Marcus winced.

The commander ignored Lance's inane comments entirely. "Lance, do you have any spells yet?" she asked.

The tall blond man frowned. "Not yet, but—"

"Then you will stay in the rear with the other new recruits. That's an order."

Lance's eyes bulged. He looked about to protest, but, smiling, Marcus clamped his arm on the mage's shoulder.

"Come away, little fish," Marcus said, "Let's go find you something to wear."

Lance sputtered and tried to resist, but as a lowly level one player, he couldn't hope to match Marcus for strength.

I grinned as Marcus dragged the idiot off. "He's going to be trouble sooner or later."

Jolin waved away my comment. "A problem for another day. Right now, we have a battle to win."

* * *

It was a further ten minutes before the murluks advanced.

The commander and I were standing atop one of the two wooden platforms. I leaned over the palisade wall and frowned as the murluk line ripple forward.

The creatures were unexpectedly coordinated. While the front lines of the murluk army were still ragged—bunched in places and spread out in others—their advance was nothing like the ill-disciplined, disjointed charges of previous battles.

I was not the only one troubled by the murluks' discipline. The creatures' advance elicited a grunt from the commander. "Those overseers are a problem," she murmured.

I knew what she meant. They were the ones enforcing order amongst their smaller kin. Even now, the overseers were wading through the ranks, beating the ordinary murluks into order with shoves and kicks. Clearly, I had underestimated the overseers' threat.

Movement from the river attracted my attention. Turning my gaze beyond the approaching front, I saw that the chieftain had begun his advance. The colossus splashed down into the water and swam swiftly to the shore, but when he reached the river's edge, his movements turned glacial.

My brows flicked up in surprise. The chieftain was struggling to pull himself out of the water. Dry land obviously affected him more than it did the murluk overseers or the rank and file of his army. Each step he took was ponderous and fraught with effort.

Land is not his natural environment.

Meanwhile, the commander's focus was on the closing front. The horde was nearing the bottom of the upper bank and still out of arrow range.

"Marcus, Petrov," Jolin shouted to the two captains who were commanding from the ground. "Get our best archers up on these platforms immediately. Their targets—their only targets—will be the murluk overseers. Understood?"

The two saluted and hurried to obey. The commander turned to me. "Begin your attack, Jamie."

"I'm on it," I said.

I drew the spellform of *fire ray* in my mind and extended it through my wizard's staff. Holding the spell in readiness, I lowered my staff and pointed it at the unmistakable—and unmissable—form of the chieftain.

When I was certain I had my target dead center in my sights, I infused the spell and hurled a focused beam of dragonfire toward the murluk leader.

The dragonfire burned a line of gold through the air and hit the chieftain squarely in the chest. Despite his size, the behemoth staggered back at the impact. Recovering his balance, he flung up his head and roared his outrage.

"Impressive," remarked the commander, studying the faint shimmer to the air in the spell's aftermath. "Now do it again."

I smiled. "Yes, ma'am." Reforming the spellform of *fire ray*, I sent a second lance of fire hurtling toward the chieftain. The murluk ducked his head, and raised his arm to shield himself, but it did him no good.

The dragonfire burned a hole through his meaty forearm. Raising his head, the chieftain glared at me in impotent rage.

I grinned in response. The twin strikes had nettled the creature. It would take more hits to bring the chieftain down, but, given his torturous advance, I was confident I could fell him before he reached the walls.

Especially if I target one of his legs.

I lowered my staff and sent a third line of flame arcing over the battlefield. It missed the knee joint I was aiming for, but still struck the murluk leader's leg, provoking another roar.

Adjusting my aim, I hurled a fourth bolt of heat and light.

It failed to hit.

What the—?

I hadn't missed. The *fire ray* had scorched through the air, as deadly accurate as my earlier bolts, but before it reached the gigantic murluk, it had been blocked by a shimmering bubble.

Startled, I rocked back. The chieftain had cast a magic shield around himself. Studying the transparent dome of arctic blue that hung over the behemoth, I recalled that the orc shaman Kagan had created a similar shield back on Earth.

I bit my lip. Just how strong was the chieftain's shield? Kagan's had held back mortar fire. This one couldn't be *that* strong, could it?

Encased within his bubble, the chieftain raised his head to the sky and bellowed in victory. I glared at him sourly. The battle wasn't over, whatever the murluk leader thought. *It's only just begun.*

A moment later, the chieftain's cry echoed through his overseers. Looking down, I saw that the murluk front was halfway up the upper bank, and hopping forward with renewed vigor.

I ground my teeth in frustration. My failure had spurred the enemy on. I *had* to burn through the chieftain's shield. Lowering my staff, I drew on my mana again.

The commander laid a restraining hand on my arm. "Wait, Jamie. He's too far away to threaten us directly. Let's observe how their front line does first."

The old lady's calm was admirable. Where my gaze was furious, hers was cool and assessing. It grated on me to leave my enemy unopposed, but Jolin was right. The murluk leader was not an immediate threat, and it would be many minutes before he reached the wall. The same could not be said for the rest of the murluk horde, which was now almost upon us.

Though I didn't like it, I followed the commander's lead. I released the spellform in my mind and steadfastly ignored the chieftain's repeated peals of triumph. Their only purpose was to goad me. I turned my attention to approaching line.

The first wave of the murluk army, exhorted onward by the overseers, labored up the bank in a frenzy to get at the human defenders.

Two archers perched on the second elevated platform took careful aim and fired. Their arrows whistled through the air toward their target—the nearest murluk overseer. But the murluk giant saw the incoming projectiles, ducked behind his wooden shield, and let the arrows thud into it harmlessly.

Disappointed, I turned away to observe the rest of the assault. The first murluks had reached the base of the palisade.

Once there, they began to hop.

I frowned. What were they doing?

The murluks were bobbing up and down, and on the spot. Slowly at first, then faster and faster, they bounced. With each hop, the creatures built more momentum and hopped even higher.

My stomach churned as understanding rushed through me. *They're going to jump over the wall.* "Commander, I think—"

"I know, Jamie," she replied grimly. Drawing a stout club from her belt, she shouted over her shoulder, "Petrov, brace the line, the murluks are about to jump the wall! And get the archers back!"

The hopping grew more frenetic as more murluks joined in. The creatures packed up tight against the palisade wall until its entire length was filled with bobbing shapes. Matters were different at the open gate. There, the murluks streamed inward, taking the path of least resistance. With bellows of their own, the cordon of spearmen guarding the gate stepped forward and engaged the horde.

My gaze flicked along the palisade, as I wondered what to do. I could see no way to stop the murluks from hopping over, if they could manage the feat.

Do I attack the chieftain? Maybe if I pierced his shield, it would demoralize the enemy. But he was still—

"Jamie, take out the overseers, starting with the one commanding the murluks at the gate," Jolin ordered. Her voice was firm, with no hint of doubt.

I didn't question her. I acted. Lowering my staff in the direction of my target, I sent a *fire ray* rippling through the air. The overseer saw the line of dragonfire burning its way toward him and tried to fend it off with his shield.

It did him no good.

The *fire ray* blew through the wooden shield and into the giant murluk. The overseer lurched backward, his eyes bulging as both his arm and his shield burst into flames.

Keeping my staff centered on my target, I unleashed a second, third, and then fourth *fire ray* at the overseer. Each lance of destruction caused him to stagger and jerk like a marionette on a string before he dropped dead to the ground.

"Good job," said the commander.

I opened my mouth to reply but was startled by a head popping over the wall. Jolin didn't miss a beat. She calmly swatted the murluk away with her club, sending it flailing into the massed horde below. Warily, I flicked my gaze left and right.

All along the palisade, murluks were bouncing over in oddly graceful arcs, only to find their deaths at the hands of the waiting spearmen.

But while the numbers of murluks breaching the wall was manageable for now, our defenders on the ground would be soon be overwhelmed.

"Jamie, focus!" snapped the commander. "Take down the other overseers. Start with that one next!" She pointed to an overseer on our right, where a section of the wall was in danger of being flooded with murluks.

I nodded sharply and set to work.

My first two rays missed. The overseer had learned from his fellow's fate that blocking would do him no good. Dancing between the smaller murluks, he foiled my aim twice over.

But I could learn too.

Anticipating the overseer's next movements and taking more care with my aim, I pinned him with my third attack. Then, while he still reeled from the flames licking at his torso, I followed up with three more *fire rays*. They were enough to leave the overseer a charred and smoking corpse.

I didn't wait for the commander's next order. Searching out another overseer, I poured dragonfire into him until he, too, collapsed.

Out of the corner of my eye, I saw that the pressure on our walls eased wherever the overseers were felled. The murluks near the dead overseers milled about in confusion. Many abandoned the attempt to scale the wall entirely and charged toward the gate, sowing even more confusion as they cut through the ranks of their fellows.

The commander was right: killing the overseers was the key to winning the battle—at least until the chieftain reached us. Without their overseers, the murluks lost their impetus.

I glanced upwards. The chieftain was still some distance off, but he was patient and steadily moving closer. I lowered my staff at my next target.

I can do this.

Chapter Thirty-Seven

386 days until the Arkon Shield falls

You have gained in experience and are now a level 21 Trainee.

I barely had time to celebrate gaining another level. We were winning. But I was running out of steam, and my stamina and mana pools were low. I couldn't go on for much longer.

With eight of the ten overseers dead, the number of murluks attempting to hop over the wall had diminished, allowing our forces to retore order inside the palisade. But our defenders still clashed in sizeable numbers with the attackers at the open gate. Despite the frantic commands of the two remaining overseers, most of the smaller murluks milling outside the walls chose to make for the gate where, unable to the bring the weight of their numbers to bear, they were held at bay.

Pausing for breath, I took stock of the battle. Only one significant threat remained.

The chieftain.

I studied the murluk leader's approach. He was laboring up the upper bank, moving even slower than he had on the lower bank. From this close, I could see that the smaller murluks moved easily in and out of his shimmering shield of blue.

So, his shield is similar to Kagan's. It appeared permeable to slow-moving objects but acted as a solid barrier against projectiles.

I chewed on my lower lip, pondering my options. The chieftain on his own could easily turn the tide of the battle against us, but his defeat would destroy the murluks.

I measured the behemoth's pace and trajectory, trying to judge how long he would take to reach the gate. We had some time yet, and I estimated that—

I frowned.

The chieftain was not making for the gate as I had assumed. Tracing his path, I saw that he was heading directly for the platform where the commander and I stood.

Jolin was leaning over the rear end of the platform, listening to a report from one of her messengers.

"Ma'am—" I began, trying to warn her.

She held up her hand, stopping me. The old lady didn't turn away from the messenger. Given her demeanor, whatever he had to say was important.

I limped closer.

"... there are thousands!" the messenger gasped. "Nearly all bear serious injuries of one kind or another. Nicholas says many are beyond his help. But that is not the worse part, ma'am." The messenger paused for breath, his chest heaving.

"Go on, Devlin." The commander pressed her lips in a thin line.

Despite the chaos around us, the messenger now had Jolin's full attention. Shifting from foot to foot, I wanted to interrupt, but the commander knew the stakes as well as I did. Whatever Devlin was on about had to be important.

"About one hundred are attacking our people," Devlin continued. "They've wrestled weapons from some of the new fishes and are killing indiscriminately. The gate guards died trying to stop them," he finished miserably.

I blinked, horrified, as I began to understand.

"They are killing our own?" asked the commander, her voice dangerously soft.

"Yes, ma'am."

"Captain Marcus!" Jolin shouted. "Take two companies and put down the trouble at the dragon temple. Show *no* mercy. Cut down anyone who resists your orders."

"Yes, ma'am!" Marcus snapped a salute as he hurried off.

Petrov stared upwards. "But ma'am, we need those men here!" he protested.

"There is no help for it, Captain," Jolin barked. "Make do!" She turned back to me. "What is it, Jamie?"

I stared at her uncomprehendingly for a moment before shifting gears. "The chieftain is making directly for us, not the gate. We need to get off the platform."

The commander peered over the palisade.

"Did I hear the messenger right?" I asked as she studied the chieftain's approach. "Are the refugees attacking us?"

"Yes," she said. "Earth is in its final moments, and people are swarming through the gate in droves. Most are in shock or injured from the natural disasters ripping apart the planet." Jolin sighed. "If it was only the terrified and wounded we had to deal with, matters wouldn't be so bad. But wherever there are large groups of people, there are crazies." She turned to study me, taking in my exhausted state. "You out of mana?"

I nodded. "You're going to have to replenish me before I can finish off the overseers."

She shook her head. "Forget about them. The murluk army is in too much disarray for them to restore order now."

Jolin closed her eyes, and a moment later, I felt restorative weaves of spirit reach out from the commander to me and to all the nearby soldiers.

"Thanks, ma'am," I said.

Jolin waved away my thanks and held my gaze. "Tell me truthfully, Jamie... can you handle the chieftain?"

"I must," I said, resolute. I wasn't certain the chieftain could be defeated, but I was determined to make the attempt.

Jolin measured my resolve for a moment. "Good man," she murmured. "Let's get down."

"I think we should—" I began.

"Wow! Now *that's* what I call a restoration spell!"

I broke off on hearing the shouts of glee. The voice was unhappily familiar.

"Come to daddy, you toady bastards! I'm gonna kill a whole lotta yah!"

My head whipped toward the gate. It was Lance, of course. The mage had pushed himself to the front of the cordon around the gate and, with a club in each hand, was bashing away at the murluks.

"Damn it!" I growled. "How did that idiot get there?"

"Damn fool," the commander murmured.

As we both watched, momentarily too stunned to act, a murluk thrust forward a spear.

Lance didn't even see it coming.

The spear skewered the mage clean through. Eyes wide and limbs twitching, he crumpled to the ground.

"Petrov," Jolin yelled down. "Send a squad to rescue our mage from the cordon." Petrov's gaze moved in confusion from the commander to me. "Not Jamie! The other one!" she snapped. "The blond idiot!"

It was all I could do not to scream. I closed my eyes and pinched the bridge of my nose. *Why did you have to do this* now, *Lance?*

Opening my eyes, I reached a decision. "Ma'am," I said, "I need to get to him. I saw the way that spear cut through him. The medics won't be able to help him."

Despite my dislike for the idiot, I knew we couldn't afford to let him die. The Outpost—humanity—needed every mage we could find.

Jolin's eyes darted between the approaching chieftain and the gate. It would be tight. If I went to Lance's aid, I might not get back in time to stop the behemoth before he reached the wall.

Indecision froze the commander—the first time I had seen her mask of certainty slip so completely. I knew she was weighing the lives of her soldiers against Lance's. It was not a choice I envied, but I couldn't wait.

"Ma'am," I urged.

"Go get him," she ordered, her expression clearing as she made her decision.

It was the right call. Lance was too important to abandon. If the mage's reckless tendencies could be controlled, he would be an invaluable asset that would save many lives.

I hobbled down the platform ladder. "After I see to Lance, pull back the spearmen if you can," I shouted to the commander, who was following me down the ladder. "Don't engage the chieftain unless you are forced to. It will be easier for me if I don't have to worry about injuring nearby friendlies!"

I didn't wait for the old lady's acknowledgement. I knew my commands wouldn't sit well with her, but I hoped she would listen.

As soon as I reached the bottom of the ladder, I skipped toward the gate, dragging my hobbled foot behind me.

※ ※ ※

It took only a few seconds to reach the back of the cordon defending the gate. I pushed my way through to the front. Most of the spearmen, recognizing me, gave way easily.

"John," I shouted when I caught sight of his squad. They were a few yards to my right, hovering protectively around Lance's form stretched out on the ground.

"Is he alive?" I called.

John glanced back. "Barely," John bellowed over the din of the battle. "But we dare not move him."

I hurried to John's side and ducked into the circle of men. Dropping to my knees, I examined the mage. The offending spear was still in place, the wound around it oozing copious amounts of blood. His health was draining fast. I feared the mage wouldn't survive the shock of its removal.

I spun mana through my hands and laid them on Lance's wound. The blue glow of life magic sank from my hands into the mage's body, repairing damaged arteries and organs.

Some of Lance's lost vitality returned, but not all of it. The spear, still embedded in his side, stopped him from healing completely.

"Pull out the spear, John," I instructed the lieutenant hovering over my shoulder.

"You sure, Jamie?"

"I am. Hurry!"

Lance's back arched as the big man yanked the spear out, but his eyes remained closed. Channeling *lay hands* again, I slapped my palms over the open wound.

This time, the wound closed all the way, leaving pink healthy skin behind. Lance gasped, and his blue eyes snapped open. Grabbing the mage by the shoulder, I forced him to look at me. "Lance, are you all right?"

The youth's eyes were still cloudy. After a moment, they focused and met mine. "I think so. Thanks—"

"Good," I cut him off. "Now *shut up* and listen," I ordered. "This little stunt of yours may cost a large number of men their lives. This world is no damn game. Do you understand me?" I glowered at him, daring him to repeat one of his fool utterances.

Lance lowered his eyes, not meeting my gaze. "I do now. I'm sorry."

"It's a start, but you have a lot to make up for," I said, my face still carved in hard lines. I wasn't sure I believed him. "Now, do *everything* John here tells you. *Exactly* as he tells you, *when* he tells you."

I rose to my feet and turned to the big man. "I have to get back to the battle, John. The murluk chieftain is nearly at the wall. Get Lance to safety, and don't let him anywhere near the murluks again."

"You got it, Jamie."

I nodded in farewell and swung away. I was slipping back through the ranks of spearmen when my world was rocked anew.

A Trials message, with flashing red text, filled my vision.

Flash alert: To all human players,

Earth is no more. The planet's core has been extinguished, its surface rendered lifeless, and its lifeforms subsumed into Overworld. All humans who have not pledged themselves to another Dominion are now citizens of the Human Dominion,

which will remain protected until the Arkon Shield falls. Days remaining: 386.

Live, strive, and grow, humans! The day you will have to fight for the survival of humanity is fast approaching!

My face drained of color.

I had known it was coming, yet the reality struck me harder than expected. All of humanity had been orphaned, thrown in a bigger pond, where the sharks were numberless and the odds of survival were questionable.

Around me, I saw that others had been similarly affected. The murluks, however, were making good use of our defenders' distraction, and injuries were mounting.

"Snap out of it, people," I bellowed. Dismissing the Trials message, I quickly made my way back to the palisade.

"Jamie, wait!" Lance cried out.

I had no time for this. Sighing, I turned to see the blond man's pale face and trembling hands. He, too, had been hard hit by Earth's demise.

Rising to his feet, the mage licked his lips. "I want to help. Let me help, please!"

I exchanged a quick glance with John before turning back to Lance. "All right. You felt that spell I used on you?"

He nodded.

"It's a life magic spell called *lay hands*. You should have read about it in the wiki."

He nodded again.

"Good. Go to the dragon temple, raise your life magic, and then try spellcrafting it if you can. John will take you to the medics after that, and you can help the wounded."

John nodded his agreement, and I swung around, limping away.

"Thank you, Jamie!" Lance called after me. I didn't turn back.

Chapter Thirty-Eight

386 days until the Arkon Shield falls

In short order, I covered the fifty yards to the section of palisade the murluk chieftain had been making for. I was pleased to see that the commander had done as I asked and pulled back the nearby spearmen.

The waiting defenders showed no sign of disorder. Jolin had moved swiftly to prevent the disruption experienced elsewhere from occurring here. With a nod to the commander in passing, I moved beyond the ready ranks of spearmen and into the open space immediately before the wall.

I glanced up at the palisade. The chieftain's blue-skinned head and shoulders were visible over its height. He had nearly reached the wall.

I exhaled a relieved breath. I was in time to stop him.

My original intent had been to slip through the gate and engage the murluk leader on the slopes of the upper bank itself. But after the delay in saving Lance, I couldn't have waded through the intervening murluks fast enough to reach the behemoth. Instead, I found myself waiting inside the palisade for the chieftain to come to me.

I was not certain how the chieftain intended to breach the wall. Would he step over and attack those within? He was certainly large enough to try. Or would he attempt to bash a hole through for his minions?

A moment later I got my answer. First one, then another clawed hand appeared over the top of the palisade, followed by the chieftain's scowling face.

The creature roared, revealing a gaping maw of shark-like teeth.

"It's nice to meet you too," I muttered. *We must seem puny to him. Small and defenseless. Easy prey.*

He would learn.

A nimbus of blue surrounded the chieftain's hands. *He's casting.* I readied myself. Whatever he was doing, it couldn't be good, but until he entered the Outpost, there was little I could do.

Lines of white frost spread out from the murluk's palms and through the wooden logs of the palisade until an entire twelve-foot span of the wall was encased in a glittering block of ice.

What is he doing?

The behemoth reached back and pulled out his seven-foot-long club. Raising it high in a two-handed grip, he slammed it down, shattering ice and palisade in a single blow.

I gulped. The palisade had offered far less resistance than I'd expected.

If he hits me just once with that club, I'm dead.

The murluk rank and file spilled through the opening created by their chieftain and headed straight for me and the defenders waiting beyond. Behind me, at the shouted orders of Jolin and Petrov, I heard the spearmen shift into a U-shaped formation centered around me and the breach.

As for myself, I didn't move. Ignoring the smaller murluks a dozen yards away, all slurping and hopping toward me, I kept my eyes fixed on the chieftain. *What will he do next?*

The behemoth slung his club back over his shoulder. Instead of advancing into the breach as expected, he swung left and stomped along the outside of the palisade.

He's heading to the next section of the wall to repeat his feat!

I couldn't let that happen.

Holding my staff horizontally in a two-handed grip, I advanced on the approaching murluks. The spearmen behind followed in my wake, moving to contain the breach.

As I closed to within a few yards of the murluks, I cast *flare* and sent jets of flames roaring along the length of my staff, forming an impenetrable shield of flame in front of me.

The murluks parted before me like a wave. But they did not flee entirely as they normally would when faced with dragonfire.

Instead, they turned aside to engage the surrounding defenders. *It's the chieftain's presence,* I thought grimly. *He must be responsible for their uncharacteristic display of courage. I have to kill him. Now!*

I limped through the streaming flood of murluks—fending them off with dragonfire—and closed with the behemoth. He was grabbing onto the next section of the wall when I reached him.

Hurrying as fast as I could, I broke through the shimmering field of blue surrounding him, letting out a sigh of relief as I did. If the field had repelled me, I wasn't sure what I would have done.

Since the chieftain's entire focus was on the palisade, he hadn't seen me—a tiny human figure less than a quarter of his height. Slinging my staff over my back, I slid up to the behemoth and wrapped my arms and legs around his massive calf. My hands barely met together on the other side.

You have engaged a creature champion on your own. You have been blessed with *slayer's boon* and *tenacious*.

Ignoring the Trials alert, I cast *invincible* and *flare*.

Dragonfire shot from my palms into the murluk. Where my hands met naked flesh, pools of red blossomed, as the hungry flames ate into the behemoth.

The chieftain shrieked. Letting go of the wall, he arched upward and slammed his leg into the palisade.

My teeth rattled and my breath left me in a rush as I crashed into the wall, but I rode the force of the impact, otherwise none the worse for wear. The palisade cracked, raining debris down on me. Yet my grip held. I clung to the colossus like a leech.

Furious, the chieftain pulled back his leg and smashed it into the wall anew. But the move only gave me time to pull myself higher up his limb. In my wake, I left a trail of reddened and smoking skin.

The chieftain was wasting time. *Good.* Every moment longer I clung to him, the more damage I could inflict.

Realizing he was not going to get rid of me by squashing me against the wall, he reached a huge hand down and yanked.

Despite my white-knuckled grip, I came unstuck.

The gigantic murluk raised me high above his head... and promptly hurled me toward the wall.

I tumbled through the air, the world flashing by in a series of disjointed images. A split-second later, the crazy kaleidoscope stopped as I slammed into the palisade and slid down.

Damn it. I rose to my feet and shook off my daze. If only I had clung to him a little longer! Knowing the murluks' vulnerability to fire, I was sure the flames would have taken on a life of their own and transformed the chieftain into a raging inferno.

Well, let's try that again. I crawled out of the rubble and limped forward, fixing my eyes on the monster's closest limb.

My single-mindedness caused me to miss the chieftain's follow-up attack entirely. My world went black as I was flattened against the hard ground.

When the light returned a moment later, I blinked. *Thank God for* invincible. *I would be dead without it.*

Spread out flat against the ground, I watched—almost hypnotically—as the chieftain's spiked club, wreathed in coils of ice, rose into the air.

The club paused at the top of its arc. Then it blurred forward again.

Spurred into action by the sight, I rolled, barely evading the frozen chuck of wood and ice.

I was running out of time.

Being felled by the club had cost me more time on *invincible* than I liked, and somehow, I didn't think the behemoth was going to let up with his current tactic. Still prone, I glanced up. Sure enough, the chieftain was winding back his club again.

Damn it. Pausing for a split-second, I flicked my gaze inward to check my Trials core. Less than five seconds remained on *invincible*.

I could not repeat my earlier approach. Even if I closed with the colossus again, he would pluck me off or smash me into the wall.

I accepted the inevitable: I would have to do this the hard way. I looked behind me. The shimmering blue curtain was at my back. I expelled a relieved breath. I remained inside the chieftain's shield.

I could still make this work.

I stole another glance at the murluk leader. His club had nearly reached the top of its arc again. I clambered to my knees and yanked my staff off my back. Drawing quickly on my mana and lifeblood, I cast *fire ray*.

Dragonfire burned a line of gold through the air and struck the chieftain in the forehead.

Aargh. I had been aiming for his eye.

The club came crashing down. I dropped to all fours and scampered away, dodging the falling mass more easily this time.

I can crawl faster than I can run, I thought wryly.

Turning onto my back, I raised my staff again. The chieftain, suspecting what was coming, flung up one arm to shield his face.

But I wasn't aiming for the chieftain—not with dragonfire, at least. With my spell readied, I touched my staff to the ground and cast *sinking mud*.

From the tip of my wizard's staff, in a cone expanding toward the behemoth, the ground underfoot rippled. A heartbeat later, the hard-packed dirt and grass around the murluk giant transformed into bubbling, sucking mud.

I smiled as, near instantly, the behemoth sank up to his knees. Sadly, the mud was not deep enough to fully immerse the monster.

The behemoth was already sluggish on land, but with his feet mired in mud, I hoped to slow him down even further, enough so to give him a hard time rotating as I circled around him. It would take only a single blow of his club to finish me, and I preferred to avoid that risk if I could.

The chieftain was studying his feet, momentarily forgetting me. Cords of muscle on the gigantic creature's legs strained as he tried to extricate them. The mud sucked at his limbs, which came free only by degrees at a time.

Leaving the murluk leader to his struggles, I scampered around the morass and cast *fire ray* again.

The behemoth roared as the dragonfire burned into his broad back. He tried swinging around, but with one leg half-raised and the other stuck in the mud, it was no easy feat. His arms windmilled before he regained his balance.

Realizing he could not get to me easily, the chieftain turned his attention to the legion of minions milling outside his shield. He barked at them. Ordering them to attack me, I guessed.

Warily, I switched my attention to the smaller murluks. When none advanced on me, I couldn't help but laugh. The little blighters appeared more afraid of me than of their oversized chief.

The behemoth hissed furiously.

Still chuckling, I unleashed another lance of dragonfire. Then another immediately after.

Both hits landed. The chieftain shrieked and snarled over his shoulder at me in helpless fury.

I met his eyes one last time. *You should have left us alone*, I thought. Then I resumed my attacks.

Launching strike after strike, I painted the air gold with *fire rays* and riddled the colossus's back with scorch marks until, overcome by the relentless onslaught, the chieftain toppled over.

You have gained in experience and are now a level 24 Trainee.

You have killed your second creature champion. Your Lone Slayer Feat has advanced to rank 2, evolving its Techniques.

***Slayer's boon*: When fighting a creature champion on your own, you are blessed with an aura that increases your damage by 4%.**

***Tenacious*: When fighting a creature champion on your own, you are blessed with an aura that reduces the damage you take by 4%.**

* * *

The chieftain's death sent a hush over the battlefield. With the glacial majesty of a crumbling iceberg, the behemoth tumbled down the bank.

A single glance at their fallen champion convinced the murluks the battle was lost. They dropped their weapons and fled for the safety of the river like a receding tide.

I slumped to the ground, wiping beads of sweat off my forehead. Even in their panicked state, the fleeing murluks stayed well clear of me. I let them go—I wanted nothing more to do with the creatures.

As the last of the murluks disappeared into the river, the commander sat beside me. "What will we do without you, Jamie?"

I smiled. It was her roundabout way of broaching the topic of me staying. "You have Lance now."

She snorted.

I chuckled. "I want to stay," I said, my amusement fading, "but I don't think I can."

"You still haven't told me why."

I sighed. "I must take the fight to the orcs before the Arkon Shield falls." For the first time, I articulated the plan I had been forming. "But to do that, I need to get stronger, much faster than I can by staying here."

The commander did not scoff at my plan, for which I was grateful. She ruminated over my words, and then asked, "Why?"

"Why do I want to take the fight to the orcs?"

She waved aside the question. "That I understand. A strong offense makes for a sound defense, assuming you can inflict more than token damage, of course. No, what I want to know is, why you are doing this? Why take up this fight at all?"

"Revenge, primarily," I answered, not shying away from my motives. "The orcs must pay for what they did to Mom. But she's not their only victim. They slaughtered millions on Earth. Many more will fall under their yoke if they are left to reign the Human Dominion. I must do this for them, too."

Jolin's iron-gray eyes scrutinized me. "And you believe you can accomplish what you set out to do?"

"I do," I replied simply.

"Then I will trust you, Jameson Sinclair."

I swallowed painfully. The commander's faith meant a lot. We fell silent, staring out over the tranquil river.

"The path you have chosen is a hard one," she murmured eventually. "Much harder than I expect you realize, and not just because of the strength of our foes. It will demand harsh sacrifices. Sacrifices that may break you quicker than any orc can." She smiled sadly. "It will be a difficult journey, Jamie. And it will change you."

Her words held such conviction that I wondered whether the path she spoke of was one she had walked herself.

"You have potential for greatness, Jamie," Jolin continued. "I do not doubt it. One day, all Overworld will realize it." Her smile turned lopsided. "*If* you live long enough."

I bowed my head, hiding my emotions, knowing the commander's steely gaze rested on me. "I hope you realize that your mission can't be completed alone. You will need others. You will need us."

I lifted my head. "I know. It is why I have stayed as long as I have. The settlement must be established—that is crucial. But it is only the beginning of what we must do here. I will return—if I am welcome."

"You will always be welcome here. On that, you have my word."

"Thank you, Commander." I blinked my glistening eyes dry.

Spying movement behind me, I looked over my shoulder. Soren and his builders were starting to repair the palisade. "Do you think we can finish the wall in time?"

"As you said, Jamie, establishing the settlement is all-important. Earth is gone. Those of us on Overworld are all that remains of humanity. We *cannot* fail. The settlement must be established. The palisade will be finished." Jolin rose to her feet. "Come, let's get back to work."

"Aye, aye, ma'am," I said, rising with her.

Chapter Thirty-Nine

386 days until the Arkon Shield falls

I didn't follow Jolin immediately.

First, I stopped by the body of the murluk chieftain and studied its gory remains. Anatomically, the chieftain was identical to his smaller kin, but built to a larger scale. A much larger scale.

How did he get so big?

Unsheathing my knife, I dissected the murluk. After a few minutes of cutting, the Trials rewarded my efforts.

You have uncovered a murluk chieftain's Technique: *water breathing*. Your skill in anatomy has advanced to level 5.

You have uncovered a murluk chieftain's Feat: Physical Augmentation, rank 3. Your skill in anatomy has advanced to level 6.

You have the discovered a champion core. The special properties of this item are unknown. Your lore skill is insufficient.

I pocketed the core and considered the Trials feedback. *Hmm... Physical Augmentation.*

I walked to a murluk overseer's corpse and repeated my examination.

You have uncovered a murluk overseer's Feat: Physical Augmentation, rank 1. Your skill in anatomy has advanced to level 7.

Physical Augmentation, again. The Trials seemed able to enlarge the size of creatures. I had a sudden vision of becoming twenty-foot-tall. *Wouldn't that be a sight,* I thought with a chuckle.

I pulled out the champion core and examined it again. It was the second core I had acquired, and even at a lore of twenty I wasn't able to divine its properties. How high did my lore have to be to identify the cores?

Remembering that I still didn't know what metal the murluks carried, I picked up one of their discarded spears and examined it anew.

You have acquired a crudely fashioned murluk spear. The spearhead of this weapon is made from aquaine and will not rust.

You are the first human to identify the metal aquaine. For this achievement, you have been awarded lore.

Lore: Aquaine is a rare metal alloy formed after centuries of submersion in fresh water. It is usually found only in the deepest rivers and lakes.

The metal's properties were somewhat disappointing. I'd been hoping for something better. *Oh well, at least I'll never have to worry about my knife rusting.* I paused as another thought occurred.

Were Marcus and I wrong about the mountains holding the closest source of metal? I glanced at the river. If there was metal to be found in it, how could we get to it? I pursed my lips. *I must tell Marcus.*

Done with my examination, I limped up the riverbank.

❉ ❉ ❉

I studied the shattered timbers of the palisade with an unhappy expression. Nothing salvageable remained of the section that had been destroyed by ice. The logs were reduced to woodchips.

The adjacent section of wall—the one I had been flung into repeatedly—was in a much better state. While many of the logs there had been uprooted, they appeared repairable.

I walked over to where Soren and his builders were animatedly discussing how to patch the damage. The head builder looked up at my approach. "Mage Jamie, nice work putting that big bugger down."

"Just doing my bit," I replied.

He grunted. "What can I do for you?"

"Actually, I'm here to help. Anything I can do? The palisade must be completed today. Are we on track?"

"What is it with you people and blasted progress reports?" Soren directed a fierce scowl at me. "Maybe if everyone just left me and my team well enough alone, the work would get done faster!"

I sympathized with the man, but I still needed to know. Smiling politely, I waited until Soren deflated.

"I apologize, Jamie, I shouldn't have snapped at you. None of this your fault. Everything was going so well, but now..." He trailed off, wrestling with his frustration. "With the twelve-foot-wide section that needs replacing, and this here portion we have to repair, *in addition* to the work continuing on the east side, well... there's no disguising that we're behind," he admitted.

"How can I help?"

He looked at me doubtfully. "Unless you have masonry or carpentry skills, I don't think—"

"I will fetch or carry if necessary," I said, interrupting him. "Anything you need done."

"Thank you for the offer, but we have ample men for that. Besides, I'm sure you have important things to do—"

He broke off as one of his men leaned into him and whispered something. He looked at the man in surprise. "That's a great idea, Dale." Soren turned back to me, "Actually, Jamie, there *is* something you can help with."

I waited for him to go on.

"What we need is to work faster, and to do that we need nails."

"Nails," I repeated, not following him.

"Nails," he nodded. "With metal being scarce, we've been fastening the logs with rope." He gestured to the riverbank, still scattered with corpses and abandoned murluk spears. "If could help the smiths create nails... securing the logs will go much faster."

"Ah," I said, understanding at last. "I'll get right on it."

✻ ✻ ✻

I drafted a squad of spearmen loitering nearby and set them to gathering and hauling the murluk spearheads to the crafting yard.

Then I went in search of Anton.

Unsurprisingly, I found him tinkering near his forge, repairing damaged tools. "Morning, Anton," I shouted above the sound of his hammering.

"Jamie!" He looked up in surprise. "How are you doing?" He frowned as he saw the two spearmen behind me, carrying the first load of gathered spears. "And what do you need?"

"I'm here on Soren's behalf. He needs nails."

Anton understood at once. "For the palisade?"

"Yep," I replied with a glance at the forge. "Any luck getting that to work?"

Anton grimaced. "Not when it comes to melting the murluks' damnable metal. I suspect we'll have to line the interior with a thin sheet of metal to better retain the heat." He eyed the spearheads the two soldiers hauled.

Sensing the direction of the smith's thoughts, I headed him off. "We can do that later. Right now, we need to be making nails."

* * *

We kept at it for hours.

Making nails was much harder than it sounded. Each nail had to be individually hammered and beaten into shape, and the builders needed hundreds of them.

At first, we couldn't make them fast enough, leaving Soren's apprentices waiting for the next batch. But, eventually, Anton and I fell into a rhythm and got ahead of the curve, growing our stockpile faster than the builders could use them.

Just after lunch—which we both missed—Anton set down his hammer. "I think we have enough now."

I blinked, jarred out of my trance by the sudden silence. "What?" I asked loudly, extinguishing the ribbon of dragonfire extending from my finger.

The nail-forging had improved my control over my dragonfire further. For the past hour I had been tapering its flow to the most minute of flames, focusing *restrained flare's* heat with pinpoint accuracy and dramatically reducing my use of mana and lifeblood.

And while I had not unlocked any new spells, I felt on the cusp of a new discovery.

"We're done, lad." Anton gestured to the neat stacks of unclaimed nails on his desk.

"Oh." I straightening up from the melting pot and glanced between the respectable pile of spearheads still waiting to be melted down and Anton's smiling face. Despite our rocky beginning, the gruff man and I had worked well together. I would miss him. "Anton, let's finish the forge lining while we are still about it."

"Nah, you're near falling over, boy. It can be done tomorrow."

"I'm leaving tomorrow, Anton," I said quietly.

The smith looked taken aback. "When will you be back?"

"I'm not sure," I admitted. "Might not be for a long while."

Anton fell silent. "All right, then, let's do it," he said eventually.

Lining the forge with sheets of metal went faster than making the nails. When we were done, and I had confirmed the upgraded forge worked to Anton's expectations, I said my goodbyes and left the smith happily tinkering with his new toy.

Where to next?

The temple first, I decided. Then on to find Soren and see how he was progressing.

As I was leaving the crafting yard, I spotted Melissa and Albert. I was surprised but pleased to see Albert back already. It meant Tara was back too, and we could finally have the talk I'd kept meaning to have with her.

I made a beeline for the pair. "Back from the woods already? No problems, I hope?"

The head logger nodded in response. "All's fine. We've brought back enough logs to satisfy even Soren!"

I smiled. "Do you know where Tara is?"

Albert's face fell. "She had to move out with her company again. The scouts spotted a band of ogres in the southern plains. The commander didn't want to risk another assault on the Outpost just yet, so she sent Tara and her people to watch the monsters and, if necessary, dissuade them from moving north."

Damn it. I have missed her again.

I turned to Melissa. "I didn't get a chance to thank you for the clothes and armor your crafters made. It fits perfectly."

"You're welcome, Jamie."

"I hate to impose, but I have another favor to ask."

"Of course, what do you need?"

"Four backpacks, food, and supplies," I said, thinking of the people who might be convinced to go with me. "I'm leaving in the morning," I added. "I'll be back, but not for a while."

Melissa nodded slowly. "I'll have the packs filled and delivered to your tent tonight."

"Thank you," I replied, turning to go.

"Jamie!" Albert stopped me. "I've got more of those saplings you asked for."

I was about to deny needing them anymore, when it occurred to me that I might still have a use for at least one. "Thanks, Albert. Will you send them over to my tent too, please?"

"Will do."

After saying my farewells to the pair, I made my way to the dragon temple.

* * *

The temple was in chaos.

Thousands crammed the space, most sporting burns or injuries. *Refugees from Earth*, I guessed. *Those who escaped our dying planet's final moments.*

With a start of guilt, I realized that the chaos of battle had made me forget all about them.

The refugees, still dressed in their basic new-fish outfits, sat huddled together for comfort. Many of the adults' eyes were glazed over. Others moaned in pain. All looked bereft and lost. Only the children appeared unaffected, laughing, screaming, or running around.

The Outpost's medics—harassed and overworked—moved between the refugees, providing what comfort they could. *I should have been here,* I thought. *These people need help.*

"Don't feel bad." Nicholas patted my arm, seeing my distraught expression as he approached. "There was not much you or anyone else could have done here." He shook his head sadly. "Even if we healed their physical ailments, there are some scars we can't mend. For that, they'll need of weeks of therapy, and even then..."

"What happened?" I asked.

"Earth died," said Nicholas simply. "These are the lucky ones who squeezed through the gate before our planet was swallowed from within. It has not left them unmarked though." He sighed. "Billions must have died back home."

I swallowed, imagining what those final moments must have been like.

Nicholas pointed out a large tent that had been hastily erected next to the dragon temple. "Come, walk with me. I was just about to check on our patients in the healing tents." He began striding toward the tent, and I fell in step behind him.

"Your apprentice is in there," he continued.

I stopped short, staring at him blankly.

"Lance, I mean. You did send him, didn't you?" Nicholas asked.

I had, but I'd forgotten. "He hasn't been too much trouble, I hope?"

"Not at all! He's been splendid. He has saved so many, I can't even begin to thank him."

I scratched my head. Were we talking about the same Lance?

"Must be nice having magic," Nicholas added wistfully.

Sometimes, but it's not without its burdens either, I thought. I remained silent, though, as we ducked inside the healer's tent.

I wasn't sure he would understand.

* * *

The inside of the tent was not as bad as I'd expected.

I had braced myself for the worst, but I was relieved to see that most of the patients were alive and resting on pallets spread out on the floor.

At the tent's far end, I spied Marcus and John tending to an exhausted-looking Lance, who was hunched over on a camp stool.

"You must eat," John insisted as we neared the trio. "You cannot go on without rest."

"No time," Lance mumbled in protest. "I have to keep going..."

I studied the mage's visage, shocked by the changes in him. The callow youth had disappeared. Lance was covered in grime, his eyes were sunken, and new lines seamed his face.

What happened to him?

"Marcus, John, is everything all right?" I asked.

Marcus looked up and nodded in greeting. "Our mage here thinks he is indestructible." He gestured to Lance, who was trying to rise despite John's restraining hand. "He won't rest."

Lance's eyes burned with a disturbing fervor. "Dude, you understand, don't you?" he asked. "I *have* to help them."

I glanced at Marcus and John. Both shook their heads. "Not right now you don't, Lance," I said. "Eat first. Rest. Or you'll be no good to anyone."

"But—"

"No buts. Listen to John, like we agreed," I added, keeping my voice stern.

"All right, man. If you think it best..." Lance finished feebly.

"I do." Gesturing for Marcus to follow me, I walked away from the mage.

"What happened to him?" I asked in a low voice. "That's not the same boy I met this morning."

Marcus looked equally bewildered. "I'm not sure. I hadn't even realized he and John were here until about two hours ago, when I found them wandering among the injured."

"It was that murdering bunch of idiots," Nicholas said, walking up to join us from behind.

I turned his way, waiting for him to go on.

"They were the ones responsible for Lance's epiphany. I'm not sure what happened at the palisade, but Lance was already shaken when he got here. When he saw those 'gamers' at work." Nicholas spat. "He was horrified."

Marcus grimaced, and I looked at him questioningly.

"A group of gamers came through earlier," Marcus explained. "But not the friendly kind. They were from a clan of PKers." As an aside to Nicholas, he added, "Player killers. They're players who hunt down other players in games."

Nicholas looked disgusted but remained silent.

"From what I could gather, this bunch thought Overworld was a game," continued Marcus. "I don't know what they were high on, but nothing got through to them. They went on a killing spree, mowed down everything in their path." He fell silent for a moment. "Children too."

My lips curled in disgust.

Marcus' face hardened. "Anyway, my men and I put an end to *that*. And them."

"I think Lance saw himself reflected in those killers," Nicholas said. "It changed him."

I sighed. There was no limit to human stupidity. *But people can surprise you for the better too*, I thought, looking back over at Lance. "Do you think he'll be okay?"

The medic pursed his lips. "Eventually. Right now, I think he needs to feel useful."

I nodded, accepting Nicholas' judgement. "We'll leave him in your hands, then. Ask John to bring Lance to see me when they're done here? I have something to speak to him about."

Before Nicholas could reply, a messenger slipped into the tent. "Captain Marcus, the commander wants to see you," he said. Seeing me, the messenger's brows lifted in surprise. "I was about to come and find you next, Mage Jamie. She wants you as well."

My brows drew down in concern. "Is something the matter?"

The messenger smiled. "No, the palisade is nearly complete. The commander wants both of you there when the final piece is put in place."

CHAPTER FORTY

386 DAYS UNTIL THE ARKON SHIELD FALLS

The last part of the wall to be finished was on the east side, where a small crowd was already assembled. At their fore was the commander and her direct subordinates: Soren, Albert, Melissa, Petrov, and Beth. Only Tara was missing. *Is she still on the southern plains?*

When Marcus and I arrived, Soren's workers already had the final pieces in hand and were awaiting our arrival so they could close the gap.

"Jamie, Marcus! Come here, please," Jolin said when she caught sight of us.

Marcus and I moved to join her.

"Gentlemen, you may proceed," the commander instructed the crew of builders.

"Great work with the nails," said Soren, stepping up to my side as the workers began to shift the final logs into place. "They worked better than we hoped. We've finished even earlier than expected!"

I nodded in acknowledgement, and then turned to the commander. "Is Tara still out, ma'am?"

"Yes," Jolin replied. "But don't worry, I've received word the ogres turned back. She will return before nightfall."

"Good," I said, expelling a relieved breath.

The commander threw me an amused glance. "I've heard you have been making plans to leave tomorrow, and with a team too."

"I was going to tell you. With the settlement established, the quicker I set out, the better. Do you mind if I ask some of your people to go with me?"

"Anyone who wishes to accompany you is welcome to do so." Jolin waved aside my concerns. "I've already given orders to that effect. Which direction are you thinking of heading?"

"East, probably. Toward the dungeon in the forest. I doubt we are in a position to attempt the dungeon just yet, but I want scout it out for myself."

"Ah," Jolin said. "In that case, you will be happy to hear that the scouts have come back from the foothills with an interesting report. Marcus, if you will?"

"We've found another dungeon," Marcus said with a grin. "Less than a day's journey east from the spider warren. This one is marked by an obelisk covered in green runes."

"Well," I breathed. "That *is* good news."

The commander raised one eyebrow. "I am guessing from both your reactions that the green runes signify something good?"

"Yes, ma'am," I replied, my eyes gleaming. "Dungeons marked like that are the lowest ranked, suitable for players under level one hundred."

She frowned.

I raised my hands to forestall her objections. "We still aren't strong enough to attempt the dungeon, but once we can get a team of players above level fifty, we stand a decent chance of beating it."

Even as I said that to the commander, my thoughts spun while I tried to figure how to attempt the dungeon even earlier. I would have to see the dungeon for myself first, though. Until I knew what creatures inhabited it, I couldn't be certain of the challenge we'd face inside.

The commander was still frowning. She opened her mouth, but then closed it with a sigh. "I will leave such matters to you and Marcus. Now," she said, turning back to the wall, "the builders are just about done."

The old lady was right.

The final log had been installed, and the carpenters were hammering at the wooden post to secure it in place.

There was no real reason to watch the palisade's completion. The Trials made certain that I, and everyone else in the Outpost, knew the exact moment it was finished. A slew of messages poured through my vision in a veritable wall of text. My mouth dropped open in shock as I scanned through them.

Location seventy-eight has been established as a village. You are within its borders and required to follow the rules and regulations of its new owner.

Settlement name: Location seventy-eight. Type: Village, rank 1. Leader: Jolin Silbright. Owning faction: none.

Human Dominion default policies are in effect. Location seventy-eight is allied with humanity's Patron, the Orcish Federation, and is neutral toward all other factions.

Dragon temple upgraded to rank 1. New facilities available for use: global messaging system.

Location seventy-eight has claimed the lair: Brown Spider Warren. For being claimed within the first 14 days of the Human Dominion's creation, the boundaries of location seventy-eight have expanded to include all territory between the village and the lair.

You own a tent in location seventy-eight and have been designated a vagrant. Apply to the village leader for full residency. Residents must comply with all settlement regulations to maintain their status. Current regulations: none.

Warning: Under the existing village charter, the villager leader Jolin Silbright has sole discretion in the approval of all residency applications.

Warning: Your status as a vagrant will be revoked if you spend more than one consecutive night away from the village.

Warning: Changing or losing your home settlement may result in dire consequences. Choose your affiliations wisely!

As a founding member of only the fifth human settlement in Overworld, you have earned the Trait Pioneer.

Trait: Pioneer. Rank: 1, common. Your Attributes are boosted by 5% when in the wilds or unclaimed territory.

"Wow," I breathed after I had read the messages. The last part claimed my attention. I had known from the Trials' feedback that when we claimed the warren that there were other teams of humans out there, fighting the same fight we were. But to find out we were not the first, but the *fifth* human village in Overworld was encouraging.

"We are not alone," I said softly. Others in the Human Dominion were battling for humanity's survival. *I will find them*, I vowed.

I looked at the others around me. They were all staring sightlessly, still caught up in their own Trials messages. The commander was the first to recover. Pulling out a flat, disc-shaped medallion from beneath her clothes, she studied it thoughtfully.

"What is that?" I asked.

She glanced at me. "A settlement core—the control device for this location. We found it outside the temple on our first day here. Now, let's see what I can do with it." Narrowing her eyes in concentration, she focused on the medallion.

A moment later, more alerts flashed through my vision.

Location seventy-eight has been renamed Sierra.
A new faction has been born: The Forerunners.
Ownership of Sierra has passed to The Forerunners.
The Forerunners have granted you Ally status.

The Forerunners have repudiated their Patron! The Orcish Federation is barred from all territory owned by the Forerunners. This resolution will be enforced by the Trials until the Arkon Shield falls.

The messages were like a punch to the gut. "You named the village, Sierra," I whispered. My hands were trembling. "How did you know?"

It was Mom's name.

The commander's expression was grave as she met my eyes. "I make it a point to know all of my people," she said. "It was the least we could do to honor your sacrifices."

I nodded. Tears streamed down my face unheeded. "Thank you," I managed before I choked up altogether. In no fit state for further speech, and feeling far too brittle to face the others, I fled.

* * *

Getting back to my tent took much longer than I'd expected. The entire settlement—or village now—had received a slew of messages. Most of the inhabitants received the Pioneer Trait. In fact, the only ones who didn't were the day-zero fishes.

All around the village, players congregated together, shouting, hollering, and cheering the village's establishment.

Almost as if Earth wasn't destroyed today, I thought.

But that wasn't fair. In spite of Earth's destruction, or perhaps because of it, people needed something to celebrate, something to give them hope.

And Sierra *was* that hope.

I swallowed painfully. The commander's gesture had caught me off guard. She had meant well. But memories I wished to keep buried had resurged. Every time I heard one of the villagers toast the village's new name, it felt like a fresh stab in the heart.

It's a good thing I am leaving tomorrow.

Pushing through the last throng of revelers in the camp, I ducked into my tent, relieved to have finally escaped the crowds.

Inside, I found Tara waiting.

CHAPTER FORTY-ONE

386 DAYS UNTIL THE ARKON SHIELD FALLS

"Jamie," Tara greeted me, her voice solemn.

"Hi," I said, recovering from the shock of seeing her here. "I thought you were still on the plains."

She shrugged. "Once the ogres turned south, my presence wasn't needed. I hurried north to see what help we could provide." She smiled. "But I see you had everything under control."

"It was close, but we managed. The village is finally established." I fell silent. Now that the moment had arrived, I wasn't sure how to broach the recent tension between us. I took a deep breath. "Tara, I'm sorry I snapped at you the other day. It was—"

"Stop, Jamie. I understand. I should have known your grief was too raw."

My brows drew down in consternation. Not that I wasn't happy by Tara's response, but her forgiveness had come swifter than I had expected, especially after her noncommittal response the last time I had tried speaking to her. Had she been dwelling on our conversation from that morning as well?

"Um, thank you, Tara. I would hate to think I destroyed our friendship over... something like that."

Tara nodded, her face sober. She didn't say anything further, and for a moment we sat in uncomfortable silence.

Eventually, Tara said, "The others said you were looking for me?"

The others? What others? It didn't matter though, because it gave me the opening to bring up the other matter I wanted to speak to her about. "I don't know if you know... but I am leaving."

"I know," she said quietly.

It was more difficult than I imagined to speak the words, but I got them out. "Will you... come with me?"

Tara let the silence draw out before answering. "Why?"

"Because we work well together." I paused, ordering my thoughts. "I trust you... like I do few others. And I have ever since my first day on Overworld when, despite everything, you took the time to school a new fish like me. And again, when you saved me countless times during my first battle. You're my friend, and I think we make a good team," I finished, wanting to add more, but lacking the courage to say any of it.

"No, Jamie," Tara said gently. "I mean, why do you *want* to leave?"

I blinked. The question caught me by surprise. "Because I have to."

"But why?" she prodded. "You've done so much for the village already. And there is so much more you can do here. Why leave now?"

I fell silent. I wasn't sure Tara would understand—not like the commander had. "Because I have to," I repeated.

Tara stepped closer, scrutinizing my face. "Is it vengeance?" Sorrow shone in her eyes. "Is that what drives you? Are you trying to avenge your Mom's death?"

I closed my eyes against a sudden throb of grief. I didn't want to discuss any of this, but I had started this conversation. If Tara was going to accompany me, she had a right to know.

"Yes." Opening my eyes, I let my rage shine through. "Yes, I want revenge... on the orcs that killed Mom, on the entire system that led to her death." I sucked in a breath and continued more calmly, "But it's not just vengeance I seek. I want to save humanity. And to do that, I can't stay here."

"Why not? Who is to say we can't build something here that can stand against the orcs?"

"I've fought them, Tara. And I'm not ashamed to say I got lucky in defeating them. Every one of them was a Seasoned player, all over level one hundred. Their shaman was a level-two-hundred Veteran."

Tara was staring at me, her face expressionless.

I leaned forward intently, willing her to understand. "Those five orcs I killed? They were just *one* hunting party. The orcs had dozens of parties roaming our world. The Orcish Federation must have thousands of Seasoned players. And they will be not be the worst we must face." My eyes unfocused, remembering. "When I entered the gate, I caught a glimpse of the orc shaman who had created them." I shivered, feeling my skin prickle at the memory. "*He* felt altogether different... godlike, even."

My eyes flicked back to Tara. "Do you know how long it takes the average player to reach Veteran status?"

Tara shook her head.

"Two years," I replied softly. "Humanity doesn't have two years, Tara. I have to get strong—fast. I can't do that staying here."

Tara cocked her head. "Jamie, humanity cannot stand against what you describe. Saving humanity sounds impossible. Why take on such a mammoth task? To even believe you can do this... isn't it a trifle egotistical?" She voiced the question gently, obviously not wishing to offend me. "Why are *you* shouldering this burden?"

She thinks I am crazy.

"Because someone has to, and because... I have gifts other players do not."

"There must be other mages."

"Not like me, Tara. None of them can do what I can."

Tara's brows furrowed as she failed to disguise her skepticism.

I sighed. "I will explain all of it if you come with me. Will you, Tara?"

She returned my sigh. "No, Jamie. I won't."

I stared at her, stunned. Despite everything, I hadn't expected her to refuse. I had anticipated resistance, obstinance, and having to work hard to convince her, but I never truly believed she would say no. "Why?" I asked, unable to disguise my shock.

She studied me in silence for so long that I thought she might not answer at all. "You are driven, Jamie. Obsessed, even. It makes you reckless." She held up a hand to still my protest. "All your victories could have turned out differently. Eventually, you will get someone killed. And I don't want it to be me."

"But—"

"No, Jamie, listen," she said. "I'm not like you. I can't take the risks you do. I can't throw myself into danger the same way. Perhaps it's what happened to you back on Earth that makes you so rash, I don't know. What I do know is, I can't do the same."

"But... but you're a warrior," I said faintly. "You take risks every day."

"*Measured* risks, Jamie," she said. "Necessary risks. I do not fight when there is no need, nor do I attempt impossible tasks."

Meaning I do. I opened my mouth, ready with another argument. Then I closed it with a snap. Everything Tara said was true. I couldn't disagree.

In my defense, everything I had done had been with a singular purpose in mind. But that was her point. I was on a crusade—one she didn't believe in herself. A crusade I was willing to die for, but that she was not.

"I will be more careful, Tara."

She smiled forlornly. "No, you will not. Goodbye, Jamie." Walking past me, she squeezed my hand for the last time.

I sat staring at nothing for a long time after she disappeared, rethinking everything I had done, wondering if it was all worth it.

* * *

I slept badly that night, pondering everything Tara had said and what it all meant. She was right: I *did* gamble with my life. But I did so knowingly and necessarily, or so I believed.

Was I a danger to others? Did I needlessly place my companions at risk? Could I lead a party out into the wilderness, knowing I might put them in harm's way?

But there isn't any 'might' about it, is there?

I was leaving the Outpost to *actively* court danger in a bid to get strong enough to face the orcs.

Was it fair to drag others along on my crusade?

Some would follow me regardless of the risks. John, for one. Probably Marcus, too. And possibly the sisters, Laura and Cass. But Tara had been the person I had been most certain of, and I had been wrong about her. I sighed.

I thought back to the moment on the wall, when the commander was forced to choose between Lance and her men. Could I make such a choice? If it came to it, would I choose my companions' lives over my vendetta?

I swallowed. I wasn't sure.

And if I was not sure, I could not do it. I would not risk John or Marcus or even Lance. A difficult path, the commander had called it, one that demanded more sacrifices than I realized.

I sighed once more. She had spoken far more truth than I realized at the time. I knew what I had to do.

I had to go alone.

Chapter Forty-Two

385 DAYS UNTIL THE ARKON SHIELD FALLS
1 DAY AFTER EARTH'S DESTRUCTION

> *"The humans and the Elders are connected somehow. It is the only conclusion I can draw from the Elders presence on the human homeworld so many millennia ago. But what is the connection?"*
> —*Arustolyx, gnomish archaeologist.*

I rose well before dawn, while the rest of the settlement was still asleep. I gazed around the tent at my meager belongings.

Other than the clothes and armor on my back, I had little of value to take—just the two mysterious cores in the pockets of my cloak.

I sighed. *I'll manage. Somehow.*

Ducking out of my tent, I stopped short at what awaited me. A sled. Loaded with four filled packs. My heart lifted at the sight.

Bless you, Melissa.

Inspecting the sled's contents, I saw that it contained far more than I had asked for, including a hunting bow, two filled quivers, and a dozen knives. The knives I was sure were from Anton. I chuckled, my dour mood evaporating.

How many knives does Anton think I need?

I tugged at the sled, judging it heavy but manageable. *Perhaps I should invest more in strength. It would make hauling the sled through the wilderness easier.*

I chuckled. It was a nice thought, but not a luxury I could afford just yet. Wrapping the sled's harness around my shoulders, I set off for the dragon temple.

* * *

The temple was quiet.

The hordes of refugees that had occupied the area yesterday were gone. *I wonder where the commander has housed them all.* Leaving the sled at the bottom of the temple, I stepped inside. A moment later, I emerged out of the gate in the center of Wyrm Isle.

Immediately, I noticed that something had changed. To the left of the gate, sitting on a large stone table, were two thick, leather-bound books, one black and the other white.

The messaging system? I wondered as I walked over to study the table and its contents.

"Welcome back, human," said a voice at my back.

"Aurora," I said, nodding a greeting.

"Are you here to use the messaging system?"

"I am, but also to increase my Discipline knowledge and Attributes."

"Well, in that case, let us attend to your advancement first," she demanded. "You players always take forever with those things." She gesturing irritably to the table.

In the act of turning back to the table, I paused. "Of course, Aurora. Please advance the same Attributes and Disciplines as I did on my previous visits. All to level twenty-four."

"Done. You have one hundred and thirty-seven Tokens and two Marks remaining," Aurora said. "Now, I will leave you—"

"One moment, Aurora."

The purple woman scowled at me. "What?"

"I require just one other Discipline advancement. Please increase my light armor to twenty-four as well." If I was going to be out in the wilderness alone, I needed to be as self-sufficient as possible, which meant improving the effectiveness of my armor.

Aurora looked put out, but with a wave of her hand, she acceded to my wishes. "Done. Now, is that all?"

I bowed smoothly to her. "It is. Thank you, Aurora."

"Good. Now I will leave you to your messages. Goodbye, human." Then she vanished.

I stared at the spot the purple woman had occupied not a second ago. She always seemed eager to escape from my visits. *What does she have against players?*

Shrugging away the mystery, I turned back to the stone table. The white book bore the title 'Incoming,' while the black book was titled, 'Outgoing.'

Simple enough, I thought, and opened the white book.

There were twelve entries, all from Eric. They started blandly enough.

Eric Anders message 1: Jamie, I've arrived. By God, this world is fascinating. So much strangeness, and so many things to do! But enough of all that. I'm in the gnomish city of Splatterpunk. Don't ask about the name! Anyway, where are you?

From there, the messages grew progressively more frantic.

Eric Anders message 2: Bud, where are you?

Eric Anders message 3: Why aren't you answering, man?

Eric Anders message 4: By God, Jamie, don't tell me you got yourself killed? No, the system is still letting me send these messages, so you must be out there somewhere.

Eric Anders message 5: C'mon, Jamie! Answer goddamn!

I touched Eric's message, penned in his own hand. My friend sounded deeply worried. *I'm sorry, Eric, I wish there was a way I could have let you know I was all right.* Sighing, I turned my attention to Eric's last message, penned two days ago. It was the longest and most interesting.

Eric Anders message 12: Jamie, I think I am finally beginning to realize why you've been silent. You're in so much trouble, I don't know how we're ever going to get you out of it.

An orcish delegation entered the city today, with the permission of the gnomish leaders. Apparently, the orcs stooping to entering a gnomish city is an event in itself. Our noble Sponsors were beside themselves, both intrigued and fearful.

The orcs entered the city for one thing only: to post a bounty notice for a human named Jamie Sinclair. Yes, bud, the orcs are hunting you. The notice included a full description of you, down to the last detail. The bounty is huge, a fortune large enough that even the gnomes, who hate the orcs more than most, seem tempted.

Questions are being asked... of your whereabouts, and your associates. No one seems to know of our friendship, so for the time being, Emma and I are safe. But we might be forced to leave on short notice. Don't be too concerned if you don't hear from me again soon. As long as the Trials' system allows you to send messages, know that I am still alive.

Anyway, bud, wherever you are, I hope you're safe. I will find you someday. I promise. Oh, and if you get this message, whatever you do, please don't tell me where you are.

Just in case.

Those last three words scared me the most. Eric had to be terrified if he thought to say that. I could never imagine a situation in which my loyal, lifelong friend would betray me, yet he must be afraid of being forced to do just that.

I opened the black book and penned a short missive of my own.

Message 1 to Eric Anders: Damn, Eric, I'm sorry you've been caught up in all this. It's the last thing I want for you or Emma. Thanks for the heads up about the orcs. I'll be doubly careful. But I am not going to avoid them. I'm going to hunt them down.

P.S. I'll find you first, bud. I promise.

I closed the book and squeezed my eyes shut to hold in my bubbling rage. It was not enough that the orcs had killed Mom to get to me, now my friends were in danger too.

I have wasted enough time.

The time had come to bend all my efforts into getting stronger. And then... then it would be time to go hunting.

※ ※ ※

Rohan M. Vider

*Here ends Book 1 of the Dragon Mage Saga. Jamie's adventures continue in **Dungeons**.* ***Out 31 December 2021!***

I hope you enjoyed this book and I would be grateful if you'd share your thoughts. [Click here to leave a review](#) and [here to follow me on amazon.](#)
Many thanks,
Rohan!

JAMIE'S PLAYER PROFILE

AT THE END OF BOOK 1

Player: Jameson (Jamie) Sinclair.
Race: Human. **Age:** 24. **Level:** 24. **Rank:** Trainee.
Tokens: 123. **Marks:** 2.
Home settlement: None.

Potentials
Might (mediocre), **Craft** (gifted), **Resilience** (exceptional), **Magic** (extraordinary).

Attributes
Magic: channeling (24), spellpower (24).
Might: strength (10), agility (10), perception (10), vigor (24).
Resilience: constitution (24), elemental resistance (1), willpower (10).
Craft: industriousness (10), artistry (10).

Disciplines
Magic: air magic (24), dragon magic (24), death magic (1), earth magic (24), fire magic (2), life magic (24), water magic (1).
Might: anatomy (7), clubs (10), light armor (24), shields (10), sneaking (1), spears (10), staffs (20), unarmed (1).
Crafting: blacksmithing (10), lore (24), scribe (6).

Traits
Unique: Dragon's Gift.
Rank 1: Pioneer, Spider's Blood.
Rank 2: Crippled, Quick Learner.
Rank 4: Mimicked Core.
Rank 5: Twice as Skilled.
Rank 6: Spirit's Invincibility.

Rohan M. Vider

Feats
Orcsbane (3), **Lone Slayer** (2), **Lair Hunter** (1).

Active Techniques
magesight, night vision, sinking mud, living torch, fire ray, restrained flare, flare, lay hands, analyze, mimic, invincible, repurpose, basic attunement.

Passive Techniques
orc hunter, burning brightly, revulsion, lair sense, slayer's boon, tenacious.

Faction relationships
Orcish Federation: hated.
Forerunners: ally.

Equipped items
wizard's staff, spider leather armor, silk clothes, aquaine knife.

Afterword

Thank you for reading **Overworld**. Please take the time to leave a review on www.amazon.com If you want to support my future work or keep up to date with the latest news on my writing, you can follow me on Patreon (click here).

Once I've begun work on book three, I will post early chapters on **Patreon**, giving readers a chance to share their thoughts and feedback.

Please feel free to drop me a message on anything related to the Dragon Mage Saga or otherwise. I look forward to hearing your thoughts!

I hope you enjoyed the book!

Best Regards,
Rohan
Support me on PATREON
Amazon Author page | Goodreads | Facebook | Twitter | Bookbub | Instagram | TikTok | Reddit |Rohanvider.com |

GENERAL DEFINITIONS

Arkon Shield: a force field around the Human Dominion.
citizen: a player pledged in service to a particular Dominion.
core: a Trials control or interface device used for controlling lairs, settlements, and champions.
dragonfire: flames imbued with the essence of a dragon, which burn hotter and brighter than any normal fire.
Elders: dragons.
faction: any group within a Dominion sharing the same goals.
faction member: a player affiliated with a particular Dominion.
Focus: a living implement used to aid a mage with his spellcasting.
Initiation: the process whereby the Trials core embedded into new players is bonded to its host and configured to closely monitor, weigh, and assess their every action thereafter.
Inductee: rank 0 descriptor applied to a level 0 player, one who has not achieved full player status.
lifeblood: a portion of the caster's blood containing some of his life and stamina.
natural learning rate: the speed at which players can advance their Attributes and Disciplines when unassisted by the Trials. This rate differs from player to player.
Neophyte: rank 1 descriptor applied to player levels, Disciplines and Attributes. It ranges from level 1 to 9.
Patron: a species that initiates another's entrance in the Trials and is awarded special rights with respect to the client species.
resident: a player who lives in a particular settlement.
Seasoned: rank 3 descriptor applied to player levels, Disciplines, and Attributes. It ranges from level 100 to 199.
settlement: a secured region, home to a population of at least one thousand and a functioning dragon temple.
spell construct: the internal design of a spell.
spellcrafting: process of creating spells.
spellform: see spell construct.

spirit weave: core of an entity's being.

Sponsor: a species that earns the right to offer refugee to a new Overworld race. Sponsors enjoy fewer special rights with respect to the client species than Patrons.

sponsored city: a settlement in a new Dominion that can act as a refugee for a new Overworld race. A sponsored city can be owned any Sponsor or Patron.

sorcery: not a true form of magic, but the use of spirit to empower Techniques.

Trainee: rank 2 descriptor applied to player levels, Disciplines, and Attributes. Ranges from level 10 to 99.

Trials Key: rare Trials artifacts that can be used to begin an entity's activation as a player. Patrons and Sponsors use this to forcibly create sought-after players and bind them to their service.

Veteran: rank 4 descriptor applied to player levels, Disciplines, and Attributes. It ranges from level 200 to 299.

TRIAL SYSTEM DEFINITIONS

agility: the quickness and speed of physical attacks and movements.
artistry: determines the quality of creations.
Attributes: a player's physical and mental characteristics that define his fundamental capabilities. Attributes represent the realization of Potential.
channeling: a measure of the amount of mana a player can draw upon
constitution: a measure of overall health.
Craft: refers to the Craft Potential.
Discipline: the knowledge necessary to employ Attributes and Potential in meaningful ways, called Techniques.
elemental resistance: the ability to resist elemental damage.
Feats: similar to Traits, but can be improved with further achievements.
health: quantitative measure of a player's health or lifeforce, and a function of the player's level, constitution, and Resilience.
industriousness: a measure of the amount of energy a player consumes when crafting.
Magic: refers to the Magic Potential.
mana: a quantitative measure of a player's magical energy, and a function of the player's level, channeling, and Magic.
maneuvers: physical Techniques.
Marks: used to enhance Attributes.
Might: refers to the Might Potential.
level: fine scale for measuring player growth.
perception: intuition and ability to anticipate.
Potentials: a player's core talents and inborn gifts, which he may or may not realize in his lifetime. They define the upper limit that a player's Attributes may reach.
rank: macro scale of measuring player growth.

Resilience: refers to the Resilience Potential.
Spellpower: determines the potency of magical attacks.
spells: magical Techniques.
stamina: a quantitative measure of a player's physical energy and a function of the player's level, vigor, and Resilience.
strength: determines the power of physical attacks.
Techniques: special abilities that may be passive or active.
Tokens: used to acquire skill in a Discipline.
Traits: specialized characteristics that may influence a player's Attributes, Disciplines, or Techniques independent of level restrictions.
vigor: a measure of stamina or physical energy.
willpower: ability to resist pain, mental assaults, and mind-altering effects.

LIST OF LOCATIONS

Brown Spider Warren: lair north of location 78.
crafting yard: crafters' area in location 78.
Elven Protectorate: Dominion of the elves.
Human Dominion: human territory in Overworld.
Orcish Federation: Dominion of the orcs.
Overworld: world of the Trials.
Outpost: Location 78.
Splatterpunk: Gnomish city.
training ground: fighting practice yard.
Wyrm Island: unknown region accessed by the dragon temples.

LIST OF NOTABLE CHARACTERS

Albert: head gatherer.
Anton: blacksmith.
Aurora: Jamie's guide in the dragon temple.
Beth: head cook.
Captain Hicks: militia captain from Earth.
Cassandra: hunter, sister of Laura.
Claire: daughter of refugee Greg.
Dale: builder.
Devlin: messenger.
Duskar Silverbane: orc warlord.
Emma: Eric's girlfriend.
Eric Anders: Jamie's friend.
Greg: parent to Claire.
Hansen: spearman.
Ionia Amyla: elven queen.
Jameson (Jamie) Sinclair: protagonist.
John: spearman, lieutenant.
Jolin Silbright: the commander, the old lady.
Kagan Firespawn: orcish shaman.
Lance: mage.
Laura: hunter, sister of Cassandra.
Lloyd: spearman, sergeant.
Marcus Smithson: captain in location 78.
Melissa: head crafter.
Michael: spearman.
Nicholas: medic.
Orgtul Silverbane: orc high shaman.
Petrov: captain in location 78.
Soren: head builder.
Sten: spearman.
Tara Madison: captain in location 78.
Yarl Sharptooth: orcish squad leader.

Printed in Great Britain
by Amazon